PRAISE FOR SECONDWORLD

"[SecondWorld] is gripping, propelled by expertly controlled pacing and lively characters. Robinson's punchy prose style will appeal to fans of Matthew Reilly's fast-paced, bigger-than-life thrillers, but this is in no way a knockoff. It's a fresh and satisfying thriller that should bring its author plenty of new fans."

—Booklist

"A brisk thriller with neatly timed action sequences, snappy dialogue and the ultimate sympathetic figure in a badly burned little girl with a fighting spirit... The Nazis are determined to have the last gruesome laugh in this efficient doomsday thriller."

— Kirkus Reviews

"Relentless pacing and numerous plot twists drive this compelling stand-alone from Robinson... Thriller fans and apocalyptic fiction aficionados alike will find this audaciously plotted novel enormously satisfying."

— Publisher's Weekly

"A harrowing, edge of your seat thriller told by a master storyteller, Jeremy Robinson's Secondworld is an amazing, globetrotting tale that will truly leave you breathless."

— Richard Doestch, bestselling author of HALF-PAST DAWN

"Robinson blends myth, science and terminal velocity action like no one else."

— Scott Sigler, NY Times Bestselling author of NOCTURNAL

""Just when you think that 21st-century authors have come up with every possible way of destroying the world, along comes Jeremy Robinson."

— New Hampshire Magazine

PRAISE FOR THE JACK SIGLER THRILLERS

THRESHOLD

"Threshold elevates Robinson to the highest tier of over-the-top action authors and it delivers beyond the expectations even of his fans. The next Chess Team adventure cannot come fast enough."

— Booklist - Starred Review

"Video game on a page? Absolutely. Fast, furious unabashed fun? You bet."

— Publishers Weekly

"Jeremy Robinson's Threshold is one hell of a thriller, wildly imaginative and diabolical, which combines ancient legends and modern science into a non-stop action ride that will keep you turning the pages until the wee hours."

— Douglas Preston, NY Times bestselling author of IMPACT

"With Threshold Jeremy Robinson goes pedal to the metal into very dark territory. Fast-paced, action-packed and wonderfully creepy! Highly recommended!"

— Jonathan Maberry, NY Times bestselling author of DUST & DECAY

"With his new entry in the Jack Sigler series, Jeremy Robinson plants his feet firmly on territory blazed by David Morrell and James Rollins. The perfect blend of mysticism and monsters, both human and otherwise, make Threshold as groundbreaking as it is riveting."

— Jon Land, NY Times bestselling author of STRONG ENOUGH TO DIE

"Jeremy Robinson is the next James Rollins."

—Chris Kuzneski, NY Times bestselling author of THE SECRET CROWN

"Jeremy Robinson's Threshold sets a blistering pace from the very first page and never lets up. For readers seeking a fun rip-roaring adventure, look no further."

— Boyd Morrison, bestselling author of THE ROSWELL CONSPIRACY

INSTINCT

"If you like thrillers original, unpredictable and chock-full of action, you are going to love Jeremy Robinson's Chess Team. INSTINCT riveted me to my chair."

— Stephen Coonts, NY Times bestselling author of DEEP BLACK: JIHAD

"Robinson's slam-bang second Chess Team thriller [is a] a wildly inventive yarn that reads as well on the page as it would play on a computer screen."

— Publisher's Weekly

"Intense and full of riveting plot twists, it is Robinson's best book yet, and it should secure a place for the Chess Team on the A-list of thriller fans who like the over-the-top style of James Rollins and Matthew Reilly."
— Booklist

"Jeremy Robinson is a fresh new face in adventure writing and will make a mark in suspense for years to come."
— David Lynn Golemon, NY Times bestselling author of RIPPER

PULSE

"Rocket-boosted action, brilliant speculation, and the recreation of a horror out of the mythologic past, all seamlessly blend into a rollercoaster ride of suspense and adventure."
— James Rollins, NY Times bestselling author of BLOODLINE

"Jeremy Robinson has one wild imagination, slicing and stitching his tale together with the deft hand of a surgeon. Robinson's impressive talent is on full display in this one."
— Steve Berry, NY Times bestselling author of THE COLUMBUS AFFAIR

"There's nothing timid about Robinson as he drops his readers off the cliff without a parachute and somehow manages to catch us an inch or two from doom."
—Jeff Long, New York Times bestselling author of THE DESCENT

"An elite task force must stop a genetic force of nature in the form of the legendary Hydra in this latest Jeremy Robinson thriller. Yet another page-turner!"
— Steve Alten, NY Times best-selling author of PHOBOS: MAYAN FEAR

"Robinson's latest reads like a video game with tons of action and lots of carnage. The combination of mythology, technology, and high-octane action proves irresistible."
— Booklist

ALSO BY JEREMY ROBINSON

The Jack Sigler Novels

Pulse
Instinct
Threshold

**The Chess Team Novellas
(Chesspocalypse Series)**

Callsign: King - Book 1
Callsign: Queen - Book 1
Callsign: Rook - Book 1
Callsign: King - Book 2
Callsign: Bishop - Book 1
Callsign: Knight - Book 1
Callsign: Deep Blue - Book 1
Callsign: King - Book 3

**The Origins Editions
(First five novels)**

The Didymus Contingency
Raising The Past
Beneath
Antarktos Rising
Kronos

Standalone Novels

SecondWorld
Project Nemesis
Island 731

**The Last Hunter
(Antarktos Saga Series)**

The Last Hunter - Descent
The Last Hunter - Pursuit
The Last Hunter - Ascent
The Last Hunter - Lament
The Last Hunter - Onslaught

Writing as Jeremy Bishop

Torment
The Sentinel

Other Books

The Ninja's Path (Humor)
The Zombie's Way (Humor)

ALSO BY KANE GILMOUR

The Jason Quinn Series

Resurrect
Frozen

Jeremy Robinson's Jack Sigler Novels

Callsign: Deep Blue - Book 1
Ragnarok

RAGNAROK

A Jack Sigler Thriller

JEREMY ROBINSON

WITH KANE GILMOUR

SEVEN REALMS PUBLISHING

ISBN 978-0-983735-09-0

Cover design copyright ©2012 by Jeremy Robinson
Interior formatting by Stan Tremblay, www.FindTheAxis.com

Seven Realms Publishing, LLC
4420 Carter Road #6
Saint Augustine, Florida 32086

www.sevenrealmspublishing.com

Printed in Canada

Visit Jeremy Robinson on the World Wide Web at:
www.jeremyrobinsononline.com

Visit Kane Gilmour on the World Wide Web at:
www.kanegilmour.com

*For Norah Kathleen Robinson
and Moira Dawn Gilmour.*

ACKNOWLEDGMENTS

Ragnarok is different from all my other full length novels in that it was a collaborative effort with Kane Gilmour. While I have co-authored with several writers in the past, including Kane, those books were all novellas and less intense. I wasn't entirely sure how this would work out, but I'm thrilled to say that the copy of *Ragnarok* you now hold in your hands exceeds my expectations and is a fantastic addition to the Chess Team universe. Kane is not only a great editor (he has edited something like twenty of my books now) but is also a fantastic author. So when you're done with *Ragnarok*, do yourself a favor and pick up his other books.

I also need to thank a new cast of characters who helped make *Ragnarok* the boldest Jack Sigler story to date. Big thanks to Kent Holloway and Seven Realms publishing, who were willing to collaborate with this demanding author and publish the trade paperback edition of *Ragnarok*. For awesome edits, I must thank Jennifer Bagdigian. For fact checking and early reading, I offer a "booyah!" to Sean Ellis (co-author of Callsign: King, for those of you keeping track). Roger "Tex" Brodeur, your advance reading and typo-checking is once again appreciated. Thanks to Stan "Rook" Tremblay for amazing interior design and cover prep, and for being a swell guy. I owe you some pancakes.

And as always, I must thank my hardcore support team: my kids, Aquila "Concho" Robinson, Solomon "Monster" Robinson, Norah "Shorty" Robinson, and my wife, Hilaree "Hoochie Mamma" Robinson. You are my clan. Without you, this stuff wouldn't be nearly as fun. Love you guys.

"The fetters will burst, and the wolf run free;
Much do I know, and more can see
Of the fate of the gods, the mighty in fight."

— The Poetic Edda

"Fear is pain arising from the anticipation of evil."

— Aristotle

"There is a fifth dimension beyond that which is known to man. It is a dimension as vast as space and as timeless as infinity. It is the middle ground between light and shadow, between science and superstition, and it lies between the pit of man's fears and the summit of his knowledge."

— Rod Serling

RAGNAROK

PROLOGUE

Fenris Kystby, Norway
The Past

THE DEEP, RESONATING beat of drums rolled through the early morning fog like the thunderous footfalls of a frost giant. In response to the sound, an alarm bell rang in the distance—tiny and pitiful. Hrolf Agnarsson knew the monastery's monks would be rising from their slumbers and arming themselves, but he wasn't concerned. He'd led many raids before, and the battle was often won before the ships even made landfall. If the drums didn't do it, the fiery torches lighting the dragonhead prows sent most of the God-fearing men running.

The drums reached a fevered pace as the ships cut through the fog. Agnarsson's beard, clumpy with debris from a hastily eaten breakfast, twitched as the man grinned. The monk's heartbeats would keep pace with the drums. By the time his raiding party reached the monastery, the men who remained would be exhausted from fear and from holding weapons in sweaty hands.

There were times when he longed for a true fight, but he wasn't ready to be sent to the halls of Asgard quite yet. Not when there was plundering to be done. *Live like a King on Earth*, his father taught him, *and be greeted by Odin as a son.*

He looked up at the gray walls of the monastery. His smile widened when he saw several men fleeing from the gates. *The Irish never put up much of a fight*, he thought.

Irish monks, persecuted refugees from their own island homeland, had decided to settle and build a small structure that had later blossomed into the gray, rock-walled monastery. Other Vikings had led raids on the Irish on their island, but Agnarsson had suggested he and his men come up and pillage the Irishmen right here at home. Monks always had good food and drink, as well as skins and books and other things that raiders could sell in the southern markets. Women would have made the raid even better, but Agnarsson had rarely found women in a monastery.

The drums beat on, and for the first time, Agnarsson let his pulse quicken.

The ship scraped over the smooth stones of the shore. The rumble beneath his feet acted like a trigger. "Hoooaaarrhhggg!" he shouted, thrusting his axe high into the air. The thirty men behind him abandoned their oars, stood and drew their weapons, joining in the war cry. Then, as one, they vacated the boat with him, jumping into the frigid knee-deep water with little thought or care.

When the two neighboring longships unloaded, each carrying thirty more men, Agnarsson actually heard screams rise up from within the monastery. *If they weren't afraid before*, Agnarsson thought, *they are pissing themselves now.*

The knowledge quickened his pace.

Rocky shoreline gave way to soft earth. His two-hundred-fifty-pound body left indentations with every step. Halfway to the monastery, he shed his skins and let them fall to the ground behind him. The furs had already begun to overheat his body, and in a moment, they would only be in the way. And his body—muscular and coated with the dried blood of previous kills—would set his foes' legs to shaking.

Agnarsson rounded the first of the outbuildings and came to a stop. There, standing before him, was something he'd never encountered before. Ten monks, armed with swords, stood waiting. He admired their bravery. Ten Irish monks against ninety Viking raiders. A ridiculous thing. Yet here they stood.

He looked into their eyes and saw their fear. *Brave, but not fools*, Agnarsson thought. *They know death has come for them.*

Ninety men stopped behind him, facing down the ten.

And still, they stood their ground.

This will not do, Agnarsson thought. He took pride in his ability to instill fear in men. That these men stood against that fear was an insult. He searched their eyes, seeing only terror. *Then why...*

Then he saw it. One of the men held his sword like he knew how to use it. He might even be dangerous.

They stand because of him.

Agnarsson laughed and lowered his axe. He looked back at his men and they laughed, too. They all knew the joke and the punch line. It was time to share it with the monks.

With a speed that belied his size, Agnarsson turned forward again and with a twitch of his arm, threw his axe. The heavy blade spun in oblong circles as it sailed through the air. It came to rest with a wet smack and buried deep in the rib cage of the brave man. Ribs split. Lungs burst. The man's heart severed in two, freeing him from this world and the remaining monks from their duty.

Swords struck the earth one by one as the nine remaining monks fled. They'd only made it five steps before the raiding party sprang into action. Waves of men surged past Agnarsson. He watched the glory unfold. Flames rose, along with screams. Monks fled, and died. Blood soaked into the earth.

With the casual gait of a man who knew that life couldn't get any better, Agnarsson strode up to the monk who held the axe in his chest. He put his booted foot upon the man's chest and pushed. The ribs flexed and cracked, loosening their grip on the axe blade. With a slurp, the weapon came free. The weight of the weapon in his hands and the sight of blood dripping from it brought a fresh smile to his face.

It grew wider still when he saw a monk fleeing toward him. The man had five raiders on his heels. And they would have overtaken the man if they hadn't seen Agnarsson waiting, axe rising up. Taking careful aim, Agnarsson wondered if he could cleave the man in two. His muscles flexed. His grip tightened. He swung.

And missed.

As the axe split the air, a brilliant flash of light, made brighter by the white snow underfoot, forced his eyes shut. Blinded, he didn't see the monk fall to the ground. The axe sailed through air and nothing more. The momentum of the missed blow nearly flung him to the ground, but he regained his balance and avoided the humiliation.

He opened his eyes to more bright light. Lightning arced through the sky above him, crackling with the sharpness of breaking trees. Then he realized that the sound, in fact, *was* snapping tree trunks. He turned around toward the source of the light and found its brightness now missing, along with a portion of earth and the trees within it. Odin had reached down from Asgard and scooped away part of the world.

As the monk behind him started praying to his "one true God," Agnarsson turned toward the man. "It is a sign," he said. "Odin takes from the earth as he desires. Just as he would have us do." He raised the axe, but the monk was spared once again.

An ear-splitting roar rolled over the monastery like a tangible spirit.

The sound reverberated off the stone walls of the buildings his men had set alight. He could feel the sound in his heart, thrumming and humming. Hardened Viking raiders fell to their knees, some of them screaming in terror. The few remaining monks passed out or pissed their robes. Every man around him screamed as if his soul was being yanked out and flung down to *Neifelheim*.

Agnarsson had known his men all his life. They feared nothing. No God and no man. But now they were weeping and blubbering like babes. Some of the men—his men—started to flee into the woods. So complete was their panic that not one of them realized they were running *toward* the sound's source, rather than away.

That's when he caught a glimpse of the thing moving like a breeze through the snows, leaping between the trees and even up onto the sides of them before springing away, almost too quickly for Agnarsson's eye to follow. Then it was gone in the shadows.

The first of his men to reach the trees was torn apart. Agnarsson didn't see it happen, but the sounds of tearing flesh and muffled screams were fodder for the mind's eye. Then the lower half of Magnus Trondheim's red-haired legs flew through the air and tangled in the lower branches of one of the half-eaten trees. Other men had bolted at that sight, but Agnarsson had stood stock still, staring in wonder. He knew whatever the creature was, it wasn't human.

The roar came again, but this time from inside the monastery.

There is more than one, Agnarsson realized.

The few men still rooted in place came unglued, and with shouts of horror, they ran without mind or any sense of where they were going. Only Agnarsson remained in place, not because he was brave, but because he was petrified. He kept a firm grip on his axe while warm piss trickled down his inner thigh.

His mind—spurred by lessons taught by a remorseless father, fought for control. *It is too cursed fast to be a bear or a wolf.*

The roar came again, dropping him to one knee.

The sound was closer, bouncing back at him from the trees and the falling snow all around him in the early morning gloom. A few of his men yet lived, but whimpered in terror. The vibration in

Agnarsson's eardrums was intense. His bones felt as if they rattled in his body. He couldn't see the creature, but he knew it was near.

Then he heard the movement. Fast. Coming right for him. He whirled around and swung his double-bladed axe wide, hoping he might strike the beast out of sheer luck and force.

Instead, the world before him transformed into the sun.

Brightness assaulted Agnarsson's sight—so intense and painful that it scorched his eyes even through his tightly shut eyelids. Thunder shouted and lightning crackled again, this time blasting out from all around him.

Guarding his eyes with his hands, he chanced a look and witnessed the giant ball of light collapse inward. Silence sucked the thunderous din away like a thirsty man slurping up the last of his mead, and Agnarsson was left alone in the dull light of early morning.

His men lay dead in the shallow snow all around him. Some of them, caught half within the sphere of light and half without, had been cut cleanly in half.

He looked down to see that his own body had been cleaved as well. His axe was gone and so was most of his axe arm below the shoulder. The wound had been closed with searing heat, the fire so hot he hadn't even noticed he was injured. Now he looked down at his blackened stump in shock.

The creatures were gone. Nothing moved in the snow. The ball of lightning and fire was gone. Everyone around him was dead. But even more shocking was that the monastery itself, along with the ninety-odd raiders and scores of monks, had vanished. All that remained was a large bowl-shaped indentation in the ground.

He stumbled away from the site, looking back at the devastation. He did not know what it was that had attacked him, or where they had come from. But at the last moment, just before the blast, he had *seen* it. One of the creatures. He lacked the language to describe what he saw, but he would never forget it.

Agnarsson lost all of his men, his axe and his arm, but he had been spared his life for some unknown reason. And he did not understand *why*. But he would remember this night for the rest of his life. It would haunt him. His father had been wrong, there *were* things in the world that mortal men simply could not fight.

THE SOUND OF FEAR

ONE

São Paulo, Brazil
The Present, 2 November, 2200 Hrs

SÃO PAULO WAS the largest city in Brazil and the largest in the southern hemisphere. It was also the sixth largest in the world in population. After today, it would be fourteenth.

The sky went bright with a loud crack and a crash of thunder. Lightning arced across the city, and a massive ball of glowing light appeared. It was yellow and swallowed several city blocks. The sphere crackled and pulsed as if it were made of pure energy. As it grew, the electrical phenomenon engulfed building after building. Security cameras around the city captured hazy, static-filled images of the creatures that eventually emerged. The first people to encounter them were torn apart. But even more people, still living, and screaming and gibbering, were dragged away into the spitting ball of fire.

After nearly twenty minutes, the globe of devastation sucked both sound and light out of the world before it winked out of existence. The crater left behind was immense. Buildings on the edge of the giant divot toppled inward, killing hundreds more still hiding in their apartments. Later, rescue workers would find that everything at the edge of the dome had been severed cleanly—buildings, roads, Metro tunnels and even human bodies, which littered the edge of the circumference of the effect. Over a million dead in just a few minutes.

Karachi, Pakistan
3 November, 0600 Hrs

AS DAWN BLED light into the sky over the city, it brought thunder and lightning. But there were no clouds in the sky.

Karachi and its environs had grown from an estimated population of five million in 1980 to over twenty million—many of them refugees from successive wars in neighboring Afghanistan, first against the Russians, then against its own people and finally against the Americans. The city eventually took measures to purify the putrid and smog-coated air by planting more gardens and building more parks. Traffic was diverted onto high-speed overpasses. Still, the city continued to grow and grow, as refugees poured in.

The newest arrival appeared just as the noisy city was waking up. The ball of light hovered in the air, just a foot off the black asphalt, between the open doors of Jinnah International Airport and the McDonald's restaurant that sat just opposite. Hundreds of crows complained at the interruption of their normal morning routine, scavenging food from nearby trash cans and along the edges of the road. They took flight, fleeing the intruding brilliance and cawing. The ball was no larger than three feet in diameter initially. But then it grew quickly and when it stopped, the fast-food franchise and a good portion of the airport were enveloped. Lightning crackled out of the center of the blinding sphere, blasting people and nearby structures.

The noise was deafening. As a repeated sound of thunder boomed, the cracks of bone-shaking sound pierced the morning air.

Screams added to the din. Then something came out of the light, tearing into anything with flesh and rending it in seconds. The attacking thing moved too quickly to be seen in the dazzling light.

Then, with no warning, the piercing noise stopped, leaving only silence in its wake.

The light disappeared.

The sphere of devastation came and went in just ten minutes, but it took a scoop of the city with it. Cleaved buildings stood with their plumbing and electrical wires exposed; the ground was a perfectly smooth crater where previously asphalt, cars and pedestrians had been. It was as if a small sun had briefly made an appearance right on the surface of the Earth, clawing away all she held, until nothing remained. The tally of the number of dead or missing would take weeks, but in the end, it would be in the tens of thousands.

Seoul, South Korea
3 November, 1000 Hrs

THE CABLE CAR that took visitors up to the top of Namsan Mountain, and the huge communications tower on top of the mountain, began to shake violently, before a blast of lightning severed the cable completely.

Fifteen people sat inside the car that had nearly reached the top of its 1900-foot journey up a graduated height of 500 feet in altitude. The car plummeted 60 feet to the ground before they began to bounce and slide down the mountainside, leaving long grooves in the soil. Despite the impacts and jolts, all fifteen people survived the fall with nothing more than broken bones, multiple contusions and various cuts and scrapes.

They were the lucky ones.

As they plummeted down the mountain on one side, a sizzling globe of death appeared on the other side of the steel and concrete

777-foot tower at the summit of the mountain, chewing a hole in everything it touched. Spreading out in an arc of chaos and destruction, the unknown phenomenon scoured the northwest side of the mountain, erasing the Jung-gu and Seongdong-gu neighborhoods before imploding and leaving nothing more than a scar on the ground that stretched three miles in diameter.

Cairo, Egypt, 3 November
0300 Hrs

AT THREE IN the morning, even a behemoth like Cairo slumbers. The incessant honking of vehicle horns dies down for just a few hours. They would start again around 5 a.m., but the cacophony would be softer than usual.

The Egyptians, even in the middle of the night, were the first to mobilize military units against the phenomenon, their forces on a constant ready standby, after the recent events of Arab Spring.

The Egyptian Army managed to get an M6-2000 main battle tank on site in time to fire its M1A1 main turret conversion kit gun, with its 20 mm shells, at the pulsing, glowing target. However, as far as the Egyptians could see, the massive shells made little difference, disappearing into the energy without a trace.

Egyptian Air Force F-16 fighters arrived on scene just in time to fire a single AGM-84 Harpoon anti-ship missile at the glowing sphere that stood hurtling lightning bolts where the InterContinental Cairo Semiramis hotel had been earlier that night. But just before the missile hit, the thundering roar and crackling light winked out, leaving an eerie silence in its wake. The remaining crater quickly began to fill with the waters of the River Nile. The missile plunged under the water and detonated at the bottom of the crater, sending up a sticky geyser of mud, water and sand. Cairo was about to get a new lake—right in the middle of the city.

Los Angeles, 2 November
1800 Hrs

RUSH HOUR WAS still grinding away when a spherical chunk of the freeway evaporated in a ball of sizzling light and blistering beams of lightning that speared through random motorists and their pastel colored minivans and coupes. Traffic had stopped anyway, so hundreds of motorists simply abandoned their cars and ran away from the brilliant orb. Most of them eluded the lightning strikes, although a few were electrocuted as they ran. One man was hit by a glancing blow that sent him into the air across five cars, only to roll off the hood of a Ford Taurus and resume his sprint as if nothing had happened.

Brian Daly sat transfixed as he watched it all happen through the windscreen of his tan Prius. He wondered briefly if he should also get out and run, as Lightning Man was doing, but then he saw the things streaking out of the ball of light. They were drawn to the fleeing people—hunting them. Daly noticed that the creatures ignored the motorists still in their cars, so he sat as still as he could, allowing only his eyes to move as he followed the carnage.

The things were fast. *Damn fast.* And hard to see. They weren't immaterial, like ghosts, but there was something strange about them. They were...indistinct, though that could also be from the fact that much of what he was seeing was in his periphery.

They were strong, too. He saw several people attacked, their limbs or heads torn away with ease. The things moved on all fours like animals, but could also stand or run on their hind legs, erect, like humans. But these things were not human. Not even close. One of the creatures raised its head, but all Daly saw was its bulbous eyes, swiveling back and forth like a chameleon's, before it ducked away, racing after anything that moved and ignoring anything that cowered.

Daly sat transfixed and somehow remained eerily calm, as if he were watching a summer blockbuster, instead of the deaths of hundreds of rush-hour drivers. Then one of the creatures clambered atop the roof of a GMC Suburban to his left. He strained his eyes for a better view, but didn't dare rotate his head. In his peripheral vision, he saw the thing lift its head to the sky like a wolf and howl.

The sound was devastating—a soul-cutting, sonic assault, unlike anything Daly had ever heard. The sound shook the bones inside his skin. He lost control of his bowels. His bladder let go and the saliva in his mouth began to pour down over his lower lip as if he'd been in a dentist's chair with a few gallons of Novocain pumped into his system. Terror took hold of him. His eyes went wide. His body shook uncontrollably.

Later, after the creatures returned to the light, and the globe of lightning flickered out, leaving behind an enormous crater and thousands dead or dying, Brian Daly's mind finally returned to some semblance of what it had been. But he would never be the same. He didn't know what he had just seen, but he knew that local police forces would be helpless against it. Whatever those things had been, even the military would be hard-pressed to stop them. Still, he needed to tell someone what he had just seen. His brother Steven was an Army Ranger. Steve was just a captain, but he might be able to get the information to someone higher up. Daly pulled out his cell phone and called his brother as fast as his shaking fingers would allow.

Philadelphia
2 November, 2100 Hrs

MOMENTS AFTER THE carnage in the other cities began, the Liberty Bell began to glow.

Currently situated in the Liberty Bell Center, adjacent to the glass pavilion that had housed the bell from 1976 until 2003, the bell is the object of visitation by over a million tourists a year. But the facility closed to visitors at 5 p.m.. Only three security guards remained on hand when the inscription on the bell, *Proclaim liberty throughout all the land unto all the inhabitants thereof,* began to luminesce. One of the three guards—the one furthest from the actual 2,080-pound copper-and-tin attraction—had just enough time to slap his hand on a large red emergency alarm before the surge of light engulfed him.

Police responded quickly. They closed 6th Street and set up barricades on Market and Chestnut, thinking people would be safe at that distance. They were wrong.

Sergeant Gina Martinez stepped out of her cruiser at the barricade to an unholy sight. A giant dome of intense light throwing forked spears of lightning. Thunder boomed despite the clear sky full of stars above her head. She stepped up to the edge of the park, her mouth agape at the sight. The spectacle washed out the strobing colors from her cruiser's light bar as well as from the forty others arrayed around her on the street and up on the sidewalk.

What the hell is *that?* she wondered.

"Clayton," she called to a plainclothes detective who was near her. "What is this thing? Terrorist attack?"

"Beats the hell outta me. We got an alarm on the bell. Thought it was a B&E or something. We're trying to keep people out of the way of those lightnin' bolts, but other than that, what the frig are we supposed to do? Fire Chief is on the way and the Mayor's got the Guard coming, too. I guess we just wait and see."

Just then, a huge bolt of lightning struck close to their position and incinerated a tall maple tree.

"Shit! That was close." Gina ducked instinctively, but by the time she had crouched, the lightning was already done with the tree. Had it hit her...

"I think it's getting bigger." Clayton sounded nervous.

"That's what she said," Gina replied, her whispered voice on autopilot. She'd spent the previous night with her girlfriends. They sat around her apartment binging on nachos, drinking margaritas and watching *The Office* until every other sentence was "That's what she said."

"I'm serious. Look. The top of the dome is above the roof and the edge is touching the credit union now."

"Damnit, you're right." Gina's hand went instinctively to the handle of her holstered Glock, before she realized how useless her weapon would be against a glistening whitish-yellow dome of lightning. Still, she kept her hand on the grip. It prolonged her life.

Four shapes bolted out of the center of the crackling energy. Gina saw them move. She dropped and rolled to the left just as one of them tore into Clayton, sending his legs in one direction and the rest of him in the other. All Gina saw was a smooth, white color and the movement of muscles, as if whatever she was seeing had no skin and was covered in skim milk.

The other shapes tore into the rest of the cruisers. Blood sprayed away from every impacted police officer. Gina could barely track them, but she drew her weapon anyway and focused on one of the creatures. She might not have had a chance to stop it, but it paused suddenly and seemed to sniff the air. What she saw was terrifying. The beast's eyes swiveled toward her and then it was in motion again, coming right for her. She couldn't see it that well, but she remembered that eye and fired five times, where she thought it would be. The thing crashed to the asphalt right in front of her, pulling a scream from her lungs.

A mistake.

The other three creatures stopped and focused their swiveling eyes on her.

What the hell are you? she had time to think.

Then one of the creatures opened its mouth and roared. The sound was so loud it vibrated her body. Sheer terror took hold of her, and her thoughts simply shut down. The gun fell from her hand and she lost all control of her bodily functions as she collapsed on the corpse of the creature in front of her. Her body shook uncontrollably. When her body was pulled by the ankle, back toward the curved, pulsating wall of light, her fear-locked mind never noticed.

TWO

Fenris Kystby, Norway
3 November, 0500 Hrs

STAN TREMBLAY LOOKED down at the blood leaking from the puncture wound in his upper arm and said, "Oh, it's on now, you pecker-noodles!"

His shoulder had only just started to heal from the trauma a few days earlier. He glanced up at the villagers surrounding him in a semicircle. Most of them were hanging back, but they wielded farm weapons, kitchen knives and even homemade torches. The man with the pitchfork, a villager he knew to be named Roald, was the closest. He reached out his bleeding arm as quick as a snake strike and snatched the pitchfork away from the man. Roald stepped back slightly, in shock. Then the glazed look returned to his eyes. A look all the villagers had.

A look of *hate*.

Roald moved forward to attack again, this time barehanded after the loss of his pitchfork. Tremblay swung the shaft of the pitchfork around in a wide arc and clocked Roald in the side of the head. The man crumpled to the grassy field. The others paused. Just long enough for Tremblay to bring the wooden pitchfork handle across his knee and splinter it like a toothpick.

"I'm done fuckin' around with you people."

The look of hatred surged in the eyes of the villagers, and then they all rushed at him.

Stan Tremblay was a pretty big guy. With his blue eyes, long blonde goatee and hulking size, he could have easily fit in as one of the local Norwegian mountain men. But his Russian accent was better than his Norwegian one, so when he had hiked into town looking for some peace and quiet, he had said he was a former Russian soldier. These people all knew him as Stanislav. None of them suspected that he was secretly a former Delta operator, one of five who made up Chess Team, a deep cover black ops group that faced threats to not only the United States, but to the whole world. When his last mission in Siberia had gone south, Tremblay, callsign: Rook, had felt he needed some time to get his head straight. After a journey aboard an Arctic fishing trawler, on his way from Russia to Norway, Rook had come ashore and just started walking. The land was desolate and windswept, and he figured if he couldn't organize his thoughts in this remote place, then he wouldn't be able to do it anywhere.

Instead of solitude though, Rook had found himself helping the locals with a predator that was eating their livestock. He had discovered some of the town's dirty laundry, but certainly not enough to warrant a mob showing up on the edge of the farm where Rook was staying. He knew some of these people. They had just been expressing their gratitude to him days earlier.

As the first man, a stoic Norwegian named Baldur, got close, Rook swung out with his left hand—still clutching the business end of the snapped pitchfork. The outer rusted tine grazed the man's cheek, but still he came on with a broad-bladed farm implement Rook had never seen before. Baldur made to swing with the heavy tool, and Rook stepped into the blow, smashing his forehead down on Baldur's nose. A gout of blood sprayed through the air as the man recoiled. Rook hoped that because his size and gruff demeanor alone hadn't been enough to make these people back off, maybe a few simple displays of violence would do the trick. He had started by talking to the crowd. But that hadn't worked. All it had gotten him from the maddened villagers was a few puncture holes in an already injured shoulder. He glanced back at the farm behind him, where he had left his .50 caliber Magnum Desert Eagle, concealed in the hay of the barn. He wished he had brought it now. Hopefully Peder, the old man that had been letting Rook sleep in his barn, would stay out of sight—or at least if he did come out, Rook hoped the man would have the sense to come out with the barrel of his well-kept shotgun leading the way.

Two more men rushed Rook. He poked the blunt end of the wooden shaft into one man's gut. A cough of air burst from the man's throat as he dropped to his knees. Before Rook could swing the pointed half of his damaged weapon at the other man, he felt a hard smack on his shoulder blade. The second man had hit him with the flat of a shovel.

A shovel? Seriously? These people were making him mad. He swung around in a full circle, bringing the wooden stick to the back of the man's knees like an Escrima stick, then he helped the man's descent to the sod by slamming the flat of the metal fork down on the falling man's chest as he went.

"So much for a few displays of violence." Rook saw that the villagers assembled against him were not backing down, and all had murder in their hearts. Even the woman, Anni, and her two children were in the crowd, each wielding some kind of improvised weapon. The thin blonde woman had a kitchen knife and her kids were armed with screwdrivers. He was about to say something about how if they wouldn't back down, he was going to have to bring his "A" game. But just then he heard a scream of anguish from behind him. Rook glanced back and saw the barn had just erupted into flames— with the horses still inside. He recognized the voice as Peder's, and he saw two more of the villagers that had circled around him were tossing kerosene cans at the blaze.

"Monkeyfu—" He was cut off by the blade of a pair of pruning shears slicing across his chest. A woman he didn't know was about to take another swing at him, and a man was swiping a 2x4 at Rook's head. He squatted low, allowing the swing to clear his head, and as he sprang back up to his feet, he let the woman have it with a left uppercut to the jaw, the wooden stick still clutched in his meaty hand. As her small body began to launch into the air, he kicked out with his left, booted foot, and caught the 2x4 man in the throat, just under his thick beard.

Another man Rook had seen in the village swung the blade of an electric hedge trimmer at Rook's left side. The damned thing wasn't even running, but the glaze-eyed Nordic man swung it anyway, as if doing so would finally end all his woes.

Rook took several steps backward. The people were getting too close. The fierce breeze in the early morning gloom would drive the flames on the barn harder. He had to ensure Peder and as many of the man's horses as possible made it out of the flames in time. But the villagers were giving him no respite. It was as if the sight of the rising flames in the barn and Rook's slight retreat had energized them. Where previously they were each taking pokes at Rook with their respective weapons, now they all simply ran at him.

"Hot friggin' pancakes, you morons won't give up, will you?"

And then the fight began. Rook started moving his feet and whirling his arms with the metal pitchfork fragment in one hand and the improvised Escrima stick in the other. Instead of waiting for the crowd to get to him, Rook headed into them and to the left. He smashed two men to the ground with his forearms, backhanded a woman with the stick on the follow-through of another strike and launched a kick at the midsection of a portly man in his fifties. Rook spun and struck with the weapons, taking down woman and man alike. When Anni's kids made it to the forefront of the fray, he simply booted them away with low kicks, not putting his full strength into it at all. They flew away and their screwdrivers were lost in the short grass.

Even as hard and fast as he fought though, Rook was getting tired. His fingers were getting numb in the cold morning air, and the size of the mob wasn't diminishing rapidly enough. Some of the men he'd put down at the start of the fight were getting back into it. Then he heard a shotgun blast from behind him in the raging flames. He glanced back just in time to see the man that had become his friend in the last weeks, Peder, fall down onto the ground, a villager standing over him with a large stick, and the shotgun falling away to the side.

Rook turned to sprint to Peder's aid when he saw the man bring the stick down hard, end first, into Peder's face.

"No!" Rook started pumping his legs but something tripped him up, and he went sprawling to the ground. His mouth filled with dirt when he hit. Then something whacked his leg hard. He rolled away from the impact and spit the dirt out of his mouth. He pulled his legs up over his head into a backward somersault, landing crouched on his feet. He had dropped the metal pitchfork stick and now had only his two-foot length of splintered wood. As his body came to a stop from the roll, he spotted what had tripped him up. It was one of Anni's kids. A little boy no taller than three feet, his long blonde hair tangled and streaming behind him, his short sharp breaths huffing, making him look like some feral jungle boy. He had the screwdriver clutched in his hand again and was driving it forward right at Rook's face. Rook swatted at the hand that held the tool's handle, knocking the thing from the boy's grip, but the kid kept coming on. Rook balled his empty hand into a fist and conked the brat on the top of his head, this time sending the little beast into unconsciousness.

Rook slowly stood, seeing perhaps twenty bodies on the ground, most of whom were writhing in agony, but a few of whom were still out after the damage he had inflicted. The problem was, there were thirty or so people still standing, and they were all coming straight at him like a tide of screaming soldiers in some sword-and-sandal epic. Rook took a deep breath. His face darted back to Peder and saw that the man's body lay unmolested in the grass. His attackers were coming right at Rook.

And one of them now held Peder's shotgun.

THREE
Mount Kadam, Uganda
3 November, 0600 Hrs

SHIN DAE-JUNG, CALLSIGN: Knight, lay perfectly still in the long, yellowed grass, with the black combat boot-clad foot of a soldier standing on his hand.

He was invisible in the long grass, with his ghillie suit covered in more of it, but if the soldier were to glance down, Knight might still be spotted. His trigger hand throbbed from the weight of the soldier's foot, but he didn't dare to flex it even slightly. Knight's left hand was clenched firmly on the handle of his KA-BAR knife, still sheathed on his chest. If the soldier made him, or worse—tripped over the camouflaged experimental EXACTO sniper rifle on the ground in front of him—Knight would launch upward and thrust the blade of the Marine Corps knife deep into the Ugandan soldier's chest. But right now, Knight's cover was more important, so he remained still, barely breathing, in tiny increments.

If it hadn't been for the damn shooting, I would have heard this bastard before he was on me. The group of soldiers he had been watching fired their weapons in the dawn sky like idiots after a rousing speech from their leader.

Knight had been deployed to Uganda to perform surveillance on a small offshoot guerilla faction. Led by Romeo Kigongo, the United Faithful Army was a militant and unruly branch of the Lord's Resistance Army. The LRA had recently come to the attention of the world for the atrocities they perpetrated on the weak and poor of rural Uganda, as well as for their incursions into neighboring African states using child soldiers as cannon fodder. The Ugandan military had been hopeless in tracking down the LRA, but eventually the world media began focusing on the group and its leader, Joseph Kony. When the world finally started clamoring for Kony's head in 2012 (the United States and other nations had labeled him as a terrorist of special interest years earlier), many of Kony's lieutenants—Romeo Kigongo included—simply formed their own splinter groups and returned to the life of privacy their smaller fiefdoms had previously provided them. Kigongo's group, the UFA, would probably have gone unnoticed for years if they hadn't made an incursion into Tanzania to steal eight hundred million dollars worth of uncut diamonds. Now funded properly, they were taking the next step in the International Bad Boy game. They were seeking a portable nuclear device.

Knight and a teammate had been sent to the grassy plateau near Mount Kadam to watch the early morning deal go down, mark the players and then, if possible, kill the UFA members with knowledge of the deal and deactivate the device. Knight and his teammate would then be extracted with the nuclear material.

The only problem was the timing. As a part of the former Delta group known as Chess Team, which was now part of a larger black ops organization known as Endgame, Knight was privy to all kinds of intelligence, but in this case, his headquarters-based handler, callsign: Deep Blue, named after the chess-playing supercomputer, had only been able to provide him with a location and a general timeframe.

No exact date.

No exact time.

Knight had been lying in the grass for three days now.

It's a wonder he can't smell me.

The soldier hadn't moved from Knight's hand in twenty minutes. Deep Blue had been tracking the operation through an NSA satellite and communicating with Knight through a tactical earplug, but Deep Blue hadn't said anything in hours and Knight guessed that was just plain bad luck. If Deep Blue had been watching, he would have warned Knight of the soldier's arrival long before Knight's digits got mashed into the soil. All he could do now was wait. If the solider moved on, fine. But if he stayed put much longer, Knight would have to break cover and risk the noise of killing the man—his hand simply couldn't take too much more.

"Please tell me that tango isn't standing near you." Knight's partner, Erik Sommers, callsign: Bishop, spoke so softly and calmly in Knight's earphone that the man could have been resting in an easy chair. Bishop was somewhere off to Knight's left across the huge field. Knight didn't know exactly where Bishop was, but he knew that the man probably would have had a great view of the guerillas down the slope of the field. He wouldn't have been keeping an eye on Knight's position for the most part. Deep Blue was supposed to do that.

Unable to respond verbally, Knight slipped his tongue out of his mouth and touched the sensitive lip-microphone he wore. The resulting sound would be an audible click in Bishop's earpiece. A *yes.*

"Is he *on* your hide?"

Another flick of the tongue. *Yes.*

Bishop let Knight hear his chuckle. "Figures. Deep Blue, you copy? Could use some eyes in the sky right now." Bishop's voice still stayed soft and level, as if he held no real interest in the fact that his teammate was close to being compromised. It almost sounded like the man was about to fall asleep.

Deep Blue did not respond, which was unusual, but far less strange than Deep Blue not warning Knight about incoming enemy forces.

"Knight, you want me to intervene?" Bishop inquired, almost Zen-like in his serenity.

Knight considered for just a moment. His hand was sore as hell, but if the soldier needed to be taken down, it would probably be better for him to do it with the knife than for Bishop to come across the field with his custom-modified XM312-B machine gun that could turn the soldier into paste, but which would also alert half of Uganda. He slid his tongue out twice to touch the lip-mic. *No.*

Knight was about to call it a day and unsheathe the knife when Deep Blue finally spoke in his ear.

"Sorry I was away. I'll explain later. Knight, I see you're in the shit. Stay down, I'm sending Bishop to you. We need to abandon this op." Deep Blue's voice, masked by voice modulation in case anyone were to pick up on their frequency, was still full of tension. Something was deeply wrong. The team rarely abandoned an operation. Anticipating the reaction of his teammates, and the questions Bishop would pose because Knight was unable to speak without giving away his cover, Deep Blue continued. "I need you both in Cairo an hour ago. Something huge is going down. Bishop, kill the tangos. Hit however many of the soldiers downfield as you can. Transport is inbound to your location and should arrive in less than two minutes. Go."

With that, thunder filled the air as Bishop stepped out of cover on the edge of the field. Despite his adopted Scandinavian-American name, Bishop was a huge mountain of a muscled man, with deep chestnut Persian skin that revealed his true heritage. He looked perfectly at home holding the long-barreled machine gun. It boomed with each shot, sending .50 caliber rounds scorching through the air at a rate of almost 800 rounds a minute. The top half of the soldier standing on Knight's hand turned to a cloud of mist with the first hit, and the man's legs fell over onto Knight's back.

Knight didn't stand. There was no point. His weapon was already aligned with the bulk of the soldiers down the field, and they had all stopped to turn and stare in Knight's direction, temporarily dumbfounded by the roar of Bishop's machine gun, which sounded like a fleet of supersonic jets each crossing the sound barrier, one after another. *Boom. Boom. Boom.* Knight swept his sore hand to the grip of the weapon, glanced down the scope and began taking out his own targets. He went for headshots, and one after the next, removed another fanatical Ugandan terrorist from the world.

Bishop began stalking across the field toward Knight, sweeping the barrel of his XM312-B to the side of him as he went, mowing down wave after wave of the enemy combatants. In many cases, Bishop's indiscriminant sweep hit the living and dead—men on the receiving end of Knight's long-range, .50 caliber sniper rounds.

"Where's that pickup?" Knight asked.

"It'll be here," Bishop said, his calm only slightly interrupted by the pounding of his weapon's vibration on his body.

The still-living members of the UFA had hit the dirt and were firing back with Russian AK-47 assault rifles, which only had an effective range of about 450 yards—nowhere near the distance away that Bishop and Knight were—but Knight had also spotted them readying a few rocket-propelled grenades and he knew those could reach his position. Still, it would take little effort for him and Bishop to hold off the 30 soldiers still in the fight.

Knight picked up his EXACTO, short for EXtreme ACcuracy Tasked Ordnance, which made hitting targets a mile away much easier thanks to its "fire and forget" ammunition, which stayed on target by changing shape while in flight. He changed positions quickly, focusing on the small breakaway group to his right, across the field. The ones with the rockets. He assumed a kneeling stance and launched a few rounds toward the group. He took two men with one bullet, piercing the first man's head and the second man's chest.

So much for—

Then the ground at the front of the field, between his position and the terrorists, erupted in a spurt of flame. Dark-colored soil launched into the air. Knight moved his eye from the scope and looked up to see an A-10 Thunderbolt II ground attack fighter. The plane was commonly known as the "Warthog" and it bristled with armaments and a GAU-8 heavy rotary nose-mounted cannon. The plane was painted olive drab green, but its belly was painted in garish, thin, black, red and yellow stripes.

At first, Knight had thought their transport was here. But the Warthog's color scheme said otherwise. The plane was one of twelve fighters in the Ugandan People's Defense Force Air Wing. The government forces had arrived, but it seemed they weren't targeting the UFA soldiers. The ground in front of Knight was chewed up by the 30 mm Gatling-style cannon on the nose of the plane, and then the cannon fire was gone as the plane blasted by overhead. The gouge in the field was almost a foot deep, as if a tractor had just come by and ploughed a furrow. The dark line was less than a yard from Knight's position in the grass. Bishop stood just to the other side of the line in the earth and looked at Knight. He had stopped firing his XM312-B.

"That was damned close," he said. For once, his reserve of calm was shattered.

Knight stood and turned to look up at the A-10 as it banked in the sky for another attack run. "Deep Blue, we need that transport, now!"

Knight ignored the scattered AK-47 fire from further down the field. Many of the UFA soldiers had fled with the arrival of a UPDF plane, but the few left were still firing at Bishop and Knight. None of them had figured out they didn't have the range to hit their targets. Knight looked at Bishop and had an idea.

"Stand still, Bish."

Bishop did as he was asked without any query. Knight walked over to him and laid the long barrel of the EXACTO sniper rifle on the man's shoulder from behind. With Bishop being almost a foot taller than Knight, the little Korean American didn't need to even squat to get the right angle. He lined up the scope on the returning Warthog and took five quick breaths, then slowed his breathing to several shallow ones.

The Warthog was lined up perfectly, on an attack run for their position, and it opened up fire with the rotating cannon spitting out a line of fire at 60 rounds a second. The fire scoured a fast approaching line into the ground. If they didn't move, they would be cut in half.

"Better know what you're doing," Bishop said. "And do it fast."

FOUR
Walt Disney World Resort, Florida
2 November, 1300 Hrs

"HOW THE HELL do I keep getting myself into these things?"

Jack Sigler, callsign: King, raced across the roof of a speeding, white public transit monorail train that ran around the amusement park on an elevated track. The man he was chasing was not going to get away.

It was an overcast day in what was supposed to be sunny Florida. A high-sixties breeze buffeted King's short-cropped hair. He missed his long shaggy hair, which he'd cut for an undercover mission in Paris and planned to grow out again. His loose-fitting black t-shirt with his hero Elvis's TCB logo rippled across his muscular chest in the warm wind. The shirt was his favorite. That was King, too: *taking care of business*. The man he chased across the roof of the fast-moving monorail was dressed in his own pair of jeans and a lightweight hooded sweatshirt with a small Jansport backpack on his back. No more than twenty-five, King thought, the man had a nervous, sweaty look to him that had first tipped King off that something wasn't right.

King had been vacationing in Florida with his girlfriend, CDC disease detective turned Endgame expert, Sara Fogg. Accompanying the pair was his adopted fourteen-year-old daughter, Fiona Lane, the lone survivor of an attack that took the lives of her grandmother, as well as the rest of the Siletz Reservation the pair called home.

As a former Delta operator and field leader of the ultra-secret Chess Team, King had met both women while on the job, and his work had severely affected each of their lives. Most of the time, Fiona was fine with her adopted family of soldiers and her life of danger, but sometimes she wanted to just be a kid. She had asked King shyly if they might take a trip to Disney sometime. After the recent events with his job in Paris, King and Sara had quickly decided it was something they all needed. A little time for each of them to be normal.

King and Sara had grown closer, too, so much so that she was naturally a part of the process now, when it came to decisions for Fiona. King wasn't sure marriage was in the cards anytime soon— after all, he was a full-time soldier dealing with threats that affected America and the globe. The level of danger was more than could be coped with by most tactical military teams. But he also couldn't deny that he felt empty on the downtime when Sara was out in the field battling microscopic enemies that all the bullets in the world couldn't kill.

Their Disney vacation had started out fine, and King found himself really enjoying sleeping in each morning. The girls were impatient with him, though, so today they had headed to Epcot early and King followed when he woke. He was taking the monorail from the hotel when he had spotted the sweaty man with the backpack.

Seated at the front of the train, Sweaty had started fidgeting with his pack, and King, trained to notice such things, had started counting problems with the man. Inappropriate clothing—the sweatshirt was too hot for the day. A bag and hands in the bag fumbling with things unseen. Profuse nervous sweating and a glazed stare fixed directly ahead. King couldn't believe it, but the man was exhibiting many of the symptoms of a suicide bomber. But he was a Caucasian man—not West Asian—so King had initially told himself that maybe he was being overly cautious. He glanced back behind him to check the rest of the monorail car for the other passengers, to see if anything or anyone else set off his security radar.

But when he turned back, he realized he never should have taken eyes off the subject. The man had stood, swept into the unlocked driver's compartment at the front of the train and pulled an automatic pistol out of his pack.

That's what I get for racial profiling.

King lunged from his seat, already in motion along the length of the car when Sweaty had conked the driver—an older man of at least sixty-five—over the head with the butt of the weapon. He was squatting and affixing a magnetic bomb to the dash of the train when King had nearly reached the door of the driver's compartment.

Passengers screamed, as King eyed the bomb.

Sweaty had turned at the last second and with no hesitation had fired a sweeping arc of eight bullets through the Plexiglas windows and back into the passenger area of the compartment. King instinctively threw himself backward as he saw the gun arm coming up, almost in slow motion. The Plexiglas shattered as he fell to the floor, fragmenting and spraying large shards over him and a row of screaming Mouseketeers. He rolled to a crouch against the bottom of the door leading into the front compartment, and one of the passengers made eye contact with him. She pointed at the front of the train.

King rose and peered through the shattered window, quickly taking in the unconscious old man, the bomb on the dash and the open side window through which he could just see the leg of the sweaty man rising out of view.

The roof, he thought. *Why do they always go for the roof on a moving train?*

King stepped into the driver's area and checked for a pulse on the old man. He was alive—just out cold. The bomb was unfamiliar to King, but clearly not a homemade job. Either Sweaty was a professional bomb-maker or he had obtained the device from one. King didn't know much about the monorail trains at Disney, or about how they worked, but he had read some things about the park on the flight from Europe. He knew that the trains had a system that prevented them from colliding and shut them down in case of an emergency. He remembered that the system was called MAPO, after *Mary Poppins*. There were lights on the dash that would indicate when the MAPO system was engaged. But a small black device with a blinking red light had been magnetically attached to the dash next to the MAPO system, and King was dismayed to see that no MAPO lights were lit. The black device was clearly interfering with the safety system of the train.

King stared at the bomb and the black box. He didn't know what to do. He knew how to disarm some simple, improvised explosive devices, but not a bomb of this complexity. He didn't know if he could just remove either the bomb or the electronic device interfering with the MAPO system. Either attempt might set the bomb off early. He glanced at the speedometer and saw the train was doing nearly 50 mph, and then looked out the front of the train at the monorail track ahead. Eventually they would hit something or the bomb would go off, assuming it had some kind of internal timer.

Gonna have to bring Sweaty back, King thought, and climbed out the open window.

THE MAN RAN toward the back of the train. King chased after him, but made ready to hit the deck should the man turn and fire the 9 mm that he still clutched in one sweaty hand. But the man didn't turn until King was nearly on top of him. Sweaty stopped on the roof of the last car and simply stood still. As King got up to him, the man turned and again brought the weapon up, but King was ready for him this time. He swatted the weapon from the man's arm and it went flying into the air. King launched a right cross and hit the man on the chin. Sweaty staggered back and all the fight went out of him. Then the man brought his eyes up to look at King.

But his eyes didn't stop on King's face. He was looking over King's right shoulder, up toward the front of the train, and King saw terror fill the man's face. The man took a step back from King, turned and sprinted off the rear of the train, his torso slamming into the concrete edge of the raised rail and his body then flipping backward to plummet to the ground forty feet below.

King watched the sweaty man fall as if in slow motion, then he slowly turned around to see what the bomber had seen. He was expecting more men. Armed men. Somewhere in the dark recesses of his consciousness, he was even expecting some hideous creature from the unknown—King had certainly faced enough far-fetched exotic creatures as a part of his work, to make the possibility of a monstrous beast one he would consider.

What he wasn't expecting was a Russian Mil Mi-24 helicopter gunship loaded with armaments on its wings and a Yak-B nose-mounted cannon pointed right at King. In fact, the massive Russian assault helicopter was probably further down on the list of things King's subconscious could have imagined than the Loch Ness Monster.

FIVE
Fenris Kystby, Norway

ROOK'S ONLY RECOURSE to the shotgun was to rush the man holding it. If he could get close enough, fast enough, he might divert the angle to the barrel on the weapon.

As it turned out though, he needn't have worried. When he got up close to the man, he watched in horror as the man pulled on the trigger, only to have nothing happen. Either Peder only had the one round in the damn thing or this man Rook hadn't met yet didn't know to cock the weapon for another shot. Rook batted the long weapon away from the man with his stick and thrust his right fist directly into the man's unprotected throat. The sound the man made was unpleasant but satisfying. The man's glazed blue Nordic eyes widened as he slumped to his knees.

Rook wasted no time; he sprinted past the other man that had set the barn on fire, and knelt down next to his fallen friend, only to find the old man dead. The blow Rook had seen him take caved in his skull. Rook stood and raced into the flaming barn with dark thoughts filling his head. He flipped the latches on the horse gates. Those animals not already aflame stampeded out of the barn and into the morning air. Unfortunately, the stall where he had been sleeping, and where he had hidden his Desert Eagle, under a pile of straw, was so full of intense flame that he couldn't get close.

Rook turned to see a few villagers had followed him into the blaze. He barreled into them, knocking them into stalls and the flaming walls. Burning to death was a horrible way to die and he didn't wish it on anyone, even his enemies, save for a few genocidal maniacs, but his desire to live trumped his guilt over laying a few Nordic nutjobs on the barbeque. For weeks, his thoughts had been a jumbled mess after the failure of his mission and the murder of his support team in Siberia. Now, his thoughts were as sharp as the edge of shattered fine crystal, focused on finding out why a bunch of seemingly normal Scandinavian villagers suddenly turned into a zombie horde. And whoever was responsible for that, and for the death of his friend, was going to find out what it's like to be a punching bag or a gun range target. Whatever got the job done. Rook wasn't picky.

The barn was a total loss. Rook bolted for the rear doorway and hoped that he might outrun the remaining villagers. But when he burst out of the door and into the fresh morning air, he knew it wasn't going to go down the easy way. The villagers had circled the barn and were waiting for him. There were still twenty-five of them and he could see another group coming across the field toward him.

No clever responses this time; he simply crashed into the first villager he saw and snatched his weapon—a scythe-like farm implement. The blade was shorter than that of a scythe and there was no handle halfway down the shaft. Still, it would do. These people had been innocent victims of something. Mind control? A virus? He couldn't be sure of anything. But it didn't matter. Now they had killed his friend. If he didn't hit back hard, he'd be next.

The gloves were off.

Rook swung the bladed weapon through the low fog that had settled. He cut or impaled any villager that got too close. Blood sprayed, coating everyone near the barn.

The horde was unfazed, pressing the attack.

Rook grunted as something slammed into his forearm, knocking the scythe from his grip. His left leg took a blow from behind him and he went down to one knee.

The mob swarmed in close, reaching for him.

He swung out backward, connecting solidly with whoever had hit him, but it was no use. They had him surrounded. Fists pummeled him on all sides, striking with raging hatred, steel and wood.

Rook kept punching and elbowing until the sheer weight of human bodies on top of him crushed him down to the ground.

SIX
Mount Kadam, Uganda

WHEN KNIGHT FIRED the shot, Bishop felt the jolt on his shoulder where the barrel of the weapon rested. He watched as the front of the A-10's canopy splintered apart, and the pilot's head exploded.

There was just one problem. The plane was still coming at them; the dead pilot's finger was still depressing the trigger on the 30 mm cannon. Bullets tore into the ground, chewing a speeding path right to where Bishop stood with his muscular legs parted.

"Move!" Bishop was shouting and flying through the air to the right as Knight was already leaping to their left. The small Korean rolled in the tall grass and disappeared from Bishop's sight as the gunfire raced past them. Bishop checked the sky to see that the trouble had not passed. The gunfire from the cannon had ripped past them through the tall grasses of the field, but the plane was crashing down toward their location now, and they were taking fire from the locals, who had closed the distance while Bishop and Knight had been distracted by the arrival of the A-10.

Before either man could move, one of the planes wing's sheared off in a shower of sparks created by a barrage of bullets raining down from a second aircraft high above. Lacking lift provided by the wing, the plane nose-dived and spun to Earth, the freed wing crashing nearby, and each portion of the ruined vehicle exploding on impact.

Silhouetted by the rising plume of burning airplane fuel, Knight picked off the last few targets downfield as their rescuer, the curved-wing transport ship known as the *Crescent*, swept past directly overhead.

The Chess Team transport plane arced gracefully and came back toward Bishop's position as he stood and watched. It kicked in its vertical-takeoff-and-landing (VTOL) thrusters, and slowed to a hover near Bishop. The craft then began to set down in the tall grass. The noise from its engines sounded low, like a hum, and the thrust of air was no stronger than a rough breeze.

The *Crescent* was Chess Team's stealth troop transport. Its half-moon shape could hold several tons of equipment, but the team more frequently used the vehicle for fast and quiet troop transport. It had recently been retrofitted for the VTOL engines, because no airports near the team's headquarters in New Hampshire had a long enough runway for it. The interior was fitted with quarters for 60 men on bunks, as well as the latest in tactical weaponry. Radar-absorbent black and gray material coated the entire vehicle, and the surface of the flying wing consisted of odd, lumpy rectangular shapes. The plane had top-notch electronic countermeasures and held a wide array of armaments for any occasion—including its own heavy rotary cannon, which had just dispatched the falling Warthog.

Bishop turned back to see a few figures fleeing in the distance and Knight casually strolling toward him, carrying his massive sniper rifle over a shoulder.

"I guess there's not much left for me to do." Bishop told him.

"Something tells me there'll be plenty for you to do in Cairo." Knight walked up to the lowered entrance ramp leading inside the stealth vehicle and Bishop followed, lugging the olive drab XM312-B.

Inside they greeted the pilots, former *Nightstalkers* men they knew only by their callsigns: Black One and Black Two. They strapped into chairs, waiting for the landing ramp to close, and the interior of the plane to pressurize, before contacting Deep Blue.

"We're on board the *Crescent*," Knight spoke into a microphone. "What's going on in Cairo?"

Deep Blue's face appeared on a monitor in front of Bishop's chair. His rugged good looks, crow's feet, and balding hair reminded Bishop of Bruce Willis. "Forget Cairo. I'm sending you to the Asian theater now. It's bad this time, gentlemen. It is very, very bad. Sending you some files right now. Read up. And if you aren't strapped in tightly, do so. I'm ordering Black One to get you to China at the *Crescent's* top speed. Deep Blue out."

Knight looked at Bishop with a raised eyebrow. Then Bishop felt the thrust when the vehicle sped up and broke the sound barrier. The computer terminal beeped in front of them, and the screen came to life with satellite imagery and video files in separate windows. The scenes of destruction and devastation were nearly incomprehensible.

The worst part was that each window was labeled with a different city name: Karachi, Philadelphia, Seoul, São Paulo, Cairo, Los Angeles, Brisbane, New Delhi and Buenos Aires. The world was on fire.

SEVEN
Fenris Kystby, Norway

ROOK PUSHED AGAINST the mound of bodies covering him, but he couldn't budge.

Couldn't breathe, either.

Fucking hell, if I go like this, it won't matter if I go to Heaven or Hell. There isn't an angel or demon that won't mock me about this. God is probably getting a good chuckle out of this.

He pushed again, but without oxygen, his muscles continued to weaken.

Then he felt the weight of bodies begin to lift off him. He heard grunting noises and shouts of pain. Then more weight shifted off him. He was lying face down on the ground, battered and bloody, with several of the villagers still on top of him and punching, clawing and poking at him. Before he couldn't move at all, but now, with the shift in weight above him, as the grunting and shouting continued, he was able to slide his arms under his broad chest. He pulled his knees up slowly to his chest and planted his toes down into the soil.

Then, with a mighty heave, he launched himself up, throwing off the last few bodies that were dog-piled on top of him. As those few villagers hit the ground—three men and two women—Rook looked around to see what was happening. The barn was still burning. The sun had pierced through the fog of the morning and lit the scene in blinding detail. A woman with long dark hair was taking it to the remaining villagers. She was throwing side and high kicks like a karate champ, and punching and gouging throats whenever they came within her reach. She moved like liquid mercury, melting from one fight, rolling and flipping to another, as if the entire battle were one long choreographed dance for which she had memorized the moves.

And she was stunningly beautiful.

This woman had clearly come to Rook's rescue, but he had no idea who she was. He wasn't about to waste the opportunity though. He leapt back into the fight, grabbing the two nearby village women by their necks with his huge hands and knocking their heads together, then punching a tall, gangly man in the solar plexus. He found a second man rushing in and drove his foot into the man's groin, lifting the now squealing bastard right off the ground with the force of the kick.

Ten villagers still stood, and another few were just staggering back to their feet, when something odd happened. The fight abruptly went out of them. Like a flock of birds communicating with each other through some unknown means, all of the conscious villagers turned as one and started slowly walking away from the battle and back toward the town. Rook's unknown rescuer kicked a few of the people as they were departing before she stopped and looked in confusion as the people calmly walked away from the fight.

A few others that had been lying on the ground staggered to their feet and limped back toward the town without a word.

Rook was bewildered. "The hell?"

The woman stood silently looking after the departing villagers. She was shorter than Rook, but in great shape. She wore black fleece tights, a loose-fitting gray sweatshirt and dark brown, hybrid, cross-training hiking boots. As if she had been out for a casual morning run when she had come across thirty blood-thirsty villagers dog-piling on him. But he didn't buy it. Her fighting skills were world class.

Then she turned to face him and he recognized her.

"Asya," he said.

She simply nodded at him. Once. Curt. Very Russian.

He had last seen her when he had put ashore in Norway. Two men had held her captive and beaten her on the boat before Rook had boarded. At first, he told himself it was none of his business—he had been trying to disappear, after all. When he had finally had enough of her whimpered cries in the hold, he had fought the two men and sent them both overboard into the frigid Barents Sea. Then he had released her from the hold. They had gone their separate ways when Maksim Dashkov, the captain of the fishing trawler *Songbird*, had used a small inflatable rowboat to get them ashore.

Rook looked at the woman and once again felt the suspicious feeling that he knew her from somewhere. He had felt the same thing when they first spoke on the boat. The bruises on her face had mostly healed. Her dark brown eyes revealed nothing. He peered at her more intently.

"What is it, Stanislav?" she asked, raising an eyebrow.

"My spider-sense is tingling," he grunted.

"Your what? I do not understand."

"Never mind. Thank you for saving me back there."

"It is only proper I repay you for saving me on the *Songbird*."

"Yes, it is. But your timing is...convenient," Rook hadn't taken his eyes off her. He wasn't sure what was going on, but now all the alarms were going off in his head. He felt that this woman was familiar. She was a serious badass, and now he questioned how she could have ended up in that situation on board the boat, tied up by two worthless thugs. And then, weeks later, after heading off in the opposite direction, here she was, just in time to bail him out.

"Why are you here, Asya? Don't get me wrong—I'm grateful for the rescue, but a lot of weird shit has been going down and you showing up out of the blue is a bit suspicious."

"I understand," she looked him in the eyes, and he felt she was about to level with him. "Those men that had me on the boat. I do not know who they were. But I have learned that they also took my parents. I do not know why. I thought I might ask you to help me locate them. It took me awhile to find you."

"Uh-huh. And your fighting skills?"

"My father trained me. He was always a big fan of the ballet and the martial arts."

Rook still kept his eyes on her. He wasn't sure about the rest of her story, but he did believe that her parents had been taken. He could see the pain in her eyes when she had spoken about it.

"What kind of work does your father do? Is he a soldier? A spy?"

She looked aghast. "No. Nothing like that. He works for an electric utility company."

"And men kidnapped him and your mother? And you want my help to rescue them?"

"Yes." She cast her eyes down, suspecting his answer would be negative.

"I'm sorry, Asya. You saw those nutbags from the village."

"Nutbags, *Stanislav*?" Asya asked with a quizzical eyebrow raised high on her forehead.

Damnit, Rook thought. He'd slipped back into his normal American accent. *Fuck it. Too late now.*

He let out a sigh and continued. "It was like they were posessed. I need to get to the bottom of this mess." He felt bad telling her he couldn't help, but he had put off getting in touch with the rest of his team for too long. They would be wondering what had happened to him after Siberia. It was time to stop feeling sorry for himself and the people who had died, his team in Russia and Peder.

"I need to bury my friend and then get to the nearest phone. I have some other...friends who need to know about what's going on here." He started to turn and walk away from her, waiting to see what would happen next. Surely, she wouldn't let him just go. There would be more to the story, he could feel it.

"Wait," she grabbed his arm. "If I come with you, and help to get to the bottom of *this mess*, as you say? Then you will help me?"

EIGHT

Above Lake Michigan, Chicago
3 November, 0100 Hrs

TOM DUNCAN SAT in the troop area of the stealth-modified MH-60 Black Hawk helicopter looking at a small array of computer screens that showed the chaos around the globe.

He was monitoring the situation, as well as orchestrating the retrieval of his various field personnel—King, Knight and Bishop—to combat the phenomenon. One of his other field agents, Rook, had been missing in action for some time, although some conflicting reports placed him in the northern part of Russia or Norway. The fifth member of the field team, Queen, was in that region looking for the man.

As the de facto leader and dispatcher of Chess Team, Duncan was known as Deep Blue, and his identity was a closely guarded secret from all those not part of his team. Only those members of his growing organization, which he had recently christened *Endgame*, were privy to the fact that Tom Duncan, former President of the United States of America, was now a global mover and shaker, in control of his own former Delta team of commandos that could be sent anywhere around the world on a moment's notice.

The formation of the team had been Duncan's idea when he was president. Along with Domenick Boucher at CIA, and General Michael Keasling at Fort Bragg, Duncan had created a crack team that could deal with terrorists the world over. But then a strange thing happened. More and more frequently, the team had needed to combat unusual threats, starting with a genetics company led by a megalomaniac that had genetically altered soldiers and animals with the blood of the recently discovered Lernian Hydra. Then there had been an outbreak of the Brugada virus, which led to the discovery of a race of Neanderthal-like creatures in Vietnam. Most recently, the team had battled golems and other inanimate objects—statues, crystals, skeletons, even Stonehenge—imbued temporarily with life.

Duncan's decision the previous year to allow an upstart senator to smear his name was part of a longer-range plan of Duncan's to step down from the presidency and out of the spotlight—so he could devote more time to Chess Team and their efforts to battle all manner of threats worldwide.

The present threat of city-devouring energy domes around the world most certainly qualified as a Chess Team-level threat. The only problem was the team was scattered. With Rook AWOL and Queen on a personal mission to find him, he had already been down two bodies when the new threat emerged.

King was on leave down in Florida; Knight and Bishop were on a mission in Uganda that he had been forced to abandon. The team was stretched too thin. He was glad he had hired a few more people to act as occasional field personnel and support—his *Black* team, as well as another group to act as security and assistants at the team's base of operations in the White Mountains of New Hampshire—the *White* team.

The continuation of the Chess theme was satisfying, but it was really more a matter of logistics. The team needed support. Their budget came from one of the Pentagon's fabled black budgets and was buried so deeply in red tape that no one would be able to discover it, even if they knew to look for it. Only Keasling and Boucher were still directly working with the military. But others were required for security at Endgame's headquarters, to fly Chess Team's transport ship the *Crescent* and the Black Hawk he presently rode in, as well as mechanics, weapons experts, scientists and computer experts like Lewis Aleman—who had been a part of the group since the beginning— and even a few spies. Over all, Endgame was shaping up nicely.

But even with the additional team members, this current threat necessitated Duncan getting out into the field himself.

"Two minutes to drop point, sir," Black Three, the pilot, turned to address Duncan. "Better suit up."

"Thanks." Duncan couldn't go into the field without disguising his identity. His face was known, far and wide, as a previous president. And the current president, his former VP, would not take too kindly to the discovery of a covert special ops team operating on US soil. Duncan felt bad for deceiving the man, but the President not knowing provided him with a buffer of not just plausible deniability, but actual deniability, and provided Endgame the freedom to act while others were slowed by politics, egos and laws.

As Deep Blue, Duncan had initially served the team as their satellite eyes in the sky, providing intelligence through his extensive use of computers and communications equipment. Aleman could cover some of those duties from New Hampshire now, but Duncan still needed to be as connected as possible. He wore a black tactical suit and donned what looked like a futuristic motorcycle helmet with a tinted faceplate. He connected its cable to a small rectangular unit on his shoulder, and the faceplate's display came alive inside the helmet. The same display from the computer monitor on the Black Hawk was now on one-half of the inside of his faceplate.

A new technology from a small Korean firm, he had managed to get his hands on an experimental prototype of the helmet. With satellite uplink, he was able to be in communication with Endgame at the base in New Hampshire, as well as with the helicopter pilot. He also had access to all manner of computing power, which ran off servers deep underground at Endgame HQ. He could even tap into the Pentagon from the small keypad on his left forearm if need be. Deep Blue was now officially mobile.

As he stood from his chair in the tight confines of the Black Hawk's hold, preparing to gather his weapons, a buzzing ringtone sounded in his ear. He depressed a button on his forearm keypad and accepted the call.

"Ale, what is it? I'm about to go."

"Deep Blue is going to want to take this call. I'm patching it over from Bragg for you." Lewis Aleman sounded amused. Duncan couldn't think of a single reason for that as he took the call.

"This is Deep Blue. Go ahead."

"Hey Boss. Rook here."

Duncan was stunned. Rook had been missing for months, and they had received no contact from him. Duncan wasn't even sure whether Rook was alive after his last mission in Siberia had gone south and all the support members had been killed. "Rook! Where the hell are you? Are you all right?"

"Well, I'm alive. I'm at a small town in Norway called Fenris Kystby."

Deep Blue had two lists with Rook's name on it. The first was a list of questions. The second was a list of harsh language to use in the event that Rook turned up alive. But there wasn't time to berate the man for going AWOL. "We could really use you right now."

"Actually, I'm kind of up to my neck in something here and was hoping for some backup of my own. It's bad, boss. Mind control type stuff. Killing hordes. Real nasty shit."

Deep Blue stayed silent for a moment, torn between relief that Rook was alive and anger that the man had the balls to request resources as though he'd been on a mission. "Just tell me you were a prisoner," he said.

"Look, I'm sorry I've been out of touch," Rook said, a touch of impatience in his voice, "but I really could use some support over here. People are dying."

Deep Blue sighed, pushing aside his mixed feelings. "Understood. But our resources are tapped."

"Tapped?" Rook said. "You've got every asset in the world's most advanced military at your command."

"And you've been gone for a while," Deep Blue countered. "Trust me. We're tapped. I'll get someone to your location as soon as possible."

"Guess that will have to be good enough," Rook said.

"If I had a choice—" Deep Blue started.

"Yeah, I know."

"Good, and Rook, stay in touch this time."

"Copy that."

"Deep Blue out."

Duncan shook his head. *The man goes off the radar for months and turns up in Norway with the Village of the Damned. Figures. Well, one problem at a time.*

Black Three nodded to Duncan, and then the side cargo door to the Black Hawk helicopter opened. Duncan looked down to the blinking lights on the roof of the John Hancock building under him. Far below that, the rest of Chicago was aglow as a dome of energy sat in the heart of the Magnificent Mile.

"After I'm gone, get out of here, Three. I have another transport coming for evac."

"Roger," the pilot said. "Good luck, Sir."

"Thanks, we'll need it."

Deep Blue deactivated the heads-up display on his faceplate, checked the altimeter on his wrist and jumped out of the helicopter to freefall a thousand feet through the Chicago night sky.

NINE
Olderdalen, Norway
3 November, 0700 Hrs

ROOK PRESSED THE End button on the phone—a cell phone he had paid to borrow from a small storekeeper in the nearest town south of Fenris Kystby. He stepped out of the shop to the quiet street where Asya waited for him by Peder's battered car, which they had used to drive the hour south.

The sky had gone overcast with a dark, heavy cloud cover. The brittle Norwegian coastal breeze ripped into him. He noticed that Asya seemed less affected by it. He supposed that was from her Russian upbringing. He himself was from New Hampshire, and he was used to both the cold and the damp sea air, but this far north in Norway was different from home. He was almost a full 30 degrees of latitude north of the chilly New England farm he knew. They were above the Arctic Circle, and Rook's body and his emotions had taken a battering over the last few weeks. He figured it was okay to admit to himself that he was cold.

"Your friend? He will send help?" Asya seemed impatient.

"Yeah. As soon as he can, someone will be here." Rook saw that she wasn't looking at him but over his shoulder and behind him as he spoke.

He turned quickly to see a long-legged blonde woman strutting up to him. She wore a fleece headband that covered her ears and the scarring on her forehead—the only blemish to an otherwise sensationally gorgeous woman—the woman Rook had begun to fall in love with: Zelda Baker, also known as—

"Queen." Rook whispered her name, then smiled wide. "Sonvabitch, that was fast!" Rook was stunned to see anyone from his team so quickly after Deep Blue's brusque brush-off.

Then she drove her right fist into his jaw, squatting slightly and using the thrust from her legs as she came back up to throw her whole weight into the blow. Rook rocked back off his feet and into the air, flying backward to slam his head against the rear window of the old Two Series Volvo, shattering it. He slid down to the pavement amidst the sprinkling of safety glass cubes, landing on his ass with a thump.

Queen looked furious. Long blonde hair streamed behind her in the Arctic air. Her cheeks were a fierce red and her eyes were filled with anger. Rook understood immediately what it meant. He was both thrilled and terrified. Thrilled because it was instantly clear to him that she had come to care for him the same way her had for her, but he was also afraid that she might have construed his recent unauthorized departure from the team as his premature death. She might never forgive him for leaving and causing her to worry so.

Unfortunately, Rook was so taken by the sight of Queen and by the power of the blow she had landed on him, that he completely forgot his companion.

Asya didn't know Queen at all and had come to a natural conclusion—only it was the wrong one. She leapt to Rook's defense.

As Rook tried to stand up, he saw Asya's black clad leg fly through the air as she executed a perfect flying sidekick. Her foot connected with Queen's face, knocking the woman back, but she managed to keep her feet. Asya landed in front of Queen and both women took a long look at each other, sizing up their opponent before the real fight started.

Rook could see what was about to happen, but his head still hurt from the impact with the Volvo—to say nothing of the impact with Queen's right cross. His body was battered and beaten from the earlier fight with the villagers and his shoulder was still brutalized from events even before that fight. He could barely move. And he couldn't get a breath into his lungs fast enough to call out a ceasefire.

Large flakes of snow, lumped together into bold shapes, fell from the sky. A single flake fell between the women, striking the ground with a barely audible *tick*.

The two women ran at each other.

TEN
Shanghai, China
3 November, 1400 Hrs

THEIR ORIGINAL DESTINATION had been Beijing, but in the time it took for Knight and Bishop to get to China—even at supersonic speed—the field of battle had changed again. Right now, all they had to go on was that giant globes of energy and lightning were randomly appearing in different population centers around the globe. In some cases, the sphere would be present only a short time. In others, it would stay long enough to disgorge a payload of creatures that were vicious and fast. The creatures could be killed, but it was very difficult to do so. Beyond those few facts, Knight and Bishop were going in blind.

On their way to Beijing, the pilot, callsign: Black One, had been informed that the portal that had opened in the Forbidden City had closed unexpectedly, without sending any of the killing creatures into the population of 20 million. Unfortunately, the Forbidden City, the former imperial palace dating from the Ming Dynasty, was carved from the face of the Earth by the devastating effects of the globe's collapse, just as other cities had been ravaged. But before the *Crescent* could be set to a new course, reports of another globe effect in nearby Shanghai had come in through Lewis Aleman, back at Endgame HQ.

News of the giant energy globes had spread rapidly around the world, so when this new globe had begun to appear in Shanghai, people had fled in terror on foot, in cars and on bicycle—by whatever means they had available to them. The People's Liberation Army had yet to arrive on the scene and even local law enforcement had bailed at the sight of the giant white and yellow crackling sphere.

So it was in relative quiet that Knight and Bishop approached their target. The *Crescent* dropped them on the street before taking to the skies again with its VTOL thrusters and disappearing. A few injured people lay on the sidewalks and in the middle of the road, but most were still moving away from the site, even if at a crawl. Bishop and Knight might have stopped to help the people, but their first priority was to guard the greater population against the creatures that sometimes came out of the energy globes.

Lightning blasted from the sphere ahead of them, arcing upward to strike the tops and sides of tall concrete, steel and glass skyscrapers. As Bishop and Knight approached the thing, debris from the ruined buildings rained down while streaks of lightning performed a spastic dance accentuated by the booming of thunder. Choreographed chaos.

"Endgame, this is Knight. As far as I can tell, the lightning strikes are completely random. They don't seem to be targeting us or anything in particular."

"Copy that, Knight. We've already had reports from Egypt that weapons fire into the sphere doesn't do a damn thing, so hold your fire. If a tank can't stop it, neither can you." Lewis Aleman sounded tired and jittery on the small earphone in Knight's ear. If Bishop was listening in, he made no indication of it. "Also, don't get too close to the thing. When they blink out, they take everything with them. Remember, you're there to fight anything that might come out of the sphere. We have reports from a Ranger, whose brother was in LA, that the things are like milky white pumas. They're damn fast, but initial reports suggest they only go after fleeing prey. So set up somewhere and be ready. If your globe closes, we'll get the *Crescent* back to deliver you to another hotspot."

"Understood," Knight said. He switched off the microphone on the side of his face and turned to Bishop. "Where do you think?"

Bishop scanned the scene. They were in a section of the city called *The Bund*. The river was to their right and a huge multi-lane road with abandoned cars was to their left. HSBC Bank and the Customs House, with its distinctive clock tower, were across the asphalt. The sphere was further up Zhongshan Road. The sun still hung overhead, but in a few hours, bright neon lights and spotlights would illuminate everything. The glow from the crackling sphere, which Bishop judged to be about 60 feet in diameter, washed out the daylight with an intensity that made him squint.

"That clock tower looks to me like a good spot for you. I'm just gonna walk along the river here and get closer."

"Bish," Knight looked concerned as he stared up at the larger man. "There's no cover along the river. If those things come out..."

"If I need to, I'll bail into the water. Let's get it done."

Without another word, Knight sprinted across the now empty multi-lane road, carrying his new favorite toy—the EXACTO rifle—strapped across his back. He wondered, as he made his way across the road to the large bank, whether this road had ever been deserted of people since its construction. He figured it hadn't. He knew Shanghai had something like 24 million people, and it had always been a crowded place.

Knight made his way into the Customs House building expecting to find cowering civilians or possibly even morons still attempting to carry out a normal day's work despite the inconvenience of a gigantic electrical ball of hellfire just down the road. Instead, he found the place completely deserted. As far as he knew, the energy effect had only started in Shanghai about thirty minutes previously. He was stunned that the Chinese had managed to evacuate the area so thoroughly in such a short time.

As he made his way into the elevator to get to the roof, Knight reflected on the fact that as the only Korean American member of Chess Team, he was their de facto Pacific Rim agent, and yet he had rarely been to China. The last time was to one of China's new ghost cities, Shenhuang. That hadn't been a fun mission. Although one positive thing had come from it: his new girlfriend, Anna Beck. She had helped the team once before the Shenhuang mission, and as callsign: Black Zero had now become one of Deep Blue's right-hand assistants back in New Hampshire. Although things were going well with Beck, he turned his mind away from her, getting his head in the game.

Out on the roof, he made his way to the huge clock tower's stairway. The structure was nearly 300 feet tall. The perfect vantage point. But as he got closer to the top of the staircase, Knight heard the distinctive *boom-boom-boom* of Bishop's XM312-B blasting away.

He was too late.

ELEVEN
Walt Disney World Resort, Florida
2 November, 1330 Hrs

FIRST THE CRAZY sweaty bomber on the monorail. Then the guy had done a swimmer off the rear of the train, splattering himself on the concrete support strut. King didn't like killing people (or seeing them killed) unnecessarily. He hadn't intended to kill the sweaty man; he only wanted to question him. Now he had turned and seen the Russian gunship pointing its nose cannon down King's throat.

For a moment, King hesitated. He wasn't sure what to do or how to react. Why in hell was there was a massive Russian helicopter hovering over Disney World? The decision was made for him. The massive helicopter turned, so its side faced King, no longer maintaining its hover over the speeding monorail train, instead letting the train pass beneath it and bringing King right up to the vehicle.

King spotted a bright, neon-yellow chess piece hastily spray-painted on the sidewall of the fuselage—a *King* piece. The picture was nearly three feet tall, and King could see the drips where the paint had bled before drying. The side door was open, and in it was a crouched US Army Ranger, who was waving King to approach the helicopter—as if he had a choice with the train carrying him to it.

The picture came clear immediately for King. He sprinted along the rooftops of the monorail cars to the helicopter and nimbly leapt into the open cargo door, rolling and hitting the closed side door on the other side of the craft. The Ranger passed him a set of headphones, which he donned. The man then started to close the open door as King seated the headset on his ears.

"Talk to me," King said.

"You're desperately needed, sir. We were told to paint that symbol outside and pick you up." The Ranger seemed apologetic as he secured the door. He was dressed in desert-style battle dress uniform, with a distinctive gold and black *RANGER* tab on one shoulder and a green and blue shield patch with a red lightning bolt on the other. King recognized it as the insignia for the 75th Ranger Regiment. The man's nametape said ORTIZ.

"I was kind of in the middle of something, Ortiz. There's a bomb on that train."

"We know, sir." Ortiz turned and smiled at King. "Everybody on board has a cell phone. They flooded the local police dispatcher

I'm going back there, and I'm going to figure out what's going on. You two can stay here and try to kill each other again, or you can come with me." Rook climbed into the driver's seat of the much-abused Volvo. Without a word—and without any haggling over shotgun—Asya slipped into the back seat while Queen took the passenger seat. Both women closed their respective doors at the same time and fastened their seatbelts.

"Alright, that's what I'm talking about," Rook said. Then from the backseat, Asya smacked her hand across the back of his head.

"Do not get cocky, Stanislav," she told him. Queen snickered.

"God help me if you two become friends."

FOURTEEN
Shanghai, China

KNIGHT BURST PAST the rusted, flaking roof access door to the balcony that ran around the clock tower, and raced to the edge of the tan concrete wall. Far below him and down the street, the energy ball still pulsed. He could feel its electrical hum in his teeth like he was standing too close to high tension power lines. Things were racing out of the globe of light and streaking down the abandoned street. About fifty feet closer to the clock tower, Knight saw that Bishop had taken cover behind an abandoned pale green taxi cab, and had set up his XM312-B across the hood of the vehicle. The big man was firing furiously at the speeding blurs as they shot from the crackling sphere, many of them clearly hit and knocked into the nearby river from the impact of the .50 caliber rounds.

But just as many of the things were getting past Bishop.

Knight quickly laid his EXACTO sniper rifle along the edge of the wall in front of him and targeted a space behind Bishop's position. Knight pulled his eye from the scope and looked for the speeding blurs. One was looping back around and heading for Bishop's back.

Damn, they're fast.

Knight barely had time to guess at the thing's speed before he fired the weapon at the empty space behind Bishop's head, hoping he could hit the racing blur before it struck his friend from behind.

The bullet blasted from the muzzle of the rifle. A cloud of white burst from the far side of the creature's head. The dead thing's momentum carried it forward and it slammed into Bishop from behind, before rolling to the front of the cab, obscuring it from Knight's view.

Bishop was knocked off his feet and simply rolled in one smooth move across the hood of the cab. He swung the barrel of the weapon back and fired at his previous position, blasting another creature and sending it smashing through the plate glass window of a cell phone shop. Broken plastic display phones skittered out of the shop across the pavement with clicking and clacking sounds, but again, Knight was denied a chance to actually see whatever it was Bishop was shooting at.

He began picking blurs and firing about ten to twenty yards in front of each, hoping to hit something. Every third shot or so, he needed to protect Bishop's six from another speeding blur, but for half of those, Bishop himself swung around in a full 360° arc, firing with his machine gun. Knight couldn't see if he was hitting the things, but he could tell, as they ducked and weaved before retreating, that Bishop wasn't killing many of them, if he was hitting them at all.

Knight saw some the things tearing back toward the globe of crackling light. Then the movement was gone.

He looked for a new target and didn't see anything moving down on the street. Knight finally had a chance to look for his fallen targets and was surprised to see so few. *Damn, I missed more than I thought.* He could see only three, and he knew there was a fourth in front of the cab.

"You seeing these things, Knight?" Bishop's voice sounded loud in Knight's earpiece as he shouted.

Knight looked through the scope of his rifle at one of the fallen bodies. He had hit it. It was missing a good portion of its muscular chest, but otherwise, the corpse provided him a pretty good idea of what they were up against. The beast was at least seven feet tall, and milky white. Long, powerful limbs were claw tipped, yet the creature was vaguely humanoid in appearance. The head was a bit blockish with a domed forehead through which he could see a white, spongy mass.

I can see through its skin, Knight realized and then wondered, *is that its skull? Or its brain?* He glanced over the rest of the body and saw bundles of long, sinewy muscles twitching beneath the translucent skin.

The creature struck him as somewhat feline, especially the way it moved, but it was really unlike anything native to Earth. The most obtrusive feature was its eyes, which were huge orbs on the outside of the sides of its face. *Like a chameleon,* Knight thought, separately mobile and stereoscopic—able to look in multiple directions at once.

"I'm seeing the fallen ones. Having a hard time tracking the moving ones," Knight replied, still eyeing one of the corpses.

"Yeah, I hear you. I'm—oh shit, here they come again."

Knight pulled back from the scope and saw several more shapes blitzing from the ball of light down the street. Bishop opened up fire on them again, strafing across the street. Knight began taking targets as they came for Bishop, one after the next. The creatures were falling this time—he'd figured out the effective range ahead of their paths to fire now—but too many of them were getting past Bishop's arc of fire, leaving Knight to pick them off. One bumped against Bishop, throwing his aim off, his stream of .50 caliber bullets passing harmlessly into the air. Knight could see more of the creatures advancing on Bishop. He fired again, taking down another creature and toggled his microphone, "Bishop, time to bug out man."

Bishop dropped to the ground just as one of the creatures was about to hit him. Instead, it leapt over him and its momentum kept it going down the street. Knight let that one pass, even though he knew it would loop back on Bishop from behind. He focused on the next wave coming out of the glowing sphere.

Then an idea came to him. As he tracked another streaking form moving close to a line of abandoned vehicles, Knight chose a car three car-lengths in front of the speeding creature and unleashed the devastation of his sniper rifle on the fuel tank of a black Audi. The tank ruptured, sending fuel onto the ground, and Knight quickly fired a second round at the pavement, the spark of its impact igniting the fuel and the speeding creature. The explosion of the remaining fuel in the car made a deep bass thump and the car flipped over backward.

Bishop was on the move, leaping over the hoods of vehicles, then firing in a sweep, and then leaping again. Knight repeated the move, rupturing fuel tanks two more times before the creatures swept over to the boardwalk beside the river, well away from the cars.

"OK, tangos are intelligent, too, Bishop."

Suddenly the staccato explosions of Bishop's weapon stopped. Knight pulled his eye away from the scope and glanced up. He saw Bishop drop the big weapon, run up the hood of a Buick, and leap into the air toward the next abandoned car on the road, throwing a grenade behind him from the apex of his leap. Bishop landed on the roof of the bright red Ford in front of him, crunching in the thin metal, as the creature trailing him reached the Buick and the grenade as it landed. Knight targeted another creature chasing Bishop just as the explosion from the grenade sent up a huge cloud of smoke and debris, obscuring his shot.

"Damn."

Bishop made for the river's edge, as he had said he would do. Knight adjusted his stance, leaning further out over the parapet. He targeted the last creature chasing Bishop and fired. Then he pulled back from the scope to see yet another wave of speeding lines making waves in the air like heat haze, down on the street. Then one of the creatures mounted the roof of the cab Bishop had previously used for cover and turned its head up to the sky and howled.

The sound was hideous.

The noise was deafening and terrible, a deep bass rumble like a horn filled with every terror in the world. It vibrated through Knight's body, rattling his bones. He dropped the sniper rifle and it fell to the next lower section of the tower. Goose bumps broke out across every part of his skin, sweat beaded and dripped as though he were clutched by fever, and a terror-filled scream that would shame him forever had anyone heard it ripped from his lungs.

Shin Dae-jung had never been so scared in his life.

FIFTEEN
Chicago, 3 November
0100 Hrs

WELL, THIS IS embarrassing.

King thought he was going to die. Clutching the pants of a dead man with one hand, and the eject lever between the dead pilot's knees in the other, King held on for dear life as the rockets on the underside of the ejection seat slammed him out of the crashing plane and across the sky laterally at close to 100 mph. He had just enough time to see that the thrust from the rockets on the seat were going to slam him, the pilot and the seat into the side of a building with darkened glass windows and five vertical stripes of dark tan concrete. Even in the brightly lit night scene, and at a point of view from which he had never seen it, he recognized it as the Park Hyatt building.

Then his next thought as the chair blasted across the sky was to try to crawl lower down the pilot's legs toward the blasting rockets— so he wouldn't end up between his impromptu getaway vehicle and the oncoming wall of stone and glass.

His brain didn't have time to complete the next thought.

I hope I don't get roasted—

The rockets died. The chute section in the headrest exploded outward with a pop, slamming into King's shins and flipping him over the footrest of the seat toward where the rockets were propelling the craft just a second before. His body arced out and away from the seat and he lost his hold on the ejection lever. He clung for all he was worth to the dead pilot's flight suit and twisted hard, scrambling in mid air to get his other hand back on the pilot before the impact.

When it came, it rattled him, but the impact was far less than he had expected. *Two men, one chair.* The normal propulsion of the seat might have pitched them through the glass and out the other side of the building, but because of the weight, the propellant had quit and their velocity had died down before the crash. The window around them shattered into tiny safety glass crumbles that rained down to the street. The chair lodged itself just inside the building, but King was dangling from the pilot's ankles and swinging from the bottom of the chair, on the outside of the building, with the wind tearing into him and lightning strikes from the several-story glowing orb below him crashing into the surrounding structure.

Well. This isn't too bad. If I can just...

King felt the chair shift and start to slide, and then it was in freefall—above King. He didn't have time to wonder whether the parachute, which had already deployed but had yet to have time or airflow to inflate, would open in the plummet to the Water Tower park several hundred feet below him. He knew it wasn't far to the ground and it would be a close thing. He scrambled up the pilot's legs, now trying to get on top of the pilot before the seat separated from the pilot's corpse.

TOM DUNCAN STOOD on the street craning his head up. He stared up at the spectacle of King's amazing ejection and wondered if it would somehow be possible for the man to survive. He had approached the edge of the glowing, lightning-spitting ball, to see if he could gain some readings from it for Aleman, when King's F-16 had come ripping into the sky overhead. Lightning struck the plane and then it faltered. Duncan could see it would crash. A second or so after praying that King would eject, he zoomed in with the camera lens on his helmet's heads-up display to see King making his way into the pilot's seat.

Then everything had gone crazy. Lightning began shooting from the glowing orb even more than it had been, striking the buildings all around the Water Tower park. The canopy on the jet burst off, and King, riding on the pilot's ejection seat with the pilot, was fired sideways through the air and straight at the side of a building. Duncan's heart was climbing up his throat like a mountaineer moving up a chimney of rock as he watched in fear for his friend.

Then a more immediate concern. The broken, crashing 20-million dollar jet was spinning and falling right for Duncan's position. With the crackling dome wall of energy that now reached close to 80 feet high directly behind him, Duncan could only move ahead along Michigan Avenue or dodge to the side in either direction, but the plane was spinning erratically as it came down out of the sky at him and he wasn't sure which way to move. Time slowed as he heard shrieks from the nearby onlookers, where the military and police had set up a cordon down by the Walgreen's store on Chicago Avenue.

The plane was almost on him and Duncan simply threw himself forward onto the rough asphalt of Michigan Ave., scraping the palms of his hands. The falling plane, its engine completely shut down, flew over his head soundlessly. The lack of noise was eerie. The crowd down the street quieted.

Duncan rolled over and sat up to look back up Michigan at the energy sphere. There was no sign of the plane or its wreckage. Duncan tapped at the keys on his wristpad and a display from a CCTV camera mounted on the John Hancock Center's roof, looking down on the street on the other side of the energy ball, appeared on his helmet's display. No sign of the jet on the other side.

The energy dome had simply swallowed the crashing plane. Then Duncan remembered King.

He scrambled to his feet and looked back up to the top of the Park Hyatt and there was King, dangling from the bottom of the ejection seat, which had lodged into what his faceplate told him was the 67th floor of the building. *Hold on, King, I'm on my way,* Duncan thought. He was about to start running diagonally across the park to the building, when the chair, its dead pilot and King, all shifted, lurched and fell.

Oh no.

Duncan watched, spellbound as the chair separated and King scrabbled up the dead man's body as the parachute inflated and slowed their descent. *Thank God.*

Then the strong winds ripping between the skyscrapers, made stronger by the atmospheric disturbance caused by the pulsing dome, slammed into King and the pilot, blasting their parachute north across the Water Tower park and directly toward the sphere of light. They were still a few hundred feet high when the roaring wind shifted and their parachute moved sideways, with King furiously working the toggle straps.

They plummeted faster, King and the dead man, just ten feet in front of the wall of electric light, and Duncan held his breath. King was 100 feet off the ground, but still too far to let go of the dead pilot and leap to safety. Lightning blasted from the sphere again, barely missing the parachute.

Duncan was sure King would make it now. Fifty feet off the ground.

The wind gusted again, hard. Duncan was almost blown off his feet. The dome was playing havoc with the atmosphere around it, like an electrical storm.

King was blown into the wall of the energy dome. He and the dead pilot swung in toward it at a 45-degree angle away from the parachute. As their bodies hit the wall of energy, they disappeared inside it, until only the lines of the parachute and the black canopy could be seen. King went into the dome at probably 30 feet off the ground. Duncan couldn't believe what he was seeing.

Then the wind shifted again and the parachute gusted back and away from the dome, yanking King and the pilot back out of it and over the park until they slammed onto the ground just to the side of the concrete fountain in the park's middle. Duncan sprinted over to the crashed men.

King stumbled to his feet, after the dead pilot's body had taken most of the brunt of the hard landing.

"King!" Duncan arrived and saw the haunted look on King's face. "What is it?"

"On the other side. I saw them. They're coming."

"How many?" Duncan pulled the strap of a Heckler & Koch MP5 submachine gun over his head and handed the weapon to King, then pulled out a Browning 9 mm from the leg holster he wore.

King looked at the MP5 and then at Duncan. "More of them than we have bullets."

SIXTEEN

Fenris Kystby, Norway
3 November, 1130 Hrs

ROOK LED QUEEN and Asya down the steep slope of the hill toward a bush at the bottom of the rise. When he reached the large squat bush, he bent down and swept some of the snow away from the base of it with his bare hands until they were wet and pink. The snow had fallen for the last few hours, through their breakfast at a small inn and their impromptu shopping trip for Rook to buy a warmer coat.

Asya had arrived with her own pack full of warmer clothing, when she had come looking for Rook. Queen had her own supplies as well. But Rook had had only the clothes on his back and the Desert Eagle pistol that was now probably melted to slag in the fire back at Peder's barn. The thought of Peder's death brought Rook to a dark place and instead he turned his mind to the present task.

He reached down for the roots at the bottom of the shrub and hauled on them with all his strength. The bush lurched upward and then sideways, as the secret entrance to the lab, concealed beneath the bush, flipped open with the fake bush on top of it. Snow blew down into the four-foot-square, darkened opening. The air smelled stale. But Rook could still clearly see the rungs of the ladder that led down the vertical tunnel to the horizontal tunnel at its bottom, which would take him to the old lab he had discovered.

"You found this when you were hunting a scientist?" Queen was skeptical.

Rook turned to her and then to Asya. Both women wore similar expressions. "Look, something was eating Peder's animals. I thought it was a wolf at first—there are several around here—but it turned out to be this Nazi scientist that had been here since the '40s, and had experimented on himself, to the point that he was nuts. The guy's corpse is down here, so you'll see for yourselves. I don't know what the hell is going on in this town, besides this old Nazi science lab, but I was told it had been shut down for ages. No one even knew Kiss was still alive. The place looks abandoned, but I figure it's the best place to start looking for information. I didn't have time to search it properly last time, because, you know, I was trying not to die."

Queen nodded at him, her blonde hair bouncing. "Booby traps?"

"Down there? Nah."

Queen dropped into the hole, her hands gripping the sides of the ladder. She slid out of sight. Asya looked at Rook and nodded. "You have strange friends, Stanislav. And strange stories."

"Call me Rook."

"Finally being honest with both of us, then?"

Rook widened his eyes to say, *Shut up!* He realized Asya had heard more of the conversation at the store than she'd let on and whispered, "Don't go listening in on people's conversations. It's rude."

"I could not hear you. Your body language said everything." Asya grinned. "You have feeling for—"

Rook raised his hand quickly, pinching his fingers together and hissing like Cesar Millan, the "Dog Whisperer," to an unruly mutt. "Not another word."

Asya shrugged and dropped into the tunnel after Queen.

Rook shook his head and grumbled, "Friggin' women, always getting in everyone's business." He looked around the field and back up the hill. Nothing moved in the snow except for his misting breath as it slowly rose from his mouth and met the frigid air. Then he dropped down the ladder, and pulled the trap door shut over his head.

At the bottom of the ladder, the stone tunnel led away down a slope toward the old Nazi laboratory. The tunnel was small, and

Rook had to stoop in places to make his way. Crumbled stone still littered the floor. The air smelled dry and dusty. Rook doubted anyone else had been down here. After five minutes of travel down the sloping tunnel, he caught up with Queen and Asya, who both stood before a metal door with a frame embedded in the rock. Queen wore a Petzl headlamp on an elastic strap where her fleece headband had been. The light illuminated the door and the word stenciled above it:

Ragnarök.

Queen turned to him with an upraised eyebrow. "Destruction of the Gods?"

"Yeah, something like that." Rook saw the confused look on Asya's face. "The word refers to the end of the world in Norse mythology. I'm sure the Nazis thought it was suitable for their kooky experiments."

The door had no handle. It was just a smooth metal slab. Rook reached past the women to the upper-right edge of the door, where he knew a small crevice existed in the frame of stone around the metal door. He remembered the worn-smooth feel of the stone on his fingers. He exerted the right amount of leverage and the metal door began to creak open. Queen stepped up and braced her arm against the wall to help Rook with the door. In her other hand, she held an M9 pistol—the only weapon any of them now had.

They stepped through into a small laboratory. It clearly had not been used in some time, but the room was still well organized, with the exception of a few bullet holes in things from Rook's recent battle with Edmund Kiss, the scientist that had experimented upon himself until he was practically a feral, yeti-like creature. But Kiss was dead. Nothing Rook had seen in his previous visits to the lab—first hunting for the creature that turned out to be Kiss, and later battling the creature he had become to the death—hinted at mind control or anything else that could be connected to the townspeople of Fenris

Kystby going glazed and attacking him and Peder at the farm that morning.

There were two doors in the room. Rook knew one was a closet. He nodded to the other door. Queen went to the door and opened it quickly with the M9 leading. Inside was a larger room with offices and two doors sporting bright orange, biohazard symbols.

"Kiss kept the wolves for his experiments down here before he started injecting himself with the stuff." Rook opened one of the biohazard doors. The room was filled with built-in metal cages that rose to the ceiling, but each was now empty, their doors ajar. "Huh. Nobody home. Fossen must have taken the wolves out of here."

"Fossen was the man that helped you find this lab and stop Kiss?" Queen asked, stepping back into the main room and making for the other biohazard door. Asya stood to the side, saying nothing.

"That's right. Don't bother with that one. Empty room." Rook walked to the other door leading out of the large office space. Queen opened the biohazard door she was near, despite Rook's explanation and peeked inside. The room was as Rook had said, completely empty. She moved with Asya, following Rook through the last door.

The new room had a single source of natural light—a small window set in a wall close to the ceiling. Most of the window had dirt packed against it, and the portion above that was nearly covered by snow. The small corner of the window that still allowed light to flow into the room was no larger than a coin.

Under the window was a set of double doors that Rook knew from a previous visit were also covered over with dirt. The entirety of the lab had been buried when it was abandoned.

Or had it?

Rook looked quickly around the room. "What the hell?"

"What is it?" Asya asked.

"Kiss is missing. This was his den. The floor was littered with animal bones. His corpse should still be here. It was only a few days ago."

"The other man...Fossen. He probably cleaned up when he left with the wolves you said were in the cages," Queen guessed.

"But there's more than that, Queen. There was a sofa here that Kiss was using as a bed."

"So?"

"So if those doors," Rook pointed at the double doors beneath the window, "are covered with earth, and there are no other ways in or out besides the tunnel we came in, how the hell did someone move a full-sized sofa out of here?"

SEVENTEEN
Chicago

"RUN!"

Deep Blue and King sprinted down Michigan Ave. toward the National Guard barrier that had been set up at the intersection with Chicago Ave., fifty feet south of the edge of the lightning-hurling monstrosity that chewed further into the buildings to either side of the wide retail strip.

Large slabs of concrete and steel debris rained down from the upper reaches of the buildings on either side of the men as lightning discharges slammed the structures repeatedly. King and Deep Blue reached the Guardsmen, who allowed them behind the barrier. A short barrel-chested man wearing Captain's bars and a nametape that said WEST, approached them.

"Who's in charge, Captain?" Deep Blue asked.

"I am. Who the hell are you guys?" West seemed shocked more than angry.

"We're Delta. You should have received a call from General Keasling—"

"Yeah, King and Blue, right?"

"Close enough." Although it wasn't strictly true anymore—Chess Team had been a Delta assault team at one time, but now they and the entire Endgame organization were so far off the books that few people knew they existed. Deep Blue and General Keasling had decided for the duration of the current threat that Keasling would notify any military presence on the ground that a Delta operations team was inbound, allowing Chess Team the freedom to act. In a situation less chaotic, they might not have been able to get away with such theater and keep it a secret from the rest of the US Military, but with energy domes popping up globally and vicious creatures darting out of the globes, no one would recall one small two-man Delta team once the dust settled. "Get your men ready to fire everything they have at the dome. A lot of targets are going to be coming out of it. And they are coming fast." Deep Blue, done talking, turned to face the dome up the street.

"Seriously?" West's face was appalled.

"Damn serious, Captain. You saw me parachute in through the dome and out again? I just saw them. They're coming. Fast. Be ready to shoot." King turned to the barrier and aimed his MP5.

The Captain passed orders to the Guardsmen—most of whom took up defensive positions around the wooden sawhorse barrier, and a few took to ordering the civilian bystanders further from the upcoming fight.

Then the lightning stopped all at once, as if the globe, which had been trying to solidify itself, finally achieved a kind of stasis. The wind died down, too, and everything was eerily silent. Time ticked by. No one spoke. But the lull was short-lived.

Eight white streaks blitzed out of the brilliant wall of the dome, racing in all directions. The Guards opened fire haphazardly, and the wall of noise from fifty M-16 rifles firing was deafening after the momentary quiet. King returned fire with the others, but the creatures were just too damn fast. He watched in horror as two of the streaks tore into the line, decimating men on either side of him.

Their blood spattered him in the breeze kicked up in the wake of the fast-moving creatures. The other racing creatures had gone in a variety of directions—some behind the Hyatt, and others toward the lake. King suspected the creatures had no specific targets in mind, but instead just ran in a variety of directions and ripped into anything they encountered.

He saw Deep Blue rolling on the ground and picking up a fallen soldier's M-16 rifle and leveling it at a creature that was returning. He fired a confident three-round burst, each round punching through the monster's rounded forehead, widening the wound, shattering what looked like a clear skull and shredding the spongy white brain beneath.

King had seen a lot of people shot in the head, but had never witnessed the bullet's progress after it entered the target. The explosive effect on the creature's brain was...horrible, but in this case, a thing of beauty.

As the life went out of the creature, it crashed through the group and over Deep Blue's head before slamming into the wooden sawhorse, sending a spray of wooden splinters and larger pieces of wood into the street beyond the small group.

"How the fuck—" King began.

Deep Blue tapped the faceplate of his helmet. "Targeting software." He fired another sustained burst of rifle fire in a direction none of the other Guardsmen were targeting. Once again, a racing creature moved from a blur to white bulk sliding on the pavement and kicking up dust into the blowing wind. "King. The Humvee."

King glanced around and saw a parked National Guard Humvee, an armored all-purpose military vehicle. He raced over to it and slipped behind its wheel. The remaining Guardsmen were firing M-203 grenade launchers at the creatures streaking through the park toward them. And King was about to drive through the maelstrom. Deep Blue took down another creature further up Michigan Ave., just as King crashed the Humvee through the one remaining wooden sawhorse. He cranked the wheel left and drove up onto the curb and into the small park that surrounded the castle-like 19th-century Water Tower. One of the creatures tore around the corner of the structure, heading right for King's vehicle.

King floored the accelerator pedal and hit the creature dead center. The impact jarred the vehicle as if it had been hit with an IED. The rear end of the Humvee tilted up and the vehicle spun, its back end slamming into the limestone monument, tearing out a small block of stone. The Humvee would still roll, but the monster was done. The corpse on the roll of steel cable attached to the snub hood of the vehicle was a mangled mess of white translucent flesh that reminded King of a jelly fish, *if jelly fish had bones and muscles.*

Up close, the thing was hideous. The misshapen head was blocky and curved down to its wide mouth, which was full of clear, sharp teeth, like jagged icicles. *It's not just the skin that's clear*, King realized, *but the bones, too.* The smooth curve of its dolphin-like forehead was marred by a pug nose and framed by two orb-like eyes positioned on either side of its head, giving it an insectoid look. The clear skin allowed King a view of the white veins, taut ligaments and coiled cables of bulging muscle beneath.

His Humvee impact had cut this creature in half at the waist, and only the head, torso and powerful arms were on the hood of the vehicle. King looked out the window for the other half. Even though the glowing energy sphere, which King decided was some kind of portal transporting these creatures from one place to another, provided abundant light, it was still the middle of the night and the park was crisscrossed by long shadows from the tower and the surrounding buildings.

King hit the gas and chased after the next creature he spotted. This one was retreating back toward the energy dome and King gave chase, moving the Humvee up to 50 mph before he felt he was pacing the beast. They were headed right for the wall of the dome.

King decided that if it went through, he would follow it and mash the fucker into the road on the other side.

The dome loomed large before him, reaching a hundred feet above the road now, and it had stretched the width of the road and through most of the buildings that had been to either side of it. The sound of lightning began to crackle again. The kinetic white creature nearly reached the sizzling yellow energy, when the wall of light winked out, muting the crackling sound. The creature continued on directly ahead.

And then down.

The dome was gone, and in its place was a crater in the Earth that stretched almost 150 feet in diameter. The creature's momentum carried it well past the lip of the crater and it arced down into the suddenly empty space.

King cranked hard on the wheel of the Humvee and slammed on the brakes. The vehicle turned an abrupt 90 degrees to the left, its thick tires screaming, but it was no use. The armored 5000-pound vehicle rolled in empty space as it plummeted down into the abyss of the ruined Chicago street and the cauterized clean edges of the crater below it.

EIGHTEEN
Shanghai, China

SHIN DAE-JUNG COWERED against the low concrete wall. His eyes squeezed tightly shut. His whole body shook with fear. He couldn't bear to open his eyes even a slice, because he knew with the certainty of a gambler on a winning streak that if he opened his eyes, his vision would fill with the sight of his grandmother having her innards eaten by one of his best friends.

Knight shook his head. His thoughts made no sense. *Why is it so dark? It was daylight. We were in a fight...*

When Chess Team had first gone up against the malevolent genetics company Manifold, run by the twisted egomaniac Richard Ridley, the company's security team captured Bishop and their scientists experimented on him. He had become what the team termed a "Regen"—one of Ridley's twisted regenerating soldiers. But there had been a heavy price attached to the regenerative healing and near-immortality. The regeneration process slowly ate the soldier's mind, filling it with aggression, until he was nothing more than a raging, hulking terror. Bishop had been well on his way to becoming such a mindless beast of anger, and Knight was the only one that had fought the big Iranian American when he was in his full-on Regen state. But Bishop had been cured, Ridley was gone and Manifold was no more. Questions formed in Knight's terrorstruck thoughts. Why was he certain Bishop had reverted to his Regen form? How had his ailing grandmother arrived in Shanghai? And why was the Regen Bishop trying to eat her?

Knight cracked his tightly clamped eyelids and daylight burst through them like stabbing skewers. He squinted and blinked a few times until his eyes adjusted to the glare. His head felt heavy and his limbs didn't want to move yet. He was curled in a ball on the concrete floor of the balcony on the Customs House clock tower. He groggily sat up. A chill ran up his back. His body was soaked through with sweat. *What the hell?*

Knight stood and swayed. Things went out of focus and he thought he would fall, but then reality reasserted itself and the world around him slammed into focus again. He looked over the wall. He had dropped the EXACTO rifle. The glowing, pulsing sphere was still crackling down the street and throwing sharp, jagged bolts of lightning to strike the street, the buildings and the river. Debris or water pluming up with each strike.

The river! Bishop!

"Bishop! Can you hear me?"

Static was the only reply. He looked over the parapet wall again, expecting to see Bishop's body on the ground with the few creatures they had managed to kill. But there were no bodies. Either the beasts had managed to get back up, or the surviving ones had pulled away the corpses of the dead.

Then a blur caught Knight's eye. One last creature streaked out of the glowing energy dome and headed to the base of the clock tower where Knight watched from above. The thing stopped its hectic race across the pavement just shy of the base of the building and slowly craned its head sideways, so its chameleon-like eye was looking up the tower, directly at Knight. *This can't be good.*

Knight was about to consider alternate means of escaping the Customs House building, but the creature didn't enter the lobby. It continued to stare up at Knight for another few seconds. Knight didn't know how its vision functioned. Maybe if he didn't move at all, the thing wouldn't spot him. The creature squatted low and lunged toward the stone base of the building. The leap carried it twenty feet into the air before its claws extended and the beast snagged the side of the building. It hung on in a crouch, its bizarre head still tilted like a dog listening to a faraway sound, its eye still glaring up the building at Knight. Then it began a galumping, leaping climb, straight up the side of the building toward Knight's position.

"Ah, shit." Knight bolted away from the low wall and quickly glanced around. At the speed the creature was climbing the building, it would be here in seconds. Without the EXACTO, he had only his KA-BAR knife and a grenade on him. "Bishop, if you're out there, I could use some help! I'm bugging out of my hide." He was still filled with the panic from earlier, although visions of his grandmother had faded and he no longer had the feeling Bishop had reverted to his Regen state. *Where had that come from anyway? Wait...the roar.* It started with the howl that one creature made.

There was no other escape beside the rusted access door from the stairs he had used to reach the balcony. Knight raced to the door and at the last second, pulled the grenade from his belt pouch. A standard-issue M67 fragmentation grenade, Knight didn't know how effective it might be on the beast, but it was all he had. He removed the safety clip, then positioned himself at the top of the stairs, inside the stairwell, holding the door ajar, with one outstretched hand. Using his thumb to remove the pin, Knight held the spoon on the side of the grenade for a second longer, his watchful eyes never leaving the edge of the wall where he expected to see the creature at any time.

But instead of one clawed hand reaching over the edge of the parapet, the beast leapt straight up into the air, clearing the edge of the wall by a good several feet, before landing on the top of it in a crouch. Knight could just see the clear claws extending from the tips of its white toes dig firmly into the concrete just below the lip of the wall.

Knight let the spoon fly and gently rolled the grenade out, before letting the door swing shut. He leapt over the side railing on the stairs, and dropped eight feet to the middle of the next flight of stairs in a crouch. In one fluid movement, he leapt forward head-first and reached his hands out side to side to grab the railings on either side of the stairs. With about a third of the flight of steps remaining, he swung his legs up to his chest and pivoted on his arms. Then he lunged down the rest of the flight of stairs feet first, releasing his grip on the rails and flying down to land on the painted blue concrete landing in another crouch. He took two steps and lunged down the next flight of stairs, repeating the maneuver, pinioning on his arms over the side rails halfway down the flight and landing on the next landing. As he crouched on that landing, he heard the rusted door above him creak open and then the grenade detonated, slamming the door shut with a booming sound that echoed down the staircase. Still, the fire door muted the explosion considerably.

Knight wasted no time wondering if the grenade had done its job. He vaulted down the next few flights of stair and then out onto the lower balcony level, searching for the rifle. He quickly found the glass door leading out to the balcony, but he could see before he went through it that the rifle was damaged—the long barrel bent at an unusual angle. He left it and raced back to the stairs.

As he reached them, he heard the fire door at the top of the stairwell slam open. He glanced over the railing and down the space between the flights of stairs. The ground floor had a large room at the foot of the stairs, beyond the blue domed ceiling of the main hall. Above the base of the stairs hung a chandelier that was suspended by a cable running up the center of the stairwell to the 5th floor, where it was secured to the steps by a horizontal bar of concrete that was no doubt reinforced with rebar.

Knight repeated his entire-flight-of-steps lunging technique for the next few flights, listening nervously as he did, to the scrambling, scrabbling noises of translucent claws scraping across painted blue concrete from above. The lower flights of stairs were covered in a rich carpet, but in typical communist Chinese architectural style, after the good impression of the first few floors, the remaining floors were a utilitarian concrete.

When Knight reached the cross-struts for the chandelier on the 5th floor, he was running out of time. He could hear the lumbering beast hurtling down each flight nearly as fast as Knight, though he couldn't yet glimpse the creature when he looked up. Knight ran down a few steps lower than the cross-struts, so he could see the underside where the electric cable and the metal support cable attached. He didn't know if the cable would support him, but at that second, he checked nervously again up the stairs and finally saw the thing. It was injured certainly. Its movements were awkward, where before it had been all grace and power and speed. It was bleeding white fluid in places too, and it dragged one of its arms— or were they front paws—as if the limb was completely limp and nonfunctional. The creature stopped and regarded him with one of its swiveling orb eyes, then opened its maw of glassy sharp teeth in what Knight thought could only be a snarl.

Knight brought his gaze back to the cables as the beast began to move again. No time to consider, he leapt out into the open space and grabbed the cables. They easily held his weight, and he swung precariously in space for a moment. The beast rounded the landing above him and was almost to the position from which he had jumped, when Knight wrapped his legs around the cables and hooked one forearm around them, then let go with his other hand and snatched a hold of his wrist. He began to descend the cables, with the sleeve of his BDU jacket on his left arm taking the brunt of the friction. He knew he could outrun the beast with gravity, but he had no idea how he would break his fall before he hit the chandelier below him, which was racing up toward his crotch.

He heard the beast frantically flinging itself down flight after flight of stairs trying to catch him. Knight tried pulling the wrist of his left arm closer to him in an attempt to brake his fall, but the tension of the crook of his elbow had no effect. He could feel the heat from the friction building up against his arm, even through the garment.

Ah no, this is going to hurt.

Knight slammed his feet into the chandelier on the end of the cables and the jolt ripped the cables loose from their mooring up at the 5th floor of the building. To Knight it felt like a slight hiccup in the rate of his descent, and then he was sailing toward the marble floor twenty-five feet below. The long cables chased him toward the floor.

He tumbled backward, the loose cable no longer keeping him upright. As he fell through the open space of the great room that served as a proper lobby after the decorative front hall, he noticed the creature come spilling off the carpet of the main staircase and scrabbling across the slippery marble floor. It slid and slipped, then came to a stop beneath him. The creature tilted its head—

staring up—just in time to see a 300-pound crystal chandelier, followed by a 150-pound Knight with an extended middle finger and 60 feet of whipping steel and electrical cables all about to smash it into paste.

NINETEEN
Fenris Kystby, Norway

ROOK OPENED THE double doors below the window just a crack, making sure they were still covered by soil on the outside, as they had been on his last visit to the lab. He didn't need to open the doors far. He could see a wall of light brown dirt. A small spray of dust and dirt tinkled down to the floor. He shoved the doors closed again.

"Must be another entrance," Queen said. She hadn't holstered the M9, and Rook could tell the place was spooking her, even though she would never admit it. "Wouldn't be the first covert lab in history to have a secret entrance hidden in plain sight."

Rook stiffened and drew a sharp breath. "Holy—you're right." Rook raced out of the room and back into the offices.

"Not sure why that's a surprise," Queen said as she gave chase.

Asya followed her back into the offices, where Rook was approaching the door to the empty biohazard room. He turned slightly as he opened the door, to look back at them. "Only two rooms in this place with nothing in them—the closet off the first room we entered and this one. But the door frame to the closet was narrower. No way you could get a sofa in there. But this room? Must be a secret door somewhere."

Rook stepped into the room and the others came in behind him. Queen's halogen headlamp illuminated the space as if it were daytime. "I never even stepped into the room the last time. Because it was empty." He smiled at Queen.

"Just like me a minute ago. Even though you told me it was empty, I looked, but I didn't go in."

"Sure. Why would you?" Rook walked back past her and Asya to the wall near the door and felt around the doorframe they had all just come through.

"You are searching for secret switch or something like that?" Asya asked.

"Yup."

Queen kept the lamp on the doorframe as Rook worked his fingers along the top of it slowly, feeling for any irregularity.

Asya turned and walked to the far wall of the room. She tilted her head slightly, and scrunched up her eyes, looking at the floor. "Queen? Light please."

Queen swiveled her head and brought the gun up in Asya's direction. The Russian woman squatted and pointed to the floor, just in front of the edge of the far wall. Queen stepped closer. The light revealed a curving arc where the grimy floor had been disturbed. It looked to Queen like the scrape marks on the floor in front of a revolving door at a fancy hotel.

She stepped up to the wall and pressed gently on it. Asya stood and stepped back as the entire wall began to spin on a well-greased central post, hidden from view.

"Nazis," Queen said, as she pushed past the slowly twisting door, with her M9 leading the way.

"I hate 'em." Rook said.

Asya looked confused for a moment before recognition filled her eyes and she smiled broadly. "Last Crusade. Great movie." She then did a horrible impersonation of Sean Connery. "I shuddenly remembered my Charlemagne, Junior." She slipped into the passage behind Queen, and Rook brought up the rear, shaking his head.

They moved through another passage like the tunnel that led them to the lab, only this one was made from small crumbling bricks and it was far wider—not wide enough to drive a vehicle through, but well wide enough to carry the bloody sofa through. Rook could almost hear the smile on Queen's face as she taunted Asya in a whisper. "They let you watch Indy in Mother Russia?"

"Oh yes. The blonde bitch plummets to her death in the end," Asya returned. Queen whipped her head back to look at Asya, her long blonde hair swinging over her shoulder as she did so. She smiled wide, showing her teeth, and turned back to illuminate the front of the tunnel again, chuckling as she did so.

"I like her, Rook. Let's keep her."

The passage continued for what Rook took to be at least a mile. At the end, they found a double set of steel doors set into a rock foundation, similar to the door at the end of the first tunnel. This set of doors also had a name stenciled above it:

Gleipnir.

"I don't know this one," Queen said.

"Beats me," Rook said, "but Ale will know what it means. Ready?"

Queen nodded. Rook took hold of the handles on the doors and pulled them open.

They moved silently. Rook made a mental note that someone must have regularly maintained the doors for them to make so little noise when moving. Perhaps Fossen hadn't told him nearly enough about what the Nazis were doing in this lab, or what he was doing with his modern wolf research.

What they encountered on the other side of the doors was so immense, it stopped them in their tracks.

They emerged on a wide metal catwalk that ran around the top edges of a cavernous space filled by a large metal structure. Eight curved struts, each rising from a concrete block in the center of the massive room, stretched up some two hundred feet, forming a sphere of metal columns that came together just beneath the ceiling twelve feet above their heads.

Rook glanced down through the catwalk's metal mesh floor. *That's a long way down.*

It looked to Rook as if the thing was missing a giant marble that would sit perfectly in its embrace. Wires and cables snaked along the length of each strut, connected to metal plates, like solar panels, spaced along the inner edges of the struts. The structure reminded Rook of an oversized version of the Faraday cage he'd seen at Boston's Museum of Science, which directed the flow of lightning.

"Like a cage of giant fingers. But what does it do?" Asya whispered.

"Or what does it hold," Queen replied.

"Doesn't matter," Rook said. "I'm probably gonna wind up breaking the fucker into tiny pieces, so don't get attached to it. These people killed Peder and nearly killed me. If that thing isn't designed to create free clean energy for the world, I'm busting it."

There were computer stations and electronics arrays at panels and desks around the base of the giant room. Along one wall was an enormous hangar-style metal door that could retract into the walls on either side. Doors lined the walls along the catwalk, on the top level where they stood, but also on several levels below, all of which wrapped around the outside of the giant room. Staircases connected each flight to the next. A vertical maze. Massive Klieg lights lit the entire scene from their housings in the ceiling of the cavern.

"Only thing missing is people," Queen mused aloud.

"They were all too busy kicking my ass this morning." Rook spotted a large door further along the same wall from where they had emerged. "One mystery at a time. I wanna know where Kiss and the sofa went."

"I'm going to take a closer look at that...thing," Queen headed for the stairs down.

Asya paused for a moment. "I will check other doors on this floor."

"Suit yourselves." Rook moved to the wide doors and opened them. They opened into an average-sized storage room with gray metal filing cabinets, cardboard boxes and the mysterious missing sofa. Fossen, or someone else, had cleaned the sofa's old fabric. There was no sign of Edmund Kiss's bloody remains. Rook looked around the rest of the room before rifling through the file cabinets. The cabinets and boxes were full of moldy documents that had clearly been around since before the '40s. The smell reminded Rook of his grandmother's house in New Hampshire, shortly before she died, when her legendary cleaning skills had diminished.

He couldn't make much sense of the documents. They were scientific and technical reports. He came across the word *Ragnarök* a few times and only once across the word *Gleipnir*. But the descriptions of the former only confirmed what he knew already—that Edmund Kiss and other Nazis had begun experimenting with wolf genes around the '40s and the man had eventually gone missing. For *Gleipnir*, all he could find were facilities reports. Janitorial supply bills and large food bills, but Rook figured in the older days, in this distant, remote part of Norway, travel to a large supermarket wasn't likely. They would have had to purchase all their necessary supplies well before the winter, and store everything here in the lab somewhere.

The technical reports discussed things that his meager German skills were never designed to decipher. Gene sequences, astrophysics, quantum mechanics and medical topics. After fifteen minutes of scanning documents, Rook had even less of an idea of what kind of research was going on in the facility than he had when he'd entered it.

He was about to give up and check out another room when he came across a manila folder that had diagrams of the gigantic octopus-like metal structure in the main room. He paused and squatted down near the floor to look at the pictures more carefully. They showed the massive device with an enormous sphere of crackling energy suspended in its center. In the diagram, lightning bolts shot out of the sphere into the corners of the room.

"Huh, maybe it *is* supposed to provide energy." Although Rook doubted the motives of the device's builders were to provide that energy for free.

Then two things happened at the same time. Rook heard the report of Queen's M9. Not just one shot. A lot of shots. And Asya was screaming.

Rook leapt to his feet and dropped the folder with its diagrams on the floor as he raced to the door, heading for the catwalk. But when he reached the catwalk, something large and white slammed into him from the side. His feet were knocked out from under him and his lower spine slammed into the guardrail around the edge of the huge machinery-filled chamber. Rook pinioned his arms, desperately trying to claw his way back to balance, but the velocity of the impact sent his upper torso flipping backward over the rail, and he was falling down through the giant room to the floor, hundreds of feet below him.

TWENTY
Endgame Headquarters, White Mountains, NH

LEWIS ALEMAN WAS returning to his senses after the sonic blast of the creature's roar in Shanghai, as he had listened in on the battle with Knight and Bishop. He had acted quickly at the sudden auditory siege, but not quickly enough. His hand had reached the toggle switch to kill the audio from the Shanghai location, but by that point, Aleman had vomited in sheer terror, before rolling out of the command chair, hitting the carpeted floor and crawling in his own stomach contents, crying and screaming.

Around the room, Matt Carrack had scrambled into a corner and was hugging his legs. Sara Fogg had also vomited. She was on the floor on her hands and knees with a long string of saliva dripping from her mouth to the floor, reminding Aleman of a drooling St. Bernard. George Pierce was nowhere to be seen.

Aleman could only remember the creature's roar, and his instantly reaching for the audio dampening switch, before his biggest fears seized him. The fear of falling was tangible and terrifying, as he rocketed out of a clear sky with a parachute that refused to open. He realized now that he had hallucinated, but his mind was once again his own. As he struggled to his feet, his mind grappled with what had happened. The creatures ripping out of the domes had a roar that somehow induced panic in their opponents.

Not opponents.

Prey.

That was the only explanation. *But what the hell can do that?* He recalled the noise of the roar had been low and keening, a little like a foghorn, then rising in pitch as if the foghorn were being tortured.

"Are you okay?" Aleman reached to help Fogg stand.

"What the fuck was that?" Fogg shouted, wiping spittle from her face.

"Some kind of sonic attack. I was terrified. Had some kind of fear-induced hallucination. You?"

Fogg simply nodded.

Across the room, Carrack popped up from where he had been huddled in the corner, pulling his M9 pistol and scanning the room for hostile targets.

"Stand down, Matt. We're fine here. Are you okay?"

Carrack blinked a few times and looked around the room again, as if he couldn't believe it was just the three of them. Then he was all business again. "Where's Dr. Pierce?"

"He ran out," Aleman grabbed a handful of tissues and wiped down the now-soiled computer seat, then climbed back into it. "Can you check on him?"

Carrack raced out of the room. Fogg looked at Aleman, shaking her head. "Thought I would never get out."

"What?"

"I have some mild claustrophobia after what happened with the team a few years ago in Vietnam. The attack made me think I was stuck in a tight cave."

"Did it sound a bit like a foghorn to you?" Aleman asked as he worked the keys to adjust the incoming audio, setting up a filter to keep out the sound of the roar should it come again, so he could continue his role of keeping the field members in touch.

"I've got a sensory processing disorder, remember? For me it was a smell. I heard it, but I also smelled it. Like wet dog dipped in dead skunk."

Aleman smiled sympathetically at her.

"That's it!"

Aleman and Fogg turned sharply to look at George Pierce, who had just reentered the room with Carrack. Pierce looked haggard. The effects of the creature's roar had affected him as well.

"What is?" Aleman asked him.

"I've been trying to remember where I had seen an image of the creatures the team is facing. I've been wracking my brain trying to come up with it and pouring over old books of mythology—but I was checking the wrong mythology." Pierce ran to a computer desk and started typing in a search as he explained. "Sara's wet dog comment jogged my memory. When the creatures run on all fours—remember, Ale, when you slowed that video down so we could all see it clearly—they moved like pumas, so my mind locked on feline features. Plus, the odd chameleon-like eyes made me keep thinking of insect species and reptiles. All of that pointed to a Greek mythology connection, which as you know is filled with creatures large and small.

"But I was in a museum in Oslo years ago, and I saw something from *Norse* mythology..." Pierce found the page he was seeking on the computer and slid his chair back for the others to see. Aleman hopped out of his ergo-chair and came over to stand next to Carrack and Fogg as they peered over George's shoulder to view a photo of a rough woodcut. The piece of wood was a thousand years old and was housed in a Viking exhibition. It showed a creature very similar to those attacking the cities of the world. The eyes were not entirely correct, squashed and elongated, but the group could see that the artist had definite carving skills. Details like the teeth and claws were carved with careful attention. The body had the same powerful shape and the head looked accurate, too, despite the obvious Norse stylization.

George turned to look at them. "This woodcut was made by a Viking named Agnarsson. A one-armed man who claimed such a creature attacked him. The Norse called it a *Dire Wolf*."

"That can't be right. Dire wolves are an extinct species of wolf in North America." Aleman frowned and jumped back in his chair, checking the screens for the battles in Chicago and Shanghai, before devoting a second to checking another screen for information on the dire wolf. His fingers flew over the split keyboard. "Here it is. The species was named by an American paleontologist named Joseph Leidy in 1854."

Pierce stepped closer. "Was he from European descent?"

"Name like Leidy? Most likely." Aleman typed a bit more. "Yep. German."

"So it's possible that this man had heard of a Norse version of such a creature and named the North American variant after it. In any case, the Norse called the creature we are facing a dire wolf. We've got a name for it, now." Pierce moved over to another desk and sat down. "There's more. The most famous of the Norse dire wolves was named Fenrir, or Fenris Wolf. It's mentioned in a lot of Norse poetry as the son of Loki, and is regarded as the lone parent of the dire wolves, whether that's the actual species of terrestrial wolf or these monsters, I can't say. But legend says it will kill Odin during the time of Ragnarok—the end of the world, which is kind of where we're headed."

"Any instructions on how to kill them?" Aleman asked. He didn't sound serious, but Pierce missed the sarcasm.

"No, but listen to this." Pierce cleared his throat and read a block of text written below the dire wolf carving. "Much I have travelled, much have I tried out, much have I tested the Powers; from where will a sun come into the smooth heaven when Fenrir has assailed this one?"

"What's that from?" Fogg asked.

"A poem," Pierce said and then butchered the title as he slowly pronounced it. "Vafþrúðnismál."

"From where will a sun come into the smooth heaven when Fenrir has assailed this one?" Aleman repeated the line. "A sun."

"Yeah, sounds familiar, right?"

Aleman nodded. "I think it's safe to say this isn't the first visit these things have made to Earth. Let's keep digging. See if we can't find a how-to on closing these portals." Aleman frowned at his screen. "Hopefully we'll find something sooner than later."

Fogg was about to take her own seat and pitch in with Pierce's research. She paused and turned back to Aleman. "Why? What is it?"

"Since this thing began, I've been tracking the appearance of these dire wolf portals around the globe. I've also been keeping track of how long each appears, how much damage is done, the size of each occurrence and so forth."

Pierce pushed his glasses up his nose "And?"

Aleman turned to him. "The globes are getting larger and they're occurring with more frequency around the world. Also, they flicker less."

Fogg turned in her chair. She was wiping her face off with a wet-wipe. "Flicker?"

"Flicker. As in the strength of the electricity coming off the portals varies in strength the way a lightbulb does when the power is struggling."

"Wait," George stood up and walked around the room. "You're saying these domes aren't at full power yet? They're already chucking lightning bolts around like a two-year-old throwing a tantrum with his toys. You're saying these domes will...what? Get more powerful?"

"Well, yes, but no." Aleman leaned his head to the side, loudly realigning the vertebrae in his neck with a clunky popping noise. "It's worse than that. They will get more powerful, but these globes of light are clearly portals for the dire wolves. So far, we've only seen a few hit-and-run incursions. They come out, they tear shit up and then run back into the portals. The portals close or collapse or whatever."

"How are portals even possible? Portals to where?" Fogg asked.

"Don't know yet, but you're all missing the point." Aleman looked at them each slowly. Even Carrack was paying full attention to every word Aleman said. "If the portals grow in strength, then like with a lightbulb, one of two things will happen. Either they will reach full power and stabilize, which means nothing could stop the dire wolves from flooding into our world...or the other thing will happen."

Fogg looked confused. "What's the other thing?"

Carrack spoke up from the corner of the room. He understood what Aleman was driving at. "You know when you go to turn on a light and the bulb is done, and the tungsten filament kind of pops? A sort of mini-explosion, but contained inside the glass of the bulb? If I understand what Ale is saying, these things could go boom."

Pierce turned from Carrack's laid-back features to Aleman's tense visage. "How big of a boom?"

TWENTY-ONE
Chicago

KING LEAPT OUT of the Humvee as it hurtled into the suddenly dark abyss, and landed on the scoured-clean side of the crater. With nothing to grab onto, he slid down the steep grade. He could see in the dim light where different pipes or cables had been before the dome had appeared, but the entire surface of the crater wall was now as smooth as glass, the lightning ball having melted soil, asphalt, concrete, metal and everything else into a smooth paste before rapidly cooling and solidifying.

He slid face down, picking up speed as he went. His hands scrabbled for purchase, trying to find a nook or hole to grab, to stop his descent. Behind him, the abandoned Humvee smashed into the center of the hole with a loud crump but no huge explosion. The twisting, shrieking sound of impacting metal was horrible enough and he was glad he had bailed, even though his body slamming into the crater had hurt plenty.

He wasn't really worried about sliding to the bottom of the crater. He was worried about what had happened to the creature. *Did Whitey make it back into the dome before it blinked out?*

He looked below him as he slid down into the dark, but couldn't see anything in the dim light. He strained to hear the beast in the dark below him, but the noise of sirens from rescue vehicles up on the panicked streets drowned out any chance he might have had to detect movement. Moreover, there was the whispering hiss of his uniform gliding on the silky-smooth crater wall throwing up a white noise barrier.

Then, instead of coming to the bottom of the crater, he felt himself lurch downward, falling through the open air. *What the hell?* But before he had time to finish the thought, he hit solid ground again unexpectedly, the force driving the air from him lungs in a loud cough. He was no longer moving.

He was laying down on a lumpy horizontal surface. He reached under his back with his hand and felt wood spaced out by concrete. *Railroad ties. But there's no subway anywhere near here.* King slowly moved to a sitting position and toggled his communications gear.

"Blue, you out there?"

"King! You're okay?"

"Bruised and battered. I'm in some kind of underground railroad tunnel that shouldn't be here. Plus I'm going to have trouble getting back to the surface. The sides of the crater are smooth."

"There were a number of mining projects after the turn of the century, King. Over 110 miles of tunnels and caverns are now under the greater Chicago area. You must have found one of them. What about the hostile you were after?"

"No sign of it. I'm going to give pursuit."

"Understood. Just be careful. I'll be down for you once we wrap of the last of them up here. Two of them didn't make it back to the sphere before it closed down." King heard the audible click of Deep Blue signing off. He stayed still in the dark of the tunnel, waiting for his ears to adjust to the ambient noise of the tunnel, before he proceeded deeper inside. There was always the chance the creature missed the tunnel and slid to the bottom of the crater, but King didn't think so. The small hairs on the back of his neck raised; he could tell the beast was in the tunnel with him.

It was colder up on the city streets, with the November wind blowing hard. In the tunnel, the air was dry and mild. The dark was inky black. King knew he would have to use a flashlight. He removed a small tactical light and laser sight from one zippered pocket on his flight suit and attached it to the barrel of his Glock 23, which the Air Force had issued him before his ill-fated F-16 flight. It took some work to get the thing attached in the dark, but he managed it.

With the lights off, he slowly stood and moved to his right. Leading with his hand outstretched, he searched for the wall of the tunnel. It took him only a few steps before his fingertips brushed the edge of the smooth rock wall. His ears strained at the silence, hoping to detect some small sound of movement, but all was dead quiet. King laid his body against the wall and took a slow breath, then flicked on the flashlight and targeting laser.

The tiny LED light and red laser beam illuminated the ten-foot wide concrete tunnel as if the sun had just been turned on. Ten feet deeper into the tunnel and hanging upside down from the ceiling by its claws, its back was to King. He was in its blind spot.

He stood stock still, moving the targeting laser to the back of the creature's head.

Almost. Almost...

King took a slow deep breath and released it, preparing to take the shot, when the bulbous white orb on the side of the creature's upside-down head swiveled back to look directly at King. He fired the Glock, but the beast was already on the ground, flipping and landing couched on all four limbs, like a cat.

Then it roared.

A huge, echoing, hideously loud roar that vibrated in King's chest like the thumping bass of a high-end car stereo. He squinted in momentary pain from the volume of the roar, but then fired another shot and dropped to a crouch of his own.

The creature lurched to the side, a gout of thick white blood spraying from its shoulder. King could smell the fluid, and it didn't smell coppery like human blood. More like spoiled fish. And metal and plastic.

The beast paused and moved its head to the side, as if it were considering something. One of the white eyes swiveled, peering down at its fresh wound.

King watched, fascinated as the bundles of cable-like muscles under the thing's translucent skin tensed and released, as the creature moved its head.

King opened up with the remaining 13 rounds in the magazine of his Glock.

The beast's head erupted with spurts of white fluid, before its perforated corpse collapsed in a heap on the dusty concrete floor of the tunnel.

King stood and ejected the magazine, allowing it to clatter to the floor, the sound of it drowned out by the still echoing gunshots. He reached into another zippered pocket on his flight suit for the only spare magazine he had.

He just finished inserting the fresh rounds when Deep Blue's voice returned.

"You alright? We heard the roar up here, although my sound dampeners in the helmet kicked in. Aleman says the fear response that the roar creates is pretty devastating."

"Uh, the what?" King asked.

"Fear response. Did you experience a debilitating terror from the roar?" Deep Blue sounded perplexed in King's earpiece.

"No. It was loud, but that was all. What are you talking about?"

"I'll explain later. Come to the edge of the tunnel, we're lowering a winch from the second Humvee."

After King was winched up, Deep Blue led him to an exterior door on the side of the John Hancock Center, where he inserted a key and a door opened to reveal a private elevator. "One of the Secret Service evac routes from when I was the President." Once inside the elevator, he used the same key to activate the lift. The men felt a tug at their stomachs as the fast-moving car raced for the roof, 100 stories above them. Deep Blue relayed the intel from Aleman about the fear response generated by the creature's roar.

"Didn't experience anything like that," King said.

"Odd. Maybe you can't hear certain frequencies, or have an odd ear structure. Whatever it is, be thankful for it. The National Guard topside were pissing themselves and screaming like little girls. Ale assures me I would have done the same if he hadn't warned me to calibrate the audio pickups in this helmet to dampen any noises on that frequency."

"We might all need helmets like that, then."

The doors to the elevator opened and the men stepped out onto the roof of the building, its two massive antennas towering over-head. A huge fixed-wing, crescent-shaped craft idled on the roof.

"Looks kind of like the *Crescent*," King said as they boarded the aircraft.

"Similar. The *Persephone*. The Pentagon is messing around with the design. Keasling is loaning it to us."

They sat and strapped in, surrounded by a complicated computer array. Deep Blue removed his helmet and contacted Aleman, back in New Hampshire. The craft launched vertically and then King felt the thrust as it banked and accelerated.

"Aleman, catch us up," Deep Blue began.

"Cape Town is gone," came the sober response.

Deep Blue sighed. "How many dead?"

"No, you don't understand. It's gone. Completely."

TWENTY-TWO
Shanghai, China

KNIGHT STAGGERED THROUGH the street, his body sore from the fall onto the creature on the ground floor of the Customs House building. The creature had remained inert after cushioning Knight's fall from the chandelier. He didn't know if it was dead or just unconscious, but he stuck his KA-BAR knife in its head five times to make sure it wouldn't get up again either way.

Now outside the building and making his way between the abandoned cars in the road, Knight felt some of his normal cool persona returning, despite the fact that all he was armed with now was the knife. The creature's roar had completely incapacitated him and he tried to analyze whether the noise had maybe triggered a dormant childhood terror, but that explanation didn't feel right. He figured something in the beast's vocalization had instigated a severe fight or flight response—except he was too paralyzed to fight and too full of hallucinatory fear to even consider taking flight.

There was no sign of the speeding white things along the road, but he had seen them go back into the glowing sphere, as if regrouping or afraid to be left behind, should this energy dome wink out like the others had. Knight squatted down low behind a garishly blue Ford and looked at the pulsing wall of light. The dome showed no signs that it was going anywhere anytime soon.

"Bishop? Where you at?" Knight tried his communicator again, but there was no response from his partner.

He moved from one car to the next, making his way toward the river. He wondered if the creatures could swim. They didn't really look built for it—all sinew and claw. Still, when the creatures were upright, they looked like bipeds. *If man can learn to swim, there's no reason to think these things can't.* As Knight stepped onto the board-walk adjacent to the water, a blur of movement in his peripheral vision made him pause.

Crap.

He could make out at least four more of the things tearing around the street. He looked for a pattern, but they moved chaotically, almost as if they couldn't see him, or didn't yet have a target. Knight glanced back to the water. Ten feet, and he could jump into the river. *But will they follow me into the water? What if they swim better than a human?*

"KNIGHT! INCOMING!" Bishop's voice bellowed from the direction of the river.

That was all it took to get Knight in motion. Unfortunately, it was also the impetus the creatures needed to unite in pursuit of him.

He sprinted blindly for the river, moving in a straight line, whereas the beasts still needed to weave in and out of the abandoned car obstacle course.

Knight reached the river's edge and saw the water level was a good ten or fifteen feet below the concrete lip of the boardwalk. But his speed carried him out over the water. A screeching noise filled the air, and Knight twisted in mid-dive to see the return of the *Crescent*.

The plane sped into the Bund historical district, firing rockets and cannon fire at the street, where Knight had been seconds before. He looked back to the water just before he hit and saw Bishop bobbing in the slow current on the other side of the river. He didn't see the cars exploding and flipping in the air behind him as the *Crescent* turned the street, and the creatures skittering over it, into a swath of white, meaty slop.

A roar ripped through the air.

Knight's mind registered what it was and what it was about to do to his body.

He tensed.

But nothing happened as his head submerged beneath the murky, polluted water. The liquid muted the fear-inducing scream, protecting Knight from its effects.

When Knight surfaced to take a lungful of air, snapping his head back to fling his shoulder-length black hair out of his face, he heard the powerful detonations on the road behind him, but no longer heard the roar of the white creatures. The *Crescent* pulled up and banked, coming in to hover over the pickup point at Bin Jiang Park, opposite the bend in the river.

Knight stroked over to where Bishop waited, a million questions on his mind, but Bishop had had plenty of time to think of the answers and preempted him.

"They can't swim or maybe just don't want to. They didn't follow me into this muck." Bishop pointed down at the thick stew of brown swirling waters. At least the current wasn't particularly strong. "I heard the start of that roar of theirs before going underwater, and it was enough for me. Aleman got in touch. Says the sound causes some kind of physiological reaction. Adrenaline dump into the heart to the point of paralysis. Could even kill you, if you got scared enough."

"I can believe it," Knight said, lowering his eyes.

"You caught the full blast," Bishop said. It wasn't a question. "I called in the airstrike. Deep Blue wants us to regroup and gear-up. Starting with getting you a new headset." Bishop swam over and pulled Knight's earpiece away from his head. Knight flinched from the move. Bishop looked at Knight without a word. He hadn't missed the flinch.

Bishop held up Knight's earpiece, and Knight could see that the plastic frame was damaged and a small wire was hanging out of it. He hadn't even noticed.

"We need some kind of headsets that'll protect us from that roar." Bishop watched Knight, his generally implacable features filled with concern for his friend.

Knight held his gaze for a moment, then looked away, still treading water. "Let's just say it was pretty fucking terrible, and leave it at that."

"Yeah," Bishop turned and stroked overhand for the shoreline. Knight followed him.

BISHOP CRAWLED ONTO a concrete boat launch and stood slowly, looking back across the river at the energy dome. Before his eyes, the dome closed in on itself, disappearing in seconds, until only a glowing dot was left at the center of its radius, *like an old cathode-ray TV set, moving down into a tiny dot of light before turning off completely. Or was it just a trick of the eye? An imprint left on my retina?*

He reached down to help Knight out of the water. The little Korean man was usually so slick and self-assured. Not only was he a stellar sniper, but as a wealthy, well-dressed ladies' man, his personality was the most confident on the team. But the sound of that roar had really rattled him.

Bishop felt more than a little rattled himself, but more so over how damn hard it had been to shoot the creatures. It was one thing to know that you could drop them with a .50 caliber round. But shooting something that moved in a blur? He shook his head. Wasn't easy. He could hit them by firing in the path of their trajectory, but it was sloppy, wasted a lot of ammunition and he still missed the damn things more frequently than he hit them. Plus, the bastards hit like a freight train. He absently rubbed his right shoulder, which he had torqued when he rolled across the pavement after one of the creatures slammed into him.

"Nice timing," he told Knight, and nodded with his head across the river, where the energy dome had been.

Knight looked across the river and sighed. "Think the thing is sentient?"

Bishop looked aghast. "The dome? No. Let's hope not. The creatures are enough to deal with."

They boarded the *Crescent* and took their seats, the vehicle launching them into the sky. Once they were at cruising altitude, Knight headed to the small galley on the ship, intending to fill up on protein. Bishop got in touch with Aleman and passed on their mission status, as well as his own personal observations about the dome.

When Knight came back, handing him a chocolate protein shake, Bishop gladly took it and leaned back in his chair, not looking at the little man. "Ale gave me good news and bad news. Which do you want first?"

Knight considered a moment, slurping liquid protein through a straw. "The good, please."

"He's got some full-body armor suits waiting for us at the next hotspot, which should help protect us in hand-to-hand against those things. They're not bullet-proof, but he says they're made of impact-resistant memory foam. Not too bulky. Should give us a nice edge, especially if they barrel into us, like that one that knocked me across the taxi."

"Nice," Knight removed his straw and gulped the rest of his shake. "Where *is* the next location?"

"London. Ready for the bad news?"

"Not really, but hit me."

"Our original destination was Cape Town, South Africa, but there wasn't just one energy dome there. There was a whole cluster of them. Cape Town is gone. The whole city. Gone."

"Damn," Knight stretched the word out. "Clusters?" His face looked ashen, as if he had seen not just one ghost, but an entire convention of them.

TWENTY-THREE
Fenris Kystby, Norway

ZELDA BAKER, CALLSIGN: Queen, was out of ammunition. She had one more magazine for the M9, but she knew she'd never have time to load it. The thing at the end of the narrow corridor moved like lightning, leaping from wall to wall, floor to ceiling. She had fired 15 times and missed every shot but the last. Now, the thing stopped, hanging upside down from the ceiling. It looked at her through one of its baseball-sized eyeballs on the outside of its blocky head.

Queen had been expecting something strange since Rook had told her about the mind-controlled villagers and the Nazi experiments that had gone on in these labs. But she wasn't prepared for this. It looked at

The knife slid into the creature's clear skull, up to the hilt, from the force of her thrust. She pushed until the beast's body toppled over. She didn't release her pressure on the knife until she felt the tip of the blade strike the stone floor.

She squatted next to the creature and wondered what it could be. She was about to remove the blade from the dead thing when a small skittering sound came from down the tunnel behind her. She withdrew the blade with agonizing slowness. *Have to make it like I'm not even moving.*

A rock rolled across the floor and hit the wall of the tunnel with a loud clacking noise.

Queen drew in a breath.

The newcomer was less than ten feet behind her. The blade of the knife came free and Queen spun in a whirl, raising the knife for another killing stroke.

But that stroke never came. Instead came a noise. A roaring vibration like a hundred jet aircraft in her head.

Her arms turned to limp spaghetti.

The knife fell from her hand.

Her legs quivered and her teeth chattered.

Her eyes watered and a thick river of drool slipped from her mouth. She never saw the second beast. Its roar filled her world, and her eyes clamped shut trying to force out the terror, but as she fell to the ground, her whole body shaking like an epileptic in the throes of a seizure, she could utter only two words:

"Daddy, no!"

TWENTY-FOUR
Manhattan Island, New York
3 November, 0630 Hrs

MAJOR GENERAL MICHAEL Keasling's permanent scowl didn't alter when he saw the UH-60 Black Hawk helicopter settle in the middle of the cordoned-off city street, but he did breathe a sigh of relief as its rotor blades whipped dust and grit into the sky. The situation in New York hadn't gotten out of hand yet, but he knew it would. He had 200 men out of Fort Dix, and another 200 on the way, but he knew they wouldn't be sufficient for this mess. He also suspected the two men emerging from the helicopter might not make much difference against such an alien threat. Still, these two men were among the most capable soldiers he had ever known, and they were both his friends.

Keasling absently raised the fingers of one hand and stroked the smooth skin under his nose, where he had worn a mustache for most of the last twenty years. With the recent receipt of his second star, he'd made a few simple but profound changes in his life. No more coffee and more time in the gym for one—although with his short, stocky barrel shape, he'd been muscular enough. He wasn't looking to become more intimidating but to increase his lifespan with cardiovascular exercises he hadn't bothered with since long before he had become a General. His wife was long in the grave from the cancer, but his daughter had just had her first little blonde-haired son, Liam, and Keasling now wanted to live long enough to see the boy become a man. *Funny how family changes everything*, he thought.

The loss of the mustache wasn't as physically life changing as the exercise, but he found his hand returning to the lack of it repeatedly, as if the loss of hair signified this new phase in his life as much as it reduced the appearance of his age by a decade. As the two men approached him on 6th Avenue, and the helicopter took to the dawn sky behind them, Keasling thought about the chaos of the present situation and wondered, not for the first time since he had received his second star, if maybe it was time to stop. He knew he never would, though. The vicious cycle of thought further fueled his gruff demeanor as he stepped forward to greet his friends.

"King, you look like the fucking Michelin Man."

Both of the recently arrived men were dressed in personal body armor suits that looked to Keasling like they were wearing sculpted pillows on their bodies. The General knew the suits were an extension of research carried out by the Pentagon and a Canadian man that started out making a suit impervious to grizzly bear attacks. Lewis Aleman's genius had been further applied to the designs and the result was an incredibly lightweight, tactical battle-suit, which, while it would not stop a large-caliber bullet, would significantly reduce damage from impacts, falls and knife—or in this case, *claw*—attacks. Keasling's people in the Joint Special Operations Command (JSOC) had been involved in the Pentagon's end of development on the suit, so he was aware of its capabilities. He understood the necessity of such body armor. Still, they looked like the Tempur-Pedic memory foam pillow he used during the few hours of sleep he got at night.

The suits had multiple sculpted angles that resembled the boxy radar-reflective surfaces of stealth aircraft, and the color scheme for the entirety of the suits was a grayish black, reinforcing the similarity. Both men wore full-face-mask helmets that kept their identities hidden as well, but Keasling knew each man by his gait.

"General," Deep Blue said from behind his armored faceplate. "If King is the Michelin Man, what does that make me?"

"Very dignified and presidential, sir."

"I was going to say *my valet*," King started, "but *dignified* works too."

"Show some respect, Delta Boy," Keasling said, but he was smiling as he said it. King and his Chess Team cohorts were all former

Delta, and they were used to a level of informality and a lack of ranks not approved of in other branches of the service. However, in just a few short years, Keasling had gone from being constantly irritated at the informality to having immense respect for Jack Sigler. The two men had become close friends.

He shook hands with both men, noting with approval how supple the gloves on the suits were. While still padded with a thin layer of the experimental armor material, the fingers would still be able to operate triggers and even keyboards if necessary.

"Sorry about the switch to the chopper, but *Persephone* would have trouble with how tight the buildings are in Midtown. Plus, no easy rooftops for VTOL nearby, like you had in Chicago. There's crap all over the roofs here." The general led the other men up 6th Avenue, along the sidewalk.

"No problem. We came in low from Jersey and couldn't see much. How bad is it here?" Deep Blue asked the general as they began walking up to West 49th, where soldiers from Fort Dix stood and crouched behind sandbags, weapons trained down the street.

"Well, let's just say that I've been wondering whether it's too late to join the Peace Corps and get assigned to the ass-end of Botswana. I can tell you it was no damn fun getting all the civilians out of these buildings in this part of town. NYPD played a big part in that, but it would have been impossible later in the day."

The men rounded the corner of a small concrete-bordered city-planning park with about ten trees, all still tenaciously clinging to their orange leaves before winter's inevitable pull. Beyond it stood five abandoned hot dog carts with brightly colored umbrellas. Keasling's stomach rumbled at the thought of wolfing down a few dogs with brown mustard and sauerkraut. They turned onto West 49th Street and saw an empty road, cordoned off a few bocks west, down the narrow corridor of tall buildings before them. Steam gently seeped up from manhole sewer covers on the asphalt, and a discarded sheet of crumpled, dirty newspaper caught an errant breeze and wafted along the street, wrapping around the leg of a squat black fire hydrant with a silver top on the other side of the street.

"Where—?" King began, his voice thick through the built in voice modulator on his helmet.

"Up gentlemen, up." Keasling said more forcefully than necessary. The situation was wearing on his nerves.

His armored companions slowly titled their heads up and took in the sight.

The Cobra Head streetlamps, stretched into their view, but otherwise, all they could see were two glass-walled skyscrapers reaching into the sky on either side of the road. The one on the right reached to 750 feet and the one on the left went almost as high, to 675 feet. But the building on their right had a glowing energy sphere embedded in it, close to the top. The globe of light stretched across the 100 foot gap between the buildings, over the street and just barely kissed the edge of the building on the left. The ball of light floated in the sky, with the right third of it clawing into the taller building. The globe was steady and solid, with none of the lightning effects Keasling had seen in video footage of the Chicago event.

"Gentlemen, the building on your right is the Exxon Building. The X part of the so-called 'XYZ buildings' of Rockefeller Center. The building on the left is McGraw Hill. The Y. Far as we can tell, the event does not actually touch the Y building, although it does look like it from where we are standing. The Exxon Building has 54 floors and floors 38 to 51 are inside the affected area. The elevators are just clear of the effect, though, so we can still get up top if we need to. I've got men in the Y building just opposite the curving wall of light, ready to fire if needed. No one in the X building though. If the creatures show up, I don't want my boys too close." Keasling turned to face Deep Blue and King in their armor. "They haven't got pillow suits on."

Deep Blue kept his head tilted upward, looking at the floating ball of light jammed between the two glass skyscrapers.

King lowered his head and looked at the General. "I think we're going to need that helicopter to come back."

TWENTY-FIVE
Gleipnir Facility, Fenris Kystby, Norway
3 November, 1300 Hrs

EIREK FOSSEN WAS so close to his freedom, he could taste it.

He sat behind a desk in one of the offices looking at three, side-by-side, 17-inch monitors. He had divided each screen into four windows displaying video footage from major world news stations. The volume on all of them was off, but he didn't need it to understand what was happening around the world. Portals were opening up. Shanghai. Chicago. Los Angeles. Istanbul. Kinshasa. Lima. Mumbai. The portals, and the pack of dire wolves that came from them, were devouring entire cities.

It was all too delicious.

He leaned back in the tilting office chair and one after the other, placed his lower legs diagonally atop the corner of the desk. He slipped his hands behind his head and prepared to enjoy one hell of a show. A portal had even opened up halfway up a set of skyscrapers in New York. He would have liked to see some of the footage of action on the ground—the dire wolves ripping into people—but none of the camera operators could get that close to the conflagrations for more than a second or two without being shredded themselves.

The door to the office opened, and Fossen looked up. Nathalie Schröder was Fossen's assistant. She was young, at 25, but highly capable. She had a brilliant mind for the math involved in their undertaking, and she was equally good with electrical engineering. She wore a lab coat, and her dark hair was back in a ponytail. Her father had worked for the project before her. Fossen liked her, but she had been asking the wrong kind of questions lately.

"How are the power readings?" he asked her.

"Good," she said, looking down at her tablet PC. "The turbines have collected a surplus and we should be ready for another test."

"How long has it been since the last test?" Fossen interrupted her.

She tapped a few times at her tablet. "Five hours. I have the statistics now. It was at 98% stability and generated over 12 gigawatts at one point, but I think we can go higher—"

Fossen waved his hand cutting her off. "I don't need the details. As long as we are at 98%, that's all that is important."

He let his eyes drift back to the screens with the scenes of destruction.

Schröder looked over his shoulder and cleared her throat. She spoke softly. "We still have no control over the global portals. They are definitely a byproduct of the experiment, but as you can see, they open at random intervals and geographic locations. There are far more of them than we ever expected."

"I know. It's beautiful, isn't it?"

"People are dying," she said. "Far more than was projected."

Fossen stood up from the chair, staring at her. Schröder lowered her eyes to the floor. "We knew this when we began, yes? Opening and maintaining the portal was always going to have side effects. One collateral portal or a hundred, it makes no difference."

"But so many people—" she began again.

"Do not matter!" Fossen finished for her. "If after all this time you are having doubts about the project, if your *faith* is wavering...you can go."

Schröder raised her eyes to him, hopefully. "You would let me leave?" Then more furtively, "*It* would let me leave?"

Fossen grimaced as though pinched, but quickly forced a smile. "If your heart is not in it, Nathalie, you have no place here. You've already performed your part. The system is self-sustaining now. If you want to leave, go."

She looked him in the eye, relief washing over her. "Thank you, Eirek."

Schröder turned to make for the door.

Fossen drew a Walther pistol from his lab coat pocket and shot her twice in the back of her head. The bullets went through her at such a close range they chewed holes into the wood of the door beyond her. Her skull detonated like a popping water balloon, before her legs gave out and her body dropped to the floor.

"You are welcome. They are not people. They are sheep, waiting for the wolf."

An intercom on the wall came to life with a clicking noise.

"What is it?" Fossen asked, disgust in his voice as if the shooting was the latest in a never-ending series of distractions and interruptions.

"Security, sir. We have intruders. The dire wolves have them cornered." The voice said through the intercom with a thick slur, as if the man attached to it was on drugs.

"I want them alive. I'll be right there." Fossen got up from his chair and made for the door to the chamber.

Oh Stanislav, you should not have come back.

TWENTY-SIX
Pinckney Bible Campground, New Hampshire
3 November, 0700 Hrs

GEORGE PIERCE SAT atop a brown picnic table with his feet propped on the bench. Pierce knew the campground would fill with people in the summer, but right now, he was the only human being in sight. When Chess Team fought the monstrosity Manifold Genetics had created from the original Greek Hydra a few years back, the battle destroyed parts of the campground.

After the fight, Deep Blue had arranged for the Army to take over the entire area, while Hazmat teams cleaned up the secret Manifold facility hidden under the mountains behind the campground. Then they had the base refurbished and refitted to house Chess Team and its extended support crew, now collectively dubbed *Endgame*.

Pierce had assisted in the project at the time, before he was formally a member of Endgame. Finally, once the base was finished and operational, its secret entrance in the mountain sufficiently concealed again, Deep Blue had accepted Pierce's suggestion of restoring the campground itself. After all, the public would become wary if a supposed chemical spill was being 'cleaned up' by the Army, but once that process was completed, they didn't turn the land back over to the public. The last thing Endgame wanted was more scrutiny from the public. Besides, the base sprawled underground over miles. There were other entrances and exits, which afforded more privacy, and which did not require movement through a formerly public area.

Still, when Pierce felt the crushing claustrophobia of the underground base weighing on him, he liked to slip out of the vehicle entrance located behind the campground, and come out here to think.

He was exhausted, after spending all night researching Norse mythology. It wasn't his field, and there was so very much to learn, although he had found little in reference to the dire wolves. In addition, the dire wolf roar had rendered him nearly useless for much of the night. He still suffered the terrifying visions that the sound induced in him, but they had lessened in their intensity, and he knew them to be nothing more than echoes of his hallucination.

Carrack had later told him he had fled the computer room at the sound of the roar, but Pierce had no memory of that. What he saw when the dire wolf roar had assaulted them over the speakers of the room, before Aleman had been able to switch off the audio, was worse than anything his mind could come up with in a normal nightmare.

And George Pierce had plenty of nightmares.

When Chess Team had gone up against Manifold a few years earlier, Pierce, much like Bishop, had been tortured and experimented upon. But unlike Bishop, Pierce had received DNA directly from the Hydra sample. His skin had changed into a green and scaly substance. He had been half-man and half-reptile by the time Manifold finished with him. The nonhuman genes attached to his body were eventually blocked and he had suffered no relapses. But the bad dreams had taken far longer to go away than his skin had taken to slough and repair itself.

Pierce sighed and watched his breath in the cool morning air. Some might say chilly, but he had quickly acclimatized to the cold, despite his years spent in Greece and even in the humidity of Peru. His hallucinatory reaction to the dire wolf roar still haunted him. It was far worse than any Hydra nightmare he had yet to experience. He'd seen Julie, King's deceased sister, his fiancée who had died long ago in a fighter jet accident—except it hadn't been her. It was Julie as she would have been if she'd been the one Manifold infected. She wore a flight suit and her skin had the same sickly green scaly look that Pierce's had when he was altered by the Hydra DNA.

It was so real, he thought. *I could smell her.*

He hadn't run from the computer center as Carrack had said. The monstrous Julie had *chased* him from the room in his hallucination.

She was going to eat me.

Julie's death had initially led to Pierce and King falling out of touch. The Hydra incident, which had begun with Pierce on an archeological dig site in Nazca, had brought them back together. Pierce's ordeal cemented their friendship.

He took another sip of the now cool coffee and vowed never to tell King about the hallucination. It was simply too terrible, and Jack Sigler had enough to deal with.

Pierce took a deep breath and closed his eyes, bringing his mind back to the present. Soft footsteps approached him from behind. He turned and opened his eyes to see Anna Beck striding toward him from the direction of the base's concealed door.

Beck, callsign: Black Zero, was Deep Blue's right-hand woman. Ostensibly, the man's bodyguard, she did far more fieldwork for Endgame. She was dating Knight, Pierce knew, or he might have asked the woman out. She was cute, although not stunningly beautiful. But she was tough and had a razor-sharp wit that often manifested in blistering sarcasm. Pierce liked her.

Beck walked across the yellowing grass. Her brown hair, pulled back into a ponytail, swayed as she walked. She wore her customary all-black military battle-dress uniform, and strapped to her leg was her ever-present sidearm. Pierce had asked her once why she was always armed. Her answer had been that the base creeped her out.

After the facility had been attacked by Manifold agents, before its restoration was complete, Pierce could understand that. Although Matt Carrack, callsign: White Zero, was officially in charge of security at the base, Pierce knew that Beck played a significant part in stopping the Manifold incursion. They had lost several security members of the team during that incident—the soldiers formerly known as White Two through White Five. Pierce understood afterward that was the reason Deep Blue had insisted on naming the White and Black team members with numbers. It would be harder on Chess Team field personnel to get attached to their support members. Replacing their identities with numbers would lessen the focus of the field team on the loss of these team members in emergencies. They were expendable. Pierce realized the strategy hadn't worked completely, especially when he saw that

Knight and Beck had become a thing. Still, Pierce was glad he hadn't been given a numbered callsign.

"What's up?" he called to Beck.

"Aleman wants everyone back for a meeting."

Pierce leapt up and strode over to her, tossing the remaining cold coffee from his cup into a nearby pine tree and shaking the drips out onto the grass as they walked.

"Everyone?" he asked.

She looked at him with a grim expression. "Yeah. Even Boucher is going to be on the call. Then I'm off to Norway as soon as we're done." Domenick Boucher was the current director of the CIA, and although Pierce hadn't met the man, he knew that Boucher was an Endgame ally in the US government.

"Norway? You're going after Rook?" Pierce asked.

"Yeah. Him and Queen both. We need everyone for this mess."

They entered the vehicle entrance in the mountain and rapidly descended to the lowest level of the part of the base christened *Labs*. The main computer lab was a ten-minute ride away by underground tram, in a different section of the expansive base known as *Central*. They sat silently on the tram, each lost in their own thoughts. Once at Central, they proceeded to the main computer lab down quiet corridors.

The main screen showed a view from Deep Blue's helmet of the massive energy globe suspended above Manhattan. Aleman was in his customary jeans and t-shirt, straddling the futuristic workstation in the center of the room. Sara Fogg stood with baggy eyes in a corner, leaning against a wall. Seated next to her was King's adopted daughter, Fiona, who wore a Disney t-shirt and pajama bottoms, and sleepily ate a colorful breakfast cereal from a porcelain bowl. Her striking Native American facial features were partially obscured by a thick shock of her long black hair that had managed to escape her ponytail. She leaned her head against Fogg's hip. Pierce was pleased to see how well King's 'family' was working out for the man.

Matt Carrack leaned against another wall, wearing his usual forest-pattern BDUs. The other five members of the White security team were standing next to him and looking anxious. No doubt, Carrack had already briefed the men on the severity of the situation worldwide. Each man was a crack soldier from the alpine 10th Mountain division at Fort Drum. Pierce had yet to learn any of their names or even speak to them. He had made that mistake with the last batch of White Team members, and now they were all dead.

Pierce knew the two White Team scientists in the room, but they were easy to recognize from their white lab coats. White Six was an unusually tall, gangly man. At just under seven feet tall, Six had to duck his head when going through most of the doors in the base. Ironically, the tall man with the dark mop of black shaggy hair hated sports. Especially basketball. When he wasn't working on chemical analyses for Endgame, the man was building models from toothpicks and popsicle sticks. The structures were incredibly intricate, and when Six chose to design something recognizable, like the Eiffel Tower, the structures were meticulously accurate to every detail. Pierce had joked with the man that he had missed his calling as an architect. Six's serious response was simply "I know." But Pierce liked the gentle giant.

White Seven, the other scientist on the team, was a short, burly man with a gruff demeanor. Pierce rarely spoke to the man, but was impressed by the scientist's wide knowledge of everything but social graces.

The White Team was completed by a weapons expert named Reggie. Reggie was technically callsign: White Eight, but despite Deep Blue's admonition that White and Black support team members each keep their names to themselves and use only their callsigns, Reggie had introduced himself to everyone at the base as Reggie, so the name had stuck. He was the consummate joker, but the sort whose jokes were more frequently directed at himself. Everyone liked the man. Plus, he knew everything there was to know about every weapon they had on the base. Reggie certainly destroyed any stereo-types Pierce had had about weapons training experts. He pictured most of them to be hard-assed drill instructor types, and he wasn't surprised to discover that King had thought much the same. Reggie was also the only one around to best King at horseshoes up on the campground.

On the other side of the room, the Black Team was under-represented, because half of them—the pilots, callsigns: Black One through Black Four—were currently out in the field. Two mechanics that repaired the team's helicopters and the *Crescent* were present. Both men wore bib overalls, and both tended to keep to themselves. Pierce had seen them around the base a few times. They were both short and skinny men, with grease caked under their fingernails from a lifetime of mechanical work. Both men were dark haired, and Pierce occasionally wondered if they were brothers. The men were callsigns: Black Seven and Black Eight.

Black Five was an overweight man of at least sixty years old. Deep Blue had introduced Pierce to the man only a few weeks earlier. Balding and always wearing half-moon glasses, Black Five probably looked older than he was. When Pierce had seen him, he was neck deep in computer programs, on the phone or both. Deep Blue had introduced Black Five as an intelligence analyst, but he had been recruited because he also had a Ph.D. in physics. Deep Blue liked team members to pull double duty, which was why Pierce was expanding his expertise into general history and even paleontology, should dinosaurs ever emerge from Antarctica. Sounded ridiculous, but the ridiculous was kind of their thing.

Black Five stood against the wall, speaking softly to a man Pierce had never met. But Pierce knew this wiry, muscular man in the charcoal suit could only be one person. Black Six was the team's only former Central Intelligence Agency member. He was a field operative.

The team's very own spy, like James Bond. But due to the nature of his work, he was usually in the field. Pierce had, until this moment, only heard of the man, and never actually laid eyes on him. Black Six was younger than Pierce might have thought—perhaps in his mid twenties. He had a strong jaw and blue eyes, but the cut of his hair was a bit long, and Pierce could easily picture the man sliding undercover as an executive one week and as a surfer the next.

Lewis Aleman cleared his throat.

"We've got General Keasling, Deep Blue and King on the line in New York. Bishop, Knight and Black One and Two are also online as they transit to Europe. Mr. Boucher, is on the call from DC. I have the rest of Endgame here with me. Here's the situation as we have it so far.

"We're dealing with a threat unlike anything we've seen before. I'm afraid most of the news I have is pretty grim..."

"Lewis," Deep Blue interrupted. "Let's start with the bad news."

"Okay," Lewis said, looking down at the floor. When he looked up again, sorrow hid behind his eyes. "The world is going to end in four days."

TWENTY-SEVEN

Endgame Headquarters, White Mountains, NH
3 November, 0715 Hrs

COMPLETE SILENCE FOLLOWED. Pierce watched as jaws dropped around the room.

"Come again, Aleman. Did you say the world was going to end in four days?" Deep Blue's voice sounded rattled.

"That's what I said. The portals are stabilizing and appearing with more regularity around the world." Aleman sounded tired, but certain.

"Portals?" Pierce recognized the gruff voice of General Keasling.

"Yes, General. King accidentally entered one in Chicago and came out again."

"I was only in contact with the portal for a few seconds," King's voice came through the speaker as clearly as if he were in the room, and Pierce found himself suddenly missing his friend. "But all I saw was darkness and multiple tangos coming at me before I was swept out by the parachute."

"Yeah, King," Aleman continued his briefing, "I've been giving that a lot of thought and cross-referencing it against all our other data on these things. Everything fired inside the portals hasn't come back out. Your F-16 crashed into one and we didn't see a sign of it after that. You came back out of one alive though. We're definitely looking at a portal."

"To, uh, to what Aleman?" Pierce recognized the always-cautious voice of Domenick Boucher, the director of the Central Intelligence Agency, and one of only a few people left in the current administration that knew of the existence of Chess Team and the entire Endgame organization. "If these energy balls are portals, then portals to what? To where?"

"That is the question, Mr. Boucher. My best guess, based on the information available, is...to another dimension."

Boucher scoffed on the other end of the call. "Another *dimension*? Like in *Star Trek* or something? You can't be serious."

"Dom..." Deep Blue's voice was stern, and the message was clear: *Give the man a chance to explain and the benefit of the doubt.* Besides being the leader of Endgame, no one on the call would ever forget that this man was also formerly the leader of the free world.

"Sorry, Lewis. Please explain." Boucher sounded as tired as Pierce felt, and he imagined the Director was up to his neck in briefings of his own, trying to explain to the new President what the hell was going on around the world.

Bishop's meaty voice came through the speaker next. "They *can* be killed. They're just fast. Enclosed spaces or battlefields with obstacles are our best bet. If they get up to speed, they're hard to hit."

Aleman spoke up again. "And their roar is devastating."

"Any theories on that?" Deep Blue asked.

"Just one," Aleman said. "Infrasound."

"Which is?" King asked.

"Any sound lower than twenty hertz, which is right at the fringe of what human ears can hear. For us to hear it, the sound pressure would have to be significant."

"It's significant," Knight added.

"At the right volume, we would actually be able to feel the sound as much as hear it. Several studies I found, published and unpublished, suggest that a seventeen-hertz infrasound, with enough punch, can induce strong feelings of fear. Test subjects reported powerful anxiety, extreme sorrow, revulsion and terror. Physical symptoms ranged from goose bumps to loose bowels, which might have also been a physical effect caused by the low frequency vibrations, rather than an emotional response. As for the hallucinations, they're probably caused by the adrenaline and other chemicals dumped into the body by the fear response, but it's worth noting that the resonant frequency of the human eye, according to NASA, is eighteen hertz. Pegging someone with this frequency can cause optical illusions, visual hallucinations and are one of the leading theories for ghost sightings. If they're pegging multiple frequencies at once, the effects match."

"That sounds about right," Knight added. "Good to know I'm not a wuss."

King, who was the only field team member to be unaffected by the dire wolf roar, was unperturbed. "So if we hear it, we'll either fight harder or run away? Not that big of a problem."

"Oh, but it is, King," Sara Fogg stepped toward the center of the room to speak. Pierce noted that her eyes were still baggy, but her face had come alive at a chance to participate in the conversation on a medical topic, with which she could relate. He also noted that she remembered to use his operational callsign, instead of calling him Jack. "In a life-threatening situation, the human 'fight-or-flight' response involves an involuntary increased heart rate, increased blood flow to the muscles, pupil dilation and a whole host of other symptoms. You won't be at your fighting best, and what's worse, adrenaline dumps into your lungs, your liver, kidneys and heart. With the dire wolf roar activating such a heightened fight-or-flight, your heart could seize up with adrenaline and crash. You'd drop dead just like with the Brugada strain from a few years ago. The dire wolf roar can actually scare you to death."

Deep Blue cleared his throat. "Lewis, you said you have a plan for dealing with the dire wolves?"

Aleman replied without hesitation. "Yes sir, I think we should nuke them."

TWENTY-EIGHT
London, England
3 November, 1600 Hrs

"*THAT'S* NOT GOOD."

Bishop tilted his head to the side and looked out the open door of the *Crescent*, as it hovered on its thrumming VTOL engines. Rain lashed the late afternoon London sky, but both he and Knight had a perfect view of the River Thames and the 443-foot tall white Ferris wheel, known as the London Eye. The bizarre cantilevered support struts and several of the steel tie rods of the structure were hidden inside a large crackling dire wolf portal that covered over a fourth of the surface of the wheel. Both Bishop and Knight understood that when the portal winked out, it would take the central hub of the giant structure with it.

But that wasn't what had caused Bishop's comment.

Despite the lousy overcast weather, the ride—one of the largest tourist attractions in Europe that saw 3.5 million visitors a year—had been full when the portal appeared out of thin air. As the *Crescent* moved the men into position above the wheel, they saw hundreds of passengers from the remaining egg-shaped capsules around the edges of the wheel. A storm of brightly colored tourists attempted to climb down the superstructure after having freed themselves from their steel-and-Plexiglas prisons. Some were still trapped in their capsules. They frantically hammered on the glass as they watched the immense sphere of pulsing light engulf the wheel like Pac Man gobbling up tasty snacks. Bishop noted that some of the people were leaping to the river far below them from the upper reaches of the rim, almost 400 feet above the water.

Others leapt off the ride on the other side—to the concrete pedestrian path and the trees, which were turning dark red from the frequent human impacts.

The panicked tourists fled in terror as the portal disgorged its swarm of milky white occupants. Hundreds of dire wolves leapt out of the yellow wall of light. Many of them lunged up the London Eye's struts and scampered across its surface like manic children on a playground.

"Get me close, Black One. Now!" Bishop shouted into his helmet microphone to the pilot of the *Crescent* and readied a rappelling line at the door. Their plan had been to keep the creatures at bay as much as possible while the Ministry of Defense arranged to get a small nuclear device to them. Domenick Boucher had handled convincing the US President of the plan to drop a nuclear device inside a portal with a timer. The device would be shut off by remote control if the timer ticked down and the portal hadn't shut. If it did close, as all of the portals had done so far, then the device would detonate, hopefully stopping the dire wolf incursion. A device would be attempted both here in London and in New York. The US President convinced the Prime Minister of the United Kingdom only an hour before the *Crescent* arrived. As far as both the US and the UK were concerned, Bishop and Knight were US Delta members, acting on US orders—not independent operators.

No one liked deceiving the President, but all involved agreed that a typical Special Forces unit would be a liability. While other soldiers would still be reacting to the freakish events unfolding around them and the dire wolves trying to tear them apart, Chess Team would be *acting*. They had grown accustomed to the strange and horrible, and weren't distracted by it. Deep Blue and General Keasling had agreed that they would deal with the political ramifications after this event, if they lived through it. Boucher had concurred and the plan was set in motion. If Bishop and Knight failed, King and Deep Blue would attempt the same strategy in New York or in the next event location.

But after seeing the chaos up close, Bishop was not content to sit and wait for the device to arrive with its British couriers.

Knight squatted in the open doorway, one arm looped through a nylon safety strap on the door's edge. He knelt to the floor of the doorway and began picking off targets. He was using a new rifle—a Barrett M82 he had snagged from an armaments closet on the *Crescent* after they had boarded in Shanghai. He knew he wouldn't find a better vantage point for sniping the dire wolves than right where he was—above them on the gently hovering troop transport plane.

Even with the new helmet he wore, equipped with sound dampener technology to protect him from hearing the roar of the dire wolves, Bishop could still feel a vibration every time Knight took a shot with the .50 caliber rifle. The climbing creatures moved slower than they did on the ground; Knight had no problem executing them one by one. Still, no matter how quickly Knight fired, more of the dire wolves darted from the portal. Bishop was tempted to open fire with his newly replaced XM312-B as well, but he couldn't risk hitting tourists. He needed to get down onto the Eye.

Bishop looked down at Knight, who wore one of the impact-absorbent suits. It seemed to double his size. *If Knight looks big, I must look like the Goodyear Blimp.*

Bishop hated the helmet. The sound dampener allowed him to hear nothing but his own breathing and he found the faceplate's view limiting. With more time, they could have had helmets that only blocked certain frequencies, but time was short, so they blocked everything, and it just about drove him nuts. Still, he wore it for protection against the fear-inducing roar. Better to have limited eyesight than to bolt in fear from a dire wolf only to realize, like Wile E. Coyote, that he had run off a cliff—or in this case, off the top of the London Eye.

He leaned down and placed his hand on Knight's shoulder, then rocked the man slightly—a tap to the shoulder would do no good with the armor. Knight quickly retracted from the doorway, allowing Bishop to exit the craft.

With two MP5 submachine guns stretched across his chest and the XM312-B across his broad, armored back, Bishop leapt out the door, splaying the 11 mm black rappelling rope out his titanium belay device at his waist. The rope ran through his gloved fingers. He cleared the *Crescent* and began his drop toward the Eye.

Black One piloted the transport ship just above the wheel's curvature. As Bishop descended, controlling the rappel with one hand, he swept an MP5 up and began pummeling dire wolves with bullets.

In thirty seconds, he was down on the top of one of the abandoned capsules that sat parked hundreds of feet above the river. Most of the passengers were below him now, so Bishop took the opportunity to fire wildly, taking out dire wolf after dire wolf, sometimes with only a grazing shot, but enough of an impact to send the target tumbling.

The rain wasn't helping either. Bishop lay down on his stomach on top of an abandoned capsule to cut the wind and rain against his body. He hadn't detached from the rope yet, and decided not to. Instead, he crawled forward to the end of the egg-shaped passenger compartment's roof and began to slide over its end toward a precipitous fall. With one hand on the rope, he allowed some slack to spool out. He grabbed the lip with his other hand and swung down and into the empty carriage, dropping to the floor. The rain spatting on the faceplate of his helmet and the wind pushing his armored body let up immediately. The view was fantastic, and Bishop knew that on a clear day you could see almost 25 miles. Today the visibility was not that good, but he could still see several more of the glowing portals that had opened in various parts of the city.

The center of the capsule had a white roof, but the ends of the egg shape were all windows. The end he'd come through had a set of double doors that retracted to the sides like in an elevator. A designer wooden bench filled the center of the space. Bishop knew from a previous visit in calmer times that the egg-shaped air-conditioned capsule rotated as the wheel moved, but at such a minimal speed that passengers barely felt the rotation. In fact, it moved so slowly that the huge Ferris wheel never stopped turning—tourists simply stepped into and out of the slow moving capsules at ground level. One complete revolution of the wheel took about a half an hour. But now the wheel wasn't turning at all. Bishop guessed the operators must have hit an emergency stop before fleeing from the spectacle of the besieged Ferris wheel.

He was glad the wheel wasn't moving, because it made aiming at the dire wolves easier. He lay down on the floor of the capsule, sliding his body next to the bench, with the barrel of his XM312-B pointing at one of the lower side windows under a pane with a huge British Airways logo in red and blue. His view was down the arc of the wheel to the next two lower capsules. He fired once, blasting the window out. Then he started obliterating any dire wolf in his field of fire. It was so easy that he started to wonder why the dire wolves kept pouring down that direction, as if they couldn't see where he was in his capsule. As if they were afraid of the height themselves. He watched the limber creatures swing and slide their clawed grips along the white metal struts to the next lower capsule, and he realized there was something wrong with the dire wolves. These were not the same creatures he had faced in Shanghai a few hours earlier. Those beasts had moved with a surety and speed he had never seen before.

Bishop stopped firing for a moment and rolled to look up through the clear ceiling of his capsule, back toward the portal where even more dire wolves were emerging. There were far more of them in this attack than in Shanghai, but they were moving much slower. Pausing to tilt their heads, as if looking for something or smelling the air. Sometimes darting their heads from side to side, like a startled dog, when it hears a far off noise. His observations were interrupted when one of the creature's heads exploded into white mist as Knight continued his barrage from the still hovering *Crescent*.

Bishop detached his rappelling line and turned to fire on the dire wolves that made their way past his shattered window, heading toward the passengers below. He fired a few volleys and then two things happened.

The first was that the rain intensified to a full-on deluge. His visibility reduced significantly.

The second thing was completely bizarre. The dire wolves—all of them, as if receiving a cue telepathically—simply stopped moving. Wherever they were on the Eye, on top of one of the capsules below Bishop's vantage point, on the white metal frame or just emerging from the portal, they just...stopped. Frozen where they stood.

"What the hell?" Knight's voice sounded in Bishop's headset inside the helmet and it startled him. He had become so used to hearing only his own breathing inside the helmet, that any external sound was freakishly loud by comparison.

"No idea, man. It's like they're afraid of something." Bishop replied, and then he began mowing down any stationary targets he could sight through the curtain of rain. Knight's fire from above resumed and soon they drastically reduced the number of dire wolves on top of the wheel.

Bishop stopped firing when he ran out of targets lower than his side of the capsule. He stood and clambered over the bench to the other side of the capsule. He knew there were thirty-two capsules—one for each borough of London—from his previous visit as a tourist. He glanced out past the twin BA logo on this side, and he could see only two capsules above him, before the wall of the portal engulfed the frame of the wheel. Those two capsules were completely empty. The doors to one were open. The capsule furthest from him still had its doors shut, but the dire wolves had smashed in windows on top and the inside of the capsule was painted in a dark red hue.

Bishop shuddered.

Those people had been first. That explained why the others had panicked and jumped to their deaths. More dire wolves squatted on the frame above Bishop's capsule, unmoving. He counted thirty of them.

Make that twenty-nine. Bishop smiled as Knight continued to obliterate the stationary targets.

The rain let up as he watched for a few seconds. Something nagged at the back of Bishop's mind as he watched the frozen beasts succumb one by one to the devastating fire from Knight's Barrett. Then, again as if controlled by one mind, they all twitched and moved their heads. Several of them stood from their crouches, and the rest swiveled and tilted their heads, their strange tennis-ball-sized eyes roaming.

Oh shit. Bishop shattered the glass on this side of the capsule and began firing the big .50 caliber rounds at the dire wolves again, still laying down a line of slaughter, but he wounded more than he killed.

The remaining creatures rushed his capsule as another wave of forty or so muscular, gleaming white beasts lunged out of the portal and onto the white steel trusses. Many of them climbed onto the roof above Bishop.

This was a fight he could not win.

Bishop heard a noise at the end of his capsule and turned to see two huge, eight-foot tall dire wolves. The first had dropped into the open doors, just as Bishop had done. The second had climbed into the compartment on the upright metal hinges of the open door on the right and grabbed the safety rail, squatting laterally on the wall of the capsule's glass as if gravity didn't affect it.

There was no time to pull the barrel of the XM312-B out of the shattered window on the side of the capsule to aim at these two, ten feet away from him on the capsule's end. Then the thought that had been tickling his subconscious came through to the front of his mind like a Japanese bullet train.

"Knight! It's the rain! They can't see in the rain!"

The dire wolves, each outweighing Bishop by a few hundred pounds of muscle and menace, charged.

TWENTY-NINE
Midtown, New York
3 November, 0830 Hrs

KING WAS SWEATING profusely inside the body armor and helmet. Although the suit contained a state-of-the-art liquid cooling system, it wasn't as comfortable as it could have been. Each time he took a step and the armor between his legs rubbed, he was reminded of the corduroy trousers his mother had gotten him at

Goodwill when he was ten. He hated those things. With the sound dampener technology in the helmet activated, he couldn't hear the noise of the armor rubbing, but he could feel the vibrations on his skin.

He knew he wasn't sweating because he was hot, though. No, he was certain the cause of his dampened skin was the small suitcase nuclear device he wore on his back.

"How you doing, King? I'm sweating like a pig in this thing," Deep Blue's robust voice came through King's helmet microphone as they rode the elevator to the 40th floor of the Exxon Building.

"Thank God, I thought it was just me." King looked at their reflections in the shiny brass elevator doors.

Deep Blue grunted a laugh. Still, King could tell the humor was forced. Neither one of them liked the current plan, but it was all they had.

"These things don't smell too good either."

Deep Blue ignored this latest quip, but King felt certain the man was cocooned in his own foam stench. The putrid smell wafted over King, threatening to ruin his focus.

"Remember you are not to engage any dire wolves if you can avoid it. I'll cover you as best I can." Deep Blue was back to business.

"I'm sure you'll be better at it than I would be. That targeting software in your helmet is kind of like cheating," King said, as the elevator reached the 40th floor and both men felt their stomachs lurch at the abrupt stop.

"Wasn't time to get you one," Deep Blue said.

"Yeah, but Christmas isn't far off," King quipped, and then as if throwing a switch, he shut off his sense of humor and readied himself to kill anything that wasn't human. If someone's pet chihuahua jumped out, it was toast.

Both men raised their MP5 submachine guns and stepped to either side of the doors as they slowly opened. King smiled briefly inside his suit. Deep Blue might have been out of action in the field for years—since he had been a Ranger and subsequently served in politics—but the man was still sharp, and he and King had very quickly learned each other's moves. They had gained an almost precognitive awareness of each other in battle—something that often took many battles for other soldiers to gain.

King moved into the lushly carpeted hallway and crouched. Water rose from the rug, surrounding his foot. Everything was saturated. "Looks like the sprinkler system went off." He eyed the sprinkler head poking out of the ceiling above him. A single drip of water maintained a tenuous grasp. It fell and smacked against his facemask. "Let's hope there isn't a fire. I don't think there's any water left in the system."

Deep Blue took up a position right behind King. About forty feet down the wood paneled hallway, the glowing yellow curve of the portal's wall emerged from the wood and seared into walls, floor and ceiling, completely blocking the corridor.

The total lack of sound was eerie. King had gotten up close to one of the portals before—*hell, I've even been though one*—but the last time, according to Aleman's theory, the portal was still 'flickering' into our world. This one was stable.

No fluctuations.

No lightning.

No sound. Though King couldn't be sure if that was just because his helmet made him deaf to the outside world. It was a tactical disadvantage, but in this case, with dire wolf roars that could incapacitate a Chess Team member with crippling fear, Deep Blue had insisted. King had pointed out his previous immunity to the roar in Chicago, but Deep Blue wouldn't be moved. Their communications between each other were voice activated as well, so unless Deep Blue or Lewis Aleman spoke in his ear, all King could hear was his own breathing. It reminded him of HALO jumping, which might have been somewhat calming if not for the nuke in his backpack.

King advanced down the hall, staying to the left, Deep Blue covered the right. The plan was simple: a few feet away from the portal wall, he would unsling the backpack, arm the heavy device it held, remove the safety remote control and pocket it, then hurl the thing through the glowing yellow wall. Keasling had a second failsafe that could shut off the device if the backpack passed harmlessly in and out of the portal and plummeted to the ground forty stories below them. The General and his men would be watching for anything to come out of the bottom of the orb. The team wouldn't take any chances with destroying New York. The city had seen enough hell already.

King squatted a few feet from the portal and pulled the strap of his MP5 over his helmet, freeing his hands. He slid the backpack off his shoulders and then slowly stood, facing the wall of light. Then he dropped the pack on the carpet and froze.

DEEP BLUE WATCHED King's motions ahead of him as if in a trance. King was getting ready to deploy the bomb and then just stopped for some reason. The man hadn't moved in a minute. At first Deep Blue thought King had heard or sensed something. But their helmets had sound dampeners and King hadn't moved at all.

Something was wrong.

"King? What's going on?"

Nothing. No reply.

Deep Blue took a cautious step backward, away from where King stood facing the portal. He pulled his arm up and tapped quickly on his wrist-keypad that he'd attached to this battle suit from his last. He tested the ambient audio. Had a dire wolf roared? He thought he would have felt it vibrating in his chest, even if he couldn't hear it because of the audio dampeners. The faceplate display in his helmet told him no such sounds were present.

"King? Are you okay?"

Still no reply.

Deep Blue activated another scanner on his wrist and waited an impatient twenty seconds, until a display came up on his faceplate indicating a foreign substance in the oxygen content of the air. Not a huge amount, but whatever it was, it was an unrecognizable chemical substance. Could be something to worry about, or it could just be the electrified atmosphere from the portal and the stench of the cleaning chemicals used in the hallway. He couldn't be sure.

But one of the small features Aleman had built into Deep Blue's new tactical helmet was an air-scrubbing filter. King's armored helmet didn't have one. *Must be something in the air.* He wouldn't know more until he approached King. But the stiff way the man stood worried Deep Blue.

He stepped forward and reached his hand out to King's shoulder.

A blur erupted from the wall of light, moving around King's static form, slamming into Deep Blue's chest. Something flung him halfway back down the corridor where he hit a wall and crashed to the floor. He was surprised that the suit took the brunt of the impacts—both when he was hit and when he landed in a heap against the wall.

The optic displays in his helmet's faceplate were going nuts.

Dire wolves.

He lifted his MP5 and prepared to stand, but one of the fast-moving creatures swept him up and threw him over its shoulder. Its claws raked across his back, but the armor deflected the blow. With his rifle arm pinned under him, the beast streaked headlong toward the other end of the corridor with him as its captive—away from King's still-frozen form. Three more dire wolves clustered around King, but they weren't attacking his inert body for some reason. Deep Blue fumbled with his free hand, searching for the knife on his left leg. He had just wrapped his fingers around the blade's handle when he and the dire wolf hit the floor-to-ceiling window at the end of the carpeted hallway.

Deep Blue's armored back smacked the glass and he barely felt the window shatter. He couldn't hear it, either. But he could see the dire wolf's mouth opened wide in a roar, as his body separated from it and they both began to fall through the shower of glittering glass particles toward the pavement forty stories below.

THIRTY

Gleipnir Facility, Fenris Kystby, Norway
3 November, 1300 Hrs

ROOK CLUNG TO the thick black rubber insulation around one of the heavy cables that ran up the curved I-beam of the metal monstrosity. He managed to snag the cable with the fingers of one hand, and now swung precariously above the concrete floor over a hundred feet below him. He reached up with his other hand and grabbed a purchase on the side of the arcing metal upright, then swung his legs in and wrapped them around the beam like a man clinging to the slick trunk of a coconut palm tree.

Once firmly attached to the curved surface, and in no danger of falling, Rook looked back up at the catwalk from which he had fallen. The metal bar was painted a deep Nordic blue. Balancing on the railing like Batman crouched on a Gotham gargoyle, was a creature, partially silhouetted by a huge Klieg light on the ceiling behind it.

Great. At least I know who to blame for knocking me over the railing.

Although vaguely humanoid, its limbs were longer than a human's and had muscles that dwarfed Bishop's. Rook could see the individual bundles of its musculature just below the soft white, slightly see-through skin of the thing. Its hands and feet were larger than a human's were, and each digit had a clear two-inch claw on it, like a shard of glass. The head was domed with large orb eyes on either side of its brain, which he could see through its transparent skin and skull. Its mouth was wide, like some kind of psychotic Cheshire Cat, and when it opened its mouth, Rook saw plenty of see-through sharp incisor teeth for tearing and ripping prey. He couldn't decide if the thing was snarling or smiling at him.

"Slap my ass and call me Susan! Finally, something I can kill. Just you wait, Milkshake. When I get down from here I'm going to introduce your ugly head to your rectum." Rook began to scramble down the curved metal, using the twining black electrical cables as handholds. He was nearly to the first panel-like metal plate below him when a distant roar sounded from far off in the bowels of the facility.

Terror seized Rook.

His eyes grew large and his body broke out in a sweat. His heart was thumping in his chest. He started hyperventilating, pulling in huge gulps of the dry air. Instead of climbing further down the metal leg of the cage toward the floor far below him, Rook gripped the cables tighter. His hands clutched the cables so tightly that blood ceased to flow through them. His knuckles turned a pasty white color. He was afraid to stay in place and he was afraid to move.

Suddenly, as quickly as the fear had beset him, Rook felt it begin to fade. His heart rate began to slow and he looked around the cavernous space in shock and wonder. He blinked a few times. Besides the creature on the railing, no one (and nothing) was in sight. He had no idea why he had temporarily been so scared of the distant howling sound. It was almost like a wolf's howl at the moonlight, but stronger.

Not a wolf.

He felt less and less afraid with each passing moment. The creature remained on the railing above him, unmoving. His breathing under control again, Rook resumed his descent down the curved metal beam. The number of metal plates, protuberances and twisting cables made climbing easy. When he reached the half-way point, he glanced back up at the white creature on the catwalk.

It hadn't moved.

He continued to climb toward the safety of the floor, seventy feet down. When he was no more than fifty feet off the ground, he glanced up again. What he saw almost made him fall.

"Sweet fuck-a-doodle-doo!" The creature's face was inches from his own. Somehow the creature had leapt to the strut and descended over a hundred feet in the few seconds since Rook had last looked up at it. And it had come down the strut headfirst and in complete silence!

Rook's heart jackhammered. He gripped his handhold tighter with his left hand, preparing to release his right. He wasn't sure how much damage he could do with one bare hand, while hanging fifty feet off the ground, but he was ready to give it a go. He pulled his arm back to fire a punch at the beast's snout, but a voice held his shoulder in check.

"I wouldn't do that, Stanislav. The dire wolf will not hurt you unless I tell it to. Or unless you attack it."

Rook kept his fist cocked back, but craned his neck around to the floor, where Eirek Fossen stood wearing a white lab coat. He was over six feet tall with short dark hair and brown eyes and a wide face. Broad and imposing, the man also held a small black pistol. Rook couldn't be sure from his height above Fossen, but it might have been a Walther PP, the precursor to the famous pistol used by Ian Fleming's infamous spy. This was the man Rook had allied himself with to fight the monster Edmund Kiss had become. Fossen raised his arm, aiming the weapon at Rook.

The alliance was most definitely over.

"I should have let Kiss eat your face off."

"I could say the same, Stanislav. Now come down, and do so slowly."

THIRTY-ONE
Exxon Building, New York

JACK SIGLER, THE man known as *King* in the field, felt fine.

Not fine. Fantastic.

He wondered if he had ever felt better. The light from the portal glowed and beautifully. He breathed in deeply and relished the taste of the air. He knew it would be even better if he took the helmet off.

He unfastened the clasps at his neck and lifted it up off his head. He didn't carefully place the helmet on the ground—he just let it fall from his fingers. The helmet thumped with a dull sound when it hit the carpeted hallway floor, but King paid it no mind, because now he could hear the portal as well as see it.

And it sang to him.

He smiled broadly. *This must be what it's like for Fiona when she hears the mother tongue.* His foster daughter was unique in her ability to see and hear the protolanguage of the world in paintings and sculptures, in music and in nature. She had used that ability to help Chess Team and save mankind on more than one occasion. But such important thoughts couldn't find a hold on the slippery surface of King's mind, lost in ecstasy as it was. Instead, he let thoughts of the team and the world fall away, like small bits of paper caught in a breeze.

It's so beautiful.

King inhaled the air deeply, smelling lush fragrance and clean mountain air all in one breath. That he stood in a sterile air-conditioned corridor in a modern building seemed a faraway notion, and because it ran counter to how good the air smelled and tasted, he let that idea go too. It fluttered away just as his worries had. In Chicago the light had been bright, glaring and full of electric danger. Now it shimmered with a luster he felt soothing and exciting all at the same time. He felt calm and in control for the first time in his life. He felt both purpose and the complete lack for a need of purpose. He just was.

King smiled again at the strange wall of light in front of his face.

He glanced around him and saw three of the dire wolves moving slowly around his body, looking both at him and down the corridor behind him. He didn't really care what they were looking at. They didn't frighten him at all, and he felt no animosity toward the creatures. He reached out his hand to touch the skin of one and found he couldn't feel it because of his glove. He pulled his hand back and removed the glove with the other hand, then reached back out to stroke the dire wolf's chest with his naked fingers.

They are so soft! The creature had a very fine downy hair on its body, almost invisible to the human eye, like the fuzz on a ripe peach. *Like the feeling of a high-end stuffed animal.*

King ran his hand over the dire wolf's chest and the creature simply stood there allowing it. The eye facing King warbled in the orb on the side of its head, regarding him carefully. King wasn't frightened of the creature at all now. Instead, he felt affection akin to love for the beast.

But somewhere small at the back of his mind was a tiny voice screaming that this whole situation was wrong. King ignored the voice and moved forward, placing his cheek against the dire wolf's shoulder. He rubbed the soft down against his face.

"You're nice," he spoke aloud and the dreamy quality of his voice made him giggle.

The dire wolf moved away from him and another came closer, sniffing at him. He liked this new one even better. *Friendly. Fiona would like him.*

But this second thought of Fiona gave power to the insistent, niggling voice at the back of his brain.

No. She wouldn't. No! This is wrong.

"Go away," he told the voice, and it died a quiet death in his subconscious. The dire wolf didn't move away from him.

He knows I'm not talking to him. Or is it an it? I didn't see any naughty bits.

King assessed the beast again, but came away from the glance only feeling better, if that was possible. His thought of determining its gender, if any, was swept away, as if a glorious breeze had just rushed by him, carrying scents of his favorite foods, the sea after a storm and gentle winds from an almost artificially green Alpine valley he had once visited in Switzerland.

This place is so good. I should bring Sara here. He grinned a huge grin.

No. The quiet voice returned. *You have to keep them safe.*

His grin faltered as images of cities being devoured by globes of devastating lightning-hurling energy filled his mind. *But the pretty—*

King tightly squeezed his eyes shut, blocking out the glistening wall of the portal in front of him. No longer looking at the soft, friendly dire wolves. The images were still in his head though. The horror of people killed and cities scooped out of the ground by a cosmic event unlike anything before it.

You have to keep them safe.

Thoughts of his girlfriend, adopted daughter, team members and friends like George Pierce filled his mind. His memories of them made resisting the euphoria that much easier. There was a nuclear weapon in a satchel at his ankles, and he remembered what he was supposed to do with it. But it was hard, so very hard. Fighting against that warm happy place, where he had been for days—or had it just been moments—was the hardest fight of his life.

He sensed his resistance slipping. He wouldn't last much longer. He yearned to go back to the bright light and the wonderful smells of autumn in Vermont, skiing in Europe, the beach in Florida...*Florida*. He remembered Disney and the Russian helicopter.

In one sudden, lunging movement, he reached down and grabbed the satchel with the nuclear weapon. He spun in a fast circle and flung the backpack into the wall of bright light before him. It disappeared as it hit the edge of the portal. He could only hope that it had gone in far enough.

Then as the warm happy feelings began to engulf him again, filling up all the empty places in his soul with a pulsing joy, the likes of which he had never even imagined existed, it happened.

That tiny voice that had brought him back to sanity for one brief moment spoke again. A doubt. A whimper. Little more than a squeak.

You didn't arm the device.

King didn't care.

The warm glory of God Himself wrapped him in a loving embrace.

THIRTY-TWO
London, England

THE TWO DIRE wolves, glistening wet from the rain, slammed into Bishop's body, knocking him to the river-facing end of the capsule. His body smashed into the glass and metal of the end of the passenger car, but with the impact-absorbing armor, it felt like little more than a light shove. He lost his hold on the XM312-B and the machine gun flipped out the shattered window, toppling away. A second weapon lost in 24 hours. Bishop swore silently.

The dire wolves stopped halfway inside the capsule. One now squatted on the center of the wooden bench and the other on the floor to its left. They waited, and Bishop wondered why. He stayed on the floor of the capsule, unmoving, watching them.

Great big eyes, but you can't see too good, can you?

He realized they couldn't see in the rain and had waited for it to abate before moving again. But it wasn't raining inside the capsule. Bishop strained to hear and then realized he couldn't hear anything but his own breathing. *The armor. Maybe they detect body heat too. Maybe they only track movement.* Then inspiration struck.

Bishop couldn't hear any external sound and his body was cushioned from impact by the armor. Slowly, he moved his hand up to his chest. The MP5s were still strapped to him. Attached to the strap of one of the rifles was an M84 stun grenade, more commonly known as a flash-bang. It didn't contain shrapnel, but instead emitted a non-lethal burst of magnesium-based flaring light and an incapacitating bang of sound. But with the sound dampener in his helmet and the impact-absorbing armor, all Bishop would have to do to avoid the effects of the grenade was close his eyes tightly. He slipped his finger into the circular pull ring and then struggled a second to get another finger into the secondary, triangular pull ring. He didn't bother depressing the safety lever. His movements were minimal, but still the dire wolf on the bench moved its head slightly at the motion.

Crap. He's seen it.

Bishop lunged to his feet, dropping the grenade on the floor of the cabin. The dire wolf on the bench turned its attention fully in his direction, but it lunged laterally, grabbing the metal railings again as it had done when it entered the capsule. The other dire wolf swiveled its eyes and lowered its head to examine the grenade as it skittered to a stop in front of the creature.

Bishop crushed his eyes shut and lunged forward toward to dire wolf on the wall. The shockwave impact from the grenade hit his armored body just before he slammed into the creature on the wall. The creature bounced off his moving body like a superball bouncing off a wall. The dire wolf was moving away from Bishop as he opened his eyes, in time to see the beast sliding out the open doors of the capsule and falling away. He looked back to see the second dire wolf stirring on the floor, where the grenade had temporarily done exactly what it was designed to—it had stunned the creature. Bishop didn't wait to see how long it took the dire wolf to recover. He sprinted for the open door and leapt out into the air.

The *Crescent* hadn't moved from its position above Bishop's capsule on the top of the wheel, so the rappelling line still hung from the underside of the huge curve-winged transport plane. But it was further away than Bishop had thought. He stretched his fingers out as far as he could. His body shot out into open space. Just when he thought he would miss the rope entirely, the back of his fingers brushed the line. He scrabbled at it and snagged it. As he moved through the air and before the rope absorbed his weight, he quickly wound the rope around his left arm once. Momentum swung him out and away from the wheel. The line wasn't long enough for him to slide to the ground, so his only option was to swing back to the frame of the Eye.

He twisted on the rope as he began to swing back. Keeping the rope wrapped around his left arm, he reached out at the apex of his swing and caught hold of the nearest tie rod. Hooking his knee around the rod, he moved his hand back to the rope and began to climb. Knight must have noticed what was going on, because Bishop looked up to the capsule he had just escaped in time to see the second dire wolf's head explode, coating the doors on the end of the capsule with a milky fluid.

He climbed hand over hand, rewrapping the rope around his left arm each time for an added measure of security. He slid his leg up the tie rod until he got to a crawlspace formed by a triangular tunnel of bars and struts that ran under the capsules—or above them at the bottom of the wheel. Knight picked off a few more dire wolves from around Bishop while the big man focused on his climbing. He could see the creatures pitching off the rails to either side of him, falling to the ground and river below. As Bishop worked his way down the tunnel of bars, heading for a capsule two away from the first one he'd entered, he could see three people still trapped inside. He also noticed that Knight's firing had stopped.

"Bishop, you read?" Knight calm voice spoke softly in his earpiece.

"What's going on?" He asked.

"They're bugging out. But there are a lot more over on the bridge by Big Ben. You okay on your own for a minute?"

Bishop glanced back the way he had come through the jungle gym of connected white bars. Upriver, he could see Westminster bridge was overrun by dire wolves and a portal had formed on the Victoria Embankment, close to, but not yet touching Big Ben, the famed British landmark clock tower at the end of the Palace of Westminster—one of the city's major seats of governing.

"Go. I'm going to help the people still trapped in the other capsules." Bishop resumed his scramble through the bars.

"We'll be right back. Try to hurry. If the portal goes, the center of that wheel goes too. You'll look pretty silly rolling to Southend." The *Crescent* suddenly peeled away from the top of the London Eye, heading for the middle of the green-painted Westminster Bridge.

Bishop continued down past the remains of his original capsule and the next, on to the one after that. Inside were three young girls that looked to be no more than sixteen or seventeen, each dressed in fashionable pink and white fleece jackets. *They probably dressed like each other intentionally*, Bishop thought. He remembered when he was younger, the girls would have been mocked mercilessly by their peers for showing up at high school or elsewhere looking like 'Twinkies'—identical and two to a package. What was considered cool had apparently changed.

When Bishop looked up from under the capsule, he saw that each of the girls had smeared eye make-up. They had been crying. Also, it was a long way up to the capsule from the bottom of the triangular passage. He would have to shimmy nearly twenty feet up one of the diagonal uprights to get to the girls.

He looked down briefly to the hundreds of feet of air and steel below him before the river, then looked back at the portal. The last of the remaining dire wolves were high-tailing it back inside.

Running out of time.

He took one more glance, this time further afield toward the bridge, where the *Crescent* lowered and Knight delivered pain from above. Bishop began to slide, climb, shimmy and shrug his way up the slick metal pole. The angle helped the climb considerably, and before he realized it, he reached his hand up for more pole only to find the upper rim of the wheel. The girls had watched his ascent awestruck, and now that he was close enough to almost reach out and touch, they started screaming for his help.

"Relax. I'm going to get you out!"

Then the unthinkable happened.

The portal disappeared. He could see its absence from his limited peripheral vision in the helmet. He turned his head to look and just as his side vision had suggested, there was a massive gaping space where the hundred-foot diameter globe of energy had been. In the distance across the city, other globes were still present, but his had gone, taking everything it had touched. A quarter of the outer rim of the wheel was now missing, along with the capsules that would have been there. The tie rods that reached from that portion of the wheel down to the hub were gone too. The hub itself and the two gigantic white cantilevered supports that held the entire wheel aloft were also gone. Bishop was holding onto a crescent-shaped incomplete wheel of steel and now-dangling tie rods and cables that were held in the air by...nothing.

With several people still trapped in capsules below him on the unaffected side of the wheel, the girls still trapped in the one above him and Bishop still holding on to the structure near the top, the London Eye began to fall over into the river.

THIRTY-THREE

Gleipnir Facility, Fenris Kystby, Norway

THE WOMAN WITH the callsign Queen disappeared. In her place was a fourteen-year-old girl with the unlikely name of Zelda. Her mother was dead. Her father was a drunk and beat her nightly. Sometimes with a leather belt. She was terrified of spiders and mice. She couldn't stand heights. Enclosed spaces would make her break down into a puddle of tremors. Lightning terrified her and made her scream. She dreamed every night that she was being devoured by wild animals. She was still alive and breathing as lions and cougars pulled her intestines from her abdomen. When she woke from her sleep, the nightmares just got worse in the light of day.

Her world was a living state of terror. If only she could find a way out of it. But she knew drugs were not the way. She had been on drugs when her son died and they hadn't helped.

Wait, that's not right. I didn't have a child at fourteen.

She struggled to make sense of the fear and the logical incongruity that crept into her mind. *I crushed the spider. I'm not afraid of spiders any more.* She knew she shouldn't think that way. He would be back and he would be angry. He would beat her again and again, and maybe this time he would go too far. *I don't fear anything. Major-General Trung tried to break me in Vietnam, but I beat him too. I am the hunter now.*

"Quiet," she whispered. "He'll hear!"

I base jump.

"He's in the hallway, right now."

I free solo rock climb!

"He has the one with the large buckle." The whispers were frantic.

I am fearless!

She moved her hand up in the darkness to touch the scar on her forehead. The brand—it was a skull encased in a star, the symbol of the VPLA Death Volunteers, Vietnam's Special Forces Unit. Trung had branded her like cattle, but she had escaped and exacted her vengeance on the bastard. Then she made the symbol her own, drawing strength from the wound. She felt the rough lumpy surface of her scarred skin beneath her fingertips and the sensation brought her fully back to the here and now.

Queen opened her eyes and looked at the small room in which she lay. There were a few wooden crates with swastikas on them and the legend *Ahnenerbe*. Queen recalled Rook mentioning the word—the name for a WWII German unit that focused on historical research and German superiority. The room had a door with no handle on it. Beyond that, she was alone in a storeroom of sorts, turned into the perfect jail cell. No window, but a lone 40-watt bare lightbulb hung from the ceiling.

She sat up from the floor where she had been lying and rubbed the brand on her forehead again, reassuring herself that she was in the present and not lost in the quagmire of her childhood. It was there under her fingers. Her old anger about the mark resurfaced, and with it bloomed a new anger at the people who ran this place and the creatures they employed. Her face felt red and hot. She could feel her heart beating faster as rage coursed through her strong body, cleaning out the last vestiges of the fear that had filled it moments before.

And then her anger turned toward Rook.

"I am *so* going to kick your ass again, Rook."

Had he called this in sooner, the team could have come together and moved through this place like the coordinated tornado of destruction they trained to be. Sure, they could solve a puzzle or two, unlock the secrets of history, science and the unknown, but they really excelled at blowing shit up. It was an art form they perfected as a team. Solo, they were dangerous. In two-man teams, they were deadly. United, they could fight the unkillable and win.

By her logic, the blame for the trouble they found themselves in lay squarely on Rook's broad shoulders.

But she couldn't stay angry at him. He'd suffered a loss in Siberia, and right or wrong, it had affected him deeply. Loss was part of the game, but Rook had never really experienced it before. Not like that. Now he was damaged goods, just like her.

She smiled at the idea. A match made in Heaven.

Or hell.

She couldn't deny her growing feelings for the man. She'd nearly come out with it back at that store, but he'd gone and used that nickname.

Zel.

It was the name her mother used for her, before she succumbed to cancer and left her alone with her abusive alcoholic father. She didn't remember a lot about her mother. Didn't think about her much, either. But that single word, Zel, was like a key to her soul. It unlocked the past and she wasn't ready to share that yet, with anyone.

She stood and examined every inch of the room until she had assured herself that there were no other ways in or out and that nothing in the room would help her pry the door open. The crates held oddly shaped scientific equipment. She didn't recognize most of it. One of the things she *did* recognize was a dirty, broken microscope that looked older than the one she had used in high school biology class, but it didn't hold her interest.

Across the room, there was a small air vent near the ceiling, on the wall adjacent to the door. It was far too small for her to fit even her head into it. She considered removing the grill over the vent and using it to pry open the handle-less gray door, but then she had a better idea. She managed to get her fingers behind the edge of the flimsy vent grill by standing on the *Ahnenerbe* crates. She pulled hard and the pliable metal popped free into her hands. No way it would be strong enough to go to work on the door. She didn't even think she could use the weak metal as a stabbing implement. Next she slid two stacked crates to the center of the room and reached up to the lightbulb.

Hello darkness, she thought and unscrewed the bulb. She climbed down and set the bulb down into one of the other crates she had opened. It might come in handy later—she didn't want to break it. Then she carefully felt her way through the dark, back onto the stacked crates where the dangling lightbulb hung. She grabbed it and tugged hard. The wire, insulation and all, came free in her hand. She pulled a long length of it out of the ceiling and wrapped it around her hand.

Now she would just wait for someone to come open the door and meet doom.

THIRTY-FOUR
Outside the Exxon Building, New York

DEEP BLUE MARVELED at how in moments of extreme action, the human mind could sometimes slow things down to a crawl and your perceptions heightened to the point where you could pick out a speck of dust floating in the air, as if it were suspended in time.

That was happening now for him. He and the dire wolf that had propelled him through the window on the 40th floor of the Exxon Building fell in spectacular slow motion. Tiny fragments and slivers of glittering glass rained down around them. Deep Blue was further from the wall of the skyscraper than the dire wolf that was already reaching out toward the wall of glass. Deep Blue drew his knife. The EOD variant of the Army M9 bayonet came up and Deep Blue thrust the wicked blade down toward the exposed rear flank of the falling dire wolf.

The upside down monster scrabbled at the slick glass and concrete surface of the building with its clear claws. At the same moment that Deep Blue plunged the sharp point of the blade into the creature's rump, its claws found purchase on the concrete space between the windows. The blade sank into the creature at an angle and a thick white fluid spurted out of the wound in a slow-motion arc, sweeping over Deep Blue's knife hand. The creature stopped falling. Deep Blue nearly lost his grip on the knife as his fall suddenly jerked to a stop, but he held on with a determined shout that filled his helmet.

Then he slipped lower.

The dire wolf's claws had found a tight grip on the concrete upright of the building. It wasn't falling anymore. But the knife, sunken deep into the beast's flesh, was too sharp. The weight of Deep Blue's body pulled the blade down, along the creature's ass and into its lower back.

Finally, the blade chewed into spinal bone—Deep Blue could see the pronounced spinal column pushing against the skin, like the bones of a hideously skinny man. The blade lodged fast into the spine and Deep Blue's descent stuttered to a halt, just as time resumed its natural pace.

Deep Blue looked back up the building and saw that the spectacular fall had only taken two stories from the shattered window up on 40. The dire wolf clung to the wall upside down outside the 38th floor. Deep Blue hung from one arm, his hand clutching the knife tightly. He looked down to the street far below him.

A mistake.

It was a long way down and the street was totally empty. There was no sign of Keasling or the Army. Then he remembered where he was. He was dangling from the creature's back over West 50th Street. Keasling and his men were on 49th, under the portal.

He turned his attention back to the dire wolf. It wasn't moving, but he suspected the beast was in pain. The muscles in its back were twitching out a samba, but it refused to move. The extra weight of Deep Blue, plus the twenty pounds of armor and weaponry he wore, were clearly taking a toll on the thing. Deep Blue wasn't sure what his next move would be.

Then the dire wolf made the choice for him.

It slid one of its rear legs backward and up the concrete pillar. The helmet's heads-up display and the camera built into the face-plate registered the motion and reported it to Deep Blue. The creature stretched the leg as far up as it could and then sank its translucent claws on that foot deep into the concrete. Then it slid one of its clawed hands higher.

Son of a bitch. He's going to try to climb backward up to the window, with me still hanging from him.

That was not going to work out well for Deep Blue. If the creature made it to the shattered window above, it would be free to attack him while he was still hanging out over the drop.

He tried King one more time through the communications link. "King! Wake up soldier! I need you!"

No response. Whatever was holding the man under its thrall was powerful.

Deep Blue reached his free hand up and grabbed the beast between its legs. The area was smooth, lacking any reproductive organs that he could feel.

Thank God for small favors.

He climbed up the creature's back as it pulled itself up the wall backward. Once his grip was secure in the beast's crotch, Deep Blue released the knife and quickly pulled an M67 fragmentation grenade—the only one he had—from a pouch on the front of his armor.

He popped the safety clip, thumbed out the pin and let the spoon flip outward into a graceful arc across the Midtown sky. He then rammed the grenade into the oozing wound left behind by the knife in the creature's ass. He let go of the device and pulled his fist back. Then for good measure, he rammed his fist back into the wound, punching the grenade deeper.

Then he pulled his feet up and thrust them against the dire wolf's back. He sprang and flew backward into the chasm of air between the Exxon Building and the Time-Life Building.

Deep Blue was still in his lateral swan dive out into space when the fragmentation grenade detonated, ripping the dire wolf in half and grotesquely sending its severed legs flying first up and then down, while its torso remained clinging to the wall for a horrible second longer, before it, too, began to fall.

With only 450 feet to fall, Deep Blue's body was moving rapidly, so he just barely had time to twist in the air and pull the ripcord on the small parachute he wore. They had only had one nuclear device, and King carried that. With battle in a vertical space, Deep Blue had thought to carry a parachute—just in case.

As his parachute popped open, Deep Blue enjoyed the relatively calm nine-second ride to the street below him. He reflected that this was now the second time in a period of 24 hours that he had needed a parachute. *I might start wearing one of these all the time.*

The ground rushed up to meet him as Deep Blue pulled and released the toggles. As he came to a landing, Lewis Aleman contacted him on the headset in his helmet.

"That was interesting, Boss. Twice in one day?"

"Shut it, Ale." His feet touched the ground and he quickly detached from the parachute and began to sprint back to the building's doors. He needed to get back inside to help King.

"Got something that might help a lot. The dire wolves don't see well with interference in the air surrounding them. Bishop reported they can't deal with rain. Anywhere you can pick up some chaff?" Aleman's voice sounded excited. They finally had a way to combat the creatures.

The collapse of the Eye had distracted him, when a wave of dire wolves had been headed his way. *Stupid!* The creature carrying him ran fast. Knight tried to grab at the creature's face with a hand, but it batted his arm away with a swipe of claws. Knight could see the tears in the armor from the beast's claws and knew if he wasn't wearing it, he'd likely be dead already. Up close and over the monster's shoulder like a burlap sack, all Knight could easily see was the creature's broad back. The muscles rippled and tensed under the see-through skin. Knight tried to push back away from the dire wolf, but it suddenly turned at the end of the bridge and began sprinting back the way it had come. The force of the high-speed turn threw its balance off and allowed Knight a look around. The other dire wolves were already heading back toward the portal from which they had come. Knight reached for the low-slung holster on his left leg, pulling out his Glock, but again, the creature swept claws at him and the gun was knocked from his hand. He watched helplessly as the gun sailed over the edge of the bridge and into the river.

Next, Knight twisted his torso, lunging his head and knocking the dire wolf in the back of its head with his armored helmet. The creature loosened its grip for just a second. Enough for Knight to slide his right hand up to his sheathed knife on his chest. The dire wolf tightened its crushing grip again and Knight's hand was trapped against his chest on the handle of the knife.

Bastard.

He struggled and peered around again to see that they were nearly at the portal, and many of the other dire wolves had retreated into it. He began frantically kicking his knee toward the dire wolf's chest and once again, the creature loosened its grasp for just a second. But this time Knight was ready for the short respite. He ripped his arm outward, pulling the knife and driving it deeply into the back of the creature's neck. He was surprised that the beast didn't drop from the blow, so he tore the blade out and began stabbing at the creature's back repeatedly, aiming for the heart—if it was where a human heart would be—and the back of the head and neck as much as he could.

The creature faltered and slowed. He could feel the descent in velocity as the dire wolf staggered. Then it began to fall forward, pulling Knight's body with it. Knight pulled his legs up hoping to spring off the creature before the weight of it pinned him to the ground, but he was too late.

The dire wolf collapsed right through the wall of the glowing energy portal, and just as it hit the ground, the energy portal closed with a sucking sound and a strong gust of wind. The portal left a crater in its wake.

And a pair of feet.

The dire wolf's.

There was no sign of Knight.

THIRTY-SIX

Gleipnir Facility, Fenris Kystby, Norway

ASYA SCREAMED AS she fell.

She had made her way to the lower level of the lab and stared up at the giant cage of metal that dominated the space before exploring the doors and tunnels that led off from the cavernous room. Many of the doors were locked, but she found old crumbling tunnels that burrowed into the earth, leading off each wall of the giant room. She had ventured into one just a few feet past the point where the lights from the main room offered any illumination.

She was about to turn back when she heard a tiny sound from deeper in the tunnel. It might have been a pebble scraping along the stone floor. Or maybe a small animal. It was impossible to tell.

The tunnel, which was wide but low, was pitch dark. Asya felt along the brick walls with her hands and moved deeper into the space. She smelled dust and something wet, which surprised her, because thus far everything in the lab had been very dry.

It was when, for the second time, she was about to give up exploring and go back to look for a flashlight that she stepped forward into nothing and toppled over in the gloom. She screamed as she fell, the sounds of her voice echoing through the tunnel. She landed on something that was soft mixed with tiny sharp pokey spines. She felt the surface under her in the dark and the sensation on her fingertips was like spongy rubber with toothpicks sticking out of it. She touched one of the sharp things and applied a gentle pressure to its side. The thing snapped, just like a toothpick would. She ran her fingers over the break and felt the tiny barbs, but they were more jagged than the fibers from a snapped toothpick—more solid too.

"Bozhe moi. What is this?" She whispered in the dark, afraid suddenly of what else might be in this pit with her. She struggled to find footing on the squishy surface and instead walked on her knees with one hand on the mushy uneven ground for balance and the other reaching out in the dark for a wall. She felt the barbs poking her knees as she moved forward, but her splayed out fingertips soon grazed brick. She ran her hand over the bricks and they felt similar to the ones that formed the tunnel up above—smaller than normal bricks today. She ran her hand left and right along the wall looking for anything different than a flat wall surface. A door or a ladder. *Or a light switch.*

The smell in this new space was wetter than up in the tunnel, but the squishing surface that made up the ground was dry to the touch. She tried again to stand but quickly gave up. It was like standing on top of a ball pit. What she had thought was solid—if rubbery—ground was actually a pile of something. Several small somethings.

Stupid! Asya suddenly remembered that she had a small LED light in a survival kit that she wore on her waist in a tiny fanny pack. She had picked it up at the store in Olderdalen when Stanislav—*no, Rook,* she corrected herself—was buying his new coat. The kit would have some wooden matches as well, but the LED keychain light would be easier to find in the dark.

She unzipped the pouch and carefully slipped her fingers inside the scratchy nylon, so she didn't disgorge the contents into the pile of mystery things on which she knelt. Her fingers found the plastic casing of the tiny flashlight. She pulled it out. Before lighting it, she zipped the pouch again, and slipped a finger through the ring on the end of the light. She didn't want to lose it.

Then she depressed the spring-loaded button, illuminating the small room around her with a garish blast of blue-tinged white light.

She wished she hadn't.

Against her will, a second scream rose up in her. This one far longer and far more distressed than the yelp she had let out when she fell.

She was in a graveyard. She was *on* a graveyard. A grave *mound.* And it was heaped with the tiny corpses of small white creatures unlike any she had ever seen. There were hundreds—maybe thousands—of the little things, their rib bones poking though the desiccated chests of the small white puppy-like creatures. They had miniscule clear claws on each paw but strange small pinpricks of eyes on the sides of their heads. They were not puppies, nor wolves. She could see their musculature under their whitish skin. They were not any animal she had ever seen or heard of.

They were something else.

Something unnatural.

Hideous.

Asya's breath caught in her chest. The mound of tiny bodies moved.

THIRTY-SEVEN

Endgame Headquarters, White Mountains, NH
3 November, 1000 Hrs

SARA FOGG WALKED with Anna Beck into the large aircraft hanger that housed the last airborne vehicle belonging to Endgame. The Black Hawk sat on the concrete floor of the hangar and Black Six, the suave young spy, stood next to it in a black flight suit. Beck wore a black flight suit herself.

"You get to ride with the hunk, huh?" Fogg joked. "I bet Knight won't like that."

"He'll get over it. Besides, Six can pilot a Black Hawk—I can't. He'll come with me to the Pease Air National Guard Base in Portsmouth where we'll wait around to rendezvous with a Blackbird out of Hanscom Air Force Base and haul ass to Norway. Half the pilots are in Europe with Bishop and Knight and the other two are in New York with King and Deep Blue."

"Would be nice to have Queen and Rook back. They'll help keep our guys alive." Fogg looked at Beck and patted her on the shoulder. The two women had become close over the last two weeks. "Be safe and kick ass."

Beck winked. "You know it."

Fogg watched as Beck strode across the hangar and lightly punched Black Six in the upper arm. "Let's go, Secret Agent Man."

Fogg turned as the two got into the Black Hawk and it rolled forward out of the massive hundred-foot-wide doorway. It then took to the sky and the computer controlled steel door slowly lowered into place from where it had been hidden in the ceiling of rock and concrete. Fogg had heard about a mishap with that door when the base was being set up and she always made it a point to not stand anywhere near it.

With the door completely shut, and the daylight gone from the hangar, it was a dimly lit and empty place. Fogg headed back to the corridor off the hangar that led to the offices and the main computer center, where she would no doubt find Aleman and Pierce still frantically trying to make sense of the strange creatures destroying the world.

Fogg had already made sense of it for herself. This was just how crazy the world had gotten. King and the rest of Chess Team were always in the thick of it. Genetically engineered soldiers, reanimated monsters, custom tailored bio-weapons and viruses, anthropological missing-link creatures, golems, artificially intelligent super computers, assassins, corporate megalomaniacs, modern-day pirates, terrorists and even black holes. This was King's world and she was now a part of it. The world would go apeshit nutso and Chess Team would stop it. That's what they did. And if they didn't, there wouldn't be a world to worry about. Armed with that knowledge, she was able to remain as calm and tranquil as a Buddhist monk.

Most of the time.

Seeing King ejecting from that plane and smashing into a skyscraper had been a jolt. So had the dire wolf roar that brought back her claustrophobia.

It's strange, she thought. *Being in this base under a mountain doesn't weird me out, but the thought of a tiny dirt tunnel so close to the surface that I could dig my way there with my fingers gives me the heebie-jeebies.*

She had a rock-solid inner belief in King's invincibility, and that got her through each new crazy thing that arose. But she also found herself wondering if maybe there would be a time soon when someone else could become 'King.' A time when she and Jack could take Fiona and go off to some isolated part of the world away from corporate madmen and bio-engineered super threats.

She knew enough about lab-created viruses from her work at the CDC to realize that it was only a matter of time before some super-plague wiped out a good swash of the world's population. Going off to live like a survivalist in a cabin in British Columbia was looking more attractive to her all the time. Of course, the forest would play havoc with her sensory processing disorder, but maybe she could learn to live with that.

As she stepped into the computer room, she saw Lewis Aleman and George Pierce, who had both clearly found the time to throw on new clothes—Aleman still in jeans and a t-shirt, and Pierce with a black sweatshirt with a white King chessman icon on the left breast. Both men hunkered over Pierce's computer terminal at the side of the room, Aleman having abandoned the ergonomic chair.

"What's up?" she asked.

Aleman stood straighter and stretched his back, turning to her. "We're tracking the portals and trying to find their origin."

"Can you do that?" she asked.

"No," Aleman smiled weakly. "But we can look at the surrounding environmental disturbances that the portals create and make some educated guesses."

"Environmental disturbances?"

Pierce placed his hands on his lower back and stretched as Aleman had done, then slid his glasses further up his nose with the tip of one finger.

"The weather," he said. "Each event creates local disturbances in the weather pattern because of the amount of electricity—even the ones that have appeared underwater or underground."

"Oh that's genius," she walked over to the screen to see a map of the globe and colored circles representing the placement and appearance of known energy portals based on storm patterns detected by weather satellites. She'd seen similar maps on the news.

"Thanks," Aleman said. He pointed at the screen. "So we've factored in the likely weather phenomenon when one of these things appears, and we're tracking the size of them as they keep appearing. They keep getting bigger. So George had the idea to try to find smaller ones from before yesterday..."

Pierce broke in, "Right, and Lewis realized we could use existing satellite data to find smaller occurrences of the portals before yesterday when the first really big ones appeared in Asia."

Aleman continued. "Right now the algorithm is searching out likely weather patterns and making a list of possible portals. But even if we can trace their origins, it doesn't mean we'll be able to figure out how to stop them. It's just something to do. More data to gather. Hopefully it will all lead somewhere."

As they watched the screen, Fogg noted the date in the upper-left corner of the screen going backward as fewer and fewer possible incidents appeared in different populated areas of the world. Eventually they got so small that she realized these events had gone unnoticed in large cities around the world. Only the portals of the last few days had been large enough to gain the world's attention. The number of portals on the screen got smaller and smaller until only two remained—in Kathmandu, and in northern Norway. Fogg pointed to the one in Nepal.

"How large would that one be?" she wanted to know.

"About the size of a panel truck, probably."

The next date, a week earlier, was of a portal about the same size, and it showed up in Norway again. It was now the last portal on the map. Then another on the previous day in Norway. Then another a few weeks earlier. These events were smaller than the one in Kathmandu. But she noticed they were all in the same town.

"Fenris Kystby. Hey, isn't that the—"

"—the town where Rook is." Aleman's face was shocked. "He's been at the source this whole time."

THIRTY-EIGHT

Gleipnir Facility, Fenris Kystby, Norway

ROOK SAT ZIP-TIED to the metal chair and seethed. Fossen had led him to a small office off the main room with the giant metal apparatus. His pet dire wolf had followed at a distance, walking on all fours, curious and sniffing the air. Some of Fossen's assistants were in the office—two men and a woman. They had secured Rook to the chair while Fossen kept his small pistol trained on him.

Rook didn't recognize the people, but he knew the glazed look they had in their eyes. It was the same look the town's villagers had that morning, when they attacked him at Peder's farm. The assistants wore lab coats like Fossen and once they secured Rook to the chair, they left the room.

Rook scanned the space, but it mostly resembled a regular office. Desks and chairs—although the styles were pretty out of date—and a few far-newer laptop computers. The walls were white, and a large glass window looked out to the massive chamber with the metal octopus-like machinery. Fossen ignored Rook and consulted a laptop at one of the desks. Rook kept waiting for the man to start monologuing like a comic book villain, but the stoic Norwegian wasn't inclined to oblige.

"You lied to me," Rook tried.

"Actually, Stanislav," Fossen looked up from the screen of his laptop and considered Rook. "If you carefully consider everything I told you, you will find that I did not lie to you at all. I told you to leave Fenris Kystby when we first met. I really didn't know what Edmund Kiss had become, or that it was he that was destroying Peder's livestock. I lost my son Jens to that monster."

Rook didn't think it a good idea to correct Fossen and inform him that *he* had killed Jens Fossen. It had been self-defense, but Rook didn't think Fossen would care. A son is a son. Peder had helped him dispose of the body. He simply disappeared. It was only natural that Fossen assumed the creature Edmund Kiss had been responsible.

"I told you the truth about my research with the wolves. I admitted to you that I had known about Kiss's lab, but that I had forgotten it even existed—because it had been shut down years ago, when this larger installation was constructed. You asked me why Kiss's lab was called *Ragnarök*. I told you I had no idea why. I really don't. It was something the German Ahnenerbe group came up with. Kiss was a part of their research. Part of their group. I didn't tell you about this installation because it wasn't your business. But I never lied to you."

Rook looked at the man in astonishment. "You just found it unnecessary to share information about this giant lab—which connects to the smaller lab upstairs. You didn't bother mentioning that Kiss was your father. You didn't mention anything about a Nazi experiment in World War II or that you had a pet marshmallow with teeth." Rook motioned his head toward the dire wolf that sat quietly in the corner on its haunches. "Is that the *Ulveria*? The dire wolf, the local woman Anni was afraid of?"

"Yes, indeed. It is." Fossen just looked at Rook with a blank expression. No questions and no more information forthcoming.

"You didn't tell me about zombie people coming to kill me. And Kiss wanted you to seal something. He said he'd seen the dire wolf and it was terrible. Looking at it now I'd have to agree with him."

"When could you have spoken to Kiss? He was beyond speech when we tracked him down and killed him. He was little more than a yeti." Now Fossen was interested. His eyebrows raised high on his pale Nordic forehead as he waited for an answer.

"He had a note clutched in his hand. It was for you. Part of it was illegible. He still retained some of his human intelligence at the end, and he wrote the note for you. He urged you to *seal* something. What was it?"

Fossen turned his head to gaze out the huge pane of glass at the giant metal cage in the main room. He turned back to Rook, then looked down to his laptop screen again and typed a quick key sequence. The clacking noise of the keyboard was loud in the small room. With a flourish, Fossen hit the Enter key.

In the other room a small sphere of yellow light appeared in the center of the eight-beam structure that still reminded Rook of an oversized Faraday cage. The light was no more than a foot in diameter. Then there was a loud popping noise. The ball grew to nearly thirty feet in diameter, filling the space between the curving struts of the structure. It threw bursts of lightning, only to be caught by the solar panel-like sheets of metal attached to the uprights. The whole thing crackled and hummed with a deep bass vibration. Rook could feel it in his chest.

"He wanted me to seal that."

THIRTY-NINE
Exxon Building, New York

KING FELT HE was losing himself inside the dreamy world that had filled his head. His vision clouded at the edges and everything in front of him looked bright and cheerful. He smiled so big his cheeks hurt.

The tiny voice at the back of his head trying to regain control needed something to hang on to—something that it could use to keep itself anchored in his brain. *Something...* But that voice was weak now. Weak and insignificant. He still stood in front of the wall of light, staring at the yellow brilliance. He could hear the hum and crackle from the portal crossing the barrier from somewhere else to his world. The dire wolves were still moving around him and smelling him. He could smell them, too, but only faintly. They smelled like talcum powder and the soft fur of stuffed animals. But had they always smelled that way?

He didn't think so.

It didn't matter. No point in worrying about it. He felt great. Happy, calm and full of contentment.

Wasn't he unhappy before the portal and the dire wolves?

Wasn't he considering spending more time with Fiona and Sara?

Fiona...

Every time he thought of Fiona and his responsibility for her, the part of his mind that really was him gained strength. The only other thing that the tiny voice could find to cling to was a question. And that small part of his mind held on to it as if it were a life preserver in thirty-foot swells at sea.

Why?

Why had he been mentally hijacked? Why hadn't Deep Blue been affected? Was it something from the light the portal emitted? No, that didn't work. He would have seen the portal too, but Deep Blue was gone now. King lazily swiveled his head around the corridor, looking away from the bright light of the portal. Several more dire wolves filled the hallway and crouched on the walls and upside down on the ceiling.

"Cool, man" he said.

No. Not cool. How did they get here? You didn't even see them come out of the portal did you?

Then he felt the tiny voice shrinking again.

Why?

Fiona. Remember Fiona.

The voice grew stronger and tried to work out the mystery of why again. How long had he been here in the hallway? He turned his head again and looked down the corridor past the dire wolves that clung to every surface.

Deep Blue isn't here anymore.

A clanging bell sounded somewhere deep inside of him, like a big red wall-mounted number used in older elementary schools. But it was so soft. Almost beyond the range of his hearing.

He was worried, that's what it was. Deep Blue was more than a teammate and former President. He was a friend.

Where is he?

The voice noticed the shattered window at the end of the carpeted hallway. The smile on his face faded slowly, hesitantly, as if it wasn't sure it wanted to contribute to a look of concern on his face. Smiling was so good and right.

Fiona. Where's Fiona?

No, the small voice shouted from the black depths of his hind-mind, *she's safe in New Hampshire.* Safe with Endgame. *Endgame. That's right. Deep Blue...*

He had turned back and stared at the wall of light again. He hadn't even been aware of turning away from the sight of the shattered window. *Damn.* He turned again to look down the corridor, but this time he did so slower and more deliberately. The smile that had crept back onto his face remained, but he was afraid to battle it. Whatever had control of him was incredibly strong, and the nature of his bliss as a weapon prevented him from even noticing when he was being attacked. *One battle at a time. Why? How?*

He dimly recalled Deep Blue wearing a parachute. *He must have bugged out. But why?* His thoughts rapidly returned to his own predicament and used the mantra that was allowing him to retain even a sliver of control over his senses.

Fiona.

How was the portal controlling him? Or were the dire wolves doing it? It wasn't the light. It wouldn't have been a physical attack or an auditory one. He was protected against that. He slowly slid his hand up to touch the side of his cheek. He felt the rough stubble there. He hadn't shaved since leaving the hotel for Epcot.

Fiona. When did I take off the helmet? He looked down at himself. He was still wearing the rest of the armor. *So I was wearing the helmet before, and the only things coming in the helmet were light and...air.*

It was something in the air. He recalled that Deep Blue was not wearing an armor helmet—he wore the special helmet Aleman had helped design for him. The black one with the computer displays. And Deep Blue had said it had air-scrubbing filters that could remove close to 98% of contaminants in the atmosphere that he breathed. So it wouldn't have been a gas that was controlling King, or else Deep Blue might have been affected, too.

Why? Fiona. What then? Something airborne but not as potent as a gas? Frustration welled up in the back of King's mind and he was surprised to find it a potent remedy for his artificial bliss. He was used to fighting, but fighting with hands and weapons on a battle-field or in an alley in some Third World backwater. He could handle frigid polar wastes and arid desert climes. This sort of cerebral fight was new to him and he wasn't sure how to go about it. He couldn't isolate the enemy, its methods or its motives.

Fiona. She's safe and that is the most important thing. The next was figuring out how to get out of the happy trap. Frustration was good. *Maybe anger will be better?* He willed himself to be angry, but soon felt himself slipping into distraction and forgot what he was trying to do. He almost lost it altogether, when his thoughts again turned to those he loved and—

Fiona!

Why?

How?

In the air.

I'm breathing it. Can I hold my breath long enough for the effect to stop?

But then another idea occurred to King. He turned his head again back to the broken window at the end of the hallway. The gaping grin was still on his face but he made no move to change that. He would need all his willpower to accomplish what he had planned. First, he took a breath and held it. Not a deep gulp but a covert intake. The dire wolves that lined the hall still looked at him occasionally, sniffing the air. If this worked, he didn't want to alert them that he was gaining control.

As he was about to initiate the second phase of his plan, an overwhelming urge to look at the portal swept through him like a tornado ripping up trailer homes in the Midwest. He squeezed his eyes shut, and still holding his breath, repeated his daughter's name again and again. His head buzzed from the lack of oxygen and from the monotony of the mantra, but he felt the urge to look at the light slip away from him.

When the desire became manageable again, he forced that small but growing voice to let out a scream in his head.

Walk!

He took a step away from the portal, toward the opening, the daylight and the city street at the end of the corridor. He opened his eyes and the hallway looked to stretch into the horizon like a perspective drawing, dwindling down into a tiny dot.

He felt dizzy now from lack of air but refused to breathe again. He took a second step. The smile on his face wanted to diminish. The artificiality of it wanted to fade. Not completely, but from a shit-eating grin to a smirk. He refused to let it and kept the grimace of a smile in place. Another step and another, past a dire wolf on the left wall. It smelled him as he passed, but made no move toward him.

He took a chance and reached out his hand and stroked the creature's neck, smiling still. The creature didn't move. Its skin no longer felt like soft down. More like rubber. *How much did this attack alter my perceptions?* But that line of questioning cost him control, so he returned his thoughts to Fiona and walking. Forcing all his will onto those two thoughts. The edges of his vision began to blur a bit, but he could still see. His lungs struggled to get to fresh air, but he denied them. Another step and past another dire wolf. Two more between him and the window.

The effort was taking its toll and he could feel a trickle of sweat on his forehead, dripping toward his left eyebrow. He closed his eyes and focused on Fiona. The grin slipped. The sweat dripped off his eyebrow and down his eyelid. He opened his eye and the lid flicked the remaining liquid away. Two more steps. The smile was down to just a notion now, and he let it go. It wouldn't matter soon. He passed another dire wolf, this one moving slowly along the ceiling toward the portal over his head. He ducked a little as it passed him, but he kept his speed the same—deliberately slow.

Then he felt it. The November Manhattan breeze on his face, gusting in from the shattered window forty stories above the asphalt. He pulled air in through his nostrils, slowly, testing it. The breath made him happier, but not loopy. *Good. One mystery solved. It was the air.* He took another step, past a dire wolf crouched on the floor. This one swiveled its head to follow his stroll. *Does it know? Does it suspect?*

Three more steps and he would be right next to the shattered window. He drew in another lungful of air and slowly exhaled. Crisp and cold, the always-static acrid tang of New York on his tongue. But happy? Not too much. He was nearly out of the zone of influence, which must have been the portal, because the dire wolf behind him was still within arm's reach. If it was emitting the bliss, then King reasoned he would still be feeling the full effect at this end of the hall.

He took another step into the fresh air and heard movement behind him.

He turned to see that all five of the dire wolves in the corridor were now keenly staring at him, their ten bulbous eyes locked on target.

King stood stock still, and smiled wide. The biggest, goofiest court jester grin he could manage.

The dire wolves, three on the floor, one on the ceiling, and one on the wall all looked back at him. They each turned their heads in unison, facing their snouts at him. Their mouths opened wide. All King could see were teeth. Hundreds of pointy incisors, like sharpened crystals. The dire wolf farthest away roared. The others rushed along the walls, ceiling and floor.

He had just seconds to act or die.

FORTY
River Thames, London, England

BISHOP HELD TIGHTLY to the metal bar, helpless to stop the fragmented Ferris wheel from plummeting into the Thames, and certain he was about to die.

The wheel warped down to the muddy river. Saving the girls in the steel-and-glass cage was no longer possible. He held on with all he had as the wheel tipped out over the river. Four-hundred feet down, but the ride took only a few seconds.

At the last moment before his capsule hit the murky brown of the Thames, he considered leaping off the structure, to improve his chances of surviving the fall. But a split second of indecision was one second too many. He was out of time.

The capsule he stood on was the last part of the large wheel to reach the river. As the base of the wheel struck and sunk, his descent slowed some, but Bishop didn't notice as the water rushed up toward him. A wave roared up, striking the capsule and slamming Bishop down against its roof. He coughed as his ribs and lungs compressed from the impact. His head spun, but he remained conscious, protected by the armor, which was living up to its reputation. Thick, brown river water coated Bishop, stealing his vision.

He dropped again, as the wave receded, and the wheel began to sink.

He looked through the capsule window; his hands still clenched around the metal bar he had used as a handhold during the descent. His grip tightened in anger. The three teen girls were dead. Their bodies had slammed against the steel and glass in the plunge. Murky tan water filled the shattered capsule. He could see two bodies floating and the third girl's fractured head looked like a split-open watermelon left to wilt in the sun.

The very top of the capsule was still above the water level, but the rest had submerged. He turned, looking behind him at the crunched and mangled frame of the London Eye, which now resembled a toy construction kit hastily shoved into a container with bits sticking up in all the wrong ways. Bishop turned his attention to the bridge, searching for Knight. But the *Crescent* had retreated further along the river. *Where is he?*

Then Bishop saw him through the murk coating his helmet's visor. He quickly unfastened the catch buckle at the side of his throat and pulled the helmet off his recently shaved head. The cold of the air hit him and the rain spattered down on his face as he watched his friend being carried away by a dire wolf toward a portal.

He nearly dove into the river with the plan to swim to the Embankment, but he wouldn't have time and his armor would drag him down into the depths of the river.

"Shit, shit, shit!" He reached to his earpiece to call the pilot back to him. But it was too late. Knight was stabbing the back of the white thing's neck over and over, but then they were in the portal.

And suddenly it, too, was gone, leaving a tremendous hole in the side of Portcullis Building's lower corner. Missing the structural support the corner of the building provided, the rest crumbled in a heap of stone, sending a plume of dust up into the rain. The billowing cloud looked like a miniature nuclear detonation.

"Black One, this is Bishop. I'm in the river, north of the bridge. Come get me before I drown." Bishop spat into the water. The remains of the Ferris wheel were still sinking slightly as water filled the capsule with the dead girls. Bishop smashed the helmet onto the glass of the capsule, his normal calm demeanor gone, along with his friend and half of London. The impact lined the glass, but the helmet bounced away into the brown swirling water and sank.

"On my way. The door or the rope?" The hovering ship banked sharply and raced back over the bridge and above Bishop's head before slowly beginning to lower.

"Rope will do." Bishop said.

The black nylon rope dangling from the still open door of the craft came within his reach. Bishop didn't bother with the belay device—he just wrapped the rope around his arm a few times and shouted, "Go!"

"Where to Bishop?" Came the reply from the co-pilot, Black Two.

"To the next nearest portal. I'm going after him." Bishop grunted as the *Crescent's* engines blasted, increasing altitude until he was nearly as high as he had been on top of the Eye. The plane accelerated, swinging him on the rope, banking away from the river and over the top of Big Ben.

"But the device the MOD is bringing..." Black Two's voice was hesitant, but he was right. The mission was to get the nuke inside the portal.

"If those lame dicks ever get here, tell them to throw the thing in after me."

Bishop could see the next portal on the edge of the duck pond in St. James's Park up ahead, filling the green clearing set aside in the middle of the gray city. He took a deep breath of the rainy air and made up his mind.

"Lower. Then do a flyover."

"Roger," came Black One's reply.

The *Crescent* dipped a bit and the rope swung Bishop directly at the globe of crackling and spitting yellow fire. As the rain pelted it, the portal spit miniature lightning bolts, making this one look like it had electric hair. Bishop could smell the singed air as he got close. The rope swung right through the curvature of the wall of bright light, taking Bishop's body with it.

A second later, as the *Crescent* sped past the globe, the rope swung out the other side of the sphere of light.

Bishop wasn't on it.

FORTY-ONE
Gleipnir Facility, Fenris Kystby, Norway

QUEEN TENSED IN the dark. As the door rattled from the other side, she prepared to lunge.

The door swung open easily and a woman in a lab coat with short spiky blonde hair stepped into the room, without any hint of caution. The woman simply stood in the darkened room as if she couldn't remember why she had come in. Light streamed in from the outside with a pulsing electrical quality that made Queen certain that it came from something large, like a spotlight.

She had been in the room for what felt like hours. She was wedged between two walls of the room, in the corner up by the ceiling. Her feet were braced in the open air vent and her hands rested on the frame over the door. Between her hands, like a garrote, she clutched the wire from the lightbulb she had pulled down. The cord's coarse black insulating rubber dug into her fingers. She was ready to kill, but she stayed her attack, even in the awkward position. The woman hadn't noticed her, and she didn't display any alarm at finding the light out or at finding the room empty.

She just stood there, looking into the empty space.

Then the woman casually turned and walked out of the doorway. The door began to swing shut after her, but Queen quickly allowed one end of her weapon to unravel from the hand that had been braced on the doorframe, balancing herself on one arm, over the door closer. Once the thick insulation was in the crack of the door, she let the door swing nearly shut, where the wire stopped it from closing entirely. She dropped to the floor, landing in a silent crouch.

She paused, straining to hear anything from outside the door, but heard nothing. She stood and cautiously peered around the door, and out the crack. The woman walked away along the high metal catwalk near the roof of the huge room where Queen had come in with Rook and Asya. But that had been hours ago. Only one of the overhead Klieg lights lit the giant room, leaving the huge space shadowed and dim. Whatever brightness had been making the gigantic space crackle before was gone now. As Queen watched, the woman in the lab coat continued along the metal of the catwalk, her footsteps clanging in the silence as she went. Her posture was weird. The woman looked like she didn't know where she was going or what she was doing. When she reached the top of the metal stairs leading down to the floor of the room and the intricate metal finger-like shape that filled it, she just stopped.

Queen ducked back into the room briefly, but when she heard no noise, she once again looked out the crack. The woman was simply standing and looking out across the massive room.

She's acting like a robot.

Queen took a halting step out onto the catwalk. The woman remained inert. Queen took another soft step out of the room and fully onto the metal of the catwalk. At this section of the walkway, a solid plate sat on top of the grill that formed the catwalk around the room. She had noticed that there was a solid plate to stand on in front of every door around the walkway, when she explored earlier. The spiky-haired, frozen woman stood on a similar plate at the top of the stairs. Queen checked her surroundings and made sure she was alone with the woman. She couldn't see the stairwell below, because of the plate's placement, but she could see the rest of the room, down to the machinery at the bottom of the cavernous space and back along the walkway behind her. She noted the door that led to the tunnel through which they had entered the facility.

It was when she took a step off the metal plate and onto the see-through metal grating of the catwalk, that she sensed something was wrong. The small wispy white-blonde hairs on the back of her neck began to stand up. She tightened her hold on her makeshift garrote and froze in place, just like the lab-coated woman ahead of her. But nothing happened. Nothing in her line of sight was moving. The robot-like woman stood statue still.

What the hell?

Every sense she had told her to run, but she couldn't detect danger from any direction. She turned and looked behind her again.

Nothing.

As her eyes scanned back toward her own position, she looked down at the grating. She could see through the grill and under the metal slab behind her.

The creature hung in a crouch, upside down, like a bat, from the underside of the catwalk, just under the metal plate. It was larger than the one she had killed, and its translucent domed head was bigger than her chest. Muscles bulged under its ghost-like skin. Its bulbous eyes, the size of grapefruits, regarded her. She could sense a silent countdown happening. Soon it would strike.

But Queen showed no fear. Instead, she returned the creature's stare, imagining a hundred different ways she might be able to kill it. Size was an advantage, but as the only woman in Special Forces, she was accustomed to fighting larger adversaries and used her lower center of gravity, surprising strength and ruthless techniques to overcome them all. Of course, most of them didn't have teeth and claws. Then again, some did.

The thing scrambled to the side rail of the catwalk and began to climb up over it. Queen rushed it with her homemade weapon, and as its head cleared the rail, she rammed the insulated cord across the beast's throat and shoved hard. The monster's white body was in an awkward position, its claws only barely holding on as it had tried to vault over the rail to attack her. The clear claws slid on the slick metal. She could hear a screeching noise as the last two nails lost traction. Then the creature shot away from her and down to the floor. The lack of resistance was so sudden that she nearly lost her own balance and went over after the thing.

She stayed leaning over the rail long enough to watch the white animal-looking thing hit the concrete at the bottom of the room, bursting into a thick oozing fluid that splattered the machinery all around it.

Good.

Then, as she shot her eyes back to robot-woman, she saw what had impeded her path. Three more of the bastards on the stairs, and now one crouched on the railing at the top, level with the woman, who stood stock-still. All three of them had their strange external eyes swiveled down to take in the sight of their fallen comrade. Then as one, they swiveled their eyes up to look at Queen.

Time to go.

She turned and sprinted for the door down the catwalk that led to the tunnel and the older, abandoned part of the lab. She could hear the claws scraping and skittering along the metal walkway behind her as she flung the door open and pitched herself into the darkness of the tunnel. Her headlamp was gone. She had no time to be careful. She just ran, remembering as she went the long brick tunnel and the secret room at the end.

But this tunnel brought back her memory of the other. She bashed her fist against the ceiling a few times, as she ran. It was so low that she could easily reach it, even though the walls were far apart. She felt the dust cascade down on her in the dark, but she didn't know if it would be enough to slow the creatures. She couldn't hear them behind her, but she knew they made it into the tunnel before the outer door swung closed, removing even a trace of light. Finally, she found a brick that was loose. She halted in the dark and took a step back, reaching her fingers up to find it again. She played her fingertips over the rough stone and the fractured mortar until she felt the wobble. Then she banged on it again, with the bottom of her fist. It lurched under her strike. She worked her fingers into the crack and tried to pry it out, but it wouldn't come loose. It was like a marble inside someone's hand—it spun freely, but wouldn't come out of the grip.

In the dark behind her, she heard a scratching noise. *Crap*, she thought. *Break the hand.* She struck the ceiling again with her fist, and then again. She punched up at the stones and pounded them with the bottom of her fist. She heard one of the surrounding bricks crack and then she heard something else sliding in the dark behind her.

Something close.

She hit the brick above her again and felt something in her own hand break. It wasn't the first time she had broken a bone in her hand. *Probably the 5th metacarpal. Boxer's fracture.* She recognized the sensation, but the urgency in her mind made her shut the pain out. She hit the ceiling again and the stones surrounding her target brick crumbled, raining debris down in the stygian tunnel. Now she attempted to pry the brick again, and it came loose in her broken hand. She swapped the insulated wire for the brick and now used her good hand to smash it into the ceiling and the gaping wound she had created by prying out the brick. She could feel more dirt cascading down around her wrist.

Then she got an idea and moved her body to the other side of the tiny spray of falling dirt. She wrapped the wire around her torso in the dark, and shoved the brick fragment between her knees. She then reached up and dug the fingers of both hands into the soil beyond the brick ceiling. When she had a good grip, she hung from the bricks and used her weight to swing forward. She kicked out in the dark and two things happened. The first was unexpected, but the second was just what she was hoping for.

Her feet connected with something solid before she had the chance to extend her legs fully. She had planted her feet on the chest of one of the creatures. She wasted no time in tugging hard with her upper body strength. Several of the bricks gave way under her weight, pulling a section of the ceiling down on top of the beast and onto her legs. The tunnel filled with choking dust, but she had been expecting it and held her breath.

With nothing to cling to anymore, she fell to the floor with the shattered ceiling. She quickly scrambled backward on her ass, shoving with her feet and clawing back with her hands. She lost her brick weapon, but there were plenty to choose from now. She checked and found the insulated wire still hanging from her waist. She wrapped it around her broken hand. Then she grabbed the first piece of rubble she could find—half a brick—with the other hand and raced deeper into the darkness of the tunnel.

As she ran, she got angrier at the creatures behind her in the dusty darkness. She took breaths as she ran and tasted dirt in the air, but it was nothing like the cloud of dust from the ceiling collapse. She kept one hand in front of her and waited for the impact with the secret spinning wall. It was farther down the tunnel than she remembered it, but when she hit it, she felt it move smoothly on its axis.

The room on the other side of the spinning wall was as dark as the tunnel, but she remembered the way well enough. She found the door and turned left, heading across the small room toward the first tunnel—the one that led her up and out. She got angrier at the thought of leaving Rook and the Russian woman behind her. But she knew she couldn't fight the white creatures here in the dark, and they had been between her and the rest of the lab, back on the catwalk. She reached the tunnel just as she heard a door slam open behind her.

Crap, they're close.

She used her fragment of rubble to smash along the wall as she made her way down the original tunnel to the metal ladder, sending small waves of sand and grit through the air in the dark behind her. She felt the dirt pelting the skin on her face as she ran. She misjudged the distance down this tunnel too, slamming her face into the metal of the ladder in the darkness. She reeled from the impact, dropping her brick fragment. She caught herself from falling backward by grabbing the ladder rung with her broken hand. A fresh wave of pain shot up her arm. She grunted, but most of the pain was drowned out by her rising fury.

Holding tightly to the insulated wire, she grabbed the rungs above her in the dark and climbed the ladder. When she reached the top, she forced her weight behind the flipping door that wore the fake bush like a feather-capped Royal attending Prince Harry's wedding. It was heavy, but it closed quickly.

She launched herself out and into a newly fallen snowdrift. Snow poured down from the sky in tiny jagged clumps—not quite sleet, but not quite snow.

Queen rolled away from the hatch and into the snow, relishing the weather. The sun had gone down, but the moon must have been up somewhere. She couldn't see it, but light was trapped between the two-foot layer of fresh snow on the ground and the low-lying clouds above her head. It reflected back and forth off the two surfaces making everything nearly as bright as day. She had seen a similar effect before, on a skiing trip in Flagstaff.

She couldn't have asked for a better battleground.

She knew she should probably run. Get help. Call in the cavalry. But that could take hours. Maybe longer. If something happened to Rook...

Queen shook her head. Not an option.

"C'mon, you see-through assholes. I'm waiting," she whispered, clutching the rubber-coated wire.

FORTY-TWO
Midtown, New York

DEEP BLUE PULLED the trigger on the confetti launcher as soon as the elevator doors parted. Instantly the hallway was a riot of white, pink, and pastel greens and blues, as shredded paper filled the air with a loud popping noise. The effect was surreal. Everything that had been moving a second earlier—King and the five dire wolves—just stopped as if turned to stone.

Even with the colorful airborne flak, Deep Blue knew he wouldn't have much time. King was near the shattered window and the dire wolves were between them, stopped where they had been and so still that he couldn't even see an eyeball moving. He wasted no time in firing on the dire wolves with the MP5. He ran through the falling confetti as he fired. He aimed at three of the beasts and drilled two of them in the eye, hitting a third in the chest, before the first two managed to fall off the walls, where they had crouched sideways.

As Deep Blue got up to where King stood, he could see that King had regained his senses but was unarmed. A quick peek back toward the portal showed King's weapon on the floor, just in front of the glowing wall. Two dire wolves stood hunched over by the walls further down the hall, between him and the rifle. It was a loss. But the other thing wasn't on the floor at all.

"Jack, where's the nuke?"

"Sorry, Boss. I chucked it into the portal when I was under its control, but forgot to arm it. The portal is putting something in the air—"

"Yeah, I got that part. I—"

"They're moving again." King pointed down the hallway.

King was right. The confetti had mostly fluttered to the floor. Deep Blue leveled the second confetti cannon he had nabbed from the nearby party supply store and fired it high in the air. One of the two dire wolves ran headlong at them and King snatched the pistol from its holster on Deep Blue's leg. He fired three shots at the creature and hit its head each time, but the beast kept barreling toward them down the hallway.

"Look out!" Deep Blue shoved King into a door marked *Stairs* that had no handle—just a metal hand plate for pushing. King slammed into the door and it opened wide, spilling him onto the landing. At the same time, Deep Blue gambled that with the confetti in the air, the charging dire wolf really couldn't see but was just striking out where it had last seen them. When the beast was nearly on him, Deep Blue lunged to the side, against the hallway wall. The dire wolf ran right past him and out the shattered window, into open space.

Deep Blue looked out the window to see the animal fall. *Olé!* he thought. Then he leveled the MP5 at the remaining dire wolf. This one had been content to wait for the confetti to settle, but its eyes swiveled in anticipation of being free to move unobstructed through the soon-to-be-clear air. Deep Blue put a burst of bullets in its cranium. The skull erupted in a gout of ichor resembling warm mayonnaise. The perforated beast sank to the floor as King was getting to his feet.

"You back to your normal self?" Deep Blue looked King up and down.

"Completely. Fresh air from the broken window helped. Shit. More of them!" King opened fire down the hallway as more of the creatures crawled and ran out of the wall of yellow light. As Deep Blue looked, he realized they wouldn't be able to hold off that many.

And he was out of confetti.

"The stairs," he said.

King stopped firing and bolted into the stairwell.

Deep Blue followed at his heels. "They were all over the outside of the building too. Keasling's men are having a hard time of it."

King leaned over the railing and looked down the stairwell, but turned quickly back to Deep Blue, his face grim. "Too many. Up!"

Deep Blue sprinted up the stairs until he hit the landing. King was still at the bottom of the stairs and fired as soon as the door opened, cracking the skull of the first dire wolf through the door. The body's momentum carried it forward and down the lower flight of stairs to the next landing.

Deep Blue covered the door from the upper landing as King raced up the industrial gray steps to meet him. Just as King reached the landing, another creature leapt through the door and Deep Blue blasted it with a carefully controlled burst.

They continued up flight after flight of stairs, carefully picking off any of the monsters that got too close. When King passed a foam fire extinguisher on the wall of the 45th floor, he halted and nimbly unlatched the bright red tank from the wall. He then leaned over the railing and blasted the contents of the extinguisher down the space between the flights of stairs. It was a narrow space, but it was enough for the burst of white foam to spatter into the air and cascade down several floors. The extinguisher ran dry as the first dire wolf reached a landing below them, stopped and opened its jaws in a snarl that looked almost comical.

Deep Blue fired two shots at it before the MP5 ran dry.

King threw the empty fire extinguisher canister down the flight of stairs, knocking the animal back and off balance slightly. Then he pulled up the pistol he had taken from Deep Blue. He had only one round left and no more magazines, so he aimed carefully and then fired.

The creature's head crumpled inward. The bullet liquefied the brains, exited the back of the skull and pulled the white slurry out with it, splattering white gore across the wall. His stomach turned at the sight. *If only I could unsee some of this shit.* He turned and raced up the next flight of stairs with Deep Blue. The much-older man had managed to reload the MP5 faster than King had ever seen anyone do.

"How many more magazines?" He asked.

"Last one. Run faster."

As though in response, the horde of dire wolves on the steps below resumed their loud pursuit, closing the distance.

FORTY-THREE
Somewhere

EVERYTHING WAS A deep rich shade of midnight blue.

Everything.

The bleak cloudless sky, the rocky ground littered with small round stones, and the distant, jagged, impossibly tall cliffs. Chunks of London that had passed through the portal were scattered around the area: building rubble, a street sign, a dead bird and half of a car, its occupants missing. As Shin Dae-jung, callsign: Knight, looked around the alien landscape, his eyes kept struggling to comprehend the complete lack of variation in the color of things. It made looking at things hurt. He had taken refuge behind some boulders to deal with the overwhelming sensation of nausea he felt while his eyes tried to perceive and adjust to the monotone surroundings. He strained to focus on the cliffs and to differentiate them from the sky. He considered removing his armored helmet for fear of vomiting inside it, but didn't think it wise. He focused on controlling his body and his stomach contents stayed down. He activated the night-vision optics built in to the helmet's visor and the night changed to a dim day. The technology amplified available light, but there wasn't much of it. Still, the shades of green in the night-vision view had a few more contrasts than the overwhelming palette of blue did.

The air tasted metallic, like dirty coins, but was breathable. He deactivated the audio dampener—it would help more at this stage if he could hear dire wolves approaching. The place was deathly still.

He didn't hear anything.

No wind, no animals or insects. Just vast emptiness.

Aleman was right. This isn't our world—or dimension—or whatever. Everything about the place is wrong, or my perception of it is.

The land was flat and rocky, except for the cliffs on the horizon. Knight stood and surveyed the sight. No sign of dire wolves on the open plain. He remembered they could really move when they were on a stretch of flat open ground, so he figured they had all just raced off to the horizon while his stomach was doing flip-flops. *That or they went underground somewhere.*

With no rifle, no pistol and now only the corpse of the dire wolf he had stabbed and his KA-BAR knife to keep him company, Knight kept scanning the plains for a sign of another portal. If he found one, he would rush for it and try to use it to get back to the world— his world.

He knelt down and examined the corpse that was missing its feet and legs below the shin. The wounds were cauterized completely. Knight poked one of the stumps with the tip of his knife to see how thick the scar tissue was. Eventually, with enough pressure, the knife slipped through the skin and a pearl of thick fluid oozed from the puncture. He looked over the rest of the creature up close. It had foggy transparent skin, like a jellyfish. It was muscular. The eyes were weird as hell. The mouth was full of clear sharp teeth ranging between one and two inches in length. The claws, like the teeth, were transparent and deadly. He picked up the creature's limp arm and placed the sharp blade against the clear skin and made an incision that cut all the way to the bone. After wiping off the blade and sheathing it, he pulled open the wound and looked at the bone. Clear. Like glass. He could see the tube of gray marrow running down its core.

He looked up at the bleak sky. Something about this world made the creatures evolve this way. He remembered what Black Five said about how alternate dimensions could be similar, but also incredibly different. Was it the atmosphere? The sun? Or simply a completely different set of physical laws? With no way to find out, and no new insights on how to kill the creatures, beyond putting a bullet in them, Knight put the arm down and stood. *One more unsolved mystery.*

The variant shades of night-vision green showed no life signs and no portals. He prepared his stomach and then deactivated the night vision and looked out through the normal visor view for a sign of a portal. The view was less unsettling now that he knew to expect the constant shade of midnight. Still, nothing that looked like a portal, a structure or a living creature. He reactivated the night vision and turned to face the distant cliffs. They were the only aberration in what seemed to be otherwise endless rocky plains.

Cliffs it is, then.

With the knife in hand, he began walking. He took only a handful of steps before he became convinced that someone—or something—was watching him. He looked around, but still saw nothing but the plains. He kept walking toward the cliffs, switching the night vision on and off occasionally, just to be sure that one spectrum of light wasn't preventing him from seeing something that the other might reveal. Nothing.

So he walked. The feeling that something was following him—or just observing him—remained. As a sniper, he knew that feeling. The feeling of having a long barrel targeting your every move, ready to send death with a few pounds of pressure on a sliver of metal. He was on the other end of that feeling, but recognized it in his targets when, as though warned by some sixth sense, they turned and looked directly at him. He was usually too far away to actually be seen, but if anyone ever did see him, they died with the image.

When he came to a small pile of waist-high boulders, he dove behind them and rolled to a stop on the other side. In the dive, he turned his head and looked back behind him. Old submarine commanders called an abrupt change of direction 'clearing the baffles.' The idea was to change course unexpectedly, allowing you to see a stealthy pursuer. But like with his other attempts to spot any pursuit, which he was convinced of now, he saw nothing.

Dejected, Knight resumed his trek to the cliffs. They were further than he had thought. He felt like he had walked for at least an hour, but the cliffs appeared no closer. He felt ravenously hungry and reached into a canvas pouch on the outside of the armored suit, withdrawing a high-energy protein bar. He squatted on his haunches, turning as he did so, clearing the baffles again, but as usual, he saw only the rocky field around him. He took off the helmet and ate the protein bar, trying not to fully taste its chalky flavor. The suit had a built in Camelbak water reservoir. He removed the plastic tube from its holster on his left shoulder and bit down on the valve, sucking the warm water into his body to flush the debris of the protein bar down. He took another gulp and then put the tube away. He didn't know how long the water would last him, but he figured it would be better to conserve it.

He put the helmet back on and activated night vision again, then resumed his walk. He checked the Suunto watch on his wrist, but found it had been damaged in the fight with the dire wolf on the bridge. The face was cracked, and a piece of the plastic bezel stuck out at a weird angle. He considered just ditching the thing, but then realized he'd be making a trail on the rocky ground. He stopped and squatted again, but this time, it was to pick up one of the many flat round stones on the ground. It looked like a flat skipping stone you would find near a river. He dropped it into a zippered pocket and resumed the march to the cliffs.

Eventually, he got tired and had to stop. The cliffs were still a distance off. He sat and removed the helmet. There was no cover anywhere, so he just sat in the middle of the rocky plain and took in the rich hues of navy blue that covered everything like a blanket of night. It felt like night to him too. He and Bishop had been on the go for how long? He looked at his watch again. Still broken. The bezel fragment had snapped off at some point. He rubbed his hand over his smooth face. He had never been able to grow a beard—with his Korean ancestry, his abilities to grow body hair were pretty limited. So a five o'clock shadow wouldn't be arriving any time in the next decade to help him determine the passage of time. Ultimately, he realized it didn't matter. However much time passed, he would get out of here as soon as he could. He would keep heading for the cliffs and he would do whatever it took.

Exhaustion began to take its toll on his body, and even though he sat cross-legged on the uncomfortable rocky ground, his head kept nodding. Eventually, he lay down on his side, his sleep-deprived mind rationalizing why it would be perfectly safe to do so, and how he would remain vigilant, nonetheless. He was a sniper after all. He was trained to stay awake in combat situations for days on end. He would be fine. There was nothing moving on the plain.

Then his mind cajoled him to allow himself just a few minutes of eyes-closed rest.

I won't go to sleep deeply. Just a few minutes, that's all.

And then he slept. Deeply.

For years.

FORTY-FOUR

Gleipnir Facility, Fenris Kystby, Norway

ASYA CLOSED HER mouth, clamping off the scream before it was truly done. She swung the tiny LED light around the space. It was little more than a brick pit, really, just twenty feet in diameter and roughly circular. She played the light around the chamber and hoped for a door or a ladder, but the walls were uninterrupted.

And the whole pit was filled with heaps of the dead and desiccated corpses. Like little white stuffed animals in one of those crane-and-claw, coin-operated vending machine games. But there was no metal claw above her—instead, something moved beneath the heap of tiny bodies.

The mound shifted slowly.

Little bodies tumbled.

The corpses were almost cute, except for the rib bones poking out of the chests. The eyes were hardly pronounced but sat on the outside of the face, like halved grapes. The creatures had white skin that she could see through to the muscles and meat below it.

She began to breathe quickly, willing herself to overcome the fear paralyzing her. The thing under the mound moved again, in a zig-zagging motion. The floor of tiny dead performed a wave like the people at a sporting event.

It moves like a snake, she thought.

And then her paralysis broke. She lunged, clawing and scrabbling across the heaped dead, heading for the brick wall. As she moved her hands through the pile, crawling to the wall, the glow from her LED flashlight flared wildly in the space, throwing fast moving shadows around the pit.

She needed to get out. This place was wrong and horrible. Unnatural. *Evil*, the word came to her panicked mind unbidden. *Evil*.

She flailed through the bodies and reached the brick unmolested, but her mind, completely unhinged by fear, couldn't comprehend that the slithering thing under the bodies had yet to grasp her ankle. She dug her fingers into the mortar between the bricks and found it was crumbly under her touch. She pulled herself up and placed her toes into the wide spaces between the bricks. She raced up the thirty-foot wall with balance a rock climber would have admired. She kept the LED light between her teeth, placed her toes and fingers into the cracks and didn't look back.

When she reached the top, she threw herself over the lip, and onto the rough stone floor of the tunnel. She could see a blazing bright light at the end of the tunnel, back in the large laboratory. It was far brighter than the spotlights affixed to the ceiling, and she clung to the idea that bright light was her salvation from the atrocities in the pit.

Asya struggled to her feet and ran headlong toward the light. She abandoned all thoughts of stealth hoping to find Rook and Queen. But when she exited the mouth of the tunnel into the room though, another strange sight greeted her. The giant hand of metal—she recalled the gleaming chrome claw in the game with the stuffed animals, only this one was absurdly large and upside down, resting on the floor with its open claws stretching almost two hundred feet up to the ceiling—held something in its clutches now. A blazing sun, easily over a hundred feet in diameter, hovered between the metal struts of the claw. Small arcs of lightning shot out of the ball of crackling energy, but the lightning curved unnaturally backward, striking the large metal plates on the claw's upright legs, harmlessly dissipating.

The light was incredibly bright, but the globe of electric fire felt appealing. It drew her closer. She stood directly in front of the pulsing light, all thoughts of her recent scare in the pit now gone from her mind. She just wanted to be near the light. It filled her with warmth, like the sun. Only this sun was for her. Her very own, personal star.

She smiled wide and exhaled a deep and contented sigh.

She didn't notice, as five large white creatures that looked like grown versions of the dead babies, crawled out of the globe of brilliance and began to sniff the air around her.

FORTY-FIVE
Endgame Headquarters, White Mountains, NH

LEWIS ALEMAN SAT alone in a side office off the main corridor in Central that ran to the tram station, which would lead to another part of the base that housed a submarine dock. He had left Fogg and Pierce in the main computer control room. He needed just five minutes to himself to process what he had learned, before he reported to Deep Blue. That his boss had not reported in yet regarding his rescue attempt for King did not bode well. It meant they were still up to their necks in battle or dead.

He would have to attempt to contact them regardless. Too much had happened. Knight and Bishop were off the grid. Queen and Rook were in the same town as the source portal—a portal that had appeared regularly over the last few months, and in precisely the same location.

Aleman realized that someone had to be regulating the phenomenon. *Not phenomenon*, he thought. *Attack.*

The portals were appearing with increasing frequency around the globe and their strategy of dealing with the fallout caused by dire wolf attacks had led them nowhere. They needed to find whatever was causing the portals to appear and eliminate it. Before there wasn't anything left of the planet. His quick research into the town of Fenris Kystby led exactly nowhere. There was no useful information about the place. It was a tiny town near the coast of northern Norway, well off the beaten track for tourists and natives alike. But the lack of any information on the Web was disturbing to Aleman. He could nearly always find *something*, about even the most obscure places in the world, even if it was just a farm report or a local carnival announcement. It was almost like any information about this place has been scoured away from the Web.

They knew the dire wolf was mentioned in Norse mythology. They had seen evidence that someone in Viking times had come across a dire wolf. They suspected repeated appearances of the portals in a town in Norway that no one had ever heard of. And Rook had called in earlier from the very same town and was facing mind-controlled people. Aleman didn't know what it added up to, but he knew that the team was wasting its time in other locations. *Norway is the source.*

He stood from his office chair and touched the ear of his communications headset, then he voice-dialed Deep Blue. He paced back and forth across the rich blue carpet between the glass-walled air-conditioned closet of routers and servers and the desk the room held. He heard the connection go live with a tiny audible click.

"Kind of busy now, Lew. There's shooting and running..." Deep Blue sounded out of breath. Aleman would keep the information about Bishop and Knight to himself for the moment.

"It's going down in Norway. Norway is the source."

"Son of a—that's where Rook is." Deep Blue's voice came between heaving breaths. Aleman couldn't hear any external sounds because of the audio dampener in Deep Blue's helmet, but he could imagine the running and shooting, just fine. He'd experienced it during his previous years as a Delta operator before an injury sidelined him.

"Actually, it's the same *town* Rook said he was in. Queen's tracking chip show's she's there with him. If they're not together, they're close. We need to get over there. Time is running out."

"What's the...projection?"

"Maybe two days if the portals keep appearing at the same rate and keep growing in size. The one in Norway seems to have stabilized in size and intensity. And there's something else. When the Norway portal has opened in the past, it hasn't stayed on for longer than a few minutes. But it's on now and has probably been activated for close to a half an hour."

"We're...on our...way. Ready everyone who can fire a weapon. The whole White team. How are Bishop and Knight doing?"

"Didn't work out." Aleman changed the subject quickly. "I'll take care of everything on my end. Anything else?"

"Nothing. Out."

Aleman consoled himself that now wasn't the time to tell Deep Blue about Bishop and Knight. Deep Blue would be checking on everything from his satellite uplink on the face display of the helmet as soon as the battle subsided enough for him to do so. He would see the complete absence of the tracking chips both Bishop and Knight unknowingly carried, with his GPS program. The man would understand the ramifications of the missing signals. They were either dead or they were trapped on the other side of the portals. Possibly both.

FORTY-SIX
Gleipnir Facility, Fenris Kystby, Norway

ROOK WAS DUMBFOUNDED. Fossen had just flicked a switch and teleported a sun into the neighboring room.

A sun!

"What the hell? Is that a...a dwarf star?" Rook turned back to Fossen, who wore a smug grin.

"No. Only a doorway."

"A doorway to what?" Rook asked. "To where?" He struggled covertly against the plastic zip ties binding his wrists to the chair behind him. He didn't think he would be able to break them, but he would try until he had no breath left.

"Another world." Fossen nodded to the creature still crouching in the corner of the room. "The dire wolves are not a native species. Surely, you can see that, Stanislav."

The man fell silent. Rook let the man do so for a while. He needed to get free from the damn chair. But then his curiosity got the better of him.

"But why, Fossen? Why open a 'doorway' to bring the dire wolves here? What does that get you? Is it connected to your work on the local wolf population? I don't get it."

The man didn't reply.

Rook looked out the window to the glowing sphere in the next room and saw some of the puppet-like lab coats walking around the room, checking on the machinery.

"Why aren't you being controlled like the others, Fossen? Or are you the one doing the controlling?"

The man leaned back in his office chair and it gave a groan from his weight. Rook looked at the man, and he appeared to be a part of the chair, as if it and he were old friends. He smiled. "The pheromones passing through the doorway help free the will of those who resist the will of my Lord."

My Lord? Rook thought. *Shit on a stick.* Religious nutjobs were always harder to handle because they were so unpredictable.

"I've heard it feels quite wonderful," Fossen added. "And they're happy to do whatever I, or my Lord, ask of them."

"I noticed that when half the town tried to kill me."

He shrugged. "I asked you to leave more than once."

"So why aren't you all happy-tappy?"

"There are some of us here, those whose goals are aligned with the Lord's, who remain unaffected. Sharp minds are required for an undertaking such as this. The pheromones only affect those who feel any degree of fear. We tested the compounds years ago, you see. But for Edmund Kiss, and your friend Peder—oh yes, he was a part of our group—we didn't need to be controlled. We *wanted* to open the doorway. We *wanted* to see what was on the other side. And what we found? *Glorious.*

"As I said before, I didn't lie to you. I just didn't tell you everything. During World War II, the *Deutsches Ahnenerbe* was set up as a group with the sole purpose of investigating potential supernatural weapons. Hitler, as you probably know, was convinced that he would find some dark art or powered talisman that would help him win the war."

"And the *Ahnenerbe* was willing to serve, right? Just doing their jobs like the jack-booted thugs at Auschwitz?" Rook looked disgusted.

Fossen surprised Rook by barking with laughter.

"No. Not at all. Hitler was a fool. He was good at getting people riled up, and he played that 'master race' card very well in public, but that wasn't his true goal. He had a limited scope of vision. The man only wanted power and more power. Once removed from the main theater of war, the small group here abandoned the Third Reich and its bigoted agenda. They even abandoned the name *Ahnenerbe*. Now we simply call ourselves 'The Group.' Kiss and Peder and the others were interested in other worlds and supernatural creatures the likes of which Hitler could not have imagined. They remained here in Fenris Kystby, dedicated to one sole ideal. Over time, some, like Kiss, gained their own ideas about how things should be done and went their own way. Others, like Peder, dropped out shortly after the war. He never had the stomach for what we were doing, but he knew to keep his nose out of our business. I was born in the '60s, when the project was well under way and the war was long over."

Fossen stood and walked to the window, his back to where Rook sat tied to his chair. "You see, we kept people out of Fenris

Kystby. No one knew what we were doing all these years. I did try to convince you to leave this town. We discovered the doorway and we figured out how the pheromones work. We even genetically tried to replicate the dire wolves, but all our attempts have been failures. We can't get any subjects to survive infancy. Even tried crossing their DNA with our local wolves. I keep trying, but it's more out of habit at this point, if I'm honest. Ultimately, we realized our true goal should be stabilizing and amplifying the doorway. It's a naturally occurring phenomenon, like a small hangnail between dimensions. What you see out there is about twenty years' worth of work to help that phenomenon become a permanent opening between worlds."

Rook was sure one of the two zip ties was loosening as he flexed his thick wrists and pulled apart with his upper arms. It just wasn't happening fast enough.

"So this is all about opening a portal for the dire wolves to come through? Why? Are they the mystery Lord you keep talking about?" He had to keep stalling the man, if he could.

Fossen leveled a serious glare at Rook.

Rook tried not to look away. He'd broken rule number one for dealing with religious kooks: *don't insult their God.*

"No, Stanislav, I wanted to *go there.* To live in Asgard and sit at the right hand of Lord Fenrir's throne."

Fenrir, Rook thought. Fossen's God had a name.

"I'm all that's left of the true believers. The others out there are all dominated by the pheromones or by Fenrir's will directly as She speaks to them. I see the look on your face, my friend. But I've already been though the doorway to the other side. I've seen it with my own eyes. It is a stark place, but it is filled with bliss beyond comprehension."

Rook thought it sounded like Fossen got a dose of Fenrir's happy gas, too. Maybe not enough to make him loopy, but enough to make him see God, and want more.

Rook pulled hard at his restraints, but then stretched his neck, as if he were merely uncomfortable in the chair. He didn't want Fossen to stop talking and start realizing his captive was nearly free.

"Have you ever wondered if Fenrir just wants to come here?"

Fossen smiled a strange distant smile, like he was remembering something amazing in his mind's eye. "Oh, she wants to come here very badly. That's why she needs me. To loosen the leash that keeps her from fully entering our world. She has been here before, several times over the ages. We've just mistaken the evidence of her passage."

Fossen had actually piqued Rook's interest. "How?"

"Impact craters," Fossen said. "Some really are impact craters, to be sure, but many are simply the footprints of my Lord entering our reality, taking what she pleases, and returning to her world until the season returns."

"Season?"

"The opening between our worlds occurs naturally, but the duration and scope cannot be predicted. Until now. Historically, many of the seasons with larger openings and longer durations coincide with mass extinctions."

"Hold on," Rook said with a laugh he couldn't hold back. "You're telling me these assholes are what killed the dinosaurs?"

Fossen shook his head. "They merely contributed to it."

"Then why in the name of Ronald Reagan's undescended right testicle would you help with something like that?" Rook's patience ran out. "Oh right, Lord Fruitloop."

Fossen seemed to absorb the comment with just a moment's discomfort. "Because, with my help, the portal will remain open indefinitely. Our worlds will become one, and everyone will serve the Lord Fenrir."

"Right, with you at *her* right hand." Rook hadn't missed that Fossen's God was feminine.

"As promised."

Rook was almost free of the plastic cuffs. "Listen buttercup, if there is one thing I've learned about megalomaniacs—human or otherwise—it's that they'll say, do and promise just about anything to achieve their goals. You're being duped."

"If you would only open your eyes and see—"

"You know they make big comic book conventions for people like you, right?" Rook said. "You'd fit right in. Pop on a pair of rubber Vulcan ears and you'd be all set. Maybe hook up with a Ferengi. I think they're ugly as shit, but you seem to have low standards."

Fossen grinned and shook his head. "Oh, Stanislav. I will miss your sense of humor." The door to the room opened and Asya walked in calmly, holding another Walther pistol in her hand, trained on Rook.

Rook's momentum toward his escape was derailed the moment he saw Asya. At first, he thought she was in on it with Fossen, but then he saw the wooden way she walked and the glazed look in her eyes.

Fossen went back to his laptop. "Take him."

Asya stepped behind Rook and cut the plastic zip tie with a small knife she produced with her free hand. She shoved him hard in the spine with the gun and said simply "Go."

He left the room and entered the main chamber with the glowing sphere—a *doorway*, he thought—and Asya motioned him toward a tunnel on the left. He hoped for a second that this was all some ploy on her part to rescue him. Maybe she was just pretending to be under the spell of the pheromones. As they left the light from the main chamber and pressed on into the darkness of the tunnel, he tried whispering to her, but she made no response other than to poke him repeatedly in the spine with the Walther.

He planned to attack her on the next poke, but she spoke to him instead.

They tumbled together, a mass of black and white bodies and limbs.

The world spun around King. He had no sense of where he was, only that he was rolling, far, with no way to stop.

While King careened across the roof, another three dire wolves emerged from the stairwell and headed for Deep Blue.

King withdrew his knife from the monster's eye with a wet squelch. The motion flipped him free and he struck the concrete roof on his stomach, sliding on his body armor. The edge of the roof over 6th was fast approaching. Slapping his hands down on the roof, King threw his body weight laterally, away from the dire wolf.

The dead dire wolf reached the end of the concrete roof and bumped up and over the six-inch high decorative wall before dropping down to the street. King scraped his knife blade across the concrete roof and spun his body just in time to plant his feet against the low wall and stop his slide toward doom.

One of the three dire wolves chasing Deep Blue let loose with the bone-shaking roar, and King once again discovered he possessed some kind of immunity to the auditory attack. He pushed himself up onto his hands and knees.

Deep Blue and the first dire wolf caromed across the roof, the dire wolf clawing at the man. Deep Blue stabbed back with a bayonet. The roof shook beneath them, knocking everyone down. They rolled and tumbled across the concrete as King struggled to give chase on the suddenly uneven surface of the roof.

"King! The roof is collapsing! Get over here!" King raced across the roof and noted the other two dire wolves bounding toward him in his periphery.

Deep Blue slashed at the dire wolf attacking him. It flailed and struggled.

King leapt atop the dire wolf and pinned the creature's head down on the ground. Deep Blue sank the bayonet onto the creature's eye.

"Go! Go!" Deep Blue struggled to his feet and lurched.

King nearly fell as the roof shifted beneath him again.

Oh my God. It's the whole building!

Deep Blue ran for the edge of the building over West 50th Street. "The portals are gone! The building is collapsing! Black Three, deploy! I repeat, deploy! And get the fuck out of our way—" The man reached the end of the building and showed no signs of slowing down. King raced after his friend, mentor and the former President of the United States of America, as the man leapt right off the roof of a 52-story-tall Manhattan skyscraper.

The dire wolves were right behind King as he reached the end of the building and without a second thought, leapt off the building and into the air, 750 feet over the city street, as the skyscraper slid backward and away from his jump. The distance his leap took him out and away from the edge of the building appeared to be super-human, but the building was collapsing—tumbling away beneath him, dumping tons of glass, steel and concrete on West 49th and the troops waiting down below.

As he fell toward the asphalt far below him, King had time to note two things that were more terrible than falling to his death for over 700 feet.

The first was that about half way down the plunge, a black Sikorsky UH-60 Black Hawk helicopter was hovering above the street, directly under Deep Blue and King, its rotor blades waiting to grind them like two scoops of ice cream in a blender.

The second thing was worse. The two dire wolves had followed him off the roof. They fell just above him, claws extended and reaching for his exposed face.

FORTY-EIGHT
Somewhere

BISHOP STRUGGLED TO comprehend what he was seeing. Everything around him appeared to be a salmon shade of orangey pink. The sky was so pallid it made him nauseous to look at it. The ground was covered in chunks and oblong protruding mounds of rocky grit. As far as he could see, the landscape was uniform. Lumps and bumps, but no mountains and no trees. No water and nothing moving.

He was on his hands and knees, disgorging the contents of his stomach onto the peculiar pasty colored soil, when he heard movement behind him. He still had two MP5s strapped to his body, but he couldn't access them quickly from his position on the ground.

He scooped up a handful of the strange grit on the ground in his left hand, as if he was struggling to stay on his hand and knees. The truth was that after vomiting, his body felt far better adjusted to the strange sights. He was almost back to normal. He just hadn't gotten up yet. He pulled a knee up, as if in agony, but actually hoped to spring up to his feet. Then he slowly dragged his right hand under his body, as if he was holding his stomach in agony. Instead, he pulled the handle of his SOG SEAL knife from its sheath on his massive armored chest. He had formerly relied on a KA-BAR, like the rest of the team, but since Deep Blue had formed Endgame and taken over the old Manifold base as a headquarters in New Hampshire, Bishop had started field-testing lots of different equipment for fun. Deep Blue obtained what he felt was the best of the best for the team, and the base had racks of armaments from which to choose. Bishop had found the 12-inch knife with the 7-inch blade and instantly fell in love. On a smaller man, the size of the knife might have made it unwieldy. But Bishop was a mountain of a man.

The noise scuffed again, just behind him.

Bishop sprang up, whirling in a 180 degree circle. It wouldn't be the first time he shocked an opponent with how quickly a man of his size could move.

His hand came whistling around, spraying the soil at the eyes of the dire wolf, which stood just taller than Bishop did. His second hand followed through on the spin and sliced out with the SOG blade. The edge raked across the beast's chest, and the creature let loose with its natural defense mechanism—the devastating aural attack that made the thick bones in Bishop's body vibrate as if they were about to explode.

Under normal circumstances, the roar would paralyze an opponent. Fear would course through their bodies at the fight-or-flight reflex the roar triggers. But Bishop had just the one major fear. It dwarfed everything else and was a fear he lived with every day. When Chess Team had first gone up against Richard Ridley's Manifold Genetics company, they had captured Bishop and experimented on him at the genetic level. Bishop had been transformed into a 'Regen.' He had developed amazing regenerative abilities, healing from minor wounds in seconds and could even grow back severed limbs like a salamander. But those amazing abilities had come with a heavy price. Each time his body regenerated, his mind lost a shred of his humanity until he became nothing more than a raging monster. He had battled the condition with meditation and eventually with a crystal from the Neanderthal city of Meru in Vietnam, which had negated the rage effects he felt with a combination of vibrations and ionization. He didn't buy into things like crystals and UFOs, but the one from Meru worked, and that had been clear to everyone.

Ultimately, his genetic structure had been fixed, removing the regenerative abilities, and with them the likelihood that he would transform into a raving maniac again. But the fear never left him.

The nightmares came nearly every night. He put on a good façade for the team, but inside he lived with the constant worry that he would one day lose control and start killing every living person around him. He lived with the fear that he would eat their bloodied corpses like a deranged African lion, pulling and tearing at the flesh in long strips and unrecognizable chunks.

The dire wolf in front of him wasn't finished howling when the fight-or-flight reflex in Bishop manifested. But for Bishop with his fear of losing all control, the reflex simply made him hallucinate that he had. He lunged forward before the dire wolf had closed its mouth and before it could move. Bishop grabbed the beast around the back of its head and sank his teeth into the creature's throat, ripping and tearing at the white translucent skin. Fluid filled Bishop's mouth as he continued to bite and tear at tendons pulled as tight as piano wires. His powerful meaty hands clutched the back of the dire wolf's head, so it couldn't escape.

The creature backpedaled, and fell over in shock, dead before it could hit the rocky salmon soil. Bishop rode the falling creature to the ground, but even the impact couldn't dislodge him.

He didn't stop eating for a long time.

FORTY-NINE
Outside, Fenris Kystby, Norway
3 November, 2330 Hrs

QUEEN MOVED AWAY from the trap door, back in the direction she had traveled underground in the tunnels and the labs. The snow drifted to above her knee in places. She found it hard to believe this much snow had fallen in just a few hours. The landscape was completely different from how it had been when Rook led her and Asya down to the secret hatch.

She moved steadily through the snow, heading toward what she expected would be a much more obvious entrance back into the facility. The room with the giant metal cage had huge hangar-style doors. She knew they must open to the outdoors somewhere. The land was hilly with small rises and valleys, but she moved at a rapid pace, despite the snow. She kept looking back, waiting for the white-skinned creatures to appear. They would blend perfectly into the snowy landscape—natural camouflage. But she knew they couldn't see properly with any kind of obstacles in the air. The sleet would play havoc with their perceptions. They might even still be back at the hatch.

She couldn't waste time. She needed to get closer to the hangar doors—wherever they were—and then find a place to make a stand. If the snow and sleet stopped, those things would be after her.

Queen crested a small rise, and ahead she could see a rectangular hill in the snow, which looked to be about four or five feet taller than the rest of the hill. *Like a bunker*, she thought.

She moved toward the shape, at times in snow almost up to her hips. As she got closer, she could see that her original thought about a bunker wasn't far off. The structure was a gray concrete, although it was difficult to see it clearly, as she approached it. Snow coated its flat roof. Small ice crystals clung to the vertical sides of the building. Its most notable feature from a distance was the small window set into the side of one wall. Light poured out of the tiny window like blasting rays of the sun.

When she reached the wall, she could see decorative swastikas carved into the cement. The bunker had the look of a WWII-era German structure. Each symbol was perfectly centered above a feature of the building—one above the small window, which was too small to climb through and not much larger than her face, and the other above a long-since-rusted metal door. The symbols had faded with time and weather, and upon closer inspection, it looked like someone had made a concerted effort to chip them away. The small bunker-like building sat atop a hill, exposing Queen to harsh winds. The top of the building's roof, just a few feet above the snow, was mostly clear of piled snow, blown away by the wind.

She inched close to the window, but couldn't make out anything more than the blisteringly bright light that streamed out, making the rest of the un-illuminated area around the bunker darker by comparison. She swept away the snow covering the door and discovered it was covered by earth as well. The upper hinge was on the outside of the door. There would be no way to get the thing open. It reminded her of the double doors in one of the abandoned labs that Rook had shown her. That room had a small window that was covered over almost entirely by soil and snow, too. She hadn't seen that window on her way to this hill. She assumed it would be completely covered by snow now.

The snow was letting up. Her hand began to throb and swell. Her gloves were long gone, so she reached into a pocket of her jacket and pulled out the fleece headband she had worn earlier to hide her brand. Her ears were cold too, but they would have to wait. She needed her hand. She used her teeth and ripped the fleece along its seam, and then wrapped her broken hand with it, using it like a bandage.

With the additional warmth and support from the fleece, she then wrapped the wire around her hand again, to use it as a garrote, when the time came. Then she looked again at the way the window cast light onto the snow and had an idea. She moved to the side of the window and began to scoop snow away from the bottom of the huge drift against the side wall. Soon she had to get on her hands and knees to move the snow out of the makeshift cave she was creating. The hole would be just large enough for her to squat in, and the top would come just a few inches under the top of the snow drift. The snow packed nicely, and she could tell that the roof wouldn't collapse in—at least not until she needed it to. Once she could fit inside the small shelter, she started scooping more snow, but this pile she placed at the entrance, sealing herself in. By the time she was nearly done, Queen was soaked with sweat. She hoped the white beasts didn't have a good enough sense of smell that they could detect her even through the natural sensory countermeasure provided by the falling snow.

She left a small window at the top of her doorway, about three inches in height—just enough for her to see out and into the field of light the window of the building provided. She could see that the sleet had lessened and turned into a light gentle flow of large, two-inch snowflakes. She had never seen such large flakes—not even in the Arctic islands of Russia, several degrees north of where she was now in Fenris Kystby. The flakes fell, but they lessened in intensity. The beasts would be coming soon. She would have to work quickly. This last part was delicate. She used the end of her electrical wire to gently prod holes in the ceiling of her snow cell. One wouldn't be enough. She made a dozen holes, enough to see the roofline above her drift.

The bunker was a natural rise. The roof would provide a natural vantage point. She suspected that at least one of the creatures would utilize both it and the light the window cast onto the snowy valley below the bunker. She saw movement through her roof holes, as one of the monsters moved past her line of sight to crouch on the edge of the roof and scan the valley below with its bizarre head cocked askew and the large reptilian eye rotating on the side of its head.

She could also see movement outside her door. At least two of them. A gust of wind howled across the hill, bringing a curtain of white sweeping along the ground with it, like nature's broom, sweeping things clean.

The movement outside the door ceased. Queen checked through the peepholes in her roof. The squatting creature above her remained locked in place, its powerful chest and arms perfectly still.

They wouldn't move until the gust of wind stopped blowing snow around.

Now.

Queen tensed on her bent legs and thrust up through the roof of her snow cave, launching her body onto the concrete roof of the bunker and rolling in one swift move. The big white monster turned its head, but it was too late. Queen leapt onto its back and threw her cord over its head, pulling tightly with both hands and leaning back like she was riding a mechanical bull at a Texas dive bar.

The beast stood and wobbled backward as it clutched at its throat and the thick insulated cord that was cutting off its air flow.

Needing to breathe is a bitch, ain't it? she thought, and held on harder as the twitching, bucking creature began to flail uncontrollably around the roof of the small 10 foot square bunker.

There were two more creatures in the dooryard of the building, illuminated brightly by the window, but snow still fell, obscuring their sense of the world.

Queen pulled her knees up and rammed them against the monster's spine, using her powerful leg muscles to add thrust to the pull of the wire across the throat.

The creature was out of air and out of time. It staggered closer to the front of the building, and tipped over the lip, head first, with Queen riding its back like a trick equestrian. They dropped toward one of the stationary beasts and at the last second, Queen abandoned her cord and leapt off the falling creature's back. As it hit the snow, she struck the head of a second beast, digging her thumb straight into its large tennis-ball like eye. The sound it made was horrendous. Not the roar that had incapacitated her earlier, with fear and trauma hallucinations, but a screeching wail of pain and dismay. She wrapped her broken hand around the other side of the thing's head as a white jelly-like substance juiced over the thumb of her attacking hand. This beast was going down too, and she rode it into the snow, then rolled.

As soon as she landed in the drift, she moved her head up to check on the location of the third white creature, and then she froze in place. A few feet away, it twisted its head, swiveling its eyes in alternating directions, trying to make sense of the white noise wreaking havoc with its strange senses.

She stood slowly.

Confidently.

Then the last beast let loose its dreadful roar. She was expecting it this time; she knew that one or all of them would try to use the roar. She didn't know how it worked, but she knew it had been responsible for her flashbacks and hallucinations last time.

Even expecting it this time, it brought her down, trembling in fear. Tears filled her eyes.

Her body shook more violently from the fear than from the cold, but the hallucinations did not attack her mind.

She knew where she was and what was going on around her, but she was scared shitless.

Drawn to her emotional fallout, as though it could *smell* her fear, the beast swiveled its eyes in her direction. It opened its maw slowly, showing a mouthful of jagged pointy teeth, all sharp and long in the front. Her fear spiked again and she shrieked.

The beast stalked toward her.

The snow stopped.

She watched in horror as the last flakes floated to the ground.

The creature opened its mouth wide enough to engulf her head. The muscles beneath its clear cheeks coiled. The jaws looked powerful enough to pulverize her skull.

The only response she could manage was a scream, but it wasn't simply a primal fear response. It was a name. And it lent her strength. "Rook!"

****

for miles. At the bottom of the cliff, the land went flat again, sweeping out as far as he could see, but the ground wasn't featureless, it was pocked with what looked like impact craters. Thousands of them. All different sizes.

He looked behind him, searching for craters. He couldn't see any, but the land was so flat and devoid of features that he could be within a mile of one and never know it was there.

He peered over the edge of the cliff again. A flicker of movement caught his attention—a small moving spot near the base of the cliff. Something living. It climbed up the cliff close to where Bishop stood.

Bishop considered his options. Climb down, walk forever to the left, walk forever backward, or walk forever to the right, toward the pinnacle of rock on the horizon. Maybe get a better vantage point. Maybe see another portal somewhere.

The final option was to wait for the climbing thing and see if it could reach the top of the cliff. The ground along the edge was scattered with large rocks and even a few boulders. Bishop had no doubt that he could nudge one of the rocks over, crushing and killing whatever was climbing the cliff face if it presented any danger. He was also sure it wasn't a dire wolf. It wasn't white, but rather was a grayish pink. Like it was coated in the salmon dust of this place.

Bishop peeked over the edge again, to look at the thing. He couldn't see it clearly enough yet to figure out what it might be. It just looked like a speck. He walked a few yards to the right until he was directly above it, then found a good-sized boulder nearby and sat down on it. He let his gaze sweep the distant plains and the craters below the cliff.

A portal appeared, far away on the horizon. The thing looked no bigger than a marble but cast its bright light far across the orange plain. He didn't think it was dark out there until he saw the portal appear, then, with its new brilliance added to the scene, he realized how dim things had been.

Several streaks of dust appeared from far off on the right, blazing direct paths toward the portal. *Dire wolves.* He considered making for the portal himself, but it was far. It would take him hours—maybe even days—to climb down the cliff and run across the plain. He leaned over the edge of the drop to check on the climbing thing. It was moving, but too far down to tell what it was or guess at its size. Bishop looked at his watch and then looked back to the portal on the pink-hued orange horizon. Suddenly the streaks in the soil from the dust clouds left in the wake of the dire wolves reappeared. This time they moved from the portal back toward the far right of his view until they disappeared. Then the portal winked out. Bishop looked at his watch. Four minutes had elapsed.

Weird. The portals were staying open for much longer back home.

Then he noticed the spot where the portal had been. A crater was left in its wake. He thought about what he had seen and what it meant. Breathing slowly, he allowed himself to fall into a meditative state. When he came out of it, he looked down the cliff again to check on the progress of the climber.

He moved back to his boulder and smiled. He knew several things now. Wherever the dire wolves were coming from, it was to his right, along the cliff's edge up toward the pinnacle or tower of rock. He didn't know if it was a natural formation or not. He looked at the rise again and concentrated on its shape. It didn't matter. If it was a natural formation, he'd have a better view from the top of it and could more easily spot the enemy. High ground was rarely a bad thing. If it wasn't a natural formation, then he would have *found* the enemy. Either way, the solitary tower was his next destination.

He also knew why there were craters here. They were the aftermath of portals having opened and closed. The plains were covered with craters, no two overlapping, with tracks of flat land between them wide enough for a racing horde of dire wolves. Very few free spaces remained. That's how he would get home. Find the dire wolf source, do what he could to stop them, and then try to anticipate the next portal's appearance by going to a spot on the plains with no craters. It wasn't much of a plan, but it was all he had, and it felt good to have that at least.

Finally, he knew what the climbing thing was, and he settled back on his boulder to wait for it. He checked his watch. Another ten minutes passed, when he saw movement at the edge of the lip of the cliff. The thing struggled up over the ledge and rolled onto the ground at the top, just a yard away from where Bishop sat cross-legged on top of his smooth orange boulder.

The thing was humanoid, with thick boots caked in the salmon grime of this place's ground. Dust also coated its body, and Bishop could see it didn't wear much in the way of clothing. The hair on the head was long—well past the shoulders, tangled and matted, not too different from a jungle boy in a Tarzan film. It lay on its back, breathing hard from the exertion of its climb.

"It's about fuckin' time, Knight." Bishop said with a grin.

The feral thing rolled to a crouch and looked up at Bishop through the filthy hair. "Bishop? How did you find me? How long have I been here?"

"By my watch, we've been here for around eleven hours, but by the looks of you, you've been here a lot longer. You okay?"

Knight stood slowly and Bishop took in the sight of him. The man was wearing shorts—the BDU pants he had worn under his armor, but the legs had been cut off. No shirt, and the rest of the armor was gone. Aside from being filthy and coated in grime, the thing that struck Bishop the most was that while Knight had been a wiry fellow before, he was now much better built. His muscles bulged as if he spent a lot of time pumping iron at the gym. And Knight's hair was longer than it had been earlier that day—about two years of unchecked growth longer. Knight's hair came down below his armpits.

The two men appraised each other.

"I'm okay. I just didn't think I'd be seeing you. Or anyone. I think I've only slept two times, so I should have only been here for a couple of days." Knight sounded clear-headed, but he wasn't making much sense.

"Shin, your hair is down below you armpits and you look like Mowgli the Korean Jungle Man. Your clothes are rags. You must have been here longer than that. Time is funny on this side. I've already figured that out."

"Huh," Knight grunted. "My watch broke. It only felt like a few nights. Hard to tell day from night, if this place even has one, what with everything being blue."

Bishop looked around the landscape at the pink and orange hues, then back to Knight. "Remember what Black Five said about other dimensions not following the same laws of physics? I think maybe our brains are having a hard time comprehending things here. Because I'm looking at everything around us—the sky, the ground, even you—and all I see are shades of orange."

"Orange?" Knight looked around him, then back at Bishop. "I see midnight blue."

Bishop was about to offer a theory on why they perceived different colors when he noticed something on Knight's back. A backpack. A very full backpack. He hadn't noticed it before because Knight's long hair covered the straps over his shoulders.

He pointed to the pack. "What's this?"

Knight grinned. "You know I hate failing missions."

FIFTY-TWO

Gleipnir Facility, Fenris Kystby, Norway
3 November, 2330 Hrs

EIREK FOSSEN WALKED into to the main lab, looking up at the ball of light that filled him with a sense of awe and power. The portal glowed brightly, larger now, but still not its full size. A few dire wolves moved slowly around the room, sniffing at the air. The Russian woman, Asya, stood quietly by the portal, smiling in the Lord's bliss.

He had told the other staff members to retire to their quarters. The pheromones made them highly suggestible. By the time its influence began to wear off and they ventured back into the lab, it would be too late.

He stared up at the glowing portal, feeling the warmth of it washing over his face. It was beautiful. Up close, the brilliance of the light was painful to his eyes; his eyelids kept trying to shut, but he willed them open until tears flowed from his face. Every time he looked at it, he remembered his one and only trip through to the other side. The colors. The landscape. The dire wolves. And *Fenrir*. He hadn't spoken to the Lord in two days. He ached to hear from Her again. Or was she a him? He honestly didn't know, but preferred to think of Her as being female. Men just weren't that beautiful.

He didn't really have anything to report. The portal wouldn't grow to sufficient size for hours yet, but he couldn't wait to hear from Her again.

He knelt on the floor and bowed his head.

One of the dire wolves came over to him and sniffed the air around him, cocking its head left and right, its huge eyes dilating from the brilliance of the portal. Then it stepped up to the wall of the energy sphere and through it.

Fossen remained kneeling on the concrete floor. His knees and shins protested, but he refused to move. Minutes passed and he stayed still, allowing his thoughts to empty, until he focused only on his breathing.

Then it came, as he knew it would. The hairs on the back of his neck raised and the skin on his arms tightened with gooseflesh.

The voice.

Her voice.

Is it ready, Fossen?

The voice was just above a whisper, but it slid through his mind like a snake. Fossen knew the voice was only in his head, and that it came from the portal. But it sounded like she stood right next to him, uttering the words into his ear. He knew that wasn't the case. If the weak-willed lab techs were in the room, they would hear nothing. But Fossen could hear Her in his mind. Only he and a select few others, like Schröder and Edmund Kiss, had been able to hear it, at first like a nagging thought in the dark recesses of the subconscious, and later something more. Fossen loved that voice with every part of his being.

"Soon, My Lord. Soon. The portal should be ready in several hours. It is still growing, but we have enough energy to open it to the full size and keep it open and stable. All our work is nearly complete."

You will be rewarded.

"Thank you, my Lord," Fossen hesitated. "We have had some problems, though. Three intruders."

I am aware.

Of course She is, Fossen thought, but continued his report anyway, if only to extend the length of their conversation. "One is now contained and another is here with me, under Your influence."

I feel her, he thought. A shiver run through his body. His mouth watered. He shared Her hunger.

And the third? The voice grew serious.

"The dire wolves are dealing with her outside. She poses little threat."

I do not wish to have anything upset our plans, Fossen. I will send more of my children. They will find her.

Fossen nodded. Of course.

I will join you soon, Fossen. We will not be apart much longer.

Fossen raised his head to see dire wolves coming out of the portal. As they emerged, the first sniffed the air and looked at him. He pointed in the direction of the door leading to the outside of the facility. The dire wolf loped on all fours toward the door. And then they kept coming, following the first toward the door.

Fossen lost count after thirty arrived and more kept coming.

"Will you send all of them, my Lord?"

These are but a few grains of sand from the beach, Fossen.

FIFTY-THREE
Gleipnir Facility, Fenris Kystby, Norway

ASYA FOUGHT THE wave of happiness overwhelming her. Being Russian, she wasn't accustomed to such radiant joy. It fit her like a too-tight sweater, choking her at the neck and chafing in her armpits. She struggled to comprehend how she had become so delighted with life. When she focused on the issue, she could remember Rook, the pit with the dead things and marching Rook at gunpoint back to the pit filled with the little corpses. It was harder to remember how she had become so happy. When she thought about the round wall of light, she felt only warmth and contentment. And then she would forget—everything—and would have to start over, by focusing on Rook.

When thinking back to Rook, and how she met him, and how she had come to this place, it made her angry. The anger countered the bliss. That, and the anger and the frustration felt more natural for her. More Russian. So, she stopped trying to focus on Rook and instead turned her attention to the abduction of her parents.

The thought that someone would take her mother and father filled her with a deep rage. That the same people would abduct her and take her aboard a ship—the ship on which she had met Rook—bound for who knew where, filled her with a desire for vengeance.

Things had gone easily for Asya as a child. But as adulthood had neared, she was given two choices: ballet, for which she had a natural talent, or medicine. Both options would be well respected and would allow her to move from the middle class to the upper echelons of stardom, or at least cement her role in the new Russian middle class.

She had shocked her family by choosing the army instead.

Her athletic abilities helped her excel in combat training, but she was too defiant to rise in the ranks, and was already hindered by the fact that she was a woman. She wasn't interested in rank, anyway. She just wanted a real experience in her life. She served her time in the infantry, and then when the chance came to leave the service, she did. She traveled around Russia and even went abroad a few times. She thought about settling down somewhere, but for now, she had been happy to keep on the move and see some sights. She was almost to that place she had been seeking—a place of inner contentment bred from pleasure with the decisions she had made instead of those decisions made for her. Then the men that Rook had killed captured her on the streets of Murmansk.

A life interrupted. Her life, interrupted.

The anger she felt filled her like an inflating blimp. She let it rise, pushing out any semblance of happiness. She could now picture the attack on Rook and the anger she'd felt toward the mob. She pictured the people and the injuries they had sustained. She understood now, after having been forced by her bliss to march Rook to the pit, that the others had been under the influence of the glowing wall of light as well.

She became furious.

An entire village of people. Controlled. Their lives stolen. Brutalized!

She let all of it feed her anger. As though a hypnotist had just snapped his fingers, her mind returned in a flash.

Asya Machtcenko opened her eyes and found she was sitting in a chair, in a dark room. It was a computer lab with several desk workstations and flat-screen monitors. All sensations of being controlled were gone. She recalled sending Rook to his doom in the pit. She also remembered handing him the LED and telling him not to drop it. She hoped he had listened to her.

And where is Queen? she wondered.

She got up and looked down at herself. At some point, she had put on a white lab coat. She grimaced. *I am no man's lackey.* She was about to take it off, but changed her mind. It might help her move through the lab unnoticed. She needed to get to Rook and see if she could help him.

How long have I been under its control? How long have I been unaware of the things around me?

She stood and scanned the computer displays. They were all on, even though no one sat at any of the stations. She wondered idly where all the money for this equipment had come from. Rook had said the town was remote and they didn't even have telephones or wireless coverage. The entire lab was covert and underground. To Asya's way of thinking, a government had to be involved. Possibly even her own.

None of the information on the displays—having to do with the weather outside the lab, the giant, curved metal cage and power levels in a 'receptor'—meant much to her. She crossed the floor to the room's only door. She opened it slowly and walked out in a very slow, dreamlike shuffle. She let the focus in her eyes loosen, careful not to stare at anything in particular. Walking was difficult at first, but the more steps she took, the easier it became.

The massive glowing sphere cast brilliant light from the center of the room. She intentionally stayed on the edge of the cavernous space, avoiding the influence of the sphere, but not appearing to do so.

She didn't see any people, but there were a few of the white creatures with the spooky eyes moving around the chamber. They looked at her with their heads turned awkwardly to the side, *almost far enough to break their own necks*, she thought, *unless they can turn their heads all the way like owls.*

She continued her dazed walk, noting whenever a creature would move in her peripheral vision, but none of them advanced on her position. They just seemed restless to her. When she reached the tunnel where she'd deposited Rook in the pit, she moved past it. She realized that she had no way to get him out of the pit.

If he was still alive.

She wanted to hurry, but the lingering creatures might notice. She needed to find a rope or something she could use to help Rook. *Something I can conceal in this coat.*

She moved to the office where she recalled cutting the plastic bands on Rook's wrists that attached him to the chair. She also recalled the gun the man had. It wasn't a rope, but if it was still in the room, she would take it. She checked her pockets and found that the gun she had held on Rook and the knife she had used to cut him free were missing. She didn't remember anyone taking those things from her, but neither could she recall giving them up.

The office was empty. No knife, no guns and even the laptop the man had used was gone. She waited in the office for a minute so it looked like she had a reason for being there if the white *watchers*, as she thought of them, were intelligent and paying attention to her movements.

Then she left the room and started around the circumference of the great room again. A few of the watchers were still in the massive space, but some of them were gone. She tried to look covertly around the room as she shuffled along the wall, looking for another place to explore. The next door was labeled with a mop and bucket symbol on the door and the legend: *Freiheitsstrafe Schrank.* She realized it was German for a Janitor closet. She didn't think she would find a rope in there, but it might do for her to check on the way back.

The next door was more promising. It had a legend of a lightning bolt on it and the word: *Sicherheitsraum*. It was one of the few German words she knew. The first part meant "security" and the *-raum* portion meant "room." She calmly walked in and closed the door behind her before reaching for a light switch.

She flicked on the light and stifled a scream.

For the second time in one day, she had illuminated the space around her to find it full of bodies.

FIFTY-FOUR
Endgame Headquarters, White Mountains, NH

The mood in the subterranean base was grim as everyone packed up for a war. Deep Blue and King had returned to the base in the Black Hawk and found the White Team members just finishing packing up. The *Persephone* was loaded up with weaponry, more of the armored suits and computer arrays. By the time the Black Hawk touched down outside the *Central* section's enormous hangar door, Deep Blue was pleased to note that Lewis Aleman was installed in a computer station inside the VTOL plane's midsection. He would be monitoring the situation from inside the plane as it sat on the pavement, instead of inside the base.

Callsign: Black Seven, and his brother, Black Eight, the team's mechanics, refueled the vehicle outside the hangar, readying it for the trip to Norway. Neither man spoke to him as he walked past them, which Deep Blue appreciated. They were focused on their job, even if it wasn't the most glorious of positions.

The five members of the White security team, with callsigns White One through White Five, were stationed around the crescent-shaped transport ship, each man in snow-battle armor and armed with white-coated Mk 17 FN SCAR assault rifles. They each looked vigilant and angry.

Good, Deep Blue thought. *Be angry and use that in Norway if you get a chance.*

Each man was from the 10th Mountain Division at Fort Drum, and there were no better men for an arctic or alpine assault force than 10th men. The White team was specifically tasked with duties at the Endgame base, and these men were tasked with keeping the base secure. In any other circumstance, they would be staying behind, protecting Fiona and Sara, keeping support team members like Lewis Aleman and even himself safe from any attack by hostile forces. What the Chess Team field members—King, Queen, Bishop, Knight and Rook—did out in the world was difficult enough, without having to worry about the people you loved or the sanctity of your home. But this situation was desperate; the entire world was in danger, and Deep Blue had two members of Chess Team already missing and presumed dead. Another two members were already on site in Norway, but he had no idea if they were alive, captured or in the thick of things. Anna Beck, callsign: Black Zero, and Deep Blue's covert operative, Black Six, were en route to Norway now.

The newly christened Endgame organization was scattered, and he didn't yet know what to expect from this stabilized portal in the Arctic. He wanted every resource close and readily available. As he approached the hangar door, which he'd had to have refitted after a security incident earlier in the year, he saw Matt Carrack approaching him. Carrack, callsign: White Zero, was the head of base security and Deep Blue's right hand in all things since his promotion to the role the previous summer. The man looked the part of his callsign, with his all-white Arctic gear and his weapons covered in white cloth wraps as well. Like the other security team members, Carrack wore the white version of the experimental impact-resistant armor. He carried his helmet under one arm as he approached Deep Blue.

"Sir. We're just about ready to go. King is inside with Jet and Professor." Carrack was referring to Sara Fogg by her security codename of Jet—a sly reference to her spiky black hair, likening her to the rock singer Joan Jett. Fiona had a security codename of Professor, because of her linguistic abilities. Neither woman was aware of the names, chosen by Carrack. The men studiously avoided using the names around the two.

Deep Blue looked at the man and nodded. He understood. King was saying goodbye. Just in case. "That's fine, Zero." In the field now, Deep Blue would refer to Carrack by his callsign, where he would normally refer to the man as Matt—one of the few team members with whom he would be so personal.

"The pilots and Black Five are aboard, as is Aleman. Rome—" Carrack had deemed George Pierce, callsign: Rome, "—is staying behind with Jet, Professor and the rest of Black Team. I'd prefer to have at least one security member with them, but I understand it's not possible."

Deep Blue nodded. "It's not."

Carrack continued. "Black One and Two will rendezvous with us just past Iceland. I'm ready to seal the base on your word. I have all the equipment you'll need waiting for you on the plane."

"Okay, just give me a minute with King." Deep Blue left the man standing on the pavement and stepped into the dim hangar.

Deep Blue looked into the glassed-in office at the back of the hangar, just in time to see Fogg and Fiona unwrap their arms from around him. A group hug. The man was lucky. Tom Duncan had always been single, even as President. And he hadn't had time to think about dating since.

No one in the office was speaking. Deep Blue walked up to the door and stuck his head inside the room.

"Am I interrupting?" He could see that their faces were drawn and tight.

Fogg wiped a stray tear from her eye. She looked at Deep Blue and said, "If you come back without him, I'll—"

"Won't happen," Deep Blue said with forced confidence.

To his surprise, Fogg wrapped her arms around his neck and squeezed him tight. "Be careful, Sir."

He felt pressure on his waist and looked down to find Fiona squeezing him. He smiled at King. They were both lucky men.

"Enough of that," King said. "We'll be fine." He leaned down to Fiona and spoke three words Deep Blue didn't understand.

Fiona's reply was just as mysterious. But then King kissed her forehead, kissed Fogg hard on the lips and headed to the door without another word.

Deep Blue followed, asking, "What did you say?" Though he had a pretty good idea.

"She's teaching me to speak Siletz," King explained. "I told her if you came back without me to keep Sara away from you."

Deep Blue laughed. He had always appreciated the team's ability to find humor before entering a lion's den, or in this case, a dire wolf den.

Aleman approached, his face grim.

All the humor Deep Blue felt quickly drained out of him. He had worked with Aleman for a long time now and could read his facial expressions and body language with ease. "What is it?"

Aleman met the two men and looked at the floor, his lips twitching. "Casualty reports from the Exxon Building portal and collapse."

Deep Blue frowned. Casualty reports with just one name on the list were hard to deal with. He knew this report would be far more difficult. But he needed to know. "How many?"

"Two thousand civilians, mostly taken by dire wolves. Despite being in New York, the number is lower than other areas because it appeared so far above the surface."

"Military casualties?" Deep Blue asked.

"Two hundred and climbing. They're still digging through the rubble. But..." Aleman squirmed. "They were able to confirm... Sir, General Keasling—he was below—he..."Aleman shook his head, then met Deep Blue's eyes and used Keasling's first name. "Michael is dead."

THE SOUND OF FURY

FIFTY-FIVE
Fenris Kystby, Norway
4 November, 0100 Hrs

ANNA BECK SHOT out of the sky at 700 mph, in a speed dive. The great thing was, she didn't feel the effects of the jump on her body beyond the sensation of falling—no wind resistance or lack of oxygen. She was plummeting to the Earth from a temporarily retrofitted and recommissioned SR-71 Blackbird, from an altitude of 80,000 feet.

Even in a spacesuit, she wouldn't have wanted to do a high-altitude low-opening (HALO) jump from such a height. But she had something much better than a spacesuit: the high-altitude, low-opening personnel orbital deployment vehicle—or HALOPOD. Resembling a very skinny egg of heat-resistant ceramic, titanium and reinforced carbon-carbon (RCC), which gave the nose of it the same black-snout look that the space shuttle had, the pod was a tiny capsule for a human to ride in. It was nose heavy, and had no motor, so it was basically a bomb.

With a human payload.

Inside the pod, Beck was cushioned in impact foam and a harness that barely allowed her to breathe. The pod performed one duty only. It protected the HALO jumper from the extremes of atmospheric heat.

When she hit an altitude of 15,000 feet, the pod would deploy its own parachute, which would jolt her speed down to a reasonable pace. She had had to sit in a special oxygen chamber with Black Six for hours before the drop, on board the SR-71, while they traveled over the Atlantic. Six was now in his own pod, dropping a hundred feet away from Beck. But she couldn't see him. She couldn't see anything. The HALOPOD had no windows. Even if it did, it was the middle of the night in the high altitude Arctic sky. It was just as dark outside the pod as it was inside. She had only one thing to look at.

She eyed the digital altimeter on the inside of her black helmet's faceplate, inches from her eye. The red LED numbers whirred in a countdown. 30,000 feet. Her speed was 753 mph. *A new world record*, she thought. Although she realized that was only compared to known and recorded feats. That the US Air Force still had commissioned and fully functional SR-71s was news to her, and she had never heard of the HALOPOD either. She wondered how many records had been covertly broken and never reported.

She didn't mind the drop. It was strange to fall for so long, but she was packed in so tightly that she was comfortable. All she had to do was wait. 20,000 feet.

At 15,000 feet, the HALOPOD deployed its parachute and the unpowered vehicle jolted to what felt like a stop in mid air. Beck felt her stomach attempt to crawl out of her throat, but then her mind was on other things. The pod hissed around her. Then small charges set in a seam around the egg vertically, detonated, shooting the two elongated halves of the pod safely away from Beck's body, and leaving her free falling again.

Now free to move her limbs, Beck pulled her arms from her sides and spread her legs, tearing open the Velcro that had kept her limbs glued to her sides. Between her armpits and her legs, the parachute fabric of the wingsuit's wings deployed, giving her the ability to glide in her second descent. The wings scooped the air, and Beck pulled her left arm in a few degrees, adjusting her trajectory. She could see

Black Six ahead of her in the distance, spinning in his yaw axis, because of the lack of any vertical stabilizer on his wingsuit.

Amateur, she thought. *So much for the sexy secret agent.*

As she watched, Black Six, simply pulled his legs and arms together to get out of the spin, and after a second or so, his body repositioned in a straight vertical plunge. He moved his arms and legs out again to scoop the air with his wingsuit, and this time, his movements were perfect.

Huh, Beck thought. *Nice recovery.*

Beck dipped and dove down a little lower and closer to Black Six, then leveled out again. It wasn't as dark as she had expected it would be at this time of night. She couldn't see any auroras, but the sky was a deep blue in places and black in others. The net effect was that visibility was far better than she could have hoped.

The counter in her faceplate kept speeding down and as it reached 5000 feet, she readied herself for the end of her flight. At 4000 feet, she moved her hand toward the pull ring for her parachute. She was supposed to pull at 3000 feet, but when she reached it, she saw that Black Six hadn't pulled his chute yet. She wanted to fall longer than him. She didn't know why she felt competitive toward the man she had only met earlier that day, but she did.

2000 feet and he still hadn't pulled his chute.

At 1000 feet she almost chickened out, but she saw his parachute start to deploy. She gave herself 'one Mississippi' and then pulled her cord. Her parachute yanked her descent into a slow fall. The sky was clear, the stars shone brightly and from the harness of her parachute, Anna Beck began examining the snow-covered ground of her landing site. But then she thought she saw something and she blinked to clear her eyes. She stared at the snow below her, squinting to see if she could spot it again. Movement. Lots of movement.

As she came down to within 100 feet of the snow-covered hillside, she heard Black Six's terrified whisper in her earpiece, breaking the radio silence they were supposed to observe.

"Mother of God, there must be a hundred of them."

He was right. Tearing through the snow 70 feet below her, in the direct path of her landing, there was a small crowd of about ten dire wolves, swarming in one location, jostling and fighting for a spot at the center and being repeatedly shoved back. The other ninety or so streaked through the snowdrifts and tried to get to the crowd from several directions. When Beck got to 50 feet, she thought the dire wolves were fighting, like in a schoolyard brawl.

At thirty feet, she recognized the combatant at the core of the brawl, punching, kicking, flinging and cussing out one dire wolf after another.

"Damn," she said. "That's Queen."

FIFTY-SIX
Over the Arctic Ocean
4 November, 0100 Hrs (Norway Local Time)

THE *PERSEPHONE* RACED through the night sky, ripping a sonic boom over the northern coast of Greenland. Deep Blue sat back in his chair at a computer desk and rubbed his eyes. While he had given up being President of the United States, he found it difficult to give up some of the perks. As President he had been spoiled by the office furniture aboard Air Force One. When he had stepped down, he made sure to kit out the *Crescent* with a luxurious office, complete with all the computing power he would ever need as Deep Blue.

But the Air Force's *Persephone*, the similarly designed ship he rode in now, was more utilitarian. It had bunks for sleeping and cargo-net type chairs for sitting in. The desk he sat at now was a small modular one that Aleman had gotten the White security team to carry aboard. His chair was a cheap office chair from Staples with no armrests. Plus, the ship had a smell to it. A smell he would always associate with the military after his days as a Ranger. Sweat, dirt, rubbing alcohol...and something else he couldn't place. That odd *something else* was always around in every military space he had ever been in, whether buildings, ground vehicles, ships or planes. Over time, he had come to think it was the smell of impending death.

He leaned back in the feeble chair a little further, and twisted his back to get comfortable. Lewis Aleman sat across the room from him at a similar desk with two laptops and a tablet computer arrayed on the small particleboard desk. Deep Blue had tried to get the man to take some sleep, but he had claimed insomnia. Looking at Aleman now, he could believe it. The man had changed into white BDUs like everyone else, and he had showered and shaved, which Deep Blue hadn't bothered to do, but he looked exhausted. Aleman looked more alert than anyone else at this point. Only a few of the others aboard were even awake. Matt Carrack remained awake, while his men slept in the bunks. Even King was asleep.

He looked back at Aleman and sighed. "Anything new?"

"Packers are doing okay."

Deep Blue chuckled. "You're a Green Bay fan?"

"No, I could care less about football." Now it was Aleman's turn to smile. But the smile spoke volumes on how grim the situation was. "But you wanted to know what was new. Most of what I've been seeing here indicates that the basic problem I told you about—the world ending soon from being turned into Swiss cheese by the portals—hasn't changed."

"What's our timeframe look like?" Deep Blue tried to sound unconcerned, like he was asking about the weather. But he had hired Aleman because the man was smarter than anyone he had ever known. He was unlikely to be fooled.

"Two to four days, but probably closer to the two." Aleman's face was grim, all traces of smiles and jocularity gone.

"What? Why? What's happened?" Deep Blue sat up straight in his chair. If he had felt sleepy before, he was wide awake now.

"Seismic activity around the world suggests the existence of portals that we're not seeing. You saw for yourself that some are opening far above the surface of the Earth."

"Oh God, inside the Earth." Deep Blue shook his head. "How deep?"

"No way to know, but a portal in the wrong place could set off massive earthquakes, floods or worst-case scenario, a mega-volcano like the one in Yellowstone park. If that happened, we wouldn't have to wait for the portals to finish chewing up the planet."

Deep Blue could see that Aleman wasn't quite done. "What else?"

"Well, going with the theory that whatever is causing the portal in Norway to stabilize is of human origin, there must be some kind of a receptor. Possibly in the shape of a bowl or a cage. Something that would regulate the size of the portal. Contain it. We won't know what that is until we get there. Also, if the thing is being powered locally, it would take one hell of an energy source too. With that in mind, I checked Arctic satellite scans for the last few weeks, and looked for heat sources. Rook's little town of Fenris Kystby has a huge power plant on the edge of town. I'm guessing that's the target. The *Crescent* is due to rendezvous with us over the Svalbard Archipelago, before we get to the mainland. They're still carrying the nuclear device the UK was going to provide to Bishop and Knight. Their man got there just before Black One was ready to leave. I think if we can't shut this thing down on the ground, we have the *Crescent* nuke the site, destroying the stabilization mechanism and the power plant all in one go."

Deep Blue looked at Aleman for a minute before he spoke. "This is crazy." Aleman looked down at the laptop screen as if his idea had been ridiculed. "No, no. It's a solid contingency plan. Let's just hope we don't have to resort to it. I'm not sure the Norwegians would ever forgive us."

"I'm not sure the Norwegians aren't behind this."

Deep Blue laughed hard. Aleman joined in with him.

FIFTY-SEVEN
Fenris Kystby, Norway, 4 November, 0100 Hrs

ROOK ACTIVATED THE LED backlight on his wristwatch and saw that it was just after one in the morning local time—he'd been down in the pit with the dead for hours.

"Fuckity McFuck Sauce," Rook hissed through his teeth, not for the first time.

He understood that the pheromones from the big energy doorway were controlling Asya the same way the other scientists working for Fossen had been. He also realized that she must have been fighting the pheromone control to some degree. She had given him the little LED flashlight and told him to hold it tightly. He just wished she had been able to stop herself from kicking him down into this hellhole.

He sat on the heap of dead dire wolves and fondled the little plastic light in his hand. He didn't activate it. He had already seen the pit and the bodies. He had scoured every part of the pit looking for a way out. He had tried scaling the walls too, but his bulk was all wrong for delicate rock climbing, and his center of gravity didn't help. Every time he got a few feet up from the pile of mashed dire wolf corpses, he would fall off the wall, landing in the spongy mass. The last time he had cracked his head on the side of the pit, too, and that had put an end to any further climbing attempts.

He sat on the pile with his back against one of the lumpy walls. His head hurt, he was ravenously hungry and his mood was as dark as it ever got. Fossen was up there, opening a freeway for monsters from the outer limits to come destroy the world. Rook's team was on the other side of the planet. He was trapped and helpless.

And Queen was up there somewhere.

Where are you, Zelda? Has that bastard controlled you like Asya? Did you run into a dire wolf? Are you lost?

Rook had done a lot of thinking on Queen during his time in Norway. He knew he had feelings for her. Couldn't deny that any longer. She was smart, bad ass tough, trustworthy and looked good slathered in head-to-toe mud.

He smiled at the memory of the two of them, covered in mud for camouflage, hiding in a tree from a bunch of human-Neanderthal hybrids. Good times. He'd been on the receiving end of Queen's fury that day, too, when she'd mistaken his muddy form for the enemy. But today was different. When he hung up that phone and turned around to see Queen...the look in her eyes. She was hurt. *Queen* was hurt. And he'd done the hurting. He regretted it, but it also confirmed what he suspected.

His growing affection was mutual.

Of course, all the affection in the world did diddly-squat for him right now.

He growled in frustration until his voice was hoarse. Then he heard a scraping noise on the other side of the pit. Something sliding.

Sonovabitch, what now?

He pressed the button on the little LED flashlight and the scene was suddenly as bright as day in the blue-white light. The grayish-white skins of the piled-high genetically engineered dire wolf pups were everywhere. He saw nothing that might have caused sound. Nothing—

A small mound of dire wolf corpses shifted to his left. Then they stopped.

Then the same pile moved again.

Something was moving under the dead monster babies.

Rook played the light around the confined space and the pile of dead shifted again. He stopped breathing and moved a hand over the light to dim it, but not extinguish it entirely. He wasn't afraid. Wasn't capable of it. He was filled with so much seething rage at his confinement that fear didn't exist. The presence of something living in the pit with him filled him with a desire to fight it. He was a hunter now and whatever it was that shared this pit with him, it was *his* prey.

Slowly, Rook moved his legs under him so he could pounce if necessary. The shifting of the mound stopped. He waited, still holding his breath. When it emerged, it happened so fast that Rook fell backward, startled.

A few of the crushed baby dire wolf bodies launched a foot into the air as a furry gray snout erupted from the pile. The creature's head was rounded but with a short elongated snout. Its eyes were beady black specks in its fur, and its nose was a black lump at the front of its head. When it opened its mouth and Rook saw the teeth, he knew without a doubt what it was. He had seen plenty of them in the woods around Fenris Kystby.

Who's afraid of the big, bad wolf? Course, you're bigger and badder than most.

Rook let the light hit the creature fully as it struggled out of the vertical tunnel it had dug through the corpses. The wolf was huge. At least six foot long, with a wet matted coat that was dark in front and gradated to white by the time it reached the hindquarters. Rook had never seen a wolf like this.

The creature had elongated, white-furred legs and no tail. Its front half looked normal, but its back half had powerful muscles that looked almost human. The rear paws weren't paws, but feet. With talons.

Damn, Rook thought. *That batshit Fossen left a half-wolf, half-dire wolf abortion down here to die. Looks like death didn't take.*

Then he realized *he* was the one who'd been left to die. There was no way Fossen didn't know about this beauty. Rook stayed perfectly still, wondering if the creature would attack or not.

Then it opened its huge jaws like a cat yawning—large enough to swallow most of Rook's face. And the thing snarled at him.

Right, that's it for you, Benji.

The hybrid lowered itself, its muscles tensing, preparing to spring. But Rook surprised it. He lunged across the the pit and slammed his body into the startled creature.

The pair crashed against the brick wall. Rook ignored the jarring impact and mashed his head down on the thing's snout as it dug its two-inch-long fangs into his shoulder, which wasn't the best move in hindsight since he helped push the wolf's top canines deeper in the meat of his shoulder. He shouted in pain, but so did the wolf. It released his shoulder, snarling and snapping at Rook's face.

Rook growled, too, as he pummeled the side of its head with his meaty fist, aiming for the soft temple behind the eyes. A hard enough strike should knock the thing out. But it squirmed and flailed, slipping from his grasp.

The creature leapt away and barked at him, then leapt at his throat. Rook tucked his chin and fell back into the soft mound of Fossen's failed experiments, pulling his legs up and kicking the flying wolf up and over him, smashing it into the far wall of the pit.

Rook, still desperately clutching the LED light in his left hand, spun around on the mound to see the beast hit. He was shocked to see the creature violently twist its body in mid air like a cat and land with its hind legs on the wall. The claws dug in, and the thing stayed attached to wall as if he had tossed a spaghetti noodle up to see if it would stick. The strange creature's front legs hung away from the wall. They looked like normal wolf paws, unable to find purchase on the wall. The wolf craned its head up and opened its mouth, showing its teeth. Rook was certain the bastard was smiling at him.

It shot off the wall and rammed his stomach, slamming him back into the wall, where he hit his head yet again.

"That's it!" He shouted. "Time for a fuckin' lupine barbeque." He doused and pocketed the LED light. He wouldn't need it in these close confines, and he needed his left hand free.

Darkness engulfed the pit.

But not all his senses were blind.

The creature smelled horribly, and Rook guessed that he did too. He could hear it breathing and it could probably hear him. They would have no problems fighting each other in the dark.

Rook rolled as the beast snapped at him again, just clipping his forearm with its long muzzle, drawing a line of blood down his arm. He couldn't see it, but he could feel the warm drip. Rook snatched out and grabbed the hybrid by the middle of both of its front legs, and rolled. His arms swung hard and the beast went with them. He slapped the entire creature's body hard against the wall of the pit. While it was stunned, he wrapped his arms around the thing's thin front legs and applied sudden, sharp pressure.

He winced at the sound of breaking bones, but the monster's pain-filled howl drowned out the noise. Feeling merciful now that the creature sounded like any other wounded dog, Rook moved a hand to the creature's neck and then moved his other hand up to join it. The wolf resisted, snapping at him, but it was a half effort. The pain from its broken limbs sapped its fight.

With a violent crack, Rook twisted the head 180° around, and the body slumped in his hands. He dropped the hybrid creature and fished out his LED from his pocket, admiring his handiwork.

"Who's afraid of the big bad Rook?" he grumbled and then felt glad no one had been around to hear that particular gem.

"Now where the hell did you come from?" He moved over to the side of the pit where the thing had clawed its way free from the tiny dire wolf corpses and he found a tunnel.

Rook thought about it for a second. He rationalized that if the creature had gotten into the pit's bottom, there must be an exit out somewhere. It couldn't have just lived down here. There wasn't enough for it to eat. The thing's fur was wet too, so the tunnel must lead to water. He tried to remember any lakes or ponds in the area around the lab, but nothing came to him. Then again, it had been pretty cold for a while, and any nearby lakes must have frozen over.

I'm gonna get halfway down the friggin' tunnel and another one of those things is gonna try to eat my head.

"What the hell," Rook said and then moved over to the hole. He pushed some of the carcasses out of his way so he could slide down the tunnel head first. About a foot under the bodies, the tunnel made an S turn, and he had to struggle, grunt and squeeze to make the turns. He kept the LED illuminated ahead of him and saw that after the S turn, the tunnel widened out and moved upward at a slanting slope. The walls and ceiling were dark damp soil, but the floor was rough with yellow, grainy sand. As his legs came out of the S turn, Rook found he could actually get up to his hands and knees and crawl. It was better than wriggling like a worm.

The tunnel continued to slope upward, but the temperature dropped the further away from the pit he moved. Rook guessed he had gone about three hundred yards when the tunnel widened out to the inside of a large stick structure. Rook quickly recognized it as an abandoned beaver lodge in the rough shape of a dome. The ceiling was still low, but the room was large enough for maybe four adults to lie down side by side. It reminded him of a camping tent.

The wolf was using this for a den after eating Mr. Beaver.

He crossed to the far wall of the circular chamber and found a puddle. He guessed that he'd be able to glide through the underwater beaver tunnel. The only question was, what he would find on the other side? Was the lake or stream or whatever this puddle was connected to, frozen?

Goodbye crazy-ass wolf, hello hypothermia.

"Here goes nothing." Gripping the LED in his teeth, Rook took a deep breath. Then he slid headfirst under the water and kicked with his feet until he was completely submerged in ice cold water.

FIFTY-EIGHT

Gleipnir Facility, Fenris Kystby, Norway
4 November, 0130 Hrs

ASYA IMMEDIATELY RECOGNIZED that the security officers with the glazed over eyes were still breathing. She thought they were dead when she turned on the light. *They were sitting in the dark!*

Even now, after she had come into the room and turned on the light, the four beefy, muscular males in darks slacks, shined shoes, white shirts and gold badges on their chests, didn't move. They sat or slumped in chairs, at desks arrayed around the room. Their eyes were glassy, and they either stared at the screens in front of them or looked off in strange directions around the room like mannequins.

Their uniforms identified them as a security team working for the lab. Asya held her breath. The men still hadn't noticed her.

They must be under control from the light. Lost in bliss.

Arrayed around the room were twenty flat-screen monitors showing footage—live she guessed—from closed-circuit TV cameras around the facility. On the wall was a hard white plastic floor plan of the lab, with the legend *Gleipnir Lab 1*. Past the men, she saw a black metal cabinet the size of a closet at the back of the room.

A weapons locker.

She debated retreating from the room. Instead, she stayed motionless and continued her own glassy-eyed stare. *What will they do? Will they ignore me?*

Then as one, all four men stood abruptly, startling her. They all turned their heads her direction, glaring at her. *Like a flock of birds. Like the villagers.*

She froze in place, tensing her muscles, waiting. She knew they would come. She was suddenly glad Rook and Queen were not here. She wouldn't have to hold back for fear of what they would think of her.

The bulky men lunged at her all at once.

The two furthest from her slammed into each other. Their frenzied attempt to get at her in the narrow space between desks was passionate, but uncoordinated. The other two men, one slimmer and the other heavyset, were closer, and they came straight at her. No finesse. No tactics. They just rushed.

Asya leapt straight up, her knee connecting with the underside of the fat man's chin. His head ricocheted off her knee with an audible *chock*. The man fell over backward, slamming his head hard against the wall. Before she could land from the leap, the taller, thinner man was wrapping his arms around her midsection. She thrust her head back, hitting him in the nose, the cartilage snapping and a gush of crimson flooded out of his nostrils, saturating his white shirt and the back of her hair.

When his grip loosened, Asya swiveled in his arms, facing him. She pushed against the underside of his arms with her hands, and slid down out of his grasp. The man tried to reassert his grip, but she surprised him, by shooting back upward, where he'd held her the moment before. She rammed the flat of her hand into his already injured nose. Blood sprayed. The shattered cartilage drove into his brain, killing him instantly. The man's body fell away from her as she was tackled from behind.

Asya turned as she fell to see one of the two remaining guards. They were both big men with Nordic good looks, short blonde hair and glistening gray eyes. Acne marred their otherwise clear skin, which she assumed to be the result of steroid use. She hit the floor by the doorway and rolled in a crouch to her feet.

The man closer to her took a step forward, lumbering and trancelike.

Asya darted through his parted legs near the floor, then spun and shot a fist into the man's groin. He buckled at the blow, but quickly recovered to stand straight up again.

It's like they can't even feel the pain. As she heard the last man step toward her from behind, she realized that she would need to kill these men. There would be no other way to stop them. Her only other choice would be to run.

And Asya Machtcenko did *not* run.

She darted to the side of the man she had hit in the groin. He reached out for her slowly, like the creature in an old Frankenstein film—a large sweeping grab, unfocussed and wild. She got around him, but he had carried the sweeping hand around, and it hit her back, knocking her against the closed door.

She moved to her left just as the man drove his fist into the door, where she had been seconds before. A solid crunch filled the air. The man broke at least one knuckle. She slipped around the other side of him, and made a run at the second, slower security man still standing.

Just before she reached him, she stepped up into the air, planted her foot on his thigh and ran up the man's stomach and chest. She pushed off his broad pectorals and her head and arms shot back toward the door and Frankenstein's guard. Her body flew horizontal, with her back to the ground, for just a foot before her arms found the lumbering guard's head and neck. She grasped his thick neck with both hands and as the man that had acted as her ladder came closer, she wrapped her shins on either side of his neck too.

Together, the three of them formed a human bridge, with each guard acting as the uprights, and Asya stretched from neck to neck as the surface of the bridge. With a sudden and violent shift of her hips, Asya rotated her entire body in a horizontal twist, like a human top that had just been launched at speed. The spinning movement broke the neck of each burly man, before all three of their bodies pitched to the floor. The report of the cervical vertebrae fracturing in stereo was tremendous, and she feared the creatures from the larger room would be coming to investigate.

Extricating herself from the dead men, she scrambled to her feet. She slipped to the door of the room and opened it just a sliver. Out the crack into the large room, none of the white beasts were making for the security room.

Good.

The first man she had hit—the overweight man—began to stir on the floor. Asya lifted her leg, as if she were about to perform a simple ballet move, but then sprang up in the air and landed on the prone fat man's neck with the bone of her knee and upper shin. The man made a sickening gurgle and grunt when his neck broke, and his eyes bulged from their sockets with the ramming impact of Asya's entire weight, dropped from a five-foot height.

She stood again and quickly checked the man whose head had smacked against the stone wall of the room. His skull was cracked. Congealing blood coated the edges of the wound. It looked a brighter red than she would have expected. *Like a young girl's nail polish, thick and glossy.* He wouldn't be rejoining the fight either.

Asya looked at the live video feeds on the monitors around the room. One showed a room full of people sleeping on beds laid out like in an orphanage. *The lab scientists*, she assumed. Another showed the glowing sphere in the main room and a few of the creatures sniffing the air around it. Another showed the empty office where she had collected Rook at gunpoint, earlier in the night.

She saw more empty storerooms and offices. She had yet to come across tunnels or corridors, though. Some of the cameras showed views of doors outside, leading into the lab. One of those doors was ajar in the snow. She didn't see any rooms that looked like they might have rope or weapons, so she would check the cabinet at the back of the room next.

A monitor screen with rows of electrical switchboards caught her eye. The room was filled with thick electrical cables. Another screen showed the entrance to the tunnel where she had taken

Rook to the pit. Then she realized something and checked all twenty screens again. Fossen, the man that ran the place, was not on any of the cameras. Neither was Queen. And neither was the entrance to the lab she had used with Rook and Queen. *A lot of blind spots in the surveillance.* Asya walked over to the plastic map and looked at the floor plan. The tunnel back to the abandoned part of the lab was not even on the schematic.

She stepped around one man's extended leg, and made her way to the black cabinet. She opened it slowly and it creaked with a barely audible squeal. Inside were a few of the Walther pistols like the one she had used on Rook, and two AR-15 rifles with black canvas straps. A hook on the inside of the cabinet door held a small hand towel. It smelled of machine oil, but she used it to wipe blood off her face and out of her hair. On the floor of the cabinet was a navy blue nylon bag. She knelt and unzipped it to find a black braided nylon rope.

Perfect.

She took the bag and threw it over her shoulder and then put two of the pistols in the pockets of the ridiculous lab coat she wore. She thought of taking the rifles, too, but she didn't think she could conceal them well enough under the coat and they wouldn't fit in the bag. She left them and made for the door. On a small hook by the door was a 6-inch plastic-barreled flashlight. She pocketed it in one smooth move.

Back in the large main lab, she once again skirted the wall in a slow shuffle and made for the tunnel back to Rook, forcing the glazed look back into her eyes. She kept expecting the creatures to see through the ruse. But the beasts ignored her as she walked.

When she reached the tunnel entrance, she almost slipped on a small puddle of liquid. She grimaced. *Urine, maybe?* She sighed and continued into the tunnel, figuring the beasts had to piss some-where. A few steps further in, and she was concealed in shadow.

She breathed a sigh of relief that she had once more passed the notice of the bulky white monsters.

That relief flooded away as she was grabbed from behind in the dark. A powerful limb wrapped around her throat and squeezed. Hard. The kind of hard that left her little doubt about what was going to happen next. *I'm going to die.*

FIFTY-NINE

Outside the *Gleipnir* Facility, Norway
4 November, 0130 Hrs

ANNA BECK TUGGED hard on the toggle of her parachute with one hand and pulled her 9 mm Browning from her leg holster with the other. She fired several shots at the dire wolves on the fringe of the melee, not wanting to risk hitting Queen by firing too close to the center. In another two seconds, her feet hit the ground. She quickly released the harness of the parachute, but the dire wolves were ignoring her and still rushing for Queen.

As she freed herself from the harness and rolled in the snow to take up a firing stance on her knee, she saw Queen viciously head butt a dire wolf under its chin, sending its head back in a whipping arc, and a spray of white liquid squirting from its snout. Before its head hit the ground, Beck put a bullet in it. She fired twice more before she heard automatic fire from behind her.

She twisted in the foot-deep snow to see Black Six firing short bursts with an MP5 submachine gun. The muzzle flash lit up the snowy white expanse of the field between the hills in splashes of orange. They had muzzle suppressors for the MP5s back in New Hampshire, but no one thought this mission would involve stealth. They were here to do some damage. She watched him drop four dire wolves, their bodies contorting in agony after the bullet impacts, and then dying far more abruptly than a human would.

She fired her Browning a few more times, dropping dire wolves with headshots. She heard Queen growl like a feral animal and saw her knock one of the dire wolves away from her with an uppercut.

"Good God," Black Six said, his voice a mixture of fear and awe. "Look at her."

"Now you know why she's in the field and I guard an underground bunker," Beck replied.

Beck raced over to the center of the fight. She fired the last few shots from her weapon at point-blank range as the dire wolves still attempted to dog-pile Queen, ignoring Beck completely.

Beck recognized the situation. Even if she didn't know why, she would take advantage of it. She fired until her magazine was empty, then holstered the weapon and drew her knife—a wide, curved blade, Gurkha Kurkri Plus manufactured by Cold Steel. More machete than knife with its swept 12-inch blade, Beck hacked at the first few dire wolves she could get to and then stabbed two more in the backs of their necks. She couldn't believe that the creatures were ignoring her until she got closer to Queen and smelled the woman.

"Oh dear God," she shouted. "What the hell is that funk?"

"I know," Queen growled while striking a dire wolf in the throat with her knuckles and then stabbing a thumb into its eye. She was coated in sticky white fluid and bleeding from several places as well. "I know! I caught one in the crotch and it sprayed me with its fuckin' goo like a skunk!" Beck could hardly hear the woman over the bursts of MP5 fire from Black Six, as the man kept the remaining oncoming horde of dire wolves further away from the skirmish.

Then Beck had an idea. She sheathed the Kurkri, inserted a fresh magazine into her Browning and started firing at the approaching dire wolves, aiming for their nether regions. Gouts of white fluid burst and pulsed from the wounds as the beasts went down to the snow, and she soon saw some of the other dire wolves going to the injured ones, instead of after Queen.

She ran over to Black Six's position, where he stood knee deep in snow, and she took up firing next to him. "Aim for the balls."

"They don't have balls!"

"Well there's something there. Some kind scent sack."

Black Six calmly adjusted his aim and mowed down the next wave of the creatures, firing at waist level. A few of the creatures' genital areas burst when the 9 mm rounds ruptured the milky white skin at the groin. White liquid sprayed.

Black Six groaned. "Fuckin' nasty."

The next wave of dire wolves, about seven of the beasts, stopped at the row of freshly dead and began clawing into the corpses. Black Six and Beck exchanged a look. "I got this," he said.

Beck raced back to Queen to help her dispatch the last two creatures, but she needn't have bothered. Despite the multiple wounds on Queen's body and the muck that coated her, the woman still moved with quick grace and powerful strikes, taking down one more beast with an eye jab and then the last by leaping up onto its chest and twisting the creature's powerful neck until a loud crack rang out. Beck counted twenty-two bodies piled on the ground by Queen's feet, and several more around the main fight, that she had shot after ditching the parachute.

Queen looked at her, breathing hard, covered in a mix of red and white gore, the bright red skull on her forehead glaring through the muck.

Beck couldn't hide the shiver that ran up her spine. She'd heard stories about Queen's hand-to-hand combat skills, but never imagined that she—or anyone else aside from some mythological God of war— could be capable of such carnage. It was horrifying, yet in these circumstances, a thing of beauty.

Queen stood bent over with her hands on her knees, breathing hard. Beck walked up to her slowly. She stopped a few feet away.

The stink was horrendous. "You gonna be okay?" Queen nodded. Beck took a step back scrunching her nose. "Ugh. Maybe roll around in the snow for a few minutes or something."

Queen stood and wiped the muck from her face and flung her arm to the side. A long sticky strand of thick white viscous liquid shot off her fingers until the strand snapped and the glob went into the snow. Beck made a face.

"Who *are* you?" Queen asked. She looked like she might be readying for another fight.

"Anna Beck, callsign: Black Zero. Deep Blue sent me."

Queen nodded. "I remember you, now. From the fight with the Hydra, right?" She wiped another stream of thick glop from her face. "Too bad Deep Blue didn't send the others too. We could use them."

"He and King and the rest of the team are two hours out," Black Six had stepped up to them, the threat of the oncoming dire wolves diminished as they all scrambled to attack the piles of their recently deceased brethren instead of Queen. "I've got extra firearms. You need anything?"

Queen looked back to Beck and smiled. "I'll take that knife, if you're willing to part with it."

"No gun?"

Queen shook her head, no. "I'm a hands-on kind of girl."

Beck nodded. "I noticed."

SIXTY

Gleipnir Facility, Fenris Kystby, Norway
4 November, 0200 Hrs

ASYA MACHTCENKO COULDN'T breathe. Something was crushing her windpipe. She fumbled a hand into one of the oversize pockets of her coat and her fingers grazed the plastic barrel of the flashlight. She had been going for the gun but couldn't reach it. The light would have to do. She swung it up, trying to pummel her assailant. She struck something solid, but all she managed to do was switch on the light, which flashed over the walls as she continued to fight.

She struggled to get even a small breath in, but the arm clamped onto her tighter with the crushing power of a bulldozer. Then she heard a gruff whisper near her ear. "Turn that friggin' thing off or I break your neck."

Rook! She recognized his voice. She complied with his request, plunging the tunnel back into darkness. She still fought and struggled to break free from his powerful grasp. Her lungs were screaming at her now. She thrust her cranium back, smashing him in the bridge of his nose, and his grasp loosened, but he didn't let go.

"Let go," she hissed. "I am okay. I am not being controlled!"

Rook's vice grip loosened, but didn't let go.

"I nearly died in that pit," he grumbled.

Asya could feel the back of her clothing soaking through. Rook was completely wet. He was also vibrating with anger.

"I was being controlled," she whispered at him in the dark, "but I was still trying to help you."

"You mean that little flashlight? Lotta good it did me down there." His voice was petulant, but he let her go.

"Why did you not climb out? I did."

"Up that brick wall? You must be Spider-Woman." Now the man only sounded tired.

She paused a moment, in the dark. All she could hear was Rook breathing. "Then how did you get out of the pit, if not up the walls?"

"You wouldn't friggin' believe me if I told you. You're sure you're free and clear from the pheromones, now?"

"I came back to get you out. I have a rope and two guns." She held out the pack. "Here, take one."

The small LED flashlight she had given him lit up. Rook was covering the end of it with his hand, so it would only cast a dim red glow, but it was enough for her to see. He was soaked and covered in mud. She reached out to him, handing him one of the Walther pistols. He took it then doused the light.

"I had to fight the influence of these 'pheromones.' It comes from the energy ball—not from the creatures," she told him as he expertly chambered a round in the Walther.

"The dire wolves," Rook corrected.

"They are in the main room. Six of them. I had to pretend to be under the influence still. Walking like a hypnotized woman. Glassy eyes. They let me pass, but they still paid attention. We have to be careful. Do not get too close to the light ball. But if it gets you, you get very happy. You feel everything will be fine. The antidote is to get very angry. Frustrated."

"Getting angry is rarely a problem for me. Where's Queen?" There was a note of deep concern in Rook's voice.

"I do not know. I have not seen her."

"And Fossen?" Rook's voice took on the glistening edge of a razor.

"I saw only four guards, in a security room. They are all dead now. I haven't seen any of the people in lab coats for hours, but I saw them in the security feeds, sleeping in beds. Also, one of the doors to the outside was open. Perhaps we should just get out of here."

"That open door was me coming back inside," Rook said. "Listen, you already figured out that Stanislav was not my real name. Queen and I are a part of an American military team. We deal with this kind of stuff. Evil nutjobs like Fossen. Weird crap like the dire wolves. It's all part of the job. I don't know exactly what's coming through that portal out there, but Fossen believes it will destroy the entire planet. We've got to stay and try to stop him."

"I understand, but what can you do?"

"There's a big machine around that glowing monster testicle. I'm gonna smash the crap out of it and hope that turns it off."

"Eloquent plan," Asya said, sounding unsure.

"What can I say," Rook added. "I'm the brains of the outfit."

He moved back to the light and Asya followed him, pulling the second gun from her other pocket and chambering it. When Rook reached the lit end of the tunnel, he moved against the left wall, shielding him from the view of any dire wolves that might still be in the massive portal chamber.

Rook held the gun up near his face and looked back at Asya. "On three, we jump out and if there's any of the dire wolves, we shoot them in the heads. Besides holding me hostage, you ever fire a gun before?"

She nodded. "I was in the army a long time ago."

"Okay. In the heads, remember. You said there were six, right?" She nodded again, holding her own pistol at the ready. "Right. One, two...

"...three."

Rook leapt out from behind cover and Asya followed, but neither of them fired a shot. "Aww. Son-of-a—"

Thirty dire wolves turned toward him. Eirek Fossen stood at the center of the pack. He stood calmly and the beasts around him held a relaxed posture.

"Stanislav," Fossen said with a nod of greeting. "I'm afraid this is where we part ways. For good." He backed away toward the portal. "The time for my ascension has come." He raised his hands out to either side, making him look like Jesus on the cross. Even tilted his head to the side a little. Then he stepped back into the light. As the glow wrapped around his face, he grinned and said, "Kill them."

Then he was gone, transported to another world.

The demeanor of every creature in the room shifted from docile to hostile in a second. Moving as one, they rushed toward Rook and Asya, some running on two legs. Others loping on all four. Each and every one of them out for blood.

SIXTY-ONE
Gleipnir Facility, Fenris Kystby, Norway
4 November, 0230 Hrs

ROOK FIRED FOUR shots—hitting a lumbering dire wolf in the head with each—and then ran across the massive chamber, remembering Asya's warning to stay far from the glowing orb that stretched to the ceiling behind the creatures. Asya stayed at his side, firing as she ran. He didn't have to tell her what to do, she just did it. Once again, the thought that there was more to this woman than she was letting on flitted through his brain. He wondered if she was a Russian spy or something. She certainly moved like it.

A dire wolf made it past the barrage of 9 mm fire that Rook and Asya sprayed around the room. It lunged low for Asya's legs, and Rook marveled to see her deftly sweep her legs up and over the creature, with the fingers of one outstretched hand resting on the back of its head. It looked to Rook like a gymnastics move. Then, while still in the air, in mid leap over the beast, she pointed the Walther down and fired a round into the back of the dire wolf's head—inches from where her hand balanced her entire body above it. She followed through on the graceful leap and landed lightly on her toes before the dire wolf's now inert body slumped to the concrete floor of the huge room.

Rook fired his eighth shot and the breech locked back, telling him his Walther was out of ammunition. Another dire wolf reached him, swiping its glassy claws across his midsection. Rook jumped back, narrowly avoiding being eviscerated, as the claws traced shallow red lines across his stomach.

Barely noticing the wound, Rook punched hard, mashing a tennis-ball sized eye into the muscle and bone beneath it. The creature howled and twisted violently, swiping at Rook with its clawed hand, but he stepped back out of its range. He was about to go for its other eye, when the orb burst into a spray of sticky white liquid. Asya had used her last bullet to shoot the thing, and while the eye had detonated, the creature wasn't dead—the bullet had not penetrated the beast's skull. It rolled on the floor in agony and blindly swept out its claws at Rook and Asya.

They were both out of bullets and the rest of the dire wolves were still coming at them from across the huge room. They were no more than thirty feet away. "The stairs!" Rook ran as fast as he had ever run in his life. He might be able to take one of these things down, but he didn't think he could take the horde, not even with Asya's *Ballet-Fu*.

She reached the metal stairs before him. They led up to the catwalk, over a hundred feet above them. She raced up the stairs to the first landing, the metal steps clanging with that *bong-thap* sound metal stairs always made. Rook raced up the first flight behind her, then suddenly swiveled around, holding the railing, and swung his booted foot down the stairs to smash into the face of the first dire wolf on the steps behind him. The creature instinctively turned its head so the large eye on the side of its cranium could see him better.

Bad move, Bonzo. Rook had identified the large eyes as the dire wolves most obvious weak spot. So he aimed for it when he kicked. His booted foot hit the delicate eye. It squelched like a smashed grape. The creature's body sprawled backward away from the assault and it slammed into the next beast behind it, sending them both flying to the floor.

Rook raced on up the stairs. He made it past the second landing before another dire wolf nearly reached him on the steps. Asya was a few flights above him. Rook glanced up the stairwell. *Too many friggin' steps.*

The dire wolf swiped at his back and he felt the claws tear through the thick fabric of his wet coat. Then instead of taking another step, he threw his body backward, slamming into the creature. They both plunged down the flight of steps.

The dire wolf hit the landing hard.

Rook landed on top of it. He turned and slammed both hands on either side of the dire wolf's head, pounding its eyes, and then scrambled to his feet. The dire wolf pistoned its legs where it lay on the landing and clawed at its now blinded face. The body turned slowly on the landing and Rook thought of the *Three Stooges*. He shoved hard with his foot and the beast's body slid to the edge of the landing and under the knee-height guardrail. With a second shove, the creature fell away from the stairs.

He saw another beast coming up the lower landing and turned to sprint back up, but stopped in his tracks as another of the creatures finished climbing over the railing onto the steps several feet above him. *Tricky bastard.* He was trapped between them. He swiveled his head back and forth so see them both and took two steps toward the upper beast. Then he moved against the outer railing, still turning his gaze back and forth as quickly as he could. Neither creature moved. They tensed instead, both about to pounce. He placed his hands on the railing behind him. They sprang for him, the lower creature diving for his legs and the upper creature coming for his torso.

Rook pulled his legs up and stamped his boots onto the railing, then lunged upward, using his legs like springs. He shot up and grabbed the metal side of the flight of stairs above him, his legs swinging widely out over the 25-foot drop to the floor. The two dire wolves crashed into each other, rolling down to the metal landing below. A loud cracking noise punctuated the creature on top smashing its head against the metal railing. The one under it was unhurt from the crash, but it was pinned under the weight of the heavier creature on top.

Rook pulled hard and moved a leg up, climbing the side rails on the outside of the stairwell like monkey bars. He flipped over the top rail and onto the steps. Below him on the other side of the stairs, he saw two more of the dire wolves climbing and leaping up the outside of the stairs as he had just done. Beyond them, he saw another one racing up the wall of the room, now several flights higher than him. They were circling around to get to Asya.

He ran higher and stopped above the two dire wolves climbing up the outside of the railings. He grabbed the rail and flipped over it, to the outside of the stairs, landing feet first on the head of the first of the two dire wolves. The impact thrust the creature off the stairs and it fell to the floor. The other creature saw what was happening and shimmied to the side.

With Rook dangling by one hand from a railing thirty feet above the floor, the creature scrambled up and across the metal steps and rails to reach him.

Rook tried to pull himself up with his one injured arm—the shoulder he had injured first in the incident with Edmund Kiss, and then again in the fight at Peder's farm and most recently when the hybrid poked four fresh holes in it. No good. Between those injuries and the similar stunt he had just pulled on the other side of the stairs, he was lucky his arm could hang on preventing him from falling.

The dire wolf leapt to dislodge him, its body flying upward through the air. Rook did the only thing he could think of.

He let go.

SIXTY-TWO

Gleipnir Facility, Fenris Kystby, Norway
4 November, 0245 Hrs

QUEEN LED THE way into the main room of the lab and found pretty much what she had expected.

Mayhem.

The giant cage of metal fingers now held a hundred-foot diameter glowing sphere of light shooting random bolts of lightning, which arced back to electrocute the metal struts. A harsh metallic smell of electricity burns hung in the air.

Dire wolves—a lot of them—were arrayed around the room, running to the metal staircase, climbing up the stairs, scaling up the outside of the freestanding stairwell or running up the walls to the catwalk. Rook was three stories up, dangling from one arm with a dire wolf climbing up to him. Asya was close to the top of the stairs, slamming her foot into a dire wolf's face as it tried to climb over the red metal railing.

She ran into the room heading for the first dire wolf closest to her, a big tall one, which stood at least a foot taller than the others. She held her broken hand in toward her body and raised the curved Kurkri knife.

Beck entered the room after her, armed with one of Black Six's spare MP5s. She fired at the legs of the dire wolf attacking Asya. The bullets raked its legs and it dropped, falling down toward where Rook hung by one arm.

"Crap," Beck shouted.

Rook let go as a dire wolf leapt at him. They crashed together in the air and began to fall together, grappling and struggling with each other.

Black Six stepped into the room after Beck and fired a shot that killed the falling dire wolf stories above Rook. He saw its trajectory would take it onto Rook's head, and fired another burst, making the creature's body spin and flip in the air until its head smacked the railing and its now punctured corpse ricocheted away from the stairwell as it continued its fall.

Rook pulled his legs up onto the chest of the dire wolf he fought, intending to use the body to cushion his fall. Instead, he stopped short of the floor, clutched in the grip of a dire wolf reaching out over the first floor railing, its claws digging into his sides.

But Rook had seen the dire wolf above him get shot. Someone was covering him. "Thanks for the catch, Deputy Dawg," he said and leaned his head to the side. He heard the buzz of the bullet as it zipped past his ear and buried itself in the creature's forehead. The talons slipped from his side.

Rook fell to the concrete, but the drop was manageable. He used the dead dire wolf below to soften his landing. The impact jarred him hard, but he turned the fall into a roll, converting the impact's kinetic force into motion.

Queen saw Rook fall, but was too busy fighting the big one to help. It was cagey and knew to stay back from her slashing blade. She had no interest in continuing the standoff. "Black Zero! Crotch shot!"

She circled the big one again with the knife as Beck heard her request and fired at several nearby dire wolves, aiming at their groins. The third target's crotch erupted with a spray of fluid, and the big dire wolf turned its head. That was all the distraction Queen needed. She leapt forward, slicing upward, and cut the thing from the middle of its huge sternum up to its throat. An arc of white blood sprayed outward from the beast, coating Queen in yet more fluid. The beast also defecated on the floor before it crumpled.

"That's just wonderful," Queen said, disgusted. Then she ran for the next living target.

Rook picked himself up off the floor, limping and holding his shoulder. He was injured.

"Rook!" Queen called to him. "Duck!"

Rook trusted Queen implicitly. He didn't need to know why she'd told him to duck, only that she had. He dropped to the floor and rolled again, this time narrowly missing being shot as Black Six expertly targeted the dire wolf that had been coming up behind Rook. Its head and chest spasmed from the two shots, then it fell over backward. Rook got to his feet and approached Beck, who was firing on the last few beasts on the stairwell.

"Who are—Hopping crap on a pogo stick. You're that Pawn that used to work for Ridley's security goons, before joining our side in the fight against the Hydra."

"Black Zero," she said, handing him her Browning. "I'm with Endgame."

Rook gladly took the weapon and aimed it at one of the last living wolves in the room. He squeezed the trigger twice, and the running creature—just getting up to its full speed in the confines of the lab—slumped over dead, its body skidding a few feet on the slick concrete.

"What's Endgame?"

Beck killed the last dire wolf on the staircase, as it tried to leap upward on the exterior of the stairs. "Support crew for Chess Team."

"We have a support crew? Nobody ever tells me these things." Rook hung his head and held his shoulder with the Browning still in his hand. He grimaced.

Queen stepped over with Black Six. The man turned as he walked, checking all sides of the room, never lowering his weapon.

"Did you know we had a support crew?" Rook asked Queen.

"Nope. I've been running around Russia looking for you for the past few months. How would I know?"

Asya had run back down the stairs and leapt off the last few steps to the ground. She hurried over to where Rook stood and was about to ask him a question, but she stopped, her mouth hanging open. Then Black Six opened fire again and all heads turned toward the portal.

Dire wolves poured out of the pulsing energy portal. There were so many that they were actually climbing over each other to get out through the wall of light—a wall that stretched at its bottom to over twenty feet wide. Rook figured as many as fifty of them. They struggled and fought to push through the yellow brilliance, emerging to race across the slick concrete floor.

Black Six stopped taking single shots and began firing bursts. Beck opened fire as well.

Queen reached over to Black Six's thigh and withdrew his Browning. She picked her shots and made them count. Body after body clogged the entrance of the portal.

Rook fired carefully, conserving the few shots of ammunition in the Browning.

Asya, unarmed now, raced behind everyone to the security room. Rook figured she was taking cover.

Even though the group had fired enough rounds of 9 mm ammunition to drop a herd of elephants, the creatures kept pouring into the room. They scampered over their dead, covering themselves in the blood of their fallen.

"This is not working," Rook shouted. "We're gonna get overrun here."

Asya reappeared with two AR-15 assault rifles. She handed one to Rook and he handed her the Browning. He racked back the charging handle, and blasted another wave of the creatures. A puddle of white blood seeped out across the floor in front of the portal's edge.

Black Six's rifle stopped spitting its deadly hail of bullets and he shouted. "I'm out!"

Asya ran to him and gave him the second AR-15, then fired the last two rounds from the Browning, killing one of the dire wolves. Black Six opened up with the new weapon, dropping several more of the scrabbling creatures. When the weapon was empty, he retreated behind the rest of the group and out of sight. Rook kept firing until he was dry too.

"Too many," Queen shouted. "Sons-a-bitches just keep coming!"

Dire wolf corpses littered the room now, and the pile at the entrance to the portal, a mound of arms and claws and bulging eyes, was at least four feet high. Seeing that the fight had nearly gone out of the group, the dire wolves slowed now as they stepped out of the light and into the cavernous room. Some squatted and sniffed the air. Others stepped forward slowly. More came through the glowing wall of energy. Rook watched as more and more came through and he lost track of the number.

They're bleeding us dry, Queen thought, *making us use all of our ammo. Fucking transdimensional rope-a-dope.*

Rook turned to her. "We are going to need an escape plan before I run out of clean pairs of shorts today."

SIXTY-THREE
Gleipnir Facility, Fenris Kystby, Norway
4 November, 0300 Hrs

THE ENORMOUS HANGAR doors disguised to look like shaded rock from the exterior split down the middle, revealing a chaotic battle that looked to King like Hell on Earth. Hidden motors concealed in the walls churned as the doors retracted on wheels set into a track in the floor of the huge space. A gust of wind blew a swirl of snow into the incredible scene before him.

The room was gigantic, and it held a sparkling energy portal one-hundred feet high. The glowing orb threw lightning and disgorged dire wolves as if they were jumping off a truck on the other side. A huge metal cage held the portal in place like an eight-digit hand holding a ball. In front of the sphere, a pile of dire wolf bodies impeded the newly arriving monsters like a barricade of sandbags. Beck's MP5 spat bullets at the creatures. Queen stood off to the side, covered in white fluid, like liquid marshmallow, firing a handgun at any of the beasts that got close.

Rook and some woman King didn't know ran toward him as he stepped into the gunsmoke clouding the air. Black Six was off to the side of the hangar doors, where he had operated the controls to let them in.

"Get down!" King leveled an FN-SCAR rifle and fired. Rook and the woman dove to the side, hitting the floor and rolling away. As the dire wolves clambered over the pile of dead, King's shots riddled their bodies until they slipped down the front of the pile or added to the top of it. A river of white blood seeped from the carrion heap, sliding across the concrete floor as slow moving rivulets.

King wore the black and gray impact armor, but no helmet. He was armed to the teeth with rifles, handguns on both hips and a bandolier of grenades across his chest. Deep Blue stood to King's left, wearing his battered black impact armor and his futuristic black helmet that made him look like he was ready to ride a motorcycle in a Japanese Shoei commercial. The man took up firing right alongside him.

To King's right stood Matt Carrack, wearing an arctic white version of the impact armor, with one of the matching white padded helmets. The five security soldiers armed in the white impact suits, carried rifles, heavy machine guns and even a few grenade launchers. Even Reggie, White Eight, their weapons expert, was suited up in one of the armored suits, but like King, without a helmet. Instead, he wore huge red and black ear muffs King had seen him use on the firing range back at Endgame headquarters.

They all opened fire and the sound was deafening in the echoing chamber.

Beck ran around the field of fire and up to the group. Her face showed that she understood what the absence of Knight and Bishop meant. Reggie supplied her with weapons and ammunition.

Reggie quickly supplied Queen, Rook and the woman with him, with a new MP5 and three extra magazines each. No words were exchanged. Just action. But even if they had tried to speak, the sound of ceaseless gunfire would have drowned out their voices.

Dire wolves continued to flow from the portal, but were met by a wall of projectiles that was impossible to pass through. And each new corpse slowed the advance of those just arriving. The floor was so cluttered with dead that King doubted the creatures could get up to speed, even without the bullets. The perfect bottleneck.

Rook staggered back against the wall, using it to prop himself up. He fired his newly acquired MP5 one handed, his other arm hanging limp at his shoulder.

Queen stayed close to the new arrivals, squatting to the floor and taking up a classic kneeling firing stance. The White security team members began to fan out to the sides, to catch any stray dire wolves that escaped the main fusillade of bullets blasting at the center front of the portal. One of the men was armed with a grenade launcher attachment under his FN-SCAR rifle and fired several shots inside the center of the portal.

The onslaught of dire wolves increased until the rate of fire wasn't enough and more of them slipped past the bullets, several coming through the portal already airborne, as though flung from the other side. Their sleek muscular white bodies leapt and hopped to the sides of the fray. They got close enough to two of the White team members to attack. The first one leapt onto White Four, throwing him to the ground and tearing at the man's armored suit. King knew it was Four by his size—short and stocky, the new White Four was a nice guy, but everyone had kept their distance. The last several White security team members had been killed in action when GenY, Richard Ridley's former security force, attacked the New Hampshire base. King blasted the creature on top of Four with a concentrated burst and it fell to the side, but the man didn't get up.

Another dire wolf ripped into the man with the grenade launcher, and the weapon skittered across the slick concrete, stopping near where the portal ate into the floor. The man pulled his sidearm and fired several shots, but the dire wolf hacked and clawed at him until one of his armored arms came loose with a pop. The creature flung the arm and it landed with a thump and a wet splat in front of Queen's kneeling stance. She adjusted her aim and unloaded until the magazine went dry. The creature shook as she perforated its long body with 9 mm slugs. She reloaded and moved the sights of her weapon back to the oncoming wave of white muscled bodies, before the dead beast hit the floor.

The woman King didn't know hung back, firing her weapon at any target that stood still long enough for her to see it. *She's a pretty good shot, whoever she is.* Deep Blue and the others took positions around the room, a few lying down, a few standing and others kneeling like Queen.

One of the White security members set up a tripod, and Reggie loaded an M2 with its chain-fed .50 caliber death. The gun overpowered the sound of all the other weapons in the room. The metallic booming of the M2 sent the oversized bullets across the room, ripping into the dire wolf hordes as they emerged.

Blood sprayed.

Limbs severed.

ROOK DUCKED TO the floor near the man dealing death with the big machine gun. He picked up a rifle from a pile near the man. It was an M-16—the standard US infantry rifle—but this one had the M203 grenade launcher attachment on the underside of its barrel. "Fuckin-A!"

Rook targeted a huge metal strut that supported the portal. It had a section that had lots of electrical cables and more than the normal amount of the metal receptor plates that ran up its length. The 40 mm grenade shot out of the launcher tube and arced through the room, smashing into the concrete base of the metal upright, just as Rook fired another grenade at a second upright.

The first metal arm sheared off completely and fell inward, swallowed by the glowing ball of light. The other strut's base exploded into fragments and the strut fell backward. Each explosion dwarfed the M2's din and filled the air with a ball of orange flame and a column of dark smoke. The detonations startled everyone and the shooting paused, as the metal support struts collapsed. Even the dire wolves paused and cocked their alien heads, looking upward at the damage.

"I told you I'd break that fucker." Rook said. "I—"

The sphere of energy, no longer fully contained by the metal cage, bulged suddenly forward and upward, like a water balloon that had been squeezed hard on one side. When it hit the ceiling of the massive lab room, it ate right through, as though it had encountered nothing but more air. The front portion of the roof collapsed toward the team. Great chunks of stone and strips of steel crumbled from the ceiling, now open to the sky.

Rook watched the debris falling toward them. "Aww, shit."

SIXTY-FOUR
Somewhere

KNIGHT BRUSHED HIS arms, attempting to dust some of the midnight blue grime off his body after the long climb. *Or is it orange?* He and Bishop perceived this world differently, but maybe neither of them saw it right.

Bishop motioned to the suitcase nuke hanging from Knight's back. "Where did you find it?" He was walking along the cliff's edge toward the distant pinnacle of rock that they had agreed was their only logical destination. Knight walked alongside the big man, but away from the cliff's edge. It had taken him hours to climb the thing and he had no desire to slip and fall off it.

"In a crater. There are craters all around. From the portals."

"Yep. Seen 'em."

"Debris from Earth surrounds most of them, like a pie crust." Knight said, pointing out to the multitude of craters they could see in the distance.

Bishop stopped walking and peered out at the collection of divots on the distant plain.

"Too far to tell," Bishop said.

"Trust me; I've visited a few. I found the nuke beside one of them."

"Seems like a lot of people had the same idea." Bishop resumed walking along the cliff's edge.

Knight stayed where he was and waited. Eventually, Bishop noticed Knight wasn't walking with him and turned, a question about to form on his lips. But he saw Knight's face, with one eyebrow raised that said *Really? Think about it.*

"Wait," Bishop said, the idea formulating in his head. "That's the nuke King and Deep Blue were supposed to place in New York?"

Knight nodded, and unslung the pack, reaching into a pocket on the exterior of the canvas sack.

"How do you know it's theirs?" Bishop asked.

Knight produced a small iPhone from the pack and handed it to Bishop. It showed a picture of Fiona smiling on the wallpaper.

Bishop glanced at it and looked at Knight with a serious face. "Did you try this thing?"

Knight's face lost all color. He looked down at the iPhone's reception—no bars. *Of course, there are no bars. I'm in another dimension.* He realized he must have checked the reception on the thing a hundred times, even though he couldn't remember actually doing it. Then he realized that the battery should have died ages ago, but it strangely showed two bars left on the power meter.

Knight took the device back and dropped it in the pack, shaking his head and continuing onward. "No reception." Bishop followed him and said nothing.

They walked along the edge of the cliff for hours. Most of the time, they walked in silence. They saw no dire wolves, but after an hour, they found a crater at the top of the cliff. It was so close to the edge that they had to go around it. The circumference was only eighty feet—small compared to some of the portals they had seen, but it had a single piece of debris at its edge.

It was the front half of a police Ford Crown Victoria. The portal had sawed the vehicle in half just behind its light bar. The front windshield had been smashed in and the driver's side door was wide open. Seeing nothing of value, they walked around the vehicle, and crater, and continued on their way.

The distant pinnacle of rock on the horizon grew larger as they trudged toward it, but it felt like an illusion to Knight, *like approaching the Rocky Mountains—they keep getting bigger, but they're still so far away.* An hour after the Crown Vic, they saw another crater further away from the cliff edge to their right.

"This one must be immense," Bishop commented.

Knight could only tell that it looked like an enormous junkyard that stretched for miles. Ragged corners of buildings were interspersed with vehicles and wreckage of every kind.

"I'm thinking we check around for a functioning set of wheels. Looks like a long way to that rock tower." Knight changed course and made for the crater's edge.

"Survivors?" Bishop asked.

"I've never seen any," Knight told him. "Seen a lot of wreckage, but never bodies."

They approached the edge of the debris and saw that this particular crater stretched for a few miles. It was deep and filled with rubble that had tumbled in from the outer edge. Several smaller satellite craters pocked the ground around it.

They walked the circumference of the wide circle, looking at the destruction. They saw buildings and whole slabs of highways, but nothing really recognizable or worthwhile.

When they came to the second satellite crater, Knight stopped in his tracks. Right at the edge of the small hole were two things—a Humvee with a flat tire and an open, empty box.

As Bishop pulled up next to Knight, he could see that the box was a medical organ supply cooler. It was empty. The Humvee was an ambulance variant. The front hood and front doors of the vehicle were the same as any other of the multipurpose military-utility vehicles. The back bumper at the crater's edge had been cleaved in half by the portal when it closed. The vehicle had what looked like an olive drab camper top sporting a big red cross painted on a white square.

As Bishop walked up to the vehicle, Knight went around the back of it and returned with a spare tire that had just missed being cut in half by the portal.

"Hold on, Knight. Let's check if it runs before we bother." Bishop slipped into the driver's seat and started the ignition. The engine purred to life and Bishop smiled. He killed the engine, got out and helped Knight replace the tire.

As they were finishing with the tire and stowing the jack in the back of the vehicle, Bishop pointed to an insignia on the vehicle with two red bars and a blue bar, with a yellow pattern that looked like a hockey trophy.

"What country is that?" Bishop asked.

"Mongolia," Knight said. "I'm driving."

Knight put the pedal to the floor, peeling the vehicle around until they faced the tower in the distance. He eased up on the gas, but kept them moving quickly.

"So where are all the people we saw being abducted?" Bishop asked, from the passenger seat, where he held one of the two MP5s at the ready.

"Got a theory, but it isn't pleasant." Knight had been able to take the vehicle up to 40 mph on the uneven surface of the ground without rattling them both to death.

Bishop looked at him, waiting.

"The dire wolves. Think about how fast they are. Know how many calories speed like that would burn?"

"I'm not sure," Bishop said. "If they needed to eat that much, what do they eat when the portals aren't open? I haven't seen anything else living here."

"Maybe the portals open to dimensions other than ours?" Knight offered. "Or maybe they hibernate."

"Mmm," Bishop said. "But they probably do eventually eat what they take, human or animal, and they've been doing it for quite some time, so the real question is, where are all the bones?

TWO HOURS LATER, they found the bones.

As they sped across the plain, the tower resolved and they could see that it was not a natural geological feature.

It was a tower of bones.

A twenty-foot high, mile-long wall led away from the tower toward the upper plain before it abruptly stopped, as if whoever or whatever constructed it just lost interest. But the tower was immense, rising several hundred feet high—a massive monolith of death. As they neared, Knight suggested they kill the engine and proceed on foot.

After a ten-minute jog, they stopped at the wall's edge. It was constructed haphazardly from a mix of white human bones, and larger, clear bones which Knight assumed had come from dire wolves. Some of the longer specimens stuck out from the tower as far as a foot. They saw femurs and skulls, ribs and spinal columns. Nothing was excluded. Even the small bones of a hand were visible. Some kind of mortar that looked like concrete filled the spaces between the bones. A layer of orange dust—blue to Knight, orange to Bishop—coated everything.

Bishop grasped one the large dire wolf long bones sticking out of the structure and tested it for strength. The bone was solid. He put his weight on it, and it held him. He turned to Knight.

"Up or around?"

Knight looked up to where the tower met the twenty-foot high wall. "Up, I guess." He tested his weight on bones that stuck out of the giant monument and quickly climbed for the spot where the wall and tower converged. Bishop followed. Twice, when Bishop put his weight on a human bone, it cracked with a dull crunching noise, leaving behind a splintered stump, which he was still able to use as a foothold.

When Knight reached the top, and peered over the wall, he turned to look back at Bishop. His face was filled with tension. Bishop reached the top a moment later and saw what had disturbed Knight.

The plains continued on the other side and ran for miles to the horizon. But the span was filled with a vast army of dire wolves. Their white see-through skin added contrast to the landscape, almost glowing. Closer to the structure of the tower and the wall, there were hundreds of small bone walls, with cells built into them like in an underground crypt. Each cell contained one or more human bodies. Some were stuffed in with their limbs folded over in grotesque ways. Others were stored in pieces, with some cells filled with only one kind of body parts—all feet or all heads.

Thousands of people.

Not one of them living.

And the bodies didn't seem to be decaying. Bishop noticed an absolute lack of insects like flies that would normally be buzzing and swarming around such a charnel house. Nor, could he smell the dead.

They're being stored, he thought. *It's like a giant pantry full of human corpses.*

Near the end of the bone wall that ran a mile away from the tower, a one-hundred-foot tall portal stretched into the sky. The army of dire wolves stood a half mile away from the tower, and equally far from the portal. They weren't lined up in rows and columns like a human army might be, but it was clear to Bishop that they were ready to begin their fight.

Not far from the portal, a wide tunnel burrowed down into the soil—eighty feet wide and just as tall. A yawning cavity in the ground.

"That portal isn't flickering." Bishop said.

Knight looked at the scene and shook his head. "What's that Elmer Fudd says?"

"I'm hunting wabbits," Bishop said, enunciating the words, but not doing a full on impression.

"The other one."

"I've got a bad feeling about this," Bishop said.

"That's the one," Knight said. "What are they all waiting for?"

Bishop put his hand on Knight's head and turned him toward the cave in front of the portal. "They're waiting for that."

A massive form rose from the depths.

Knight had been trying to deal with the horror of this place through joking, but all trace humor fled his body as fast as the blood from his face.

"Let's move," Bishop said.

"Move where?"

Bishop motioned to the Humvee. "Let's take a ride. See if we can't lead the charge."

"I don't know if I love or hate the way you think," Knight said, starting to climb down. "No, wait. I hate it. I definitely hate it."

SIXTY-FIVE

Gleipnir Facility, Fenris Kystby, Norway
4 November, 0315 Hrs

QUEEN DOVE TO the side as wreckage rained down around her. She rolled on the floor and came up in a firing stance, ready to fight, but found herself in a cloud of choking dust and grit. It would have been the perfect time to take down all the dire wolves. She figured they were all frozen, stock still, waiting for the airborne particulates to clear, so they could see their prey.

But Queen couldn't see them either. All the shooting had stopped as the giant slabs of masonry fell with explosive force, shattering on the floor. She scanned the area around her and found Black Six lying face down, his torso and upper legs pinned under a slab of the massive roof. She lay down on the floor, put her feet against the stone and prepared to pull the man out by his legs. She pulled and he came free easily. When she looked down, she saw that she had freed only the man's legs, from the upper thigh down. The rest of him was crushed under the rock slab.

Man down, she thought, but there wasn't anything she could do.

She dropped his legs, growled, stood and looked for something on which to vent her anger.

Sand and grit scratched her eyes. She pawed at it with a filthy, muck-coated hand. As the cloud began to clear, she could see the snowy sky above through the fractured, opened roof. The portal, which was not quite a sphere anymore, stretched up through the roof. Gunfire erupted again as those still living found targets in the murky air.

A shift in the dusty air alerted her to the presence of a dire wolf. She turned and found it right behind her, frozen in its macabre statue-like stance. *Like a street-performing human statue.* She swept the curve-bladed Kurkri from the sheath on her hip, slicing the stationary creature's head off in one vicious swipe. The body strangely stayed erect on its feet as the head rolled to a stop next to gray rubble. The headless corpse disturbed her, so she kicked it in the chest and the carcass toppled over.

She could see the man that wore the earmuffs over by the now inactive M2. A six-foot tall spire of steel I-beam had killed him, impaling him through his chest. Falling wreckage had bent the M2's barrel like a paper clip. Two of the white-armored troopers were hunkered down behind another pile of stones, firing at the dire wolves as they slowly emerged from the gloom, although most still stood motionless, waiting for the air to clear. Queen raised her

MP5 and loosed a barrage of bullets toward every creature-statue she could see.

She held the trigger down as snow fell into the expansive room. She saw King helping Deep Blue remove his cracked black helmet. Beck was helping Asya up.

She lingered on Asya. The woman looked incredibly familiar, but Queen couldn't put her finger on why. The way she fought. The way she moved. The look in her eyes, or her eyes themselves. The two women moved over to Deep Blue and King, and the idea that had been scratching at the back of Queen's head since she had met the Russian woman burst into her frontal consciousness.

Son of a bitch. I know who you are, lady.

She didn't see Rook anywhere, until she heard him, and his voice distracted her from her new revelation about Asya. He stood across the room, covered in dusty grime.

"Like it hasn't been a bad enough day," Rook shouted. "I had to drop the friggin' ceiling on everyone. Goddamned, buck-toothed, white marshmallow lookin' cocksuckers!" He sprayed bullets from the M-16, mowing down the stationary dire wolves, dropping three of them before his rifle ran out of ammunition. "Bastards!" He dropped the M-16, and charged toward the remaining six dire wolves that stood still.

"Rook," King called out.

Rook ignored him, pounding forward. He drew a Browning pistol he must have picked up during the fight. He walked right up to the first dire wolf, placed the weapon up to the creature's head at a distance of no more than two inches, and fired. The far side of the dire wolf's white head exploded outward. Rook headed for the next creature. It turned toward him as he got close, but he still shot it from point-blank distance, before it had time to react.

"Rook!" King called out again. Rook ignored the call as he walked up to another dire wolf and executed it. The creature's body jolted from the shot and flopped onto a pile of dirt. "Rook!"

Then King called out again, and Queen and Deep Blue lent their voices to the call.

"ROOK!"

ROOK ANGRILY TURNED to face the team by the open hangar doors across the wreckage-strewn floor. "For the love of—What? What do you want?"

Deep Blue, King, Queen, Asya, the woman Rook knew as a 'Pawn' from a previous mission—now called Black Zero—and three of the soldiers in the white armor all stood still. Only some of them had their mouths hanging open, but each and every one of them was looking at Rook.

No, Rook thought. *Not at me.*

Above me.

Rook spun around. A ten-foot tall mound of white goo, like a massive clump of melted Gozer the Gozerian Stay Puft marshmallow, stood in front of the portal. When a stiff breeze carried away the smoke, he saw it wasn't goo at all.

It was loose skin.

On a foot.

The size of an SUV.

The ridges at the base of the mound were not ridges, but toes. Three thick digits, each the size of a man, coiled and twitched, as though in anticipation.

Rook stepped backward, looking up, up and further up as he moved.

The ten-foot-tall foot connected to a powerful leg that went another twenty feet up before bending at a knee, and disappearing into the light.

Rook stumbled backward over rubble and went down on his ass.

Above the backward-bending leg, a gigantic chest appeared. Ten-foot-tall cloudy-skinned sacks dangled from the torso like pendulous breasts. Two. Then four. Then six. They kept coming. Inside each were dire wolves in different stages of growth, floating in mottled white and red fluid.

The room shook as the monster took a step forward, bringing a second leg through the portal. The sacks swayed back and forth, the fluid inside them gurgling. Then the head came through.

In many ways, it resembled the smaller dire wolves. The rounded snout held a flat nose just above a wide, curving mouth full of shovel-sized, transparent teeth. Its round chameleon eyes, each the diameter of a hula-hoop, twitched back and forth, taking in the entire room as they swiveled independently of each other. But the skin, while transparent, hung in loose folds that warbled and swayed. And while quasi transparent, it also glistened, like it was covered in millions of tiny scales.

The giant's brain, which was visible beneath the clear skin and skull, was the size of a VW Bug, but it looked better formed than the sponge-like dire wolf brains. And it moved, pulsing inside the head, like a heart.

As the top of the torso slid out of the portal, a pair of shorter arms emerged. They were connected to the body below the head, but set back. The fifteen-foot-long limbs resembled *Popeye's* arms, thin at the top, but with muscular forearms. A three-fingered hand tipped each arm.

When a third leg stepped into view, Rook had seen enough and for the first time in his life, he tried to speak and found himself speechless.

SIXTY-SIX

Gleipnir Facility, Fenris Kystby, Norway
4 November, 0330 Hrs

KING WATCHED AS a fourth massive foot stepped out of the portal, this one crushing a dead dire wolf under foot. He'd seen a lot—the Hydra reborn, living stone giants, man-eating praying mantises—but this...this put them all to shame. At eighty feet tall, it was by far their largest adversary, but it was also just plain nasty.

Rook scrambled backward on the floor over the rubble with his hands and feet, shoving to gain some distance from the titanic creature. "Thing is fugly!" He turned and climbed to his feet, racing across the room to the others.

Deep Blue, King, Carrack, and the remaining three White team soldiers all heard Lewis Aleman's voice over their earpieces. He was seated back on the *Persephone*, outside the lab. "I've lost visual contact. Not sure what's going on inside. Be advised. I've done linguistic analysis on the name you saw above the hangar doors outside the place. *Gleipnir*. It was a mystical cord used to capture *Fenrir*, a giant wolf in Norse mythology. Not sure how much that helps, but watch out for giant wolves I guess."

Deep Blue touch activated his microphone and the others heard his reply, "Nice to know, Lew. Better late than never, I guess. See what else you can find on Fenrir. Like how to kill it."

"Seriously? Is now the best time for—oh shit. Really?"

"Well, it's not a wolf," King said. "But it's off its leash for sure."

"Somebody please shoot it," Rook said.

King opened fire on the creature with an MP5. The bullets ripped a line into the creature's chest. It raised its head, below which hung a white, fleshy waddle.

It tilted the head back.

The waddle expanded.

And it howled.

The sound shook the facility's walls. Ceiling fragments rained down, crashing into Beck and the Russian woman. The floor shook like a 7.7 earthquake, knocking people off their feet. Some of the team fell to their knees in abject terror. Those who had yet to deal with the roar of the dire wolves were unprepared for the effect.

King remained unaffected, as he had been the last time, with the roars of the dire wolves in Chicago and New York. Queen had mastered battling the effect with her rage, so Fenrir's roar only made her feel weak. The men in the white armor—Carrack, White One, White Three and White Five—were shielded by the audio dampeners in their helmets. They each opened fire on the gargantuan creature. Deep Blue wasn't wearing his helmet and he fell to the floor in a fetal position. The roar affected Rook, too. He fell to a sitting position, curled into a ball on the floor and rocked back and forth.

King fired again at the creature, this time aiming up near the ceiling of the huge room, at the giant beast's head. The White team kept shooting and Queen fired at the narrowest parts of the creature's leg in a concentrated burst, sending globs of fish-like meat spinning off in an arc from the limb. The wounds looked large until King looked at them in context. They were like scrapes to the giant. Barely noticeable, if at all.

As bullets ripped into the beast's hide, a meaty, salty scent wafted across the room, adding to the electrified stench of the portal and the choking dust from the roof collapse. This new smell made King's stomach turn. He wondered if they had hit a weird gland on the creature.

Then he noticed that the shooting had stopped. He looked behind him to see Queen standing calmly next to four of the white armored men, all of them with their weapons lowered. He couldn't see Beck anywhere. The woman that had been with Rook looked to be okay, as she staggered to her feet from under fallen debris. Deep Blue and Rook were out of it. He didn't see Black Six either.

He looked up at the giant and saw that one of its eyes was locked on him, the other on Rook's friend—the only two still with it.

"What the hell?" King was about to ask why no one was doing anything, but instead, Fenrir spoke.

In his head.

Why are you here, children of Adoon?

Adoon? King wondered.

Does it mean, children of Adam? King knew that in the Bible, human men are sometimes referred to as "sons of Adam." So men and women are "the children of Adam." But Adoon? That was a new one. And the question was irrelevant. This was his planet.

"Why are *you* here?" King asked.

The time of Ragnarök has come. The devouring has begun anew.

"You've come to Earth before?" King asked. He was curious, but he was really just hoping someone would snap out it and launch an RPG down the monster's throat.

The giant head swiveled, but the eye locked onto him never moved. *You know this already.*

Is it reading my mind? King wondered, but then decided against it because he *didn't* know that already.

Rook's friend took a bold step forward and shouted with a thick Russian accent. "We will stop you!"

King *felt* the thing's humor at this comment, though he did not hear a laugh, audibly or in his mind.

This world does not belong to you, children of Adoon. The fracture between worlds will remain open. Leave now...or—

"I'm not going anywhere," King interrupted.

The giant eye watching him shifted to the side, landing on Queen. She turned toward King and raised her weapon.

She's being controlled!

King dove to the floor, rolling behind rubble as she fired at his position.

Asya stood wearily, but when the white-armored men leveled their weapons at her, she reacted quickly, firing two shots from her handgun. She crouched behind a 12-foot slab of the ceiling propped up at an angle.

King stood and looked to where Queen had been, but the woman had abandoned the gun and was rushing him from the side. He rolled out of the way to avoid a devastating kick that would have knocked him down, although he doubted it would have injured him through the body armor. Few people could match Queen in a hand-to-hand brawl, but the armor would help. He leapt and swung his leg as he went, aiming his shin for Queen's head. She nimbly ducked at the last second and King cleared her, landing in a crouch. He turned and swept his leg, catching her by surprise and sending her flying.

He looked across to see the Russian, the only other person around that wasn't affected by the fear effects of the roar or the mind control. She leaped clear over Carrack as he lunged at her in his body armor. She landed in a crouch, just like King had done, and spun in a 180-degree arc, sweeping her leg out to catch Carrack off guard. The man toppled from the impact of her leg behind his knees.

King was stunned. The move wasn't part of a martial art or something he'd been trained to do. It was a part of his natural fighting style. He wondered if the woman had some kind of physical eidetic memory, and had copied his every move, but then she rolled backward and sprang from her feet to a twisting side kick that connected hard with the back of Carrack's helmet. King had never seen such a strike, and he certainly couldn't do it himself.

Distracted by Asya, King almost got clobbered as Queen struck again. If it hadn't been for the armor and the fact that he turned at the last second, she might have done some serious damage with the combination of strikes she landed.

Her fists hit his chest repeatedly in a pattern he recognized from Queen's barehanded fighting style. *She has her instincts and practiced moves, but she isn't thinking, or she'd be attacking my face.* He also noticed that one of her hands was all swollen and red, but she was using it as if it were uninjured. *That's gonna hurt like a bastard, later on.*

He struck out hard at Queen's midsection and she pivoted away as he knew she would. But if she had complete command of her senses, she would have been far more aware of her surroundings.

She wasn't.

The woman planted a foot backward, expecting level ground. What she got was a jumble of metal wreckage that had fallen from the cage struts around the portal. Her foot landed badly and the ankle buckled. As she turned to see what happened, while falling, King struck hard with the side of his hand to Queen's neck, knocking the merciless combatant to the ground. He was grateful he wasn't fighting her with all of her senses intact, or he might not have survived the encounter.

King removed two of the grenades from the bandolier he wore across his chest, and rolled behind a pile of rubble. He came up next to Rook. The man's eyes were glazed and he slowly rocked on the floor. King set one of the grenades down and slapped Rook's face. "Rook," he hissed. "Snap out of it. Rook!" He slapped hard a second time and the glazed look on Rook's face dissipated.

Rook looked startled and his eyes darted around the room, confused. When his eyes landed on King, they cleared and his face moved from surprise and fear to serious. "What the—"

"Shh," King silenced him. "Time to blow some shit up."

SIXTY-SEVEN
Gleipnir Facility, Fenris Kystby, Norway
4 November, 0345 Hrs

KING AND ROOK stood from behind their rubble barrier, each
with two grenades in hand. One of the White security men, who
had already been in mid-leap, immediately tackled Rook. The two
bodies sailed past King, but he kept his focus on his target—the
colossal monstrosity, whose body *still* had not fully emerged from
the glowing portal. He had removed the safety clips behind the
rubble. Now, he pulled the pins for both grenades and let the
spoons fly. He counted two seconds and then threw both grenades
across the room where they landed near Fenrir's massive feet. The
first to land bounced and disappeared in a crevice, in a pile of
white stone rubble. The second landed close to a foot.

Both devices detonated, the first grenade sending up a shower
of flame and stone debris. The other grenade exploded near
Fenrir's leg and the creature wailed. When the initial blast of
churning black smoke from the explosion cleared, King could see
that Fenrir had lost the outermost toe off the foot.

One toe. We're gonna need a bigger explosion.

Then another of the White security men was firing at him. Bullets
ripped into the rubble near his legs and King fell over backward in
surprise. He tried to turn it into a roll, but found himself stuck to
some jagged pieces of rubble that clung to his armor like oversized
Velcro hooks. No matter which way he moved, the armor would not
let him get up. He reached his hand under the plating on his left side
and found the buckles. He unclasped them and the chest plate was
free to hinge open on his left side. He slithered out of the chest and
back armor. The lower abdomen and sleeves of armor plating
attached to a black neoprene-like suit woven through with impact
resistant fabric. Those parts of the armor came with him as he slid

out of the chest plate. He stood up and turned to find a jagged piece of metal skewering the back plate of the armor. He slipped his hand behind his back along the neoprene suit and felt a small tear in the suit, but the skin under it was not ruptured. The suit had saved his life. The piece of metal piercing his armor's back plate would have gone through his heart.

King looked up to see Rook wrestling with the White team member. He raced over to help, but the White soldier that had shot at him was now plowing toward him. He dodged to the side, running up a small hill of rubble, then spun around and jump-kicked at the man's head. Although the soldier wore the armored helmet, King hoped the kick would at least knock the man unconscious. But the soldier ducked the kick.

As King flew over the man, he saw Beck was up and duking it out against Matt Carrack. And the Russian still fought one of the other White security men. She leapt nimbly and gracefully, while her opponent bull-rushed her.

King landed on his feet, glancing at the woman. She looked incredibly familiar to him. He couldn't understand exactly why. He had never met her.

The woman slipped up the soldier's back, wrapping her legs around his upper chest, then her hands quickly found the buckles on his helmet and pulled it off. King saw that it was White Five, a quiet man with blonde hair and an always serious face. Five threw himself over backward with the hope of crushing her with his weight. She unwrapped her legs from his chest, and cartwheeled away from the impact of his body. She arrested her spin, reversed and leapt. A second after White Five hit the floor, her hand chopped at his neck. Then she was up and away.

The neck strike was the same he'd used on Queen.

He tried to remember where he'd learned the move, but couldn't.

King heard Rook growling behind him and turned to see his friend hefting a massive slab of concrete and dropping it on the armored chest of his opponent. The armored man struggled but didn't have the leverage or the abdominal muscles to get up from under the slab. Then Rook sat down heavily on top of the slab, adding his 200 pounds of muscle.

King almost laughed.

Then he heard a scream. He looked behind him. Fenrir had stepped further into the room, and as King turned, a giant three-fingered hand swept across the floor, scooping up one of the still-helmeted White security soldiers and flinging him against the wall of the room—over sixty feet up. Then the man's armored body plunged to the floor, crashing hard again. King hoped the body armor could withstand such blows.

Fenrir stepped further into the room, revealing two more legs and its hind quarters, a stubby lump of loose flesh stained with defecation. Nearly fifty liquid-filled sacks dangled from its body. Some of the creatures inside were waking up, twisting and clawing. With a gust of viscous liquid, one of the pouches ruptured, disgorging a fresh dire wolf onto the battlefield. The creature landed on all fours, shook the fluid away like a wet dog and sprang into action, joining the fray.

King twisted just in time to avoid yet another strike. The White soldier returned, launching himself at King. Up close, King could see a small Chess Piece insignia of a King on the man's shoulder plating with a number 1 in the center. It was a quick homemade job, but King appreciated the sentiment anyway. White One again ran at King, all power and no finesse. King ducked a swinging punch and came up behind the man, his hand quickly sliding to White One's neck and the helmet buckle restraints. He only got one before the man turned and kicked. King caught the kick in the stomach. It had been aimed at King's unprotected chest, but he diverted the blow with his forearms, driving it down to the armor plating covering his lower body. The kick still had enough force to drive King backward, but not enough to knock him down.

Beck was still battling Matt Carrack—her opposite number with the callsign of White Zero—and their battle shifted closer to King's. She was holding her own, but both combatants looked exhausted to King.

White One again rushed at King, who threw himself forward into the man's chest. He wrapped an arm around White One's middle and threw his other hand to the back of the neck, getting the second clasp. As they fell, King wrenched the helmet free, and still gripping it, swung his arm back at the man's head, smashing the helmet against his head. The man fell and King worried that he might have hit the soldier too hard. He didn't want to kill him—he was being controlled. King reached down and pulled off his armored glove. He reached for the man's neck, checking for a pulse.

Before he could, a roar tore through the air, but it sounded nothing like Fenrir, or any of the dire wolves. It didn't even sound organic.

Two glowing eyes emerged from the portal, followed by a white, boxy creature.

Not a creature, King realized as the shape became clear. *A Humvee!*

The battered vehicle, covered in white, gelatinous gore, skidded to a stop, flinging a dead dire wolf from its hood. Another dead dire wolf, this one missing it's lower half, was jammed into the front wheel well. A coil of clear intestines slid down the driver's side door. The thing looked like it had plowed through an army of the things.

The door flung open, sending the guts to the floor.

Bishop, still wearing his body armor, but no helmet, stood from the vehicle looking like a warrior from some other world. He looked down, saw a grenade launcher one of the White team had dropped and bent to pick it up.

Knight slid out behind him. "Punch line, Bishop. You can't make an entrance like that and not have a punch line." When his boots hit the rubble covered concrete floor, Knight didn't miss a beat. He ran across the room in what appeared to be a loin cloth. His hair was back in a ponytail and whipped around him as he ran. He was covered in white dust. As he ran, he scooped up a discarded rifle.

Despite Knight and Bishop's sudden arrival being a shock, King recovered quickly enough to notice a familiar shape strapped to Knight's back.

It can't be...

Fenrir looked down at the disturbance in time to see Bishop fire a 40 mm grenade right up at her belly, where a curtain of still-growing dire wolves hung in their liquid-filled sacks.

Before the first grenade had hit, Bishop fired another at her ass.

SIXTY-EIGHT
Gleipnir Facility, Fenris Kystby, Norway
4 November, 0400 Hrs

THE EXPLOSION WAS tremendous. The shockwave sent Bishop flying backward into the portal, where he disappeared through the bulging, straining wall of brilliant light. Flames leapt up from Fenrir's gut, but were quickly extinguished as several of the sacks burst, spilling their fluids and partially formed young to the floor. Fenrir let out an anguished roar that could have been fueled by pain or anger of the loss of her children. Its big body tensed and closed what looked like several large pores running along its flanks.

From one side of the giant room, away from the fight, a door opened and several bewildered people in lab coats with blonde hair ran out and raced for the small door that led outside the lab. Wind and snow still swept into the chamber from the ruined ceiling and the open hangar doors that Fenrir had been heading for, before Bishop's grenade attack.

Knight ran to the metal stairwell with the FN-SCAR rifle he found and raced up the steps. Queen stood from where she had lain, rubbing her neck and squinting hard, as if she had a vicious headache. Carrack stopped fighting Beck, and looked around at the chaos around him. Beck recognized that Carrack was no longer under control. She moved away and toward the hangar door, looking for another weapon in the ruins. Deep Blue stood up from behind a long steel I-beam and looked wobbly on his feet.

King saw all of it happening around him. He threw another grenade at Fenrir's front feet—his last—then ran to join Beck and look for another weapon.

Rook was standing, still favoring one shoulder, but he had opened fire on the creature with an MP5 dropped by one of the White team. He focused his fire on Fenrir's flattened pug nose, and as the creature moved its head away, Rook followed it with the stream of bullets. The MP5 was equipped with a Beta C-Mag—the cartridge looked like two flat drums on either side of the weapon's barrel. It held 100 rounds of ammunition, and Rook had found more of them at his feet in a black nylon bag next to Reggie's impaled body. He kept the stream of fire sizzling through the air and then was joined by FN-SCAR fire from the stairs as Knight climbed, and by more MP5 fire, from Queen.

Bishop stepped out of the portal again, only this time, he backed into the room. After another step backward, he was fully into the room, backing toward Fenrir and firing his rifle into the portal, sweeping the barrel left and right.

Then they came.

Dire wolf after dire wolf poured out of the opening toward Bishop. The first wave of them crashed into him, sending him flying toward Fenrir, where his armored body slammed into Fenrir's second left-side leg, just as it lifted from the floor and stepped forward. It was like getting hit by a bus. The impact launched him back into the room. He hit the floor hard and slid for a few feet before coming to a stop. He didn't get up.

King saw twenty, then thirty, then forty of the creatures enter the room, some so eager that they climbed over each other. Fenrir had recovered from its wounds, or was simply ignoring the thirteen ruptured sacks hanging from its underside like popped balloons. It turned its slathering jaws toward the weapons that were barking at it, spitting bullets like vicious hornet stings. Carrack, Beck and Deep Blue had all added their weapons fire to the melee, but even added to Queen's, Rook's and Knight's fire, they were not able to hold back the tide of oncoming dire wolves.

King looked up at Knight and the pack sitting next to him. He whistled to the man through his fingers and shouted, "Knight!"

Between shots, Knight glanced down. King pointed to the pack. Knight pushed it over the side without hesitation. King bent his knees and snatched the heavy bundle from the air, squatting to absorb the impact. He opened it up to confirm its contents.

The suitcase nuke. *His* suitcase nuke.

As the melee came closer, King did the only thing he could think of.

He turned and ran.

SIXTY-NINE

Aboard the *Persephone*, Fenris Kystby, Norway
4 November, 0415 Hrs

THE HUGE FLYING-WING aircraft settled gently in the snow, the thrusters of the engines blasting the white flakes in all directions, clearing a landing spot for itself.

Lewis Aleman sat in the computer room with the makeshift desk and chairs, frantically searching for more information about portals, alternate dimensions, Fenrir and dire wolves, as were Sara Fogg, George Pierce and Black Five back in New Hampshire. He could feed anything they found to Deep Blue over the earbud communicator in their leader's ear.

"So, we're thinking that this Fenrir thing might be secreting scent out of glands. The scent could carry pheromones, and that would explain the control over some of the team. Look for something that looks like a sphincter, or large pore. If you could..."

Deep Blue cut him off. "Timing, Lewis, timing. I think that problem is solved for now." Aleman could hear tons of background noise on the line. He knew Deep Blue's helmet was off, but at the moment, his anonymity wasn't a concern. "We're seeing increasing numbers of dire wolves, too, and we're down several men. We need a way to stop these things and to kill the portal. We might have to go with your plan for the *Crescent*."

"Working on it."

"I know," Deep Blue said. "But work faster." He clicked off and Aleman's earpiece went quiet.

Aleman shouted in surprise as the metal door to the room slammed open.

King stood in the doorway, dirty, bloody and missing the top portion of his armor. He was out of breath from his sprint through the snow drifts to the *Persephone*.

When he spoke, his voice sounded like a growl. "I need you to do exactly as I say."

That's when Aleman noticed the suitcase nuke clutched under King's arm.

SEVENTY
Gleipnir Facility, Fenris Kystby, Norway
4 November, 0430 Hrs

KNIGHT HAD A bird's eye view of the entire conflict. He still
didn't feel like himself after his ordeal on the other side of the
portal. His brain felt loose, his thoughts all erratic. He had a hard
time remembering what had happened in all the time he was on
the other side. But he and Bishop were able to agree that Knight
must either have been on the other side for much longer—and they
realized time worked differently on that side—or else his body had
aged at an accelerated rate in the short span of time he was there.
Either way, Knight was a few years older now.

Although strangely, Bishop wasn't.

According to the big Iranian American, they had both been on
the other side for about the same amount of time—Bishop having
entered a portal on a rope like Tarzan just moments after Knight
had been carried through the one on Westminster bridge. In the
end they came to agree that time had worked differently for each
of them, either because they had gone through different portals, or
because Knight spent most of his time on the lower plane while
Bishop entered the other world atop the cliff. Knight knew that
time ran slower the further you got from Earth's surface. You
needed an atomic watch to see the difference, but the effect might
be exaggerated in Fenrir's dimension.

What Knight hadn't told Bishop was that, when they met at the
top of the cliff, Bishop had been covered in dried white dire wolf
blood. It covered his armored chest and the side of his face.
Bishop told him about his encounter with the dire wolf, that he'd
hallucinated his worst fear—becoming a Regen once more, but
Knight suspected the man had actually attacked, killed and eaten
a dire wolf. Having personally survived Bishop as a Regen, it was a

nightmare neither man wanted to think about, so Knight didn't. He put the memory out of his mind with no intention of ever telling Bishop.

A burst of gunfire brought him back to the battle.

Knight focused on the chaos below him. Deep Blue fired on leaping dire wolves. Queen was back to her preferred method of up-close devastation with a wickedly curved blade, moving with a display of predatory violence that put the dire wolves to shame. Carrack, Beck and Rook were all near each other, unleashing a barrage of bullets at the giant creature's sack-covered chest, which didn't seem to hurt it as much as distract it.

In a perfect sniping position, he focused on the largest target, the behemoth. He considered the chest, but rupturing the hanging wombs wasn't doing any real damage. Instead, he targeted the eyes, thinking if he couldn't kill the gigantic animal, he could at least handicap it.

He lay on the metal catwalk and supported the FN-SCAR under the barrel and sighted one of the creature's round eyes. The SCAR was a Belgian rifle with an effective range of about 1200 feet. He was less than a hundred feet from the beast. Of course, the monster was eighty feet tall; it would be an easy target from any distance.

He fired twice into the beast's left eye and the creature roared, shaking the foundations of the underground lab. The metal catwalk rattled, shaking Knight to the point where he wondered if the whole catwalk system might come down.

The team continued their assault on Fenrir. It struck out wildly, unaware of where the bullet strike to its eye had originated. Its torso spun from side to side, swinging its arms and flailing the dangling sacks so hard that some burst open, dropping dire wolves sixty feet to their deaths. The giant snapped its tremendous jaws at the soldiers on the ground and pounded its feet, trying to crush them.

Knight waited until the creature turned again to snap toward Rook's position. Rook ran out of the way and leapt over a pile of rock and sand, sliding down the other side. The beast's head lunged at Rook, and then swung back to snarl at Anna Beck—Knight's girlfriend—as she fired on the creature from behind, helping Bishop to his feet with her other hand. He was once again firing at the newly arriving dire wolves as they entered the fray through the portal.

The right eye stayed frustratingly out of Knight's view, so he took a few more shots at the already damaged and closed-over left eye.

Then he heard a new kind of roar. This one was loud and higher pitched, more like a whine.

A mechanical whine.

When Knight looked to the hangar doors, he understood that he didn't need to hit the creature's right eye. King was back, and he was going to hit the eye—and everything else.

SEVENTY-ONE

Outside the *Gleipnir* Facility, Fenris Kystby, Norway
4 November, 0445 Hrs

THE *CRESCENT*, CHESS Team's personal stealth, troop transport ship, looked like a giant croissant that had gone gray and black from mold. Radar-reflective material covered the ship from one tip of its half-moon shape across 80 feet of breadth to its other tip. The giant, flat plane could carry 25,000 pounds of load and travel at above Mach 2. Its newly designed VTOL engines could run in a silent stealth mode, which sounded like little more than a strong wind with an undercurrent of high-pitched metallic squeal. When the engines were running without the stealth technology, the massive engines roared like the sound of twelve 747 jumbo jets. It cost 500 million dollars, not counting the billions in research and development for the prototype.

Today, Jack Sigler, the man known as King, intended to crash it.

He was flying the huge plane alone. The pilots wanted to come with him on his suicide mission, but he hadn't allowed it. He had been taking flying lessons, and had been at the helm of the *Crescent* in the air and on takeoff. He had yet to land the plane, but for today's exercise, that wouldn't matter.

Sitting on the co-pilot's seat and strapped in with a seatbelt was the suitcase nuke King had lost in Manhattan. The goal was to get the bomb through a portal and close the portal before the timer detonated. If for some reason the portal couldn't be closed—or the device didn't make it into a portal, there was the remote control he held in his hand.

King looked at the device.

He pictured Sara. Her sarcastic smile. Her sharp eyes. He could hear her voice, whispering in his ear, but he didn't like the words. *Do it Jack, you have no choice.*

I have a daughter, he thought. *I can't.*

Fiona came into his thoughts like a specter, her voice, high and raspy, sounded like a breeze. *It's you or the world, daddy.*

King knew the words were his own thoughts, imagining what he thought they might say, after weeping, shouting and threatening to kill him themselves. It had to be done. They would understand that.

The remote clattered to the floor where King threw it.

"Love you guys," he whispered, then focused on aiming the world's largest boomerang.

King had swept the sickle-shaped transport out over the Norwegian Sea, before bringing it back toward his target—the open hangar doors on the side of the lab. He could see how cleverly the facility had been built into the landscape, using the night vision features built into the cockpit of the vehicle. The doors were hidden from pretty much everything except a direct approach from the sea—and this far north along the Norwegian coast was well off the standard shipping lanes. The timing for this stunt would be crucial. He sped up on approach and then slowed just as he was reaching the open doors, carefully adjusting his aim.

He tightened the seatbelt strap crisscrossing over his chest and prayed the high tech crash gear did its job.

The plane slipped through the massive open hanger.

Then everything happened at once.

Fenrir turned to the hangar doors and saw the fast-approaching black plane. The monster opened its gaping mouth wide to howl.

King hit the gas.

The *Crescent* rammed into the creature's open mouth, snapping off its mighty lower jaw and plowing into the beast's flaccid-skinned chest. The thrust from the plane knocked the giant back as it flailed in pain. The *Crescent*'s engines roared, pushing the giant back and together, they slipped through the portal.

KING OPENED HIS eyes to a world of white.

He was still alive, but where? He reached out a hand and found the world around him was pliable, like a cushion...or an air bag. King was surrounded on all sides by nylon airbags designed to protect pilots from controlled crashes. While his crash wasn't exactly controlled, he wasn't moving at Mach 2, either.

King drew a pocket knife, flipped it open and stabbed at the airbags. One by one, the bags popped and deflated. King's head spun as he fumbled with the seatbelt. His chest ached. Broken ribs, he thought. Could have been worse.

He looked at the seat next to him. The suitcase nuke was still in place, held tight by the belts.

Still might work.

King flinched when a pair of hands reached around him.

"Slow down, killer," Rook said and quickly unbuckled his teammate.

"Rook, what are you doing here?"

"Same thing as you," Rook said. "Playing the big hero so maybe I can get laid tonight."

King laughed, but groaned as his chest filled with pain. "Seriously."

"Seriously?" Rook said. "I lost a lot of men in Siberia. I ain't losing you, too."

King looked in Rook's cool blue eyes and nodded. "Let's go."

Rook helped King through the back of the plane, which seemed to be largely in one piece. They stumbled when the *Crescent* shifted underfoot.

"FYI, that Fenrir bitch is beneath us."

A shadow shifted at the back of the plane, where the loading ramp was bent open.

"Shit," Rook said, then led King to a chair. "Stay," he ordered like a dog trainer. He ran into the plane's armory and returned a moment later carrying two chrome Desert Eagle magnum handguns. He kissed them one at a time. "I've missed you, girls."

He handed one to King and walking as one with Rook helping to support King's weight, they made for the back of the plane. The Magnums only held seven rounds each, but the .50 caliber bullets would take a dire wolf's head clean off. Just about any hit would be a kill shot. And Rook had four spare magazines in his pocket.

As they exited the plane, King raised his gun and fired. The bullet struck a waiting dire wolf's shoulder removing the arm and dropping the beast. It wasn't dead, but it would be soon.

They moved as one, leaving the plane, scrambling over Fenrir's squishy body, which was slick with slime from its burst wombs. They ran, and fired, and scrambled and fired some more until their bullets ran out. Both reloaded fast, fired twice more each and then ducked into the brilliant portal, leaving the other world, which Rook had seen in shades of green and King in white, behind.

They emerged on the other side, but King didn't feel safe.

The nuke he'd left behind would detonate in four minutes.

SEVENTY-TWO

Gleipnir Facility, Fenris Kystby, Norway
4 November, 0450 Hrs

QUEEN SIGHED WITH relief when Rook and King hobbled out of the portal. She was covered in cuts and scrapes, her ankle was twisted, maybe broken. Her hand was swollen like a red balloon, she was coated in dried dire wolf blood and secretions and she could only move by hopping on her unaffected foot, but she still laid down fire on the dire wolf army that turned toward Rook and King as they separated.

Beck had seen the situation and moved over to help support her and share the last of her ammunition—two normal-sized curved 32 round magazines. Together, they covered their teammates as the men scrambled toward them.

Bishop moved to the high ground of the metal stairs in the corner of the giant room and fired down on dire wolves. A pile of ten of the creatures lay dead below the landing where he stood; an effective barricade.

Rook and King split up. King held his chest, but seemed to be recovering from whatever wound had slowed him down. Rook caught Queen's eyes and pointed to Bishop. "To the stairs," he called.

When he saw Queen take a limping step, he shot the leg off a dire wolf and ran to her aid. But instead of helping her run, as he had King, he scooped her over his shoulder and carried her.

"Rook!" she shouted angrily.

"I'll run, you shoot!" he replied. "We're running out of time!"

Queen's body shook with every step, but she managed to trace a line of bullets across the chest of a dire wolf pounding toward them.

"Time for what?" she asked.

ACROSS THE ROOM, Deep Blue ran to meet King. The Russian came over to them from behind her barricade of dire wolf corpses, now coated in thick white blood.

"Seriously, Jack? My 500-million-dollar stealth plane? You couldn't come up with a better plan than that?" Deep Blue fired his MP5 twice, hitting dire wolves that ran at them. His face showed only concentration as he focused on hitting his targets.

King couldn't tell whether the former President of the United States was joking with him or really upset, but decided he didn't care.

"It worked. We need to find a way to shut down the portal. Knight found the suitcase nuke on the other side and brought it back. I remembered to arm it this time. Probably would be good if we could shut down that portal before it goes off in..." King checked his digital watch, "three minutes."

"We need to completely destroy the containment apparatus. The metal arms that Rook blew up before—" Deep Blue began. He fired another volley of bullets at the oncoming dire wolves and his weapon was empty.

"That didn't work out so well last time," King said, pulling out a new magazine of 9 mm bullets from one of the Velcro attachments on his suit and handing it to the man.

"Ale says Rook was on the right track. We need to get them all— not just the two. And cut the power."

"Wait," the Russian woman spoke up. "I have seen it. A power relay."

Both Deep Blue and King turned to her and at the same time said, "Where?"

"Follow me. I saw it on a video camera. There was a map."

"Go with her," Deep Blue ordered. "We'll take care of the cage."

The woman circled around the side of the energy ball, moving along the wall, back behind the side of the sphere where the dire wolves were still coming through. King followed her, while Deep Blue provided cover fire.

ONCE KING AND the woman were out of his sight around the portal, Deep Blue crossed in front of the open hangar door to the other side of the room and made for the stairwell. Bishop, Rook, Queen and Beck were on the third flight of steps, firing on any dire wolves that came near. Knight offered cover fire from his perch in the sky.

Are they all that's left?

Deep Blue needed the cover fire. He ran out of bullets halfway to the stairs. Each of the four soldiers on the stairs turned their attention to protecting their leader. Deep Blue didn't bother looking behind him to see if any dire wolves were about to make him a snack. He knew his team would kill each and every one of them before they laid a claw-tipped hand on him.

When he reached the underside of the second flight of stairs, he leapt up and grabbed the railing, climbing up and over the side. "Up! Make for the catwalk," he shouted.

Bishop stopped firing, slung Queen over his shoulder before she could protest and sprinted up the steps. Rook was fast on his heels. Beck kept up her cover fire until Deep Blue passed her on the steps. Only then, did she turn and take to the stairs. Knight began firing from the catwalk to the base of the stairs, where dire wolves were crawling up the exterior of the metal railings—easy shots—or were racing up the steps.

As they ran up the metal steps, Deep Blue shouted to the others between breaths. He was in great shape, but even an Olympic athlete would be panting after the day he'd had. "We need to destroy the metal support arms around the portal."

"*That* was not a good idea the first time," Rook shouted back.

"Ale says it would have helped if all the struts were down—not just two!"

"There's six of the things left," Rook said. "I don't know about anyone else, but I've only got one grenade left." Rook held up a found FN-SCAR with an attached grenade launcher.

"I've got two," Bishop yelled from the lead, as he reached the catwalk with Queen and set her down gently. She grabbed the railing for support and then began hopping toward where Knight lay.

"You look like shit little man," she told him as he fired on dire wolves getting too high up the stairs.

"You have no idea. We'll talk," he said calmly, picking his next target and firing.

"I have two M67s," Beck added, once she reached the catwalk.

"You kids and your toys," Deep Blue said. "Let the old man show you how to blow something up." He opened a buttoned pocket on his left thigh and removed a gray brick of C4. He reached into another pocket and pulled out a handful of detonators. "We've got about a minute left. Whose got a good arm?"

SEVENTY-THREE

Gleipnir Facility, Fenris Kystby, Norway
4 November, 0500 Hrs

KING FOLLOWED THE woman around the energy portal, away from the side of the globe where dire wolves continued to run and climb out. On the far wall from the hangar door was a normal set of double doors with a symbol of a black jagged lightning bolt on a yellow triangle, universal for "electrical hazard." The door was locked and it opened outward, so King couldn't easily kick the door in.

He stepped back from the door and fired a burst of 9 mm bullets at the upper and lower hinges on the right side. The door simply fell outward and onto the floor. The woman rushed in first, followed by King, who skidded to a halt.

There wasn't a turbine, or a generator, but there were banks and banks of electrical switches and fuses, circuit breakers, switchboards, electricity meters, transformers and fire alarm control panels. This was a power distribution room—not the power generating station.

"I'm not an electrician," King said, "but I think this will do."

He pulled a small brick of tan-colored C4 explosive from Velcro straps on the outside of an armored thigh, and then a tiny detonating blasting cap from his belt, which he inserted into the brick. He tossed the brick to the far end of the small room.

"Ten seconds and counting," he said before pushing the Russian toward the door, though he was more concerned with the second countdown running in his head, the one that was at twenty seconds.

King ran for the door, and then grabbed the woman by the arm and tugged her to the side of the wall by the broken door. They ran three more steps when the C4 detonated. The explosion ripped out the room's other door and hurled it into the portal. A good ten feet of the brick wall on either side of the double doorway spat brick and mortar. A second larger explosion ripped through the main chamber. The concussion shook the walls and another huge portion of the ceiling over the giant room collapsed, taking catwalks with it.

****

DEEP BLUE REACHED the southwest corner of the catwalk and threw his large, brownie-sized block of C4. Anna Beck, who played college softball, threw three more blocks, aiming for the concrete bases of struts, though anywhere near them would do the trick. Bishop handled the remaining two, lobbing them far across the large room.

The timers were set for twenty seconds and set to go off as one. If someone dropped one, or didn't throw it in time, they were dead. But this knowledge motivated them and the C4 bricks all landed around the room with seconds to spare.

Several things happened at once—the electrical room on the ground floor exploded, billowing fire and smoke that obscured the view of the portal.

The six bricks of C4 in the main chamber detonated all at once, pulverizing the concrete holding the struts on the floor and killing the remaining dire wolves.

The rest of the ceiling over the eastern part of the portal fell, taking parts of the northern catwalk just after Bishop leapt away.

The portal bulged and distorted as it ate the falling wreckage. The eastern catwalk broke loose on the northeastern end, and began to fall down.

Rook, closer to the upper end of the now slanting metal slide, grabbed the railing. Queen was back by the stairwell—the most structurally sound part of the room at the moment. Beck was with her. Knight slid down the angled catwalk, scrabbling with his fingertips to get a hold in the metal grill.

With a groan of bending metal, the catwalk tipped and fell, jolting to a stop a few feet later as one of the giant curved struts fell back against the wall, and the catwalk above, pinning the whole structure to the wall.

Then all the light and sound vanished.

They were plunged into darkness.

The portal was closed.

SEVENTY-FOUR
Somewhere

EIREK FOSSEN SPUN around as an unfamiliar whine tore through the air, standing his hair on end. He had walked with dire wolves and plotted with a God, but none of them frightened him like this sound.

It portended doom.

His doom.

When he saw the sound's source, he braced himself against the massive bone wall, growing week in the knees.

"Lord Fenrir," he said, his voice oozing fear.

A giant plane, in the shape of a crescent, crashed through the portal, pushing Fenrir up and over. The giant toppled backward as though in slow motion. It roared in frustration and something else. Pain? Fossen didn't think it was possible, but then saw his Lord's lower jaw dangling loosely.

"No," he whispered. "No..."

The ground shook as Fenrir and the plane stumbled back from the portal and crashed to the ground, pulverizing hundreds of dire wolves and scattering more.

Fossen took a step toward the portal. But what could he do? The plane was obviously a move of desperation. Things were not going well for their enemies on the other side. Fenrir might be injured, but it wouldn't stop. As soon as it freed itself from the plane, it would return to the other side. And it would heal.

Something hard jabbed Fossen's back. He spun, not realizing he'd been walking backward, away from the portal.

He found a cage, a fifteen-foot cube, built of bones—human and dire wolf—held together by some kind of solidified secretion. He stepped back from the cage, eyes widening at the sight of the human bodies that filled the cage. The corpses were hacked into pieces—arms, legs, heads, torsos—all packed inside, floor to ceiling. The body parts glistened and he realized that they, too, had been covered in some kind of secretion.

Preserved, he thought, stepping back from the cage, but bumping into a second.

He leapt away from the second cage and spun around, finding himself surrounded by a field of the structures. Fear rose in his chest, but he squelched it. He knew Lord Fenrir killed and ate human beings, among other things. But she did not, *would not*, eat Fossen.

Gunshots rolled across the plains bringing his attention back to the portal. Lord Fenrir lay on Her back still, but was beginning to stir. Two figures ran over her body, heading back toward the portal. Fossen squinted his eyes. He couldn't see the mens' faces, but the shape and gait of one of them was familiar.

Stanislav.

He shouted the name, "Stanislav!"

But a moment later, the two men disappeared through the portal.

The crescent-shaped airplane shifted and fell partly away from Fenrir, who shrieked. She was getting back up, recovering from the blow, but slowly.

Fossen, came Her voice. ***You have failed***.

"No," he said, feeling a tremble in his legs. "The portal is stable!"

But it is not secure. You brought the children of Adoon to my doorstep.

"The children of what?" Fossen's thoughts became panicked. "I didn't know. How could I have—"

Fossen's twitching body froze. Dust rose in the distance between him and the portal. He saw this world in shades of monotone gray, like old photos of his father, Edmund Kiss. It had unnerved him, but not nearly as much as what he saw now.

Dire wolves.

Perhaps a hundred of them.

Running toward him.

He'd been around the creatures a lot. He understood their moods. Their body language. These hundred predators were out for blood.

His blood.

"My Lord, why?" Fossen shouted.

No reply. Fossen ran away from the approaching horde, quickly arriving at the bone wall. Gripping the protruding bones, he climbed as fast as he could, reaching the top just as the hundred dire wolves arrived at the base and launched up toward him.

"The portal is open!" he shrieked.

He turned toward the glowing sphere.

Fenrir stood again, the plane falling away. The giant's head turned toward him, its jaw dangling sickly, its body covered in white blood and ruptured wounds, looking very mortal.

Not a God.

Tears welled in Fossen's eyes.

He stood still.

The portal winked out, drawing a gasp from his lips.

"We can start again," he whispered.

The leash remains.

Her voice sounded almost sad now, as though filled with a disappointment more deep and complex than anything he had felt before. It brought tears to his eyes. He fell to his knees, weeping, waiting for the dire wolves to reach him and exact the punishment he now knew he deserved.

But then, as though by magic, the portal returned, blooming brighter than ever before. Fossen flinched away from the light, covering his eyes with his arm. A hot breeze washed over him. He chanced a look and in the fraction of a second he had left, he recognized the mushroom cloud rising into the gray sky. Then the shockwave hit, first melting and then obliterating his body, the dire wolves and the massive bone tower, leaving only dust and one more crater.

SEVENTY-FIVE

Outside the *Gleipnir* Facility, Fenris Kystby, Norway
4 November, 0520 Hrs

KING STUMBLED INTO the cold night, leading the remaining members of Endgame through the dark. Deep Blue, Knight, Queen, Bishop, Rook, Beck and the Russian woman had all survived the final confrontation and explosive finale. But they'd lost Carrack and the whole White team, Reggie and Black Six, not to mention Keasling in New York. Deep Blue hadn't talked about it yet, nor had King, but Keasling was a good friend to them both. They would feel his loss for years, both personally and professionally, as he was their only trusted liaison to the US Military.

He pushed through a low-hanging pine branch laden with snow and held it. The clearing beyond was lit brightly by the *Persephone's* spotlights. As the team hobbled into the clearing, the pilots and Aleman rushed out with med-kits.

With a smile, Aleman said, "Reports from around the world are coming in. Looks like you did it." Then he saw their condition and grimaced. He tapped the med-kit in his hand and asked, "Who's first?"

"Take her," Rook said. He held Queen over his shoulder. She looked none too pleased about it, still, but wasn't complaining. The two pilots laid a stretcher on the ground and helped Rook lower her. When he grunted in pain, one of the pilots saw his ruined shoulder and said, "You better come, too."

"What about you?" Aleman asked King, who was clutching his side.

"Broken ribs," King said. "Not a big deal. It can wait."

Aleman shook his head. "You might be the only person on the planet who would say those three sentences in that order."

King laughed, then grunted in pain.

Aleman turned to the Russian. "Who's this?"

"Name's Asya. She's with me," Rook said, as he helped the pilots guide Queen's stretcher toward the plane's loading ramp. "She's okay."

Aleman turned to Deep Blue who gave a nod.

But King wasn't satisfied. When she turned to the plane, he took her shoulder and said, "Hold on." She faced him, looking in his eyes. She stood nearly as tall as him, but he wasn't interested in her height. He was interested in her face. *So familiar.* When their eyes met, he noticed she was looking at him the same way.

"Do I know you?" she asked.

"I don't know," he replied.

"Haven't figured it out yet?" Queen called as she was carried up the *Persephone*'s loading ramp. "Who taught you how to fight, King?"

A lot of people had taught King how to fight. Hand-to-hand combat instructors, martial artists, every enemy he fought, even Queen had taught him a thing or two.

As Queen disappeared inside the plane, she shouted one more time. "The *first* person."

King's eyes widened. The story, which he'd told the team over beers one night, came back to him in a flash. He was ten. Got the snot beat out of him by a couple of kids. While his mother, Lynn Sigler, pursued typical childhood diplomatic channels—calling the other kid's mothers—King's father, Peter Sigler, took him in the back yard and taught him how to fight. Some of the moves became part of his natural fighting style. He'd used a few in the brawl inside the—

So had Asya.

He staggered away from her as though he'd seen a ghost, shuffling through the deep snow. Recognition slammed into his gut now. The face. The eyes.

"What is it?" Asya asked, stepping toward him.

Deep Blue rushed over, placing a hand on King's shoulder. "Aleman, get a—"

"It's fine," King said. "I'm okay. I—I just know who she is." He stood straighter, looking into Asya's eyes. "She has my mother's eyes."

Deep Blue looked like he'd been slapped. He whipped his head toward Asya, staring at her eyes. "My God."

"Her eyes?" Asya said, still confused. "How—"

"Your last name," King said. "Is it Machtcenko?"

She looked surprised. "How did you know?"

"Because it's my last name, too," he said. "My *real* last name. My parents were Russian spies. Their cover name was Sigler. My father taught us both how to fight. Fenrir's roar didn't affect me, probably because of a genetic trait passed down by my parents. You have that same trait."

Asya's eyes began to widen.

Despite being completely unnerved by the development, a smile crept onto King's face and tears threatened to spill from his eyes. Since Julie's death, he'd felt a void in his life. He'd grown up with a sister and missed that relationship greatly. But now...maybe he had a second chance? "You're my sister."

EPILOGUE

SNOW FELL HEAVILY outside the immense open hangar door of the Endgame base, hidden under the large rocky face of Mount Tecumseh, in the White Mountains. King drove a black Humvee into the large hangar and parked it next to a Black Hawk helicopter that sat dormant, its rotor blades strapped down lengthwise along the vehicle with nylon webbing to metal rings sunk into the gray concrete floor.

He climbed out of the driver's seat, and Asya stepped out on the other side of the vehicle. Before they had fully emerged, the massive metal door that retracted into the ceiling of rock above the doorway began to lower. Soldiers in white battle gear operated a newly installed guard shack that had a door leading from a shack on the inside of the hangar to an identical shack on the outside, adjacent to the massive door.

Some of Deep Blue's new White security team. King knew they were top-notch soldiers from Fort Drum, just like their predecessors had been. He just hadn't taken the time to get to know any of them. If they lived long enough, he knew he would. The only thing he knew about them was that Deep Blue had foregone the Chess-themed numbering and hired ten men to be security members, where previously they had numbered only five.

There was a lot to think about and process in the wake of the assault, which had hit the team hard, but the world even harder. Millions were dead or missing. Cities were destroyed or simply gone. The world economy was in turmoil. The silver lining was that most governments recognized that the threat was not of this Earth and threatened every nation. The damage was extensive, but governments were entering a new phase of cooperation as they lent aid, rebuilt and prepared to fight global threats as a unified force rather than as separate nations. King wasn't naïve, though. There would be some who deviated from the plan. Over time, alliances would fade. Greed would divide nations. Eventually, without a second attack, the world's governments would be back to fighting each other.

Despite all of that, King had only one focus right now: finding his parents. He and Asya had been hard at it for weeks, tracking down every lead. Asya had been temporarily given the callsign: Hammer for the mission, which began as a joke with Queen referencing how well Asya had fought in Norway, and also referring to the symbol from the old Soviet flag. Asya liked it.

They were a natural team and bonded quickly. Asya reminded King of his mother and he of her father. They swapped childhood stories, marveling at how their parents had led double lives, in two countries. And for the first time in his life, King knew where his father had *really* been during the ten years he'd been missing. Asya had also become fast friends with Sara and enjoyed being called "Auntie Asya" by Fiona, who also enjoyed rubbing in the fact that the women in King's life now outnumbered him three to one.

As King and Asya headed down the hallway toward the main computer lab to check in with Deep Blue, they came across Rook and Queen, heading the other way. Rook was dressed in shorts and tennis shoes, with a rock t-shirt that read Primal Puppy Dogs on the front and showed a silhouette of a medium-sized dog, lifting its leg and urinating on a guitar leaning against an amplifier. As a native of New Hampshire, things like winter didn't faze him. Even when they would go outdoors to local restaurants as a group, Rook wore shorts year-round. Over his t-shirt, he wore his arm in a blue medical sling. His shoulder would still need a few more weeks to recover from the surgery he had undergone to repair his rotator cuff.

Queen wore tight-fitting jeans and a loose navy sweater that accentuated her lithe physique. She also wore a black pneumatic medical fracture boot on her ankle that allowed her to walk short distances while her ankle healed. Her right hand was in a blue cast from the fingers to just beyond her wrist.

King noticed that she held Rook's hand with her left hand as they approached, and they were not shy about it. He smiled at them. "How's it going?"

"Pretty good," Rook said. "Together we make one functioning human body." Queen elbowed him in the rib, and he smiled broadly at King and Asya.

"I never did ask you, Rook," King said, a grin forming, "That plan we discussed on the *Crescent*, while we were on the other side."

Rook's eyes widened with a look of *Shut up, King!*

"How'd that work out for you?"

"Wouldn't you like to know," Rook said.

"What's he talking about?" Queen asked.

"Nevermind him, Zel." Rook tried to lead her away.

"Oh, ma puce," Queen said, "Are you afraid I'll learn about your plan to save the world and get in my pants?"

Rook laughed and shouted, "You told her! You son-of-a—"

Just then, Deep Blue came rushing around the corner of the corridor from the direction of the computer lab. "Been waiting for you to get back," he said looking at King, then he turned to Rook and Queen. "You two should hear this as well."

He was holding a piece of old-looking, yellowed parchment in his hand. He gave it to King, and King read aloud:

You handled Fenrir well.
I needed the laptop, so I helped myself.
Don't pursue the issue. Peter and Lynn have enjoyed
my hospitality so far but if you push, King...

The note was signed with a symbol King had seen before: a circle with two vertical lines through it, making a stylized letter H.

It was the symbol for the mysterious Herculean Society, a group that controlled and altered the historical record to hide the truth of past events. But it was also used as the signature for the group's leader, Alexander Diotrophes.

Hercules.

Previously the man had assisted Chess Team during the Hydra affair—after all, he was the one that had dealt with the Hydra in ancient times. He had rescued Fiona from the massacre at her reservation in Oregon and delivered her to King for safekeeping. Then the man had even been an active ally in the fight against Richard Ridley and his Machiavellian schemes.

"The laptop?" King asked. "What laptop?"

Deep Blue looked to the floor, lost in thought for a moment. "Before we bugged out of Fenris Kystby, Lew was able to access the servers wirelessly. He download three terabytes of data covering nearly seventy years of failed experiments: the dire wolf hybrids, as

well as personnel files, notes, photos, security logs—*everything*—
including the schematics and very detailed plans on how to build
the portal device."

"Why haven't I heard of this until now?" King asked, doing nothing to hide his ruffled feathers.

"Lew hadn't decrypted the files until this morning," Deep Blue
answered. "You were going to be briefed later today."

"But now we've lost everything?"

Deep Blue shook his head, no. "Lew transferred the files to our
servers, but the information was never deleted from the laptop.
How Alexander could have known about the laptop or that it
contained anything worthwhile is beyond me. But now he has it.
And I have no idea how he could have gotten past our security. It's
been significantly beefed up since the GenY incursion. And..."
Deep Blue paused for a second, shaking his head as if he couldn't
imagine how it was done. "I was looking at the laptop two days ago,
before I put it back in the safe. The base has been fully populated
since then. Everyone was here. He walked right past all of us and
got out again unnoticed."

King scowled. He had known that Alexander was a tenuous ally
from the start, but now the man had stepped over the line. Immortal
or not, demigod or not, he had infiltrated their headquarters, stolen
hard-earned intel and abducted King's parents.

He had just declared himself an enemy of Endgame *and* the
Machtcenko family.

Asya snatched the paper from King's hand and read it. "Who is
this man?"

"His name is Alexander—you might have heard of him being
called Hercules—and I think I'm going to have to kill him."

ABOUT THE AUTHORS

JEREMY ROBINSON is the author of seventeen novels including the highly praised, SECONDWORLD, as well as PULSE, INSTINCT, and THRESHOLD, the first three books in his exciting Jack Sigler series. His novels have been translated into ten languages. He lives in New Hampshire with his wife and three children.

Visit him online at: www.jeremyrobinsononline.com

KANE GILMOUR has visited or lived in over 40 countries around the world. A former rock climber and mountain biker, he now kayaks, and still explores the furthest reaches of the world, as time permits. His first two adventure thrillers in the Jason Quinn series, RESURRECT and FROZEN are available now. He lives in the wilds of central Vermont with his wife, son, and daughter.

Visit him online at: www.kanegilmour.com

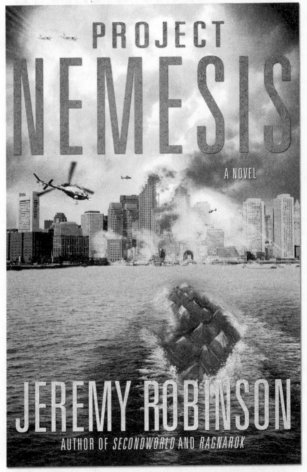

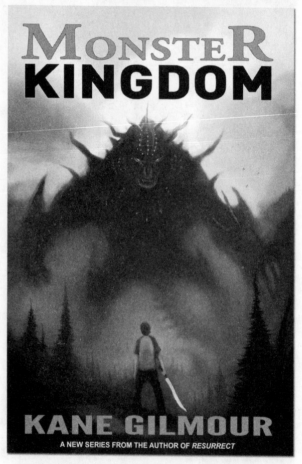

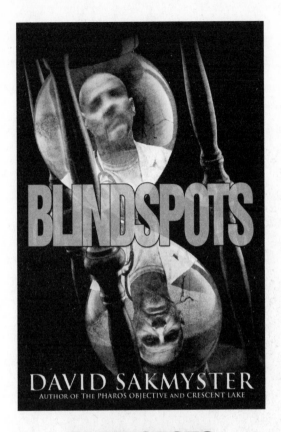

BLINDSPOTS

Six strangers from across the globe, all afflicted with *Prosopagnosia*—a disease that renders the sufferer unable to recognize faces—find themselves drawn to a Vermont clinic specializing in the disease. Once there, to the shock of their lives, these six find they're not only able to *see*, but somehow recognize each other. But before they can learn the amazing truth about their connection, they are targeted by a preternaturally-gifted killer who has been waiting, more than one lifetime, for their arrival.

Available wherever books and ebooks are sold.

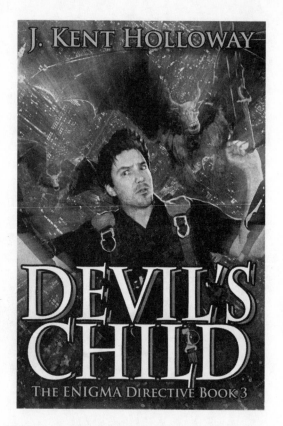

**IF YOU THINK MONSTERS ARE SCARY,
YOU DON'T KNOW JACK!**

What would you do if you only had two hours to find a helpless
cryptid infant hidden somewhere in the heart of New York City
before twelve full-grown Jersey Devils begin tearing up the
city in search of their kidnapped spawn? The Jersey Devil
is about to take a bite out of the Big Apple. Will Jack and the
ENIGMA team be fast enough to stop it? Find out in the
third ENIGMA Directive adventure...

DEVIL'S CHILD
Coming November 2012

THANKS FOR READING

FOR MORE JACK SIGLER AND CHESS TEAM ACTION VISIT
WWW.JEREMYROBINSONONLINE.COM

Kathmandu
& the Kingdom of Nepal

front cover: Bodhnath Stupa
back cover: Kathmandu temple

Kathmandu & the Kingdom of Nepal

Published by
Lonely Planet Publications
PO Box 88, South Yarra
Victoria 3141, Australia

Printed by
Colorcraft
Hong Kong

Photographs by
Tony Wheeler

First Published
1976

This Edition
July 1983

National Library of Australia
Cataloguing in Publication Data

Raj, Prakash A., 1943-
Kathmandu & the Kingdom of Nepal.

4th ed.
Previous ed. : South Yarra : Lonely Planet, 1983.
Includes index.
ISBN 0 908086 46 6.

1. Nepal — Description and travel — 1951- —
Guide books. I. Title.

915.49'604

© Prakash A Raj. 1983

Prakash A Raj was born in Nepal in 1943 and spent five years in the 1960s studying at universities in the USA. He also studied in the Netherlands, England and Norway and travelled extensively in Europe. In Nepal he has worked on the English language daily as a journalist and for the planning agency of the Nepalese government. He has also worked for a year at the United Nations Secretariat in New York and at OECD in Paris. Prakash has written several books in English and Nepali and also speaks German, French and Spanish.

PREVIOUS EDITIONS, THIS EDITION & THE NEXT

The first edition of this Nepal guide was actually published in Nepal by Prakash in 1973 with the delightful title *Nepal on $2 a Day*. Prakash devised his interesting technique of adding short comments from visitors to Nepal in that first edition and has today interviewed more than 1000 visitors to his country. The first Lonely Planet edition emerged in 1976 and this new edition is the fourth.

Apart from Prakash's work thanks must also go to Peter for the illustrations, Joy for new maps and additions to the old ones, Isabel for typesetting, Evelyn for pasting up, Andy for proof-reading and Mary for editing. Travellers who wrote with useful suggestions and information include Felicite Young, Lena Liefe, Magnus Lindgren, Bill & Benita Mikulas, Paul D Travell and Cathryn Hugh.

Things change — prices go up, good places go bad, bad places go bankrupt and nothing stays the same. So if you find things better, worse, cheaper, more expensive, recently opened or long ago closed please don't blame us but please do write and tell us about it. As usual the best letters will score a free copy of the next edition or of any other LP guide if you prefer.

The cartoon on page 48-49 is by Tony Jenkins.

Lonely Planet travel guides
Africa on the Cheap
Australia — a travel survival kit
Alaska — a travel survival kit
Burma — a travel survival kit
Bushwalking in Papua New Guinea
Canada — a travel survival kit
Hong Kong, Macau & Canton
India — a travel survival kit
Israel & the Occupied Territories
Japan — a travel survival kit
Kashmir, Ladakh & Zanskar
Kathmandu & the Kingdom of Nepal
Korea & Taiwan — a travel survival kit
*Malaysia, Singapore & Brunei — a travel
  survival kit*
Mexico — a travel survival kit
New Zealand — a travel survival kit
North-East Asia on a Shoestring
Pakistan — a travel survival kit
Papua New Guinea — a travel survival kit
The Philippines — a travel survival kit
South America on a Shoestring
South-East Asia on a Shoestring
Sri Lanka — a travel survival kit
Tramping in New Zealand
Trekking in the Himalayas
Thailand — a travel survival kit
Turkey — a travel survival kit
USA West
*West Asia on a Shoestring (formerly Across
  Asia on the Cheap)*

Lonely Planet travel guides are available around the world. If you can't find them, ask your bookshop to order them from one of the distributors listed below. For countries not listed or if you would like a free copy of our latest booklist write to Lonely Planet in Australia.

Australia Lonely Planet Publications, PO Box 88, South Yarra, Victoria 3141.
Canada Milestone Publications, Box 2248, Sidney, British Columbia, V8L 3S8.
Denmark Scanvik Books aps, Store Kongensgade 59 A, DK-1264 Copenhagen K.
Hong Kong The Book Society, GPO Box 7804, Hong Kong.
India UBS Distributors, 5 Ansari Rd, New Delhi.
Israel Geographical Tours Ltd, 8 Tverya St, Tel Aviv 63144.
Japan Intercontinental Marketing Corp, IPO Box 5056, Tokyo 100-31.
Malaysia MPH Distributors, 13, Jalan 13/6, Petaling Jaya, Selangor.
Nepal see India
Netherlands Nilsson & Lamm bv, Postbus 195, Pampuslaan 212, 1380 AD Weesp.
New Zealand Caveman Press, PO Box 1458, Dunedin.
Papua New Guinea Gordon & Gotch (PNG), PO Box 3395, Port Moresby.
Singapore MPH Distributors, 116-D JTC Factory Building, Lorong 3, Geylang Square,
  Singapore, 1438.
Sweden Esselte Kartcentrum AB, Vasagatan 16, S-111 20 Stockholm.
Thailand Chalermnit, 1-2 Erawan Arcade, Bangkok.
UK Roger Lascelles, 16 Holland Park Gardens, London W14 8DY.
USA (West) Bookpeople, 2940 Seventh St, Berkeley, CA 94710.
USA (East) Hippocrene Books, 171 Madison Ave, New York, NY 10016.
West Germany Buchvertrieb Gerda Schettler, Postfach 64, D3415 Hattorf a H.

Contents

Introduction

The number of travellers who are tired of travelling to the conventional, tourist infested resorts increases year by year. Among young people especially, there is a genuine yearning for a place which is really different, where the rhythm of life is not as fast, where the way of life is older and less altered by the modern world. With young people Nepal has almost become a legend.

After visiting Kathmandu recently a French writer said:

> . . . . the traveller starts to realise that the travel agencies have not told him everything. Some have talked of Kathmandu as being situated in the shadow of Everest (which is not true), others have described it as the Mecca of the hippies (which is only half true), but the most important thing has been left unsaid. It has been forgotten to mention that Kathmandu is the Florence of Asia, the city of art par excellence, a wonder of the modern world where Europe of the middle ages can still be discovered.

Perhaps that is why the number of tourists to Nepal is increasing so dramatically.

Nepal has many things to offer to a visitor, such as its unique combination of works of man and nature. The flourishing of art and architecture is amply demonstrated by the temples of the Kathmandu Valley; the beauties of nature by soaring peaks like Mount Everest and others, not so high perhaps, but even more spectacular in appearance.

Nepal is one of the best places in the world for trekking. Not only is trekking comparatively safe but in remote villages every household would consider it its duty to extend hospitality to a weary traveller. Nor are there many countries in the world where the contrast between old and new is so striking. In the streets of Kathmandu you will see the latest model Japanese cars while only a few minutes away from the capital people cultivate their fields with bullocks. For them things have changed very little in the past five centuries.

The Kathmandu Valley has been called one big museum — a vast storehouse of Hindu and Buddhist art with more shrines and temples per square km than any-

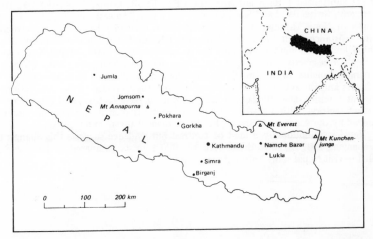

where else in the world. Two hundred years ago, in a statement that still has a wisp of truth in it, the English author Kirkpatrick said:

> The valley consists of as many temples as there are houses and as many idols as there are men.

Nor is this a dry, dead museum — Nepal celebrates countless festivals every year and has developed institutions such as the *living goddess* to ensure that this is a live museum. The Nepalese even boast of having developed the pagoda style of architecture and successfully exporting it to China and Japan.

Nepal also contains an amazing mixture of ethnic and racial groups. In the streets of Kathmandu one might think passers-by were Japanese, Chinese, Indonesian, Indian, Arab, Greek or Latin American but it is entirely within the bounds of possibility that they would all be Nepalese. Nepal is the only Hindu kingdom in the world, but Hinduism and Buddhism have co-existed amicably for centuries and many people profess both religions. Buddha's birthplace is in Nepal and one of the largest Buddhist stupas in the world can also be found here.

Nepal is one of the few windows looking on to Tibetan life and culture. Tibetan refugees live in many parts of Nepal and run some excellent restaurants and curio shops in Kathmandu. Near the Chinese border some Nepalese also speak Tibetan.

In terms of per capita income, just US$130 in 1979, Nepal is one of the least developed countries in the world. It was also, until 1973, one of the countries where the smoking of hashish was tolerated — some would even say legal. This was one of the reasons Nepal gained a name as a hippie paradise. Overland travellers consider Kathmandu, with its abundant and varied supply of restaurants, the best place to eat east of Istanbul. As a place to get away from it all and relax at the end of a long trip it can hardly be surpassed. Nor can there be many places in the east where you will run into so many visitors from so many different countries in so small an area.

Nepal is a tiny country, sandwiched between the two largest, in terms of population, in the world — India and China. Perhaps as a result of this it has managed to get substantial foreign aid from the USA, USSR, China, India, the UK, West Germany, Switzerland and Israel to name just a few. The east-west road running the length of Nepal through the southern jungle is divided into sections constructed with assistance from India, the USSR, the UK and the Asian Development Bank. China and India have each aided the construction of roads linking Kathmandu with their respective frontiers. India, China and the USSR have each built power generating plants, while the Swiss have helped in the rehabilitation of Tibetan refugees and the setting up of a cheese factory, the Germans in the restoration of ancient temples, the Russians in setting up a cigarette factory, and the Chinese a leather factory. Within walking distance of each other in Kathmandu are libraries opened by the Americans, British, French, Indians, Russian and Chinese.

Nepal is undoubtedly a land of contrast but evidence suggests this Shangri La is changing fast. In 1981 there were 181,000 tourists compared to just 6200 in 1961 — visit Nepal soon, before it is too late.

Facts about the Country

HISTORY

In the course of history the area of Nepal has shrunk and expanded. Sometimes it consisted only of Kathmandu and neighbouring principalities, at other times it extended further east and west from its present boundaries. Nepal's history is a long one. A stone pillar erected more than 2000 years ago by the Indian emporor Ashoka at Lumbini in southern Nepal marks it as the birthplace of the Buddha. During those 2000 years Nepal has seen a steady migration of people speaking Indo-European languages from the western Himalayas and the plains of India on one hand and Mongoloid people speaking Tibeto-Burmese languages from Tibet on the other.

The first known rulers of the Kathmandu Valley were the Kirats who had come from the eastern part of the country. Little is known about these people but one of their kings did rate a mention in the *Mahabharata*, and it was at this time that Buddhism arrived in the country. The Lichhavis came to power from north India during the 4th century AD to the early 7th century. Again comparatively little is known about them but at the temple of Changunarayan a stone inscription can be seen dating from this period.

During the 17th century the three independent, sovereign kingdoms of the Malla dynasty in the Kathmandu Valley created great numbers of works of art, statues and temples. The kingdoms minted their own coins and maintained standing armies. At this time all Nepal was divided into small principalities and kingdoms. Western Nepal alone had 22 and there were a further 24 in far western Nepal.

From one of these small kingdoms, Gorkha, where kings of the Shah dynasty ruled, King Prithvi Narayan Shah set out to unify Nepal. In 1768 he defeated the Malla kings and Nepal has been ruled by Shah kings ever since. For half a century after 1768 Nepal continued to extend boundaries until in 1817 Nepal lost a war with Britain. As a reward for its support during the Indian Mutiny Nepal regained part of its lost territory in 1858 and assumed its present size.

In 1846 Jung Bahadur, Prime Minister of Nepal, took over real power, after the *Kot massacre* where his supporters managed to kill almost all his opponents. For over a century the hereditary family of *Rana* Prime Ministers ruled the country and did very little for development. While almost all the countries of Asia and Africa were being colonised Nepal managed to preserve its independence and was never ruled by a colonial power. Throughout the Rana period Nepal was virtually isolated from the rest of the world. Visitors were rarely admitted and then only with severely circumscribed freedom of movement. In 1951 King Tribhuvan overthrew the Rana regime with support from India. It was a unique situation as the king had led a revolution against an oligarchic system. King Tribhuvan died in 1955 and was succeeded by his son King Mahendra, father of the present king.

Nepal became a member of the United Nations in 1955 and was even elected a member of the Security Council for a two year period in 1969-1970. After a decade of experiments in parliamentary democracy, including elections for parliament in 1958, King Mahendra introduced a system of partyless *Panchayat* democracy in 1962. King Birendra ascended the throne after his father's death in 1972, but his coronation did not take place until an auspicious date in February 1975, three years later, had been selected by astrologers. Many foreign dignitaries attended the colourful coronation ceremony in the historic old royal palace.

King Birendra was educated at Eton in England and Harvard in the US. He is

9

intensely interested in the development of Nepal and the country has made significant progress under his leadership. Nepal has been divided into four development regions: Pokhara (western Nepal), Surkhet (far western Nepal) and Dhankuta (eastern Nepal) are the regional development centres away from Kathmandu. In 1980 a national referendum was held to decide whether to continue with the partyless Panchayat system or to change to a multi-party form of government. The decision went, narrowly, to the Panchayat system although significant changes are expected to be made.

GEOGRAPHY, POPULATION & ECONOMY

Although Nepal is a small country of only 141,577 square km it contains the greatest altitude variation on earth, from the lowland Terai, almost at sea level, to Mt Everest, which at 8848 metres is the highest point on earth. The country is about 800 km long and from 90 to 230 km wide. A cross-section shows four main areas to the country. Close to the border with India is a low fertile strip of jungle land known as the Terai. Until comparatively recently malaria made this an inhospitable region but its eradication has led to a rapid population increase.

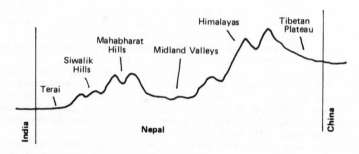

Above the Terai rise the Siwalik foothills and beyond them the higher, more barren Mahabharat range. The bulk of the population of Nepal is found in the fertile intermontane valleys, such as the Kathmandu Valley and the Pokhara Valley, north of the Mahabharat range and at altitudes between 1000 and 2000 metres. North again rises the sweep of the Himalayan range forming a barrier between Tibet and Nepal. In general the border runs along the peaks of the range, Mt Everest straddles the border, but in western Nepal at the country's widest point a portion of the high arid Tibetan plateau forms the legendary Mustang province. The Terai also disappears at a point where the Indian border comes right up to the Siwalik foothills.

The population of Nepal is about 12 million and that of Kathmandu, the main city, about 300,000. Like the geography the population of the country is extremely diverse. Some tribes, such as the Sherpas living in the eastern Everest region, have won fame as mountaineers while others, like the Gurungs, Magars and Chetris in the west and the Rais and Limbus in the east have made their mark as Gurkha soldiers. The original inhabitants of the Kathmandu Valley, the Newars, have made significant contributions in the development of art and architecture. Nepalese living in the Terai have close ethnic and linguistic ties with people across the border in the Bihar and Uttar Pradesh states of India.

Tamang girl

Nepal's main exports are rice and jute which are grown in the Terai. Tourism is now superseding the Gurkha earnings as Nepal's chief foreign currency earner. Mineral wealth in Nepal appears to be limited and inaccessible, a result of the country's geological newness. Nepal has vast potential for the development of hydro-electric power.

Development in Nepal is concentrated on improvements in communications, agriculture and education. The road building programme is continuing to link previously isolated parts of the country. In agriculture the green revolution has had a major impact on Nepal, particularly in the fertile but heavily populated Kathmandu Valley which is now able to feed itself. Nevertheless Nepal's steep population growth will continue to put pressure on agricultural potential. Birth control programmes are a major part of the educational development which it is hoped will reduce the illiteracy rate from its current levels of over 70% amongst males and over 90% amongst females. However, 69% of primary school age children are now attending primary school.

In 1970 the average life expectancy was only 40. Much remains to be done to increase the number of hospitals and doctors as there is only one doctor for every 96,000 people. Since most of the doctors are living in Kathmandu, this disparity is even more extreme in the remote areas of the country.

CULTURE & CUSTOMS
Nepal is the meeting place of two great religions, Hinduism and Buddhism; two races, caucasian and mongoloid; and two civilisations, Indic and Sinic. The population has a variety of ethnic groups each with distinct cultural identity.

Polygamy was, and still is, practised in many areas of the country although legislation has banned it in the last decade. In the northern hill areas polyandry, the custom of a wife having more than one husband, was also practised. Ethnic groups such as the Brahmins and Chetris are prohibited from drinking alcohol and sometimes follow vegetarian restraints. Widow remarriage and cousin marriages are not

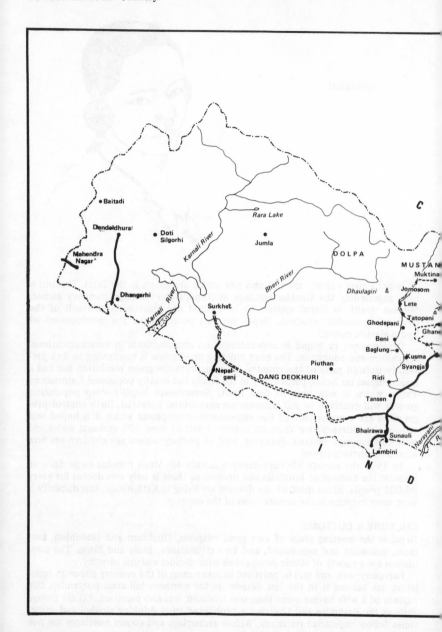

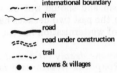

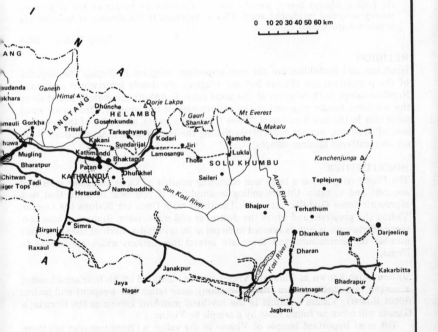

socially acceptable in some groups and amongst Brahmin families a man first meets his wife on the day he gets married. On the other hand the Gurung group have an institution called *Rodighar* intended to bring people together before they contemplate marriage. The Sherpas have a remarkably free and easy moral code.

When going inside rooms in Nepali homes it is polite to remove your shoes. Westerners should not try to enter Hindu temples and never touch the deity although they are quite free to watch from outside. Public displays of affection are not good manners, nor should one swim naked in lakes or rivers. Like many parts of Asia the sight of men and boys walking hand in hand is quite normal and does not have the same connotation it does in the west. Many young Nepalese children have started coming to trekkers and asking for money, this is one of the bad effects of tourism and should not be encouraged. The speed and intensity of change in Nepal in the past two decades has been surprising and it will be a great shame if this process of westernisation has too great an effect on Nepal's unique culture.

To anyone deeply interested in Tibetan Buddhism it is a Tibetan custom to visit the Rimpoche (reincarnate lama) of the nearby monastery. Generally the purpose is to receive his blessings and consult him concerning important matters, often to ask questions concerning dharma and sometimes only to take an offering to the monastery. A Khata gift scarf, available at any Tibetan shop for about Rs 1.50 is always taken, usually with a donation of butter or tea or perhaps money wrapped inside the scarf. This is presented to the Rimpoche held loosely between both hands.

Philip Wolcott, USA

RELIGION
Hinduism and Buddhism are the two important religions in Nepal. The majority of the population are Hindus but the religions are closely intertwined and many Nepalese adopt both religions at the same time. Buddhists are mainly found along the northern border area and in the eastern part of the country. Hindus are most numerous in the south and west. There is a small number, about 3% of the population, of Moslems, mainly concentrated along the border with India although there are also scattered Moslem villages.

HINDU DEITIES
The Hindu religion has a large and confusing number of Gods and their attendant consorts and animals. Understanding is simplified if you bear in mind that each represents some God-like attribute. The three main Gods are Brahma the creator, Vishnu the preserver and Shiva the destroyer and regenerator. Brahma, whose consort is Saraswati, is not as revered in Nepal as he is in India. Each of the Gods has a number of incarnations and there are several incarnations which are unique to Nepal.

Vishnu Also known as Narayan, Vishnu can be identified by his four arms holding a *sankha* (sea shell), *chakra* (round weapon), *gada* (stick like weapon) and *padma* (lotus flower). Vishnu's animal is the mythical man-bird known as the Garuda; a Garuda will often be found close by a temple to Vishnu.

The most important temple of Vishnu in the valley is Changunarayan but there is also a very good image of the 'sleeping' Vishnu at Budhanilkantha. Vishnu has 10 incarnations one of which is Krishna, who is often blue — there is a particularly well-known Krishna Temple in the Durbar Square of Patan. Narsimha, the man-lion is another incarnation of Vishnu, see the beautiful image inside the old Royal Palace. Some Hindus consider Buddha to be one of the 10 incarnations of Vishnu. His wife, Laxmi, is the Goddess of Wealth according to Hindu mythology.

Garuda

Garuda The Garuda is well known for its aerial abilities and its intense hatred of snakes — Garuda devours snakes at the door of almost all the temples of Kathmandu. You will see a Garuda in front of temples of Vishnu. Indonesia has named its national airline Garuda after this same famous man-bird but the Indonesian Garuda is less man and more bird than the Nepalese variety.

Shiva Pashupatinath, which is another name for the God, is the best known temple to Shiva in the valley. Shiva is often represented by the *lingam* or phallus as a symbol of his creative side. Shiva's animal is the bull, Nandi, and there is a giant sized Nandi in front of Pashupatinath. The image of Pashupatinath itself contains five heads, this is not common in other temples of Shiva. The weapon of Shiva is the *trisul* or trident. According to Hindu mythology Shiva is supposed to live in the Himalayas, smoke a lot of hashish and wear a garland of snakes. Bhairab is a representation of the terrible form of Shiva and there are numerous images of Bhairab in the valley.

Parvati Parvati is the consort of Shiva and like her God she has a peaceful and a fearful side to her activities. She is shown in her terrifying form holding a variety of weapons and her animal is the lion. Dasain, celebrated in her honour, is characterised by the sacrifice of animals. Daxinkali is the best known of her temples.

Hanuman The monkey god Hanuman is the legendary figure from the epic Ramayana who helped rescue Rama's wife Sita from the clutches of the demon Rawana. Rama is yet another of the incarnations of Vishnu and Hanuman was his faithful servant. An image of Hanuman guards the Hanuman Dhoka, entrance to the old Royal Palace of Kathmandu.

Ganesh Easily recognised by his elephant head, Ganesh, the God of Learning, has many temples in Nepal. The animal of Ganesh, which he rides as his 'vehicle', is the mouse! In the course of general worship Ganesh is the first of the deities to be worshipped and the Maru Ganesh temple near Durbar Square in Kathmandu is visited by a large number of devotees from dawn until late at night.

Shiva, Ganesh's father, is said to have returned to his wife Parvati after a journey lasting 14 years. Arriving home at night he found Parvati asleep with a young boy beside her. Suspecting her of infidelity he immediately lopped off the boy's head and then discovered it was his own son. Shiva was very sad and said he would bring his son back to life if the first living thing seen in the morning was brought to him. The first living thing turned out to be an elephant and Shiva took its head and joined it to the trunk of his son who became Ganesh.

FESTIVALS IN NEPAL

Few people in the world can celebrate as many festivals as the Newars of Kathmandu Valley. Hardly a month passes without a major festival or feast, but the three months from August to October is a real festival season and you're bound to see some picturesque festival if you visit Nepal during that time. Major festivals include:

August

Gai Jatra or Cow Festival Hundreds of garlanded and costumed people walk in a long procession accompanied by cows and crowds of happy people. If there has been a death in the family it is expected that a group consisting of two people, usually a boy and a person dressed as a *sadhu* (saint), and a cow, will be sent to participate in the day-long festival. The curious practice originated from the belief that people who happen to be holding a cow's tail at the moment of death have precedence at the hall of justice!

Krishnastami The best place to watch the celebrations of Krishna's birthday is at the Krishna temple in Patan. Sacred devotional music is played all night if you can manage to stay awake. Go early in the evening.

Teej This is a special festival for women and all married women are supposed to fast all day and bathe in the holy waters of the rivers. The entrance to Pashupatinath is a good place to watch as crowds of women, dressed in brightly coloured saris with red marks on their foreheads, come down to the river. It is believed that their married life will be long and happy and they will not lose their husbands if they celebrate this festival. Red is a symbol of joy and happiness in Nepal and the colour used for marriage ceremonies. Married women are expected to wear a lot of red but widows are forbidden to do so; white is the colour of mourning in Nepal.

Thousands of women dressed in saris flock to the temple of Pashupatinath on fasting day to do their obeisance to Shiva and his consort Parvati. One or two days later there is a ritual of washing in the holy waters of the Bagmati River in which everyone washes everything 360 times. One can go, unobtrusively, to the more sacred spots on the river bank and witness the marvellous crowds of women singing and joyously cleansing their bodies and souls.

Meg Levine, USA

Unfortunately it's not all sweetness and light at this festival, as this photograph of three western 'gentlemen' illustrates.

I was disgusted to see the behaviour of some tourists at the Shivaratri festival at the Pashupatinath Temple. It is a very holy day for Nepalese Hindus who come to bathe in the Trisuli River. Millions of pilgrims had made the trip, some saddhus coming from the Punjab and further afield. As I took this photo (with a 135 mm lens) the embarrassment of the Nepali ladies trying to bathe and pray discreetly was evident. Upon approaching these three quite politely and asking them if they were aware of the discomfort they were causing amongst these women I was told in no uncertain terms to 'F ... off!'

The Shivaratri festival is a photographers' dream, full of colour and made for fantastic photos of 'the people'. But surely people who travel through these lands must realise after a very short time in the country, if they are at all sensitive to the new cultures they are experiencing, that the local women are generally very camera-shy and certainly when pointing your camera at someone it is obvious whether they approve. Efforts must be made not to upset the locals and make a worse name for tourists in these lands.

Kim Ellis, England

September
Indrajatra The Indra festival, in honour of the ancient Aryan God Indra, God of Rain, marks the end of the monsoon and the beginning of the best season of the year, which lasts for two months. The living goddess, Kumari, is taken in procession through the streets of Kathmandu and the king receives blessings from her. The image of White Bhairab, behind the Black Bhairab in Kathmandu's Durbar Square, is unveiled for three days each year during this festival. Traditional Newar folk dances are performed in the streets around the Durbar Square, Basantapur Square and the Indrachok area. On this same day, in 1768, King Prithvi Narayan Shah conquered Kathmandu and took the major step in the process of unifying Nepal. The festival continues for four days.

October
Bada Dasain This is the biggest festival in Nepal and lasts 15 days in all although the main festivities are concentrated in nine days during which all schools and government offices are closed. On the seventh day, called 'Fulpati', you can see, around noon or early afternoon, a procession of government officials in national dress preceded by a band from the old Royal Palace in Durbar Square. On the ninth day, thousands of goats and buffaloes are sacrificed around noon in the courtyard called 'Kot' behind Durbar Square and a stream of blood flows. Similar sacrifices are made in the temples of goddesses through the country and on this day every household in Nepal eats meat. The tenth day, Bijaya Dashami, is the highlight of the festival and all Hindus and many Buddhists go to the relatives and elders in order to receive a 'tika', which is rice immersed in a red liquid placed on their forehead. On the streets of Kathmandu on this day you will hardly see a person who does not wear this red mark. In late afternoon, if you walk two blocks from Durbar Square to the temple of Naradevi, you can see the Festival of the Sword (Khadga Jatra). This day is supposed to represent the victory of good over evil; according to legend the Goddess Durga killed a demon on this day.

The final day of the festival, a full moon day, is marked by much gambling in some Nepalese households. Dasain is not only the biggest festival but a happy one because the weather is perfect, and the rice is ready to be harvested. It is a pleasant time for walking in the hills which makes the visits to relatives enjoyable. In the villages large swings are set up for the children to play on.

November
Tihar The third and fifth days are the most important of this five-day festival. In western India it is the biggest Hindu festival and in Nepal it is second only to Dasain. On the first day crows, the messengers of death, are honoured and fed. The second day is in honour of dogs, the guardians of the dead and the mount of Bhairab. The third day is set aside for cows as the incarnation of Laxmi. This day is called Deepavali, the festival of lights, and all the households of Kathmandu are illuminated by lamps to the Goddess of Wealth. This festival always falls on a new moon so the effect is particularly delightful. It is said that the Goddess Laxmi will shun any household not illuminated on this day, which is also an occasion for gambling.

The new year for the Newars of the valley also starts from this day. The Nepalese national new year starts on 13 April and 1983 in western terms is 2040 in Nepalese. The Newari calendar equates 1983 to 1103. The Tibetans living in Nepal also have their own calendar.

The fifth day of the festival is Bhai Tika and is meant especially for brothers and sisters who are supposed to get together on this day. There is a small ceremony and they mark each others foreheads with *tikas*. The sister also puts oil on her brother's forehead and offers sweets and fruits, in return he pays her small sums of money, say Rs 5 or 10. On this day the bazaars of Kathmandu are full of sweets and fresh and dry fruits.

Ekadashi On the eleventh day after the new moon Vishnu is supposed to wake up after having slept for four months. There will be many pilgrims at Pashupatinath but the best place to view this festival is at the temple of Changunarayan or at the temple of the sleeping Vishnu at Budhanilkantha. The activities of Budhanilkantha are equally interesting on the next day when a long line of devotees queue to touch the feet of the deity.

December
Bala Chaturdashi People come from all over the valley and beyond to the temple of Pashupatinath to take part in a ceremony which consists of scattering seeds of different kinds and burning candles in memory of their dead relatives. The evening is the best time to observe the ceremony as you will see many pilgrims performing religious rites and singing and dancing. The best place to watch is from across the Bagmati River which gives a good view of the illuminated temple and pilgrims worshipping. Many pilgrims from far away villages spend the night around the temple.

February
Tibetan New Year There are religious celebrations in Bodhnath Stupa around noon-time and the Buddhist monks give blessings. This festival is essentially a family affair when friends and members of the family get together.

Maha Shivaratri The birthday of Lord Shiva usually falls in the cold month of February but many pilgrims come from the warm weather of the Terai or the north Indian plains to worship at the temple of Pashupatinath in a colourful yet deeply serene ceremony.

During the festival of Shivaratri, the most impressive feature was the mass of colour and simple dignity of the pilgrims as they performed the ritual bathing in the holy river. Some Sadhus covered with ashes lay on a bed of thorns and also impaled their tongues with thorns.

John Hayward, England

March
Holi or Fagu This festival of rejoicing occurs in the springtime on the day of the full moon in the Nepalese month of Falgun when a pillar is installed in Basantapur Square in front of the old Royal Palace. The festival used to last for eight days and was marked by throwing coloured water and red powder on acquaintances and even people passing by on the street. The festival now takes place only on the day of the full moon but visitors should watch out for the coloured water. If you happen to be on the Helambu trek the village of Tarkeghyang has a colourful festival celebrated with dancing and singing until the late hours. The Sherpas in the mountains do without the water throwing.

April
Chaitra Dasain Also called small Dasain in contrast to October's big Dasain, this

festival is similar in many respects, and many goats and buffaloes are sacrificed to the Goddess Durga at the Kot Square. An image of the Goddess is pulled on a chariot through the streets.

Bisket Festival   A wooden pillar is erected in the evening on the first day of this Bhaktapur festival. On the second day, which is also the first day of the year by the Nepalese calendar, a chariot is pulled from the pillar to the temple of Bhairabnath in the same square as the five-storey Nyatapola Pagoda. The chariot is very old and looks on the point of collapse — as it is pulled every part shakes violently and it makes a tremendous spectacle. The pillar is shaken violently in the evening and then lowered with great rejoicing. The chariots of Ganesh and the Goddesses Mahakali and Mahalaxmi are carried on the shoulders of the devotees.

May

Birthday of Buddha   Since Nepal is the birthplace of Buddha and there are still many Buddhists amongst the Nepalese, this festival is celebrated with especial pomp. Swayambhunath and Bodhnath are particularly popular centres and pilgrims will gather at Swayambhunath from early in the morning.

Rato Machhendranath   The festival of Red Machhendranath takes place in Patan over a period of two months and is one of the most complex festivals. During the celebrations a chariot bearing the image of Machhendranath, revered by Hindus and Buddhists, moves in a series of daily stages through the streets of Patan.

July

Naga Panchami   Images of the serpent Naga are stuck over the doors of houses during the festival of snakes. Since snakes are believed to have power over the monsoon rainfall, it is important that they are appeased — their image also keeps evil from entering the home.

Janai Purnima   All high caste Hindus wear a sacred thread over their left shoulder and tied under their right armpit. On this day each year the sacred thread is replaced after a day-long fast. Kumbheswara temple in Patan and the holy lake of Gosainkunda are important places for this festival.

> *Two times a month, on the eleventh day after the full moon and the new moon, a concert of classical Indian music is given in the Narayan Temple very near the new Royal Palace. The best Nepalese musicians, especially tabla and sitar, and several singers of all ages will sing in the evening.*
>
> *Nadine Beautheac, France*

Marriage Ceremony

Marriage ceremonies in Nepal are supposed to take place only in five months of the year — mid-January to mid-March, mid-April to mid-June and mid-November to mid-December. Astrologers select auspicious dates within these periods on the basis of the positions of the stars. It is quite common to see several marriage processions on the same particularly auspicious date. The marriage ritual differs in the various communities but almost always has a procession preceded by a band. The bridegroom spends a night at the bride's house where a big religious ceremony is held during which the bride and groom walk around a fire on a platform so that the fire 'witnesses' their marriage.

FESTIVAL CALENDAR

Almost all of the festivals in Nepal are celebrated according to the lunar calendar so it is difficult to tell in advance the exact dates when they will take place. The festival calendar, made after consulting the lunar calendar, covers major festivals for 1983 and 1984.

Name of Festival	Place	1983	1984
Bisketjatra — Festival of Bisket	Bhaktapur	Apr 13, 14	Apr 12, 13
Buddha Jayanti — Birthday of Buddha	Kathmandu	May 26	
Gaijatra — Cow Festival	Kathmandu	Aug 24	
Krishnasthami — Birthday of Krishna	Patan	Aug 31	
Teej — Festival of Women	Pashupatinath	Sep 9	
Indrajatra — Festival of Indra	Kathmandu	Sep 21	
Bijaya Dashami — Big Dasain	All over the country		
Navami	"	Oct 15	
Tika	"	Oct 16	
Tihar — Festival of Light	"	Nov 4	
Bhai Tika	"	Nov 6	
Big Ekadashi	Pashupatinath and Budhanilkantha	Nov 16	
Bala Chaturdashi	Pashupatinath	Dec 2, 3	
Basantra Panchami	Swayambhu	Jan 19	Feb 7
Sivaratri — Birthday of Shiva	Pashupatinath	Feb 11	Feb 29
Holi — Festival of Colour	All over the country	Mar 28	Mar 17
Ghodejatra — Festival of Horse Racing	Kathmandu	Apr 12	Apr 1
Chaitra Dasain	All over the country	Apr 20	Apr 9
Tibetan New Year	Bodhnath	Feb	Feb
Mani Rimdu	Solu Khumbu	Nov	Nov

LANGUAGE

English is understood by many people in Kathmandu and Pokhara. The national language, Nepali, is related to Hindi and belongs to the Indo-European family of languages; it is a fairly easy language to learn. Many of the Nepalese ethnic groups speak their own language — the Newars of the Kathmandu Valley speak Newari and distinct languages are spoken by the Gurungs, Magars, Rais, Limbus, Tamangs and Sherpas. In the Terai, Hindu and Maithili are widely spoken and understood.

Although learning a few words of Nepali is a good idea and widely appreciated there is one word every visitor should learn — *Namaste*. This universal Nepalese greeting translates literally as 'I salute all divine qualities in you' but is used as 'hello, how are you, pleased to see you, see you again' and is generally a nice thing to say.

Some useful words

English	Nepali		
how much?	kati?	good, pretty	ramro
less	kam	here	yaha
where?	kata?	there	tyaha
OK	theek	today	aaja
thank you	dhanyabad	yesterday	hijo
more	badhi	tomorrow	bholi
little bit	alikati	stamp	ticket
that's enough	pugyo	envelope	kham
I do not have	chhaina	money	paisa

cheap	sasto	bridge	pool
expensive	mahango	descent	oralo
		ascent	ukalo
On the trail		left	baya
		right	daya
way, trail	bate	cold	jado

give me	malai dinos
wait a minute	ek chhin parkhanos
I like this	malai yo ramro lagyo
I do not like this	malai yo ramro lagena
where is the market?	bazar kata parchha?
where is the road to?	jane bato kata parchha?
I do not feel good	malai sancho chhaina
is there a village nearby?	najikai gaun parchha?
where is the porter?	bhariya kata gayo?
please give me tea	malai chiya dinos
I want to sleep	malai sutna man lagyo
I feel cold	malai jado lagyo
I do not need it	malai chahinna
I do not have it	ma sanga chhaine

Food Words

food	khana	water	pani
boiled	umaleko	rice	bhat
vegetable	tarkari	tea	chiya
sugar	chini	spicy	peero
tomato	golbeda	egg	phool
meat	masu	chicken	kukhura
bread	pauroti	milk	doodh
salt	noon	curd	dahi
pepper	marich	tastes good	meetho chha

Numbers

one	ek		
two	dui	twenty	bees
three	teen	thirty	tees
four	char	forty	chalis
five	panch	fifty	pachas
six	chha	sixty	sathi
seven	sat	seventy	sattari
eight	sath	eighty	assi
nine	nau	ninety	nabbey
ten	das	one hundred	saya

two hundred	dui saya
five hundred	panch saya
one thousand	hazar
one hundred thousand	lakh
one million	das lakh
ten million	crore

1	2	3	4	5	6	7	8	9	10
९	२	३	४	५	६	७	८	९	१०

Facts for the Visitor

VISAS

Nepal has embassies or consular offices in most European countries, the USA and in most of its Asian neighbours. Overland travellers generally collect their Nepalese visas in Bangkok or Calcutta if west-bound; in New Delhi if travelling east.

Visas cost US$10 or equivalent and are valid for 30 days. Further extensions, up to a maximum of three months cost Rs 75 per week (or Rs 300 per month) for the second month, and Rs 150 per week (or Rs 600 per month) for the third month. When extending visas it is necessary to provide proof of official currency exchange of US$5 for each day of extension — for a 30-day extension therefore you would need US$150.

A seven-day visa is available on arrival at Kathmandu airport or at any of the border entry points for US$10. This can be further extended for three weeks at the immigration office in Kathmandu or Pokhara at no cost.

The immigration offices (tel 12336) at Maiti Devi in Kathmandu, or near the lake in Pokhara, extend visas and also issue trekking permits. Local police offices can also extend visas for up to seven days at a time. Nepalese visas are endorsed as being valid only in and around the Kathmandu and Pokhara Valleys and at Chitwan. This permits travel along all the major roads and short treks around the valley. If you intend to take a longer trek you must obtain a trekking permit for the route you intend to walk. Trekking permits are only available in Kathmandu and Pokhara and can only be extended there.

It is possible to get visas for longer than three months by studying, teaching or undertaking research work at the university or any institution recognised by the government. Recent practice has made it easier to extend visas for an additional month after the three month limit has expired. This is given by the Ministry of Home and Panchayat on the recommendation of immigration. But you must have a good reason for applying — waiting for money to arrive; intending to watch a festival to be celebrated a month later, etc. Many foreigners go to India after their visa has expired, obtain a new one-month visa at the Nepalese Embassy and then re-enter Nepal. Generally the immigration office now expects the traveller to have spent at least one month outside Nepal before re-entering the country. It is also possible to get a visa extension by obtaining a trekking permit which costs Rs 60 per week (ie Rs 240) for the second month, and Rs 75 per week (ie Rs 300) for the third month. It is therefore cheaper to extend visas by getting a trekking permit and going trekking. Although you do not have to go trekking, immigration does sometimes check to see if you have actually gone. If caught you might be made to pay the difference that you would have paid had you applied for an extension without a trekking permit.

If travelling to India after Nepal, visas are not required for Commonwealth citizens or nationals of a number of European countries. Nor are they required if you arrive in India by air and have outward ticketing within 21 days. This concession does not apply if you are entering India by road and would normally need a visa.

Nepalese Diplomatic Offices

Australia	3/87C Cowles Rd, Mosman, NSW 2088 (tel 02 960 3565)
France	7 Rue Washington, Paris 75008 (tel 359 2861)
West Germany	53 Bad Godesberge im Haag, Bonn 2 (tel 34 3097)

India	1 Barakhamba Rd, New Delhi (tel 38 1484)
	19 Woodlands, Sterndale Rd, Alipur, Calcutta (tel 45 2024)
Sri Lanka	92 Chatham St, Colombo 1 (tel 26393)
Thailand	189 Soi 71, Sukhumvit Rd, Bangkok (tel 391 7240)
UK	12A Kensington Palace Gardens, London W8 (tel 229 6231)
USA	2131 Leroy Place NW, Washington DC 20008 (tel 667 4550)
Nepalese UN Mission	711 3rd Avenue, Room 1806, New York, NY 10017 (tel 986 1989)

OTHER PAPERWORK

An international driving permit is worth having if there is any chance you may be driving. Experienced budget travellers do not need to be told how useful an International Student Identity Card can be -- if you can get one do. If you are youth hostelling then YHA membership may be worth having — there is a youth hostel in Patan in the Kathmandu valley. If you are travelling elsewhere in the region you'll find many in India and in south-east Asia. It's always worth carrying a stack of photos for visa applications, trekking permits and so on. You won't find western-style coin-in-the-slot photo booths in Nepal of course, but Kathmandu's photo studios will do good quality passport photos at way below western prices. Health insurance is a wise investment. If you take out trekking insurance make sure it covers helicopter rescue services as well — being flown out by helicopter is not cheap!

HEALTH

A number of vaccinations are highly advisable both for your own safety and for regulations governing return to your own country, although they may not all be required for entry to Nepal. Diseases to avoid include:

Smallpox Vaccination lasts three years but if your current immunisation is getting old re-vaccination is a good idea. Just a painless scratch.
Cholera Another important immunisation, usually given as two injections spaced two weeks apart and valid for six months.
Typhoid and Paratyphoid Also highly recommended, this can be given with the cholera shot as TAB.
Tetanus Since the TAB shot can also immunise against tetanus as TABT, this is a worthwhile extra precaution.
Malaria Particularly if you are visiting the Terai during the wet season, malarial prophylactics are advisable. The usual procedure is a weekly chloroquine tablet or a daily dose of paludrine. In either case start taking the tablets before you arrive in Nepal and continue for two weeks after departure. Malaria has been virtually eradicated from the low lying Terai but care is still advisable.
Hepatitis The best protection against this infectious disease is to take care to eat and drink only clean food and drinks. Gamma globulin injections have a limited and doubtful efficacy and should be taken as closely as possible to your departure date.

Your doctor will record immunisations in your International Certificate of Vaccination which must then be stamped by your local health department. With a little care there is no reason for anyone to catch anything in Nepal. Nepalese pharmacies stock a reasonable range of western pharmaceuticals including aspirin (useful for high altitude headaches if trekking) and cough syrup (often necessary in the cold dry winter air).

MEDICAL FACILITIES

The government hospital in Kathmandu, known as the Bir Hospital (tel 11119), is modern and does cholera and typhoid vaccinations and issues international health cards. The Santa Bhawan Mission Hospital was closed recently but the new Patan Hospital (tel 22266, 22278, 22286) also receives assistance from western missionaries. It is located in the Lagankhel area of Patan, near the last stop of the Lagankhel bus. The Shining Mission Hospital is a good mission hospital in Pokhara.

There is a Japanese-trained Nepalese dentist named Dr Mesh Bahadur (tel 12282) just behind the fire station in New Rd. His clinic hours are 5 to 7 pm. Dr S K Pahadi (tel 12331) is a general practitioner with a clinic in the same compound as the Nepal Bank, close to New Rd. The clinic of Dr L N Prasad (tel 11801), an eye, ear, nose and throat specialist, is near the National Theatre. Gamma globulin shots can be obtained at the Kalimati Clinic (tel 14743) for Rs 65.

Many westerners interested in Ayurvedic medicine have found Dr Mana (tel 13960) to be good. Some even claim he has cured them of hepatitis! His clinic is situated on a street near the Bir Hospital.

CLIMATE & WHEN TO VISIT

October-November and February-March-April are the best times to visit Nepal. In October and November the weather is excellent, neither too hot, nor too cold. As it is immediately after the monsoon there are no clouds or dust in the atmosphere and visibility is extremely good; the Himalayan range will be clearly visible. Rice is harvested in Nepal during these months and two of the biggest festivals also take place – the Nepalese people will be in a happy and festive mood. This is also the best time for trekking.

In the February to April period the weather is still excellent but due to dust in the air visibility is not quite so good. On the other hand if you go trekking you can see the blooming of flowers at high altitudes especially Nepal's brilliant rhododendrons. The weather in mid-winter, December and January, is still fine and clear but it can be quite cool especially at high altitude where nights can be exceedingly bitter.

The monsoon lasts from the second week of June to the first week of October and this is not the best time to visit the country – although it will be cool and pleasant compared to the plains of India. Trekking is impossible during this season as the trails are slippery and difficult to walk on, rivers may be impassable and Nepal's horrendous leeches will be out waiting for you. Roads can also be blocked at this time due to landslides and the Himalayan peaks are rarely visible due to the constant cloud cover. However many festivals are celebrated in Kathmandu during the second half of the monsoon (August-September) which may make your stay rewarding.

If you visit Nepal in this period a one-week stay in Kathmandu should be adequate with just a short visit out of the valley. If you come in the dry season from October to June a two to four-week stay is better. A week can easily be spent in and around the Kathmandu Valley followed by a week's stay in Pokhara including a short trek. If you have time, a 10-day trek can be made to Ghodepani or Ghandruk from Pokhara or to Helambu from Kathmandu. The long trek to the Everest base camp can even be squeezed into two weeks if you fly back to Kathmandu from Lukla.

Maximum summer temperatures in Kathmandu approach 30°C and even at the height of winter a daily maximum approaching 20°C can be expected. Night temperatures in mid-winter can fall to nearly freezing point, 0°C, but it never actually snows in the valley. Pokhara is generally somewhat hotter due to its lower altitude. Nepal's great altitude variations make for some considerable climatic variations from the summer heat on the lowland Terai to the intense cold of the high Himalayas in winter. The Himalayas in Nepal are about 1500 km nearer to the equator than the European Alps — one of the reasons the snow line is so much higher. Apart from the brief winter monsoon, lasting just a day or two in late January, all the rain falls during the monsoon. The lack of precipitation in the winter is another reason for the high snow line, the mountains usually have more snow during the summer.

MONEY

The Nepalese unit of currency is the Rupee which is divided into 100 paisa. There are approximately 12 Nepalese Rupees to the US dollar. Indian and Nepalese Rupees are freely convertible and 100 Indian Rs equals 145 Nepalese Rs. You get a better rate for travellers' cheques than cash. At the time of going to press the official exchange rates in Nepal were:

1 US dollar	Rs 13
100 Indian rupees	Rs 145
1 German mark	Rs 5.33
1 French franc	Rs 1.90
1 Sterling pound	Rs 22.86
1 Australian dollar	Rs 11.50
1 Canadian dollar	Rs 10.55
1 Swiss franc	Rs 6.30
1 Swedish kroner	Rs 2.14
1 Dutch guilder	Rs 4.86
2109 Japanese yen	Rs 100
7414 Italian lira	Rs 100
113 Austrian Schilling	Rs 100

Nepalese currency consists of:
Coins of 5, 10, 25, 50 paisa
Banknotes of 1, 5, 10, 50, 100, 500, 1000 rupees.

The major banks in Nepal are located in New Road. There is a big Nepal Bank building near the statue and park which is open from 10 am to 2 pm on Sundays to Thursdays and from 10 am to 12 noon on Fridays. There is also an office of the Rashtriya Bank located on the first floor of the supermarket. The Rashtriya Bank also has an exchange office in the Thamel area of Kathmandu. Most travellers' cheques can be exchanged at these offices or, usually for resident guests only, at the main hotels. Unlike many other countries, the exchange rate in hotels is identical to the banks. It is wise to get some of your money in smaller rupee denominations. The Rs 100 notes may be difficult to change, particularly in the hills if you go trekking.

Upon entry to Nepal visitors are given a currency exchange card which they are advised to have filled and stamped each time they change money or travellers' cheques. If not, get one from a bank, but don't expect to change $ back. When leaving the country you can re-exchange Nepalese currency providing the amount does not exceed 10% of the total changed or the last amount exchanged — whichever is greater. There is an exchange counter in the international terminal of the airport.

There is a bank office in Pokhara and money changers operate at border points such as Birganj. Elsewhere in the country you could expect to have difficulty changing travellers' cheques although US dollars can still be changed in major towns. It is advisable to carry sufficient Nepalese currency when trekking to last the whole trek. Until comparatively recently paper money was almost unknown outside the Kathmandu Valley. Mountaineering expeditions in the 1950s would have to have several porters simply to carry the operating money for the expedition and porters' wages — in coins! Several books on expeditions in Nepal speak of the proud swagger of the porter entrusted with carrying half his weight in cash.

Getting Money Sent to Kathmandu
This might involve long delays unless you choose the right bank and do it properly. Many of the major banks in the west (ie Westpac in Australia, Standard Chartered Bank in the UK, Chase Manhattan in the USA) are correspondent banks of the Nepal Bank. The head office is located near the park in New Rd. Money can be sent by telex or other means to Nepal and you can then collect it from the bank. Be as specific as possible when having money transferred internationally and if possible arrange that you yourself are notified when money is transferred as well as the bank.

GENERAL INFORMATION
Working Days
Saturday is an inauspicious day and most shops and all offices and banks will be closed   Sunday is a regular working day.

Time
Nepalese time is 5 hours 40 minutes ahead of GMT, noon in London is 5.40 pm in Kathmandu. The odd 10 minutes is intended to differentiate Nepal from India which is 5 hours 30 minutes ahead of GMT.

What to Wear
During most of the year light summer clothes are all you'll need in Kathmandu and the valley. An umbrella is a vital addition during the monsoon and in the depths of winter you'll want a sweater during the day and a warm coat at night. In the mountains, even in mid-winter, the days will be warm but the nights bitterly cold. The burning power of the sun at high altitudes is phenomenal — sunglasses and covering unprotected skin are advisable.

Film and Camera
Although Kathmandu has a number of camera shops, obtaining film is both expensive and difficult. What film there is available has usually been sold by visitors and is of doubtful age and quality. If you are using an SLR camera a telephoto lens is a virtual necessity for good mountain close-ups when trekking. Remember also to allow for the exceptional intensity of mountain light when setting exposures at high altitude. Most Nepalese people are quite happy to be photographed but they may demand baksheesh for posing. Sherpa people are an exception and can be very camera shy.

Electricity

Electric current, when available, is 220 volts/50 cycles throughout Nepal — American 120 volt electrical items will require a transformer.

Tipping

Tipping is not a normal practice in Nepal so don't make it one. Taxi drivers certainly don't expect to be tipped nor do budget hotels and restaurants. Only in the more expensive establishments will there be a 10% service charge added to your bill.

Police

The police phone number is 11999.

Airline Offices   * Fly to Nepal

Air France, Annapurna Hotel Arcade, Durbar Marg (tel 13339)
Air India, Kantipath, Kantipath (tel 12335)
Bangladesh Biman*, Durbar Marg (tel 12544)
British Airways, Durbar Marg (tel 12266)
Burma Airways Corporation *, Durbar Marg (tel 14839)
Indian Airlines*, Durbar Marg, (tel 11196)
Japan Airlines, Trans Himalayan Trekking, Durbar Marg (tel 13854)
KLM, Gorkha Travels, Durbar Marg (tel 14896)
Lufthansa, Annapurna Hotel Arcade, Durbar Marg (tel 13052)
Pakistan International Airlines, Durbar Marg (tel 13052)
Pan American, Durbar Marg (tel 15824)
Royal Nepal Airlines*, New Road (tel 14511)
SAS, c/o Thai International
Thai International*, Annapurna Hotel Arcade, Durbar Marg (tel 14387 & 13565)
TWA, Kantipath (tel 14704)

Postal Services

The Kathmandu *GPO* is on the corner of Kantipath and Khichapokhari close to the Bhimsen Tower and opens from 10 am to 5 pm daily; a small stamp counter opens earlier. There is a separate *International Post Office* for parcels and a *Telecommunications Office* both situated quite close to the *GPO*. The Poste Restante counter is in the *GPO* and is quite efficient. But as with any other Asian country you are advised to ask that your surname is printed clearly and underlined if you are having mail sent to the Poste Restante. There is also a post office counter at the airport.

Postal Rates

Aerogrammes	2.50 Rs
Air mail postcards	1.75
Air mail to 20 gm —	
Africa, Europe	5.25
Australia, USA	6.00
Registration	

Government Offices

Immigration and other government offices are open from 10 am to 5 pm from Sunday to Friday and from 10 am to 4 pm during the three winter months.

Government Tourist Office
The tourist office on Ganga Path by the Basantapur Square (tel 11203) has a large variety of brochures and maps and shows films on Nepal.

Travel Agencies
Annapurna Travels, Durbar Marg (tel 13940)
Continental Travels & Tours, Durbar Marg (tel 14299)
Dolkha Travels & Tours, Kantipath (tel 15392)
Everest Travel Service, New Road — Basantapur Square (tel 11216)
Gorkha Travels, Durbar Marg (tel 14895)
Himalayan Travels & Tours, Durbar Marg, Ranipokhari (tel 11682)
International Travels (tel 12635), Ramshah Path
Kathmandu Tours & Travels, Dharma Path — New Road (tel 14446)
Natraj Travels & Tours, Durbar Marg (tel 15021)
President Travel & Tours, Durbar Marg (tel 15021)
Pokhara Tours & Travel, New Road (tel 14613)
Shankar Travels & Tours, Shankar Hotel, Lazimpat (tel 13494)
Trans Himalayan Tours, Durbar Marg (tel 13871)
Universal Tours & Travel, Kantipath (tel 12080)
Yak Travel & Tours, Durbar Marg (tel 15611)
Yeti Travels, Durbar Marg (tel 12329 & 11234)

Foreign Embassies
Bangladesh, Naxal (tel 15546)
Burma, Pulchowk (tel 21788)
Egypt, Jawlakhal (tel 12945)
Federal Republic of Germany, Kantipath (tel 11730)
France, Lazimpat (tel 12332)
German Democratic Republic, Tripureshwar (tel 14801)
Great Britain, Lainchaur (tel 11588)
India, Lainchaur (tel 11300)
Israel, Bishramalaya-Lazimpat (tel 11251)
Italy, Baluwatar (tel 12743)
Japan, Lazimpat (tel 13264)
Pakistan, Panipokhari (tel 11431)
People's Republic of China, Toran Bhawan, Naxal (tel 11289)
Poland, Kalikasthan (tel 12694)
Republic of Korea, Thamel (tel 11172)
Thailand, Jyoti Kendra Building, Thapathali (tel 13912)
UNDP, Lainchaur (tel 16444)
USA, Ranipokhari-Maharjganj (tel 12718)
USSR, Dillibazar (tel 11255)

Trekking Agencies
Annapurua Mountaineering and Trekking, Durbar Marg (tel 12736)
Mountain Travels, Box 170, Kathmandu 12808)
Sherpa Co-Operative Trekking, Kamal Pokhari (tel 15887)
Great Himalayan Adventure, Kantipath (tel 14424)
Sherpa Trekking Service, Kamaladi (tel 12489)
Himalayan Journeys, Kantipath, PO Box 989 (tel 15855)

Getting There

ENTERING NEPAL BY LAND
It is possible to enter Nepal by land via three main routes. Most of the 20% of foreign visitors who arrive in Nepal by these land routes are overlanders making the trans-Asian trip from Europe. If you are travelling by Indian train this is a very cheap way of getting to Nepal but it can also be very slow. The trains running up to the Indian border towns travel on *metre gauge* instead of the much faster *broad gauge* lines, as is the case between Delhi and Calcutta. It is faster and more convenient to take a bus from Muzaffarpur or Gorakhpur to the border.

The most popular land entries are from Sunauli near Lumbini, north of the Indian city of Gorakhpur, then by road to Kathmandu via Narayanghat or to Pokhara directly. As Kathmandu is now only seven hours away by express bus from Sunauli, anyone travelling from Delhi or Varanasi will find it more convenient to enter from Sunauli. On the other hand, those travelling from Calcutta or Patna will enter Nepal from Raxaul and will travel to Kathmandu via Narayanghat. Because of the opening of the connecting road from Narayanghat to Mugling on the Pokhara-Kathmandu road there are now very few buses using the old Rajpath, constructed by India in the 1950s. However, the Rajpath (from Hetaura to Naubise along the Birganj-Kathmandu route) is more scenic and has some beautiful spots to view the Himalaya in the autumn. There is also a third possible entrance route to Nepal, at Kakarbitta in the east, near Darjeeling.

The road from Birganj was constructed with Indian assistance in the late 1950s and named Tribhuvan Rajpath after the late King Tribhuvan. The Sunauli to Pokhara road was also built by the Indians but in the late sixties. It is named the Sidhartha Highway after Buddha whose birthplace at Lumbini is near its Indian starting point. Sidhartha is another name for Buddha. The road between Pokhara and Kathmandu was constructed with Chinese assistance in the early seventies.

During the monsoon, the road from Sunauli to Pokhara may be closed for a few days by landslides. However, the road to Kathmandu via Narayanght and Mugling is unlikely to remain closed due to its economic importance. The eastern route from Darjeeling may also be susceptible to monsoon blockages in which case it would be necessary to travel by train from Siliguri to Raxaul before entering Nepal.

TO KATHMANDU FROM SUNAULI
Sunauli on the Indo-Nepal border can be reached by a Rs 9 bus ride from the city of Gorakhpur. If you want to visit Lumbini, Buddha's birthplace, you should make an overnight stay in the city of Bhairawa. If not you can get buses heading directly to either Kathmandu or Pokhara.

Sunauli is just Rs 50 and a seven-hour bus ride from Kathmandu. Buses leave either early in the morning or at 1 pm. There are also night buses but you are not advised to take them. The bus passes through Bhairawa and then the city of Butwal, in the Siwalik Hills, the outermost of the Himalayan ranges. Here you turn east on the East-West Highway. This sector from Butwal to Narayanghat was constructed with British aid in the 1970s. For two hours you roll across the plains of the Terai, before crossing a small hill at Barghat where you enter the intermontane valley known as the 'Inner Terai'.

You then cross the River Narayani, one of Nepal's three biggest rivers, and reach the town of Narayanghat. This is the main town of the rich agricultural area known as Chitwan. Chitwan is also the name of the national park famed for its rhinoceros and the game reserve is only a couple of hours drive from this city. From Narayanghat the bus follows the Trisuli River north to Mugling at the Pokhara-Kathmandu Highway. From here you drive through the towns like Benighat and Gajuri before reaching a fertile valley where guavas and sugar are grown. The road finally crosses a ridge and descends into the Kathmandu Valley.

TO KATHMANDU FROM RAXAUL

A one rupee rickshaw ride will take you from the Indian border town of Raxaul to the town of Birganj. Unless you arrive very early in the morning you will have to overnight here. Almost all of the cheap lodges are found around the bus station. Birganj is not really a very pleasant place to stay but you don't really have much choice in the matter! See the Terai section for more details on this small border town.

The buses to Kathmandu leave between 6 and 9 in the morning and charge Rs 29; knock off 20% if you hold an International Student ID card. If you can find a spare seat in a truck you can travel for Rs 15 to 20. Or you can go by more comfortable mini-bus for Rs 40 and enjoy a better view of the surroundings. Several bus companies operate this route, some of the better ones are *Das*, *Yatayat Sansthan* and *Pradhan* Transport. Try to get a seat within the bus wheelbase, seats right at the back give an uncomfortable ride.

Birganj has a population of about 30,000. A sugar factory and an agricultural implements factory have been constructed here with Russian assistance. The Tribhuvan Rajpath runs 200 km from Birganj to Kathmandu and reaches a maximum altitude of over 2500 metres. Although the scenery is very spectacular most people prefer not to make this trip too often, it takes over eight hours by bus and is extremely tiring due to the constant ups, downs and arounds. In a car the time could be cut to five hours.

North of Birganj you can see the heavily forested Siwalik Hills. The southernmost and youngest mountains in Nepal. The almost treeless Mahabharat range is visible beyond and if the weather is clear the main Himalayan range can be seen still further to the north. The road from Birganj runs through the flatlands known as the Terai as far as the town of Amlekhganj. The people in this area have close linguistic ties with India but since the eradication of malaria in the Terai during the 1960s there has been much migration from the hill country. Eleven km before reaching the foothills the road passes through a dense Sal forest.

From Amlekhganj the road climbs over the Siwalik hills then descends to Hetaura, the biggest town between Birganj and Kathmandu. Situated in the rich intermontane Rapti Valley this town is the regional administrative headquarters

Kathmandu Valley

a Shiva and Parvati look out from their temple in Kathmandu
b Nepalese house beside the path to Swayambhunath
c Wood carving on Basantapur Durbar in Kathmandu

and has a small industrial estate where Nepal's first brewery produces Star Beer with German assistance. In the 1920s, long before the road was constructed, an aerial ropeway was built between Kathmandu and Hetaura. It still carries goods to this day. If you wish to make an overnight stay at Hetaura the *Hotel Rapti* charges Rs 12 for a single with bath.

After Hetaura you enter the Chitwan Valley, well known both as an agricultural region and as the home of the Royal Game Reserve and the Chitwan National Park. If you are interested in wildlife you can make a stopover in Tandi Bazaar, en route to Narayanghat, and stay overnight in one of the hotels or cheap lodges.

Before the construction of the road from Narayanghat to Mugling, buses would continue from Hetaura directly north to Kathmandu. Bhainse is beyond Hetaura and from here you travel through the Mahabharat range and soon reach the highest point known as Sim Bhanjyang. A few km away at Daman, 80 km before Kathmandu, there is a view tower at 2300 metres from where you can see an incredible view of the entire Himalayan range in Nepal, stretching from Dhaulagiri to Kanchenjunga. There is a guest house here if you want to make an overnight halt. Daman also boasts a Nepalese government horticultural farm.

The road continues to the Palung Valley at 2300 metres, an area famous for the cultivation of potatoes. All along this route you can see marginal land on the slopes being cultivated, a clear indicator of the population pressure in the hilly areas. The road passes through a serpentine series of curves, known as *seven turns* in Nepali, before descending to the tropical village of Dhunibesi at 750 metres. The valley is an important producer of guavas, mangoes and bananas and from the town of Naubise in this valley the road to Pokhara branches off. A steep 700-metre climb then takes you over the final hill before descending to Thankot, the first village in the Kathmandu Valley and only a short drive from the city.

If you want to fly from Birganj to Kathmandu you must first take the short bus ride to Simra, where the airport is located. RNAC make two flights daily on this short sector. The fare is Rs 205 and the flight takes less than half an hour.

TO POKHARA FROM SUNAULI

The easiest way to get to Sunauli, at the Indo-Nepal border near Nautanwa, is to take a bus from Gorakhpur. The UP Roadways buses are slower and more crowded. It is better to take a tourist bus at Gorakhpur (near the bus and railway station) and you can reach the border in less than three hours for Rs 9. There is also a railway service between Gorakpur and Nautanwa near the border but it is slower and less frequent and, therefore, not recommended.

If you arrive late in the evening and would like to go to Kathmandu or Pokhara

Kathmandu Valley

a   Peacock window in Bhaktapur
b   Temple strut at Changunarayan
c   Bodhnath stupa

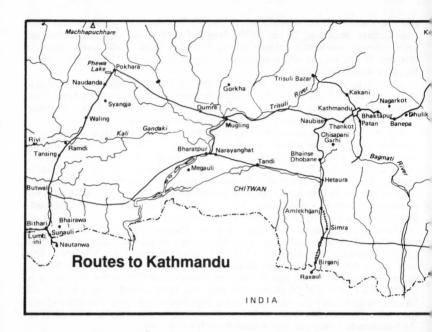

Routes to Kathmandu

early in the morning, there is *Mamata Lodge* at Sunauli near the border. Doubles cost Rs 35 and a bed Rs 10. It is very basic and may be OK for overnighting. If you want to stay in a better place you have to go to Bhairawa, three km away — see the Terai section.

At 7, 9 and 11 am express buses leave Bhairawa for Pokhara and charge Rs 35. It is better to backtrack to Sunauli on the border where the buses start to make certain of getting a good seat. From the town of Butwal, a few km to the north, buses leave almost every hour but they take longer to reach Pokhara as they operate a local service.

Like the road between Birganj and Kathmandu this road was constructed with Indian assistance and is about 200 km long. It is, however, a better road. It crosses the Terai to Butwal then climbs over the Siwalik and Mahabharat ranges. Two hours out you reach the beautiful town of Tansen, which at 1271 metres is pleasantly cool if you have just left the hot Indian plains. Around the bus terminal you can have a meal at one of the many good *bhattis*, hotels run by the local Thakalis. Nearby is the *Siddhartha Hotel*, if you wish to stop for the night. If you do stay then make sure of climbing the hill, known as Srinagar, to admire the Himalayan view stretching from Dhaulagiri to Manaslu. Tansen is a small town inhabited mainly by Newars. It used to be the most important town in west-central Nepal and was the administrative headquarters for the area.

Continuing northwards the road passes through the small town of Arya Bhanjyange then descends steeply to the Kali Gandaki River, one of Nepal's largest, and crosses it at Ramdighat at 375 metres.

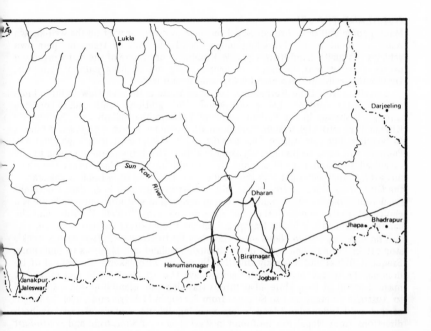

A series of ascents takes you to Waling at 700 metres, a town which has grown tremendously after the construction of the road. The road then passes through the towns of Syangja and Naudanda, the starting point for the direct trail from Pokhara to the Annapurna sanctuary and Jomosom, and finally enters the Pokhara Valley from the south.

TO KATHMANDU FROM DARJEELING

You can also enter Nepal from Kakarbitta near the eastern border across the Mechi River which forms the boundary with India. A bus or jeep will take you to the border from the Indian town of Siliguri. Buses to Kathmandu from Kakarbitta cost Rs 98, student card holders get a 25% discount, and take at least two days including an overnight stop at the Terai town of Janakpur. Until you meet the Birganj to Kathmandu road this route runs through the Terai just a few km south of the Siwalik Hills. Dense forest and new settlements are visible north of the road and the bus also passes through Biratnagar, a major industrial area and the centre of the jute industry. Later you will see the beautiful foothill town of Dharan and cross the barrages of the mighty Kosi River which causes much damage by flooding. The road as far as Janakpur was constructed under Indian assistance and from there to the intersection north of Birganj was constructed by the Russians. This route is often impossible in the monsoon as there are few bridges built yet. It is possible to fly from Bhadrapur, only a short bus ride from Kakarbitta, to Kathmandu on Mondays and Fridays for Rs 760. Sometimes, the Bhadrapur-Kathmandu flight may be cancelled. But there is always a flight between Biratnagar and Kathmandu.

OVERLAND TRAVEL

Many people still pass through Nepal on their way east or west on the well-known Asian overland route. Travelling independently by bus or train, in their own vehicles — usually Land-Rovers or VW Kombis — or on one of the many organised overland expeditions, thousands of people make this exciting journey each year. Despite the problems presented by Afghanistan and Iran.

Travelling west from Kathmandu the usual route is through New Delhi in India and across the border to Lahore in Pakistan. The traditional route used to continue through Peshawar in the Pathan region of Pakistan then climb over the historic Khyber Pass into Afghanistan. That fascinating country is now very much off-limits to travellers but it is still possible to skirt south of Afghanistan through Quetta in Pakistan and cross to Iran directly from Pakistan. This is the route now used by the organised overland expeditions and by intrepid travellers. Many other travellers, however, simply leap right over the trouble zone by flying from India or Pakistan to the Gulf or to other centres in the Middle East like Amman in Jordan. The traditional route, on the other hand, continues across Iran and into Turkey. There is a choice of routes across Turkey but most people pass through Erzurum and the capital Ankara before finally leaving Asia at the Bosphorus crossing in Istanbul.

Travelling east from Nepal most travellers fly to Bangkok, often with a week's stop-off in Burma, then travel down through Thailand and Malaysia to Singapore. Frequent flights and a weekly ship link Singapore with Jakarta, the capital of Indonesia. There are several routes across Java through Jogyakarta and on to the magical island of Bali. More adventurous travellers can 'island hop' south from Bali to Australia or cross over to Sumatra from Penang in Malaysia and travel the length of that wild Indonesian island before reaching Jakarta. Details of travel in both directions from Nepal can be found in *West Asia on a Shoestring* and *South-East Asia on a Shoestring* both published by Lonely Planet Publications.

A number of companies operate expeditions from Kathmandu to London and vice versa over a variety of routes and at a wide range of costs. Average time from Kathmandu to London is 70 to 90 days but there are shorter and longer trips.

ENTERING NEPAL BY AIR

Kathmandu is off-line for all the international airlines. Most air travellers from Europe will fly up from Delhi by Royal Nepal Airlines or Indian Airlines. Travellers from North America or Australasia generally enter from Bangkok by Thai International, Burma Airways Corporation or Royal Nepal Airlines. It is also possible to fly to Kathmandu from Hong Kong via Royal Nepal Airlines; or from Rangoon in Burma; Dacca in Bangladesh; or Calcutta, Varanasi and Patna in India.

Airfares in mid-1982 were:

Bangkok	— Kathmandu	US$243
Hong Kong	— Kathmandu	US$344
Delhi	— Kathmandu	US$132
Calcutta	— Kathmandu	US$ 89
Patna	— Kathmandu	US$ 38
Varanasi	— Kathmandu	US$ 66
Colombo	— Kathmandu	US$289
Dacca	— Kathmandu	US$ 92
Rangoon	— Kathmandu	US$190

Flying from Bangkok it is possible to include, at no extra cost, a seven-day stop-over in Burma. Visas for Burma can be obtained in Bangkok or Kathmandu. International Student Card holders under 26 years of age are allowed a 25% reduction on external and internal flights of Royal Nepal Airlines. A similar discount is given to under 30-year-olds in Indian Airlines. There is also a 25% discount available from Indian Airlines to under 30-year-olds, even if they are not students, if the fare is paid in convertible currency. Foreign residents of India and Nepal (those employed in missions, volunteers, etc) can get a 25% discount on a round trip fare between Kathmandu on the one hand and Delhi, Calcutta and Varanasi on the other. However, the trip must be completed in two weeks.

Travelling between Kathmandu and Delhi the budget conscious traveller can more than halve costs by flying to Patna and then continuing by train to Delhi in less than 24 hours. Total costs by this method will be less than US$40. Curiously the cost of a Kathmandu-Patna and a Patna-Delhi ticket is also less than a direct Kathmandu-Delhi flight. By travelling this way, a saving of US$10 can be made. It is possible to make Patna-Delhi reservations for the same day's flight from Kathmandu.

The flight into Nepal will give you a superb view of the mountains in clear weather -- if you choose the correct side of the aircraft. Flying from the east -- Bangkok, Rangoon or Calcutta - try to be on the right side of the aircraft. If you are flying from the west -- New Delhi or Varanasi -- then try to be on the left side of the aircraft. Kathmandu's International airport is named Tribhuvan Airport after the late king. It used to rejoice in the name Gaucher -- cow pasture, field!

ENTRY AND EXIT

Nepali customs are fairly lax on entry but quite systematic on departure to ensure visitors do not export antique works of art or marijuana. The usual, rarely enforced, regulations apply to how much of what you're allowed to bring into the country. The only requirement it might be advisable to worry about is the per person limit of twelve rolls of film. If you intend being considerably over these limits it may be wise to check with the Nepalese embassy before departure.

On departure there is a Rs 40 airport tax; domestic flights are also subject to a Rs 10 airport tax. The airport has a duty free shop selling the usual range of cigarettes and liquor which must be paid for in US dollars. The experienced shoestring traveller will no doubt be familiar with the considerably greater value of these items in other Asian countries. A carton of 555 cigarettes and a bottle of Johnny Walker Red Label is a very advisable investment if Burma is your next stop.

Approximate costs and times for rail travel, 2nd to 1st class, between major Indian cities and the rail heads for Nepal are:

for Kathmandu				
Calcutta-Raxaul	23 hours	Rs 42	to	Rs 145
for Pokhara				
New Delhi-Agra	3 hours			
Agra-Varanasi	13 hours	Rs 52	to	Rs 203
Varanasi-Nautawa	11 hours			

If you are planning to tour India after Nepal, Indian Airlines offers a worthwhile excursion fare. Fourteen days unlimited travel on domestic services can be obtained for US$375. Indian Airlines domestic flights are, however, very heavily booked and to make the best use of this opportunity it is wise to plan your itinerary carefully and make reservations well ahead. Indian Airlines also offer a 25% discount to people under thirty years of age but fares must be paid for in convertible currency.

ARRIVING IN KATHMANDU

After arriving at Kathmandu one should sit on the steps of the temples of Durbar Square and just watch people walking and buying.

Andre Christoph, France

If you arrive in Kathmandu by air you will find the hotel reservation counter as soon as you depart from customs and immigration. Only the more expensive and heavily booked hotels take reservations here, if you're heading for a cheap hotel you will have to front up and ask. Outside you'll be immediately surrounded by people claiming to be agents for the hotels and lodges — usually the cheap ones. If you go to the hotel they have in mind for you they may even offer a free ride. If you are paying look for a metered taxi — the ride into town should not cost more than Rs 25 at the most and by a direct route with a good meter could be less than Rs 20! Make sure the meter is turned on and working!! Royal Nepal Airlines and Indian Airlines offer a bus service into town for Rs 6 per person. The Royal Nepal Airlines office is at the top of New Road, the main shopping street in Kathmandu, only a short walk from the town centre. If you are on a budget, and don't have much luggage, you might also take the local bus from the airport to Ratna Park for only Rs 1.

Arriving by road from the Indian border or from Pokhara the bus will take you almost to the centre of town at the foot of the Bhimsen Tower near the post office. This is only three blocks from the town centre, some of the minibus services will run you right into the centre. By whatever means you get into town, taxis or bicycle rickshaws around town are very cheap, a rickshaw ride should rarely cost more than Rs 5.

The best way to visit Kathmandu is to wander without aim, then you see everything — by getting lost you discover the most.

Gilles Callet, France

Getting Around

FLYING
Royal Nepal Airlines operate a number of scheduled and charter flights around the country. Aircraft used are Avro 748s on the major routes and short take-off and landing — STOL — Twin Otters and Pilatus Porters to the smaller places mainly for trekkers. These trekking flights are not scheduled but during the season departures are frequent and tickets can be obtained from the trekking agents. It is advisable to book flights (domestic) seven to 10 days in advance.

Regular Destinations
Central Nepal: Baglung, Bhairawa, Bharatpur, Gorkha, Janakpur, Jomosom, Pokhara, Rumjatar, Simra

Western Nepal: Dang, Dhanagadi, Jumla, Nepalganj, Rukumkot, Sanfe Bagar, Silgarhi Doti, Surkhet

Eastern Nepal: Bhadrapur, Biratnagar, Lamidanda, Rajbiraj, Taplejung, Tumlingtar

Charter Destinations The following are the main destinations for trekking flights, remember you are only allowed 10 kg of baggage on these small aircraft. It may be possible to charter helicopters although RNAC does not do it any longer. However, it is still possible to charter Twin Otter and Pilatus Porter aircrafts through RNAC to such destinations as Jomosom, Lukla, Langtang and Manang.

Lukla or Shyangboche: 45 and 50 minutes flight from Kathmandu, in the Solu Khumbu region on the route to Everest.

Langtang: 25 minutes north of Kathmandu

Dhorpatan: 90 minutes west in the Dhaulagiri mountain range area

Jumla: 120 minutes east on the route to Rara Lake

Jomsosom: 60 minutes flight east towards the Annapurnas

GUIDED TOURS
Travel agencies in Kathmandu organise scheduled conducted tours and private tours by car or coach to places of touristic interest. If your stay in Nepal is too short to permit exploration on your own, then it is best to join a conducted or private tour.

Everest Travel conducts a Rs 60 tour to the Durbar Squares of the three cities of Kathmandu Valley each Monday and Thursday morning. A conducted tour to Nagarkot on Monday, Wednesday and Friday to watch the sunset and sunrise over the world's highest peaks cost Rs 80 per person not including overnight accommodation. On Wednesday and Sunday afternoons they run conducted tours to the temples of Pashupatinath, Bodhnath and Bhaktapur for Rs 50.

Kathmandu Travel has conducted tours to Pashupatinath, Bodhnath and Bhaktapur on Monday, Thursday and Friday mornings for Rs 55. Tours to Kathmandu City, Swayambhunath and Patan on Monday, Wednesday, Thursday and Friday afternoons cost Rs 55. On Tuesday and Sunday mornings there is a Rs 75 tour to watch the sunrise on Everest from Nagarkot.

These agencies and others such as *Yeti Travels*, *Third Eye Travels* and *Gorkha Travel* will also arrange private tours if requested, at widely differing prices. Most agencies will arrange tours to Budhanilkantha to see the sleeping Vishnu. *Kathmandu, Gorkha* and *Shankar Travel* all arrange tours to the temple of Changunarayan. Almost all agencies organise a trip to Dhulikhel along the road to the Chinese border and to the border itself. Some agencies, like *Kathmandu Travel* for Rs 50, organise conducted tours to the temple of Daxinkali to watch the animal sacrifices on Tuesday and Saturday mornings. Occasionally overland bus companies will use their vehicles for tours during the periods between their trips.

DO-IT-YOURSELF TRANSPORT

Cars can be hired through *Yeti Travels* or *Gorkha Travels* in Kathmandu but the cost is fairly high both in terms of initial hiring charge and fuel — over US$3.50 per gallon. Taxis, on the other hand, are quite reasonably priced — any ride around town should come to less than Rs 20 and a taxi can be hired all day for Rs 200 to 300. Taxis add a percentage to the meter reading because of fuel price increases. A group of people can tour the valley quite cheaply by taxi. A number of garages, particularly around Freak St, hire out motorcycles by the day or week but at about Rs 150 per day they are quite expensive. Recently, metered autorickshaws have become quite common in Kathmandu and cost as little as half of what you would pay for a cab.

Bicycle rickshaws only cost Rs 3 for any ride around town but be certain to agree a price before you start. For the fit and healthy bicycle hire is the ideal way to get around — the valley is sufficiently compact and flat to make riding a pleasure. Daily hire charges vary from Rs 3 to 5; get up early for the best selection of bikes and make sure you lock your bicycle when leaving it. Check the brakes before taking it out!

> *To discover the Kathmandu Valley with its three cities there is no better way than by bicycle, it costs less than Rs 5 a day and they can be hired in different places around the city.*
>
> *Joelle Lambelle, France*

but

> *If you do not like bicycles the bus service is inexpensive and well organised but during the monsoon enquire about the condition of the roads.*
> *Genette Katz & Nadine Cals, France*

PUBLIC TRANSPORT

Bus travel around Kathmandu and the valley is very cheap although often equally crowded. Less sardine-like but also inexpensive are the smaller minibuses and the curious little three-wheeler tempos. The three main bus stations are all situated around the parade ground.

Post Office and Martyr's Gate: Buses and tempos to Patan
Bhimsen Tower near the Post Office: Buses to Pokhara and the Indian border
Bagh Bazar, near the Park and Clock Tower: Buses east to Bhaktapur
City Hall: Buses to Pokhara, Janakpur and the Indian border, Dhulikhel and points along the road to the Chinese border, Kakarbitta (eastern border of Nepal near Darjeeling).
Opposite the park near the clock tower: Buses to Bodnath, Kirtipur, Pashupatinath, Patan and the airport

Balaju, Lazimpat and Maharajgunj Tempos leave from the same National Theatre location for these three places and charge Rs 1. Many of the embassies are located in the Maharajgunj area.

Patan Buses leave along the park near the clock tower, they depart every 15 minutes and charge 75 paisa. Tempos depart from the Post Office and the park beside the Clock Tower, as soon as they have six passengers, cost 75 paisa and take just 10 minutes to reach Patan.

Bhaktapur Buses leave every 20 minutes between 6 am and 8 pm from the stop across Durbar Marg from the Park Restaurant. The minibuses charge Rs 1.25. You can also get to Bhaktapur by the new trolleybus service which runs from the statue at Tirprusewar through Thimi to the outskirts of Bhaktapur for 50 paisa. It is a 15 minute walk from the trolleybus terminal to the city centre in Bhaktapur.

Budhanilkantha Buses to the Sleeping Vishnu leave from the National Theatre near the lake and charge Rs 1.25 or you can travel by tempo for Rs 2.

Daxinkali Buses to the temple of Daxinkali where animal sacrifices are performed, leave from near the park and the Clock Tower on Tuesday and Saturday mornings. A cheap way of doing it is to take a bus to Pharping from the Martyr's Gate in the morning and get off at the boarding school near the temple.

Dhulikhel & along the Chinese border road to Lamosangu Buses to these places leave from the big bus terminal near the City Hall. There are departures almost every hour for Dhulikhel or Banepa and the fare to Dhulikhel is Rs 3.70. Buses to Barabise or Lamosangu out towards the Chinese border depart at 6 am, 10 am and 2 pm.

Pokhara Buses leave in the early morning near the Post Office or at the big bus park near the City Hall. It is advisable to reserve seats and buy tickets at least a day in advance.

Indian Border Buses to Birganj and Raxaul or Janakpur and the eastern border near Darjeeling can be found at the City Hall bus park.

Bodhnath Minibuses charge Rs 1 to Bodhnath and leave from in front of the Park Restaurant, they depart when full. Pashupatinath is an intermediate point and the name of the stop is Gosala.

Kirtipur & the University Buses charge Rs 1 and leave every 15 minutes from the Park Restaurant, there are also mini-buses.

Godavari To go to the botanical garden take a bus to Lagankhel and change.

Trisuli To reach this starting point for the Langtang trek go to the main dairy at Lainchaur near the British Embassy. Walk three blocks west on the road leading in that direction until you reach the bus station known as Sorakutte Pati, buses also leave here for Kakani.

Around the Valley

KATHMANDU VALLEY

If you arrive by air the Kathmandu Valley will be the first place you visit in Nepal. As far as art and architecture are concerned your visit to Nepal need go no further than the valley. Three important cities stand in the valley, the most important being Kathmandu itself. Patan, the most 'Buddhist' of the three is across the Bagmati River to the south of Kathmandu, but so close as to be almost an extension of the capital. It is known to this day for its excellent works of art and carvings in wood and bronze. Bhaktapur, also known as Bhadgaon, is the most 'mediaeval' of the lot and is situated in the eastern part of the valley. While Kathmandu and Patan have undergone great changes in the two decades since Nepal ended its long isolation, Bhaktapur has changed very little and is still much as it was three decades ago; some would say three centuries.

Kathmandu stands at about 1350 metres and the valley is surrounded by hills of an altitude around 2400 metres. The original inhabitants of the valley were a people known as the *Newars* and they still form a majority of the population. Typical Newar towns in the valley are Thimi, Bode, Chapagaon — south of Patan and Sankhu. There has also been much migration from other parts of the country, mainly by Brahmins and Chetris who can be found in suburban areas of Kathmandu and Patan, and in villages to the western side of the valley. Many of the people living in the hills surrounding the valley are Tamangs.

Until Nepal's unification process from small principalities and kingdoms started two hundred years ago, there were small independent kingdoms in the valley. The kingdoms of Kathmandu, Bhaktapur and Patan all had amazingly sophisticated art and architecture, especially during the 17th century which was the golden age for the construction of temples and palaces in the three cities. It makes a romantic picture to think of these three mediaeval kingdoms nestled in a fertile valley in the Himalayas — sometimes fighting each other, but more often celebrating numerous feasts and festivals, and competing in the building of temples and other works of art. In the same era temples and idols were being indiscriminately destroyed in India. The affluence of the valley was assured by its strategic position on a major trade route between Tibet and the north Indian plains. The kings in the valley were sometimes Hindu and sometimes Buddhist.

Then in 1768 King Prithvi Narayan Shah started his campaign to unify Nepal. The three kings of the valley were defeated and the foundations of a united Nepal were laid. The use of the Nepali language, one of the Indo-European family of languages, replaced the Tibeto-Burmese Newari language of the valley as the language of administration.

Today the valley is the most developed part of Nepal with a network of roads and electricity in most of the villages. The availability of improved seeds, fertilisers and extensive irrigation has allowed the farmers to cultivate wheat as well as the traditional rice. Two decades ago rice was often the only crop. Land reform programmes have allowed the farmer a larger share of produce which once had to be given to the landlords.

KATHMANDU

Kathmandu is both the capital of Nepal and the largest city in the country. Most of the interesting things to see in Kathmandu are clustered around the old part of town between the old market place and the new shopping area along New

Road. Around the central Durbar Square are the old Royal Palace, a number of interesting pagoda and Indian style temples and the Kumari Devi, residence of the living goddess. Some of the interesting things to see in the Dubar Square area include:

Kalo Bhairab (39) This huge stone-image of the terrifying Black Bhairab was once used as a form of lie detector. Suspected wrongdoers were forced to touch the feet of the god and swear whether they had committed the crime. It was said that lying brought immediate death!

Sweta Bhairab (18) Hidden behind the lattice work on the temple wall behind Black Bhairab is the even more terrifying aspect of White Bhairab. This figure was built in 1794 by King Rana Bahadur Shah, the third king of the Shah dynasty, and it is used today as the symbol of Royal Nepal Airlines. The windows are opened for only a few days each year to reveal the image during the Indrajatra festival in September. You can peer at him through the lattice.

Taleju Temple (45) This beautiful three-storey golden pagoda style temple was dedicated to the family deity of the Malla kings. It was built in the 16th century but unfortunately entry inside the temple is not allowed to foreigners.

Stone Inscription (44) Walking along the outside wall of the palace from the Taleju Temple towards the statue of Hanuman you come across a stone inscription written in eighteen languages, including English and French. It was set up by King Pratap Malla in the 17th century; he was both a poet and scholar. Legend says that milk will flow from the spout in the middle of the inscription if somebody manages to read all the different languages.

Hanuman Dhoka The statue of the legendary figure from the Ramayana stands cloaked in red at the gate to the old Royal Palace. His face has long been obscured by the red paste placed on it by faithful visitors. The figure is protected by an umbrella and flanked by two poles with the unique double triangle flag of Nepal. Entrance to the palace costs Rs 5.

White Bhairab

I went for a walk down to the centre of Kathmandu during my first day. I felt as if I was going through a trip back in time, a pure fantasy. I did not judge, believe or disbelieve. I just looked at what seemed like an exhibition — a street panorama of mediaeval living. The only jolt to remind me of the present century was the odd car honking its way through the narrow streets. In fact, the sight of cows, goats and chickens going their way alongside the colourfully clad human inhabitants of this mediaeval town was bizarre to say the least.

Craig Bailey

Royal Palace The old Royal Palace takes its official name, Hanuman Dhoka Palace, from the figure at the entrance door — it translates as 'the palace with the statue of Hanuman at the gate'. The palace was originally built by King Pratap Malla in the 17th century but was renovated many times later as the Shah kings lived here till the end of the 19th century. There are many courtyards inside the palace. You can enter the most famous one, the **Nasal Chowk** (24), and climb to the top of the ancient nine-storey **Basantapur Tower** (25) that overlooks it.

As you enter you will see a very artistic and beautiful image of **Narsimha** (35) killing a demon with its nails. The picture gallery on the left contains portraits of the Shah kings and the seats used by the Malla kings. It was on the platform in the centre of this main courtyard that King Birendra was crowned in the 1975 coronation ceremony. A horse, which is believed to be a deity and which no one is allowed to ride, is sometimes walked around the platform.

UNESCO are renovating the four red coloured buildings around the courtyard and the tallest has been completed. These four buildings are supposed to represent the four ancient cities of the valley — Kathmandu, Bhaktapur, Patan

and Kirtipur. They are the Bangla or **Kirtipur Tower** (26), the Laxmi Bilas or **Bhaktapur Tower** (29) and the Bilas Mandir or **Lalitpur (Patan) Tower** (30) as well as the dominant **Basantapur (Kathmandu) Tower** (25). The Malla kings were supposed to be born on the first floor of the Basantapur Tower and granted audiences on the second floor. With their queens they would watch dancing from the third floor. From the fourth floor the kings would look out over the town before meals, to ensure smoke was coming from every household — food was being cooked and no one was going hungry. The view from the very top looks down on New Road, Freak Street and Durbar Square today, and far over the valley. The courtyard next to the white building to the south-east has a small temple where Malla kings, whose bodies were not taken to the burning ghats on the Bagmati, were cremated. There is also a small museum inside the Palace which contains a collection of items connected with the life of King Tribhuvan (1906-1955), who played a very important role in bringing democracy to Nepal in 1951. You can also see the royal throne of Nepal and a numismatic museum.

King Pratap Malla (32) The statue of a king seated with folded hands, surrounded by four sons, and situated on top of a pillar facing the palace temple, is supposed to be this most famous Malla king.

Drums and Bell (13) The giant drums, across the road next to the police station, were built in the 18th century, as was the bell, which was erected sixty years after those of Patan and Bhaktapur. At that time any unique addition to one of the valley towns' Durbar Squares was immediately copied by the others!

Kumari Devi (9) The three-storey building with the artistic windows looking out on to Durbar Square, and its door guarded by stone lions, is the Kumari Devi — house of the living goddess. The continued veneration of a young girl, as if she were a living goddess, is part of the magic that makes Kathmandu a 'living museum'.

The big gate beside the Kumari Devi conceals the huge chariot which takes the Kumari around the city of Kathmandu once a year. Entering the house you reach a courtyard surrounded by balconies with 18th century masterpieces of woodcarving. Perhaps you might catch a glimpse of the goddess at the windows. She is a young girl and easily recognisable by the black shadowing around her eyes which extends as far as her ears, and by her hair which is piled up over her head. Photographing her is not allowed. The courtyard contains a miniature stupa with a symbol of Saraswatic, the goddess of learning, on its side, looking like a star of David, and a mandala on a lotus. Non-Hindu or Buddhist people are not allowed to go beyond this courtyard.

The Kumari is not born a Goddess nor does she remain one all her life. She is usually chosen from a caste of Newar goldsmiths when she is about five years old. It is essential that she has never been hurt or shed blood. After careful screening by a number of people, including the astrologer, the selected candidates, about 10 in number, are locked in a dark room where fearful-looking masks and freshly slaughtered buffalo heads are kept. Frightening noises are made from outside and the girl who shows least fear is selected. She is installed on a throne in the room she lives in, during the Dasain festival. The spirit of the goddess is said to enter her body after this ceremony. As soon as she reaches puberty the Kumari becomes human once more and a new goddess must be chosen.

For three days each September dur-

Kumari

ing the festival for the God Indra — marking the end of the monsoon season — the Kumari is taken by chariot around Kathmandu. The Kumari also blesses the King of Nepal on this occasion, putting a red tika mark on his forehead and receiving a gold coin in return. It is said that the Kumari gave her blessing to the grandfather of the present King very reluctantly in the year that he died. People say that she was feeling very sleepy and had to be literally forced to mark his forehead. The Kumari goes out officially five to six times a year during major festivals including the big and small Dasains in October and April when she appears at the old Royal Palace, Hanuman Dhoka.

The present Kumari was only five years old when she was selected in the early seventies. When she reaches puberty she will return to her parents' home only three blocks from the Kumari Devi. Her expenses are paid by revenue from Guthi, the lands under the ownership of temples or deities. These funds provide adequate amounts of rice, salt and dal but meat and firewood have to be

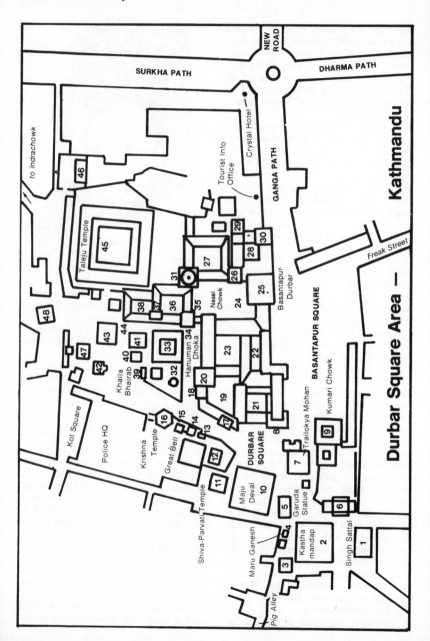

Durbar Square Area — Kathmandu

DURBAR SQUARE SITES

1 Sing Sattal Temple
2 Kastha Mandap
3 Shiva Temple
4 Maru Ganesh
5 Laxmi Narayan Mandir
6 Kabindrapur
7 Trailokya Mohan
8 Gaddi Baithak
9 Kumari Chowk
10 Maju Deval
11 Vishnu Temple
12 Shiva-Parvati Temple
13 Great Bell
14 Stone Vishnu
15 Saraswati Mandir
16 Krishna Mandir
17 Bhagawati Mandir
18 Sweta (white) Bhairab
19 Masan Chowk
20 Degutaleju Mandir
21 Hnuluche Chowk
22 Lam Chowk
23 Dakh Chowk
24 Nasal Chowk
25 Basantapur Durbar
26 Bangla Tower
27 Mul Chowk
28 Basantapur Chowk
29 Laxmi Bilas
30 Bilas Mandir
31 Panch Mukhi Hanuman
32 King Pratap's Column
33 Jaganath Mandir
34 Hanuman Statue
35 Narsimha Statue
36 Mohan Chowk
37 Mohan Chowk Tower
38 Sundar Chowk
39 Khaila (black) Bhairab
40 Indrapur
41 Vishnu Mandir
42 Kotilingeshwar Mandir
43 Kakeshwar Mandir
44 Stone Inscription
45 Taleju Temple
46 Tana Deval
47 Maha Vishnu Mandir
48 Mahendreshwar Mandir

...And the wildest dreams of Kew

Are the facts in —

Kathmandu

R. KIPLING

Dropouts, deadbeats
freaks, geeks
poseurs, mutants
& hangers out —

THE SCENE IN DURBAR SQUARE

Hair hnted red, yellow and green

USA
XXX
GRADE A
FLOUR

DAD TRYS HIS WINGS

.... lounging on the temple steps

purchased separately. The Kumari also gets a considerable sum in offerings from devotees. The Kumari is not supposed to go to school, but the last one had a visiting teacher and the present Kumari is also being educated. When she retires she receives a government allowance of Rs 50 a month until she marries when a lump sum of Rs 1000 is paid as dowry. She gets no further allowances after marriage.

There is a popular belief that a man who marries an ex-Kumari may die within six months and should, therefore, be strong both physically and mentally. This could lead, not unexpectedly, to a general reluctance to marry a Kumari, but many people now believe this is simply superstition and cite cases of husbands outliving an ex-Kumari.

The institution of the Kumari dates back at least two centuries to the last Mala king of Kathmandu, Jayaprakash Malla. He once had intercourse with a pre-pubescent girl and as a result the young girl later died. The king was then told in his dreams to start the institution of the Kumari, worship her, and once each year convey her around Kathmandu as penance for his sins. The institution may have existed even earlier and only the custom of the Kumari visiting the city by chariot started at this time. The last Malla king of Kathmandu was defeated on the day of the Kumari festival, and the first king of the present Shah dynasty received his blessing on that same day as was customary.

There are many other interesting sights to see around the Durbar Square apart from the continual bustle of Nepalese life itself. A pleasant hour can easily be spent sitting on the platform of the Trailokya Mohan Temple (7) or the Maju Deval (10) and watching the flute salesmen, trishaw riders, fruit and vegetable sellers, postcard hawkers and tourists below. The three-roofed Trailokya Mohan is easily identified as a temple to Vishnu by the fine Garuda

kneeling before it. The large three-roofed Maju Deval with its nine-stage platform has some interesting erotic carvings and gives a good view over the square and out to Swayambhunath. From here you can look across to the Shiva-Parvati Temple (12) where images of the God and his Goddess look out from the window on the activity below. The white neo-classical building looking highly out of place in the exotic Durbar Square is the Gaddi Baithak (8) which was built as a palace during the Rana period.

Erotic Carvings   There are several temples in the square with erotic carvings on the struts but the best carvings are those on the Jagnath Temple (33) beside the monkey god Hanuman. There are a number of explanations for the presence of these carvings on so many temples, but the most pleasing is that the goddess of lightning is a chaste virgin and would not consider striking

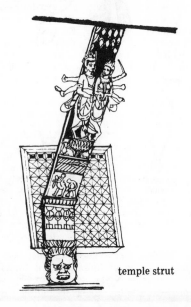

temple strut

a temple with such shocking goings-on.

At the top of Pie Alley, across from the Kasthamandap Temple is the small **Maru Ganesh** (4) temple dedicated to Ganesh and a constant hive of activity — Ganesh is a very popular god. The **Shiva Temple** (3) slightly down from this is used by barbers who can usually be seen squatting on the platform around it. Many of the temples in the square were badly damaged in the 1934 earthquake and have subsequently been restored, rebuilt or modified. An excellent and highly-readable description of the history, significance and architecture of many of the Durbar Square buildings can be found in *An Introduction to Hanuman Dhoka* published by Tribhuvan University and available very cheaply in Kathmandu.

Kathmandu will provide many other interesting sights to the casual wanderer. Set out from the centre and explore the mazed alleys and crowded squares of the market area north of the Durbar Square. You'll find many surprises. The white, minaret-like **Bhimsen Tower** was constructed as a watch tower by a prime minister and is of no particular significance but serves as a useful landmark. It was renovated after suffering serious damage in the 1934 earthquake.

> *It is interesting to visit Mahakal Temple opposite the hospital in downtown Kathmandu. There is a legend that Mahakal, great death, enters this temple every Saturday. I felt a definite presence there one Saturday, a kind of excitement in the air as people streamed past the image. Perhaps it was the ancient God or maybe just the effect of many people, bells, incense, etc — go and find out some Saturday.*
>
> *Richard Schifman, USA*

Hidden away close to the busy market place of Indrachowk is **Sweta Machendranath** the temple of White Machendranath. Religious music is played here every evening and this is the best time to visit this interesting temple.

> *Listen to the Tibetan prayers at Swayambhunath at 3 in the afternoon; picturesque and representative of the familiarity that exists between men and Gods.*
>
> *R Michel, France*

flute seller

PATAN

Patan — sometimes called Lalitpur, the city of beauty — is Kathmandu's near neighbour, the second biggest city in the valley and the most Buddhist. Patan can be reached easily from Kathmandu by bicycle or you can travel by bus or tempo. Buses and tempos stop at the large **Gate to the City of Patan** from where it is a 10 or 15 minute walk along narrow alleyways to the Durbar Square.

In the last few years a very large number of small handicraft shops have opened in Patan and it is an ideal place to buy fine bronzes and woodwork at reasonable prices.

Patan reminds me of Venice because of its red brick, the peaceful surroundings and the serenity of its people. But most of all, it reminds me of the beauty of Nepal.
Erberto Lo Bue, Italy

Hiranya Varna Mahabihar Walking from the bus stop, shortly after passing the cinema and before the road turns right, a sign to the left points to one of the most beautiful Buddhist monasteries in Nepal. The monastery, built in the 12th century, takes its name from the gold-plated roof which was dedicated by a rich merchant. Patan once had many such families who became quite affluent from their Tibetan trading. Inside the monastery there are many prayer wheels and scenes from the life of Buddha on the walls. The courtyard has a richly decorated three-storeyed temple with an image of Buddha; this monastery is quite unlike anything else in Nepal.

Kumbeshwar This five-storeyed temple to Shiva can be found further down beyond the Hiranya Varna Mahabihar. The water in the courtyard spring is said to come directly from the holy lake of Gosainkunda.

Durbar Square Another five minute walk brings you to the Durbar Square where the ancient royal palace of Patan is located. The British writer Landon had this to say of the square at the beginning of this century:

As an ensemble, the Durbar Square of Patan probably remains the most picturesque collection of buildings that has been set in so small a place by the piety and pride of oriental man.

Most of the buildings in the square were built in the 17th century by the famous Malla King of Patan, Siddhinarsingh Malla. The Royal Palace and

Taleju Temple stand on the left side of the square while the temple of Krishna and a host of other temples stand on the right. Patan's biggest market place, the Mangal Bazaar, is also around the square.

Bhimsen Temple The first temple on the right can be discerned by the pillar in front with a lion on top. Bhimsen was a figure from the epic Mahabharata and according to the legend one of the strongest men who ever lived. The three-storeyed temple has a golden-coloured facade on the first floor.

Shiva Temple The second temple with two stone elephants guarding the door is that of Shiva. Shiva's animal, the bull, is on the other side of the temple. The first floor is quite artistic and there are erotic carvings on the roof support struts.

Krishna Mandir The third temple, dedicated to Krishna, is the most famous in the Durbar Square. Built by King Siddhinarsingh Malla in the 17th century it was influenced by Indian architecture, not the usual pagoda styles. The mythical man-bird Garuda sits with folded hands on top of a pillar since Krishna is the incarnation of Vishnu and the Garuda was his animal. The stone carvings at the top of the first-floor pillars tell the story of the Mahabharata while the second floor carved scenes are from the Ramayana. A major festival is held here in August on the occasion of Krishna's birthday. A characteristic feature of this temple is that there are no nails or wood and the construction is entirely of stone.

King Yoganarendra Malla This king ruled Patan in the early 18th century and his statue tops the tall pillar. A bird stands on top of the statue and legend says that one day it will fly away.

Other Temples Next to the king is a

white Indian style temple and then a Shiva temple of three storeys with many erotic carvings. The big bell beside the Shiva temple was supposed to be rung by people wishing to draw the attention of the king to the injustices they were suffering. A small stone temple of Krishna completes the left side of the square.

Water Tap Starting again on the right side of the square the big stone water tap is the first thing seen. When the bird atop the statue of the king flies away the legend foretells that the stone elephants guarding the entrance to the Shiva temple will walk across to the tap for a drink.

Royal Palace The golden gate and artistic wooden and bronze windows mark the Royal Palace of Patan. In a room in this palace the spirit of one of the Malla kings is supposed to continue to exist; to this day a daily offering of tobacco in a water pipe is made.

Krishna
Mandir

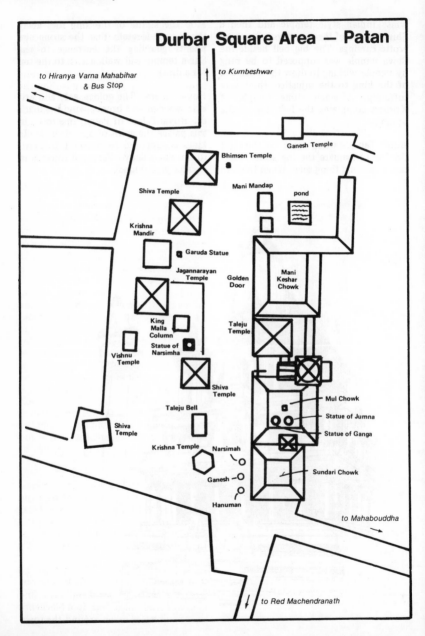

Durbar Square Area — Patan

to Hiranya Varna Mahabihar
& Bus Stop

to Kumbeshwar

Ganesh Temple

Bhimsen Temple

Mani Mandap

pond

Shiva Temple

Krishna Mandir

Garuda Statue

Mani Keshar Chowk

Jagannarayan Temple

Golden Door

Taleju Temple

King Malla Column

Statue of Narsimha

Vishnu Temple

Shiva Temple

Taleju Bell

Mul Chowk

Statue of Jumna

Statue of Ganga

Shiva Temple

Krishna Temple

Narsimah

Ganesh

Sundari Chowk

Hanuman

to Mahabouddha

to Red Machendranath

Taleju Temple The three-storeyed temple of the Goddess Taleju was built

in the mid-17th century and has excellent wood carvings. If you enter and go into the courtyard you will see a beautiful four-storeyed pagoda with statues representing Ganga, the River Ganges and Jumna, the River Jumna, guarding the entrance. The main palace is towards the end of the courtyard and outside stand statues of Ganesh, Narsimha and Hanuman. The entrance leads to Sundarichowk or the 'beautiful courtyard'. There is very beautiful woodwork on the first floor seen from the courtyard and the royal bath with a small replica of the Krishna Temple.

Mahabouddha Temple The temple of one thousand Buddhas is about 10 minutes' walk south of the Durbar Square. It is slightly out of the way and you may have to ask directions as it is located in a courtyard surrounded by buildings and not easily visible despite its height. Originally constructed in the 14th century, the terra cotta, Indian-style temple was severely damaged in the 1934 earthquake and later rebuilt. Each of the bricks in this building contains an image of Buddha. Inside there is a shrine dedicated to Maya Devi, the mother of Buddha. It is said that this temple is similar to the one in Bodh Gaya where Buddha was enlightened. You can climb the buildings around the courtyard to photograph the temple and obtain a fine view over the rooftops of Patan.

Rudra Varna Mahabihara This monastery is situated in a courtyard near the temple of Mahabouddha and is similar to the monastery near the city gate. There are many images of Buddha as well as much artwork on the walls.

Rato Machendranath The temple of Red Machendranath is a little way out from the centre of town and has a fine image of Avalokiteshwar, Red Machendranath, which is taken around the town

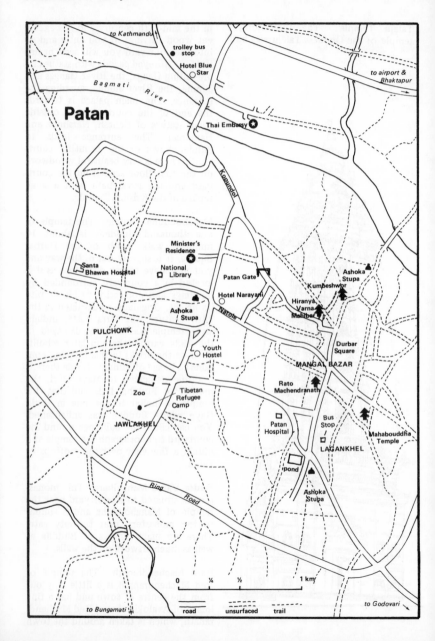

during his festival each year.

Ashoka Stupas During his visit to the valley 2500 years ago the Indian Buddhist emperor Ashoka erected four stupas indicating the boundaries of Patan. You can see the grassy humps where they stood once.

Jawlakhel The Tibetan refugee camp is only about 10 minutes' walk from the centre of town. Here you can see carpets, rugs and pullovers being made. The camp is closed on Saturdays. Prices may be slightly lower than elsewhere in Kathmandu. The handicrafts centre was set up with Swiss assistance. The only zoo in Nepal is situated close to the camp but is not particularly interesting.

To visit a typical Newar village go to Chapagaon, south of Jawlakhel. Just take a dirt road and continue walking till you reach a very densely populated village.
Jane Wolff, USA

The zoo at Jawlakhel in Patan has many specimens of Himalayan and Terai wildlife which you are unlikely to see in the wild: barking deer, Bengal Tiger and an incredible array of unusually beautiful birds.

From the small village of Bhainsepati, south of Jawlakhel, you see a beautiful view of the Himalayas, Kathmandu Valley and the gorge of the Bagmati River.
Thorwald Ritter, West Germany

BHAKTAPUR

Bhaktapur, also called Bhadgaon (batgown), is both the most mediaeval and the least transformed by progress of the three valley cities. It's also been called, unkindly, the dirtiest. Perhaps its distance from Kathmandu at the far end of the valley accounts for the slower pace of change here. Much of the art work in this town was constructed at the end of the 17th century by King Bhupatindra Malla, one of the famous Malla kings who ruled the valley at that time. Bhaktapur is well known for the manufacture of Nepali caps, for pottery and for its delicious curd.

Travelling by bus or mini bus to Bhaktapur you disembark at the walled water tank called Siddha Pokhari, a short walk from the town. If you travel by Chinese trolley bus you have a longer walk from the stop. The fastest way is to take an Express Bus.

One of the specialities of Bhaktapur is its curd known as Jujudhau which means the king of curds in Newari. During autumn and winter it is perfectly safe to taste it in one of the several shops recently opened near the bus station.
Judy Crawford, USA

Statue of Goddess and Bhairab If you walk up from the bus stop past the Hindi movie cinema you come to a gate flanked by stone statues. They are considered to be excellent examples of 17th century Nepalese art, showing the Goddess Ugrachandi on the left and Bhairab on the right. The goddess has several hands and is in the process of killing a demon. After producing these statues the poor sculptor had his hands cut off on the orders of the king to prevent him from reproducing these magnificent works.

Art Gallery A few more steps brings you into the Durbar Square of Bhaktapur with the Art Gallery on your left. Admission is only 20 paisa and the gallery contains many rare paintings and manuscripts from mediaeval Nepal. The paintings showing Hindu and Buddhist styles of Tantrism are particularly interesting as are the fine miniatures and the stone figure of Hari Shankar — half Vishnu and half Shiva.

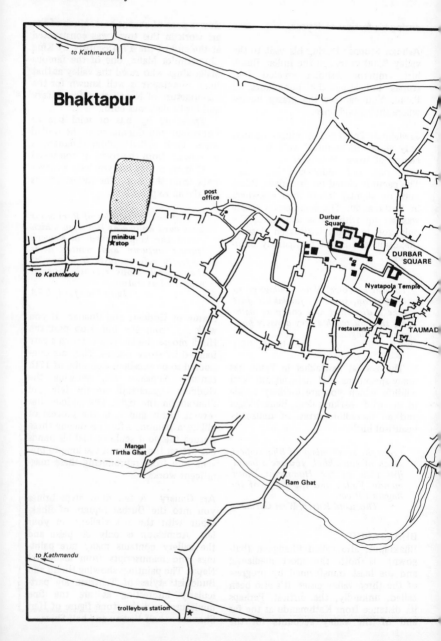

Bhaktapur

to Kathmandu

to Kathmandu

to Kathmandu

post office

minibus ★ stop

Durbar Square

DURBAR SQUARE

Nyatapola Temple

restaurant

TAUMADH

Mangal Tirtha Ghat

Ram Ghat

trolleybus station ★

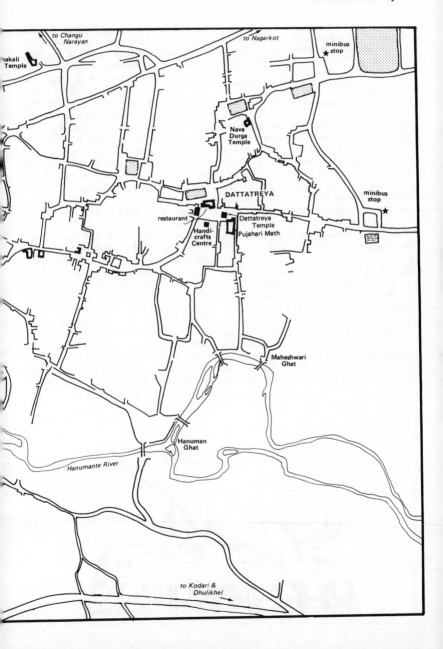

It is very interesting to watch the potters making pots out of clay. Just wander for about five minutes around Durbar Square and you will come across several potters making different kinds of utensils and pots.

Heinz Aulenbach, Austria

Golden Gate Adjoining the gallery is the Golden Gate of Bhaktapur built by the last Malla king in the middle of the 18th century. According to Percy Brown, who visited Nepal in 1912, this was the liveliest work of art in the whole of Nepal. A Garuda, the vehicle of Vishnu, tops the gate and is shown eating serpents, its traditional enemies. The other, multi-headed, figure riding the Garuda is the Goddess Kali.

Statue of King Bhupatindra King Bhupatindra Malla, one of the most famous of the Malla kings, was responsible for much of the buildings and works of art in Bhaktapur in the late 17th century. His image sits with folded hands on the top of the pillar facing the gate. This representation of the king on a pillar, and a similar one in Patan, was copied from the one in Kathmandu's Durbar Square.

Fifty Five Windowed Palace On the other side of the gate stands the palace which was first constructed in the 15th century and renovated in the late 17th. Opposite the palace is a large bell known as the *barking bell*. King Bhupatindra set it up in the late 17th century to avoid the effects of a bad dream, even today people say that dogs bark and weep when the bell is rung. The Durbar Square also contains a replica of the Pashupatinath Temple, built in the 15th century, with some athletic erotic carvings on the struts.

Nyatapola Temple The five-storied Nyatapola Temple is both the highest temple in the valley and one of the finest examples of Nepalese architecture and craftsmanship. The temple is visible from the Durbar Square and only a powerful than the preceding one and even the wrestlers at the bottom are 10 times as strong as any mortal man. One of the finest views of the temple can be had from the road running out of the valley towards the Chinese border. The whole town of Bhaktapur can be seen backed by the mountains and with the five storeys of the temple rising majestically over the lesser buildings.

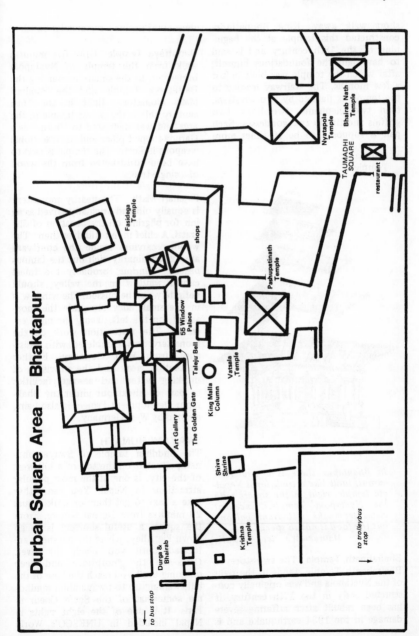

Durbar Square Area — Bhaktapur

to bus stop

Durga & Bhairab

Krishna Temple

Art Gallery

The Golden Gate

King Malla Column

Taleju Bell

Shiva Shrine

55 Window Palace

Vatsala Temple

Fasidega Temple

shops

Pashupatinath Temple

to trolleybus stop

Nyatapola Temple

Bhairab Nath Temple

TAUMADHI SQUARE

restaurant

short walk away. King Bhupatindra constructed this temple at the beginning of the 18th century and is said to have laid the foundations himself, after which the temple was built in just a few months. The stairway leading to the temple is flanked by two wrestlers, then two elephants, two lions, two griffins and finally two goddesses. Each pair is supposed to be 10 times more

Nyatapola
Temple

In Bhaktapur there is a new restaurant, built like a traditional Nepalese temple, right in the square with the Nyatapola Temple. Excellent views from the restaurant balcony but the food is not so special.
Maureen Wheeler, Australia

Bhairabnath Temple The two-storeyed Bhairabnath Temple stands to the right of the Nyatápola and was originally constructed early in the 17th century. It has been rebuilt after suffering severe damage in the 1934 earthquake and is

unusual for having a rectangular base.

Dattatraya Temple Only five minutes walk from the temple of Nyatapola brings you to the square containing the Dattatraya Temple and the Pujahari Math monastery. Built in the 15th century this is the oldest temple in the area and was dedicated to Vishnu; as a Garuda-topped pillar and his traditional weapons indicate. The temple is said to have been constructed from the wood of a single tree.

Pujahari Math The nearby monastery is equally old and originally served as an inn for pilgrims on the occasion of Sivaratri. A chief monk still lives there. The wooden carvings inside the courtyard are extraordinarily rich but the famous *peacock window*, probably the finest carved window in the valley, should definitely not be missed. The window is in the small alley alongside the monastery, on the left, facing the main entrance. The restoration work on the monastery was completed with assistance from West Germany. Further restoration work and the provision of drinking water and sewage facilities to part of Bhaktapur under the Bhaktapur Development Project is also being assisted by West Germany.

SWAYAMBHUNATH
The Buddhist temple of Swayambhunath, situated on the top of a hill west of the city, is one of the most popular attractions in Nepal. You can either take a taxi to get there or walk in just 20 minutes from Durbar Square. From the square a useful shortcut is to go down Pig Alley, where the pie shops are located until you reach the river. Cross by the footbridge and keep on going until you reach the base of the hill, walking up to Swayambhu reminds me somewhat of the Sacre Coeur in Paris. It is one of the eight sights in Nepal included in UNESCO's World

Heritage List.

The stairs leading to the temple from the east are quite steep and you might prefer the gradual climb from the southern part of the hill where the restaurants are located. The temple has also been called the *Monkey Temple* as there are numerous monkeys roving around the place which thrive on offerings made by the devotees. They will entertain you by sliding down the handrail as you climb the steps. Be careful of them and do not carry any packages as they may snatch them from you.

The ever watchful eyes of Buddha on the central stupa, the countless prayer wheels and the huge thunderbolt (Bajra in Sanskrit or Dorje in Tibetan) at the top of the stairs have long impressed visitors. Beside the stupa there is a large image of Buddha while the pagoda-style temple on the north-west side of the stupa contains a beautiful image of the goddess Hariti. She was the goddess of smallpox and used to devour children until Buddha made her stay near him and give up this bad habit. The complex also contains two Indian style temples, giving the visitor a chance to view a wide variety of architectural types. Swayambhunath gives a panoramic view over Kathmandu, particularly striking in the evening when the city is illuminated.

If you are lucky enough to be in Nepal during a full moon, try to spend part of it right up at Swayambhunath. Be sure to wander round the rear of the main stupa. There are many white stupas that glow peacefully under a full moon.
John Vogt, USA

Swayambhunath's stupa is reputed to be the oldest in Nepal. Although the earliest written reference to the place was made in the 13th century, there is little doubt that the site is very old — perhaps as much as 2000 years. Geologists now accept that the Kathmandu Valley was at one time a lake and according to legend this hill was then an island. Later in the 14th century, invaders from the south broke open the stupa to search it for gold.

When the horns of taxi cabs and music in the cold drink bars becomes too much, a short walk across the suspension bridge to the green hillside of Swayambhu will quickly relax you. Smile at the monkeys and see what happens.
Jonathan Hill, USA

Spend an afternoon, or a whole day, at Swayambhu, the monkey temple. It is a good bike ride from Kathmandu and then a steep climb up to the temple which is the centre of a tiny little village as well as a cluster of beautiful shrines. When you come down you can get good rice, dal and tea at the small roadside cafe at the foot of the hill.
Sara Jolly, England

A Warning Don't leave bikes near the shops on the way up unless you're prepared to pay protection money — otherwise they deflate your tyres. They own the only pumps for two km.

KIRTIPUR

Situated on a ridge to the south-west of Kathmandu, the mediaeval town of Kirtipur is interesting and attractive to visit. To get there by public transport you should take a bus to the university and stroll up the hill to the ridge where the town is located. Kirtipur is a centre for cloth weaving, and dyed yarn hangs from many upstairs windows, while the clatter of looms can be heard from inside. The ridge also offers a fine view back over Kathmandu with the Himalayas rising behind.

When Kathmandu was being conquered by King Prithvi Narayan Shah of Gorkha, about two centuries ago, he met stiff resistance at this strategic point in the valley. Only after suffering heavy losses in men and materials was the king, who went on to unify all of Nepal, able to subdue Kirtipur. In order to avenge the deaths of so many of his soldiers the king cut off the nose of every able bodied man in the town. It is said that to this day the citizens of Kirtipur have noses that are shorter on average than anywhere else in the valley.

The campus of the university was named after King Tribhuvan, grandfather of the present king, and may also be worth a visit. The university library has the best facilities to be found in Nepal.

BALAJU

In the last decade the site of this beautiful park was just a village but seems now to be growing into a town and even merging with Kathmandu. You can get there by tempo from the National Theatre or walk in less than an hour as it is situated close to the northern outskirts of Kathmandu. The industrial district around Balaju is the most important in the valley but it does not affect the quiet surroundings of the park in any way.

Admission to the park costs just 20 paisa and inside there are beautiful bamboos and other trees, ponds with fish and the twenty-two gushing waterspouts that gave the park its name, 'Bais dhara Balaju'. There is also a modern swimming pool where you can enjoy swimming in the summer and a smaller image of the sleeping Vishnu at Budhanilkantha.

In front of the sleeping Vishnu a small, typically Nepalese, temple is flanked by a row of Hindu images including elephant-headed Ganesh, Buddha protected by the hood of a serpent, and Bhagawati. A stupa-like structure shelters a many-armed goddess, unusual in a Buddhist stupa and an image of Harihar — half Vishnu and half Shiva. The hands on one side hold *trisul*, a symbol of Shiva, while on the other side the hands hold *chakra* and *sankah*, the symbols of Vishnu. There is also a small phallically-shaped lingam surrounded by four pillars and an image of the bullock Nandi. The site is not more than three centuries old but makes an interesting visit due to this curious juxtaposition of Hindu deities.

PASHUPATINATH

Pashupatinath is the most famous temple in Nepal and is located on the route to Bodnath. Although non-Hindus are not allowed inside the temple you can cross the river and view the temple from the hill on the other side. Near the entrance you will see many people selling flowers, incense and other offerings to be made to the deity. Inside is the golden pagoda and on the river banks you can sometimes see dead bodies being cremated on platforms. The Bagmati is a holy river like the Ganges and, like Varanasi in India, there is a burning ghat.

Pashupati, Lord of the Animals, is supposed to represent Shiva and the black image inside the temple has four heads. The temple itself is about three centuries old. It was renovated when

Kathmandu Valley

a Looking down from the Bodhnath stupa
b A typical rural scene in the valley
c Turning the prayer wheels around the stupa

the previous structures became decrepit. The idol is 600 years old, an earlier one was broken by Moslem invaders in the 14th century.

The big bull, Shiva's animal, inside the temple was built in the last century. The small bull in front of the temple is about three centuries old. Last year I visited the temple with a minister of the French government. He was so overcome at the site of it, he said: 'there are places like this where the spirit moves'. Some people are also reminded of Lourdes in France by this place.

The best time to visit the temple is on *Ekadashi*, a day which occurs twice each month. On those days there will be many pilgrims and a special ceremony in the evening called *Arati* characterised by the ringing of the bells. There may also be devotional music and illuminations. In the month of February there is a big fair at the temple to celebrate Shiva's birthday and another fair takes place in November.

NEPAL MUSEUM

The Nepal museum is close to Swayambhu and slightly to the south, a convenient visit on the way back to the city. The museum is open daily, except Tuesdays, from 10.15 am to 3.30 pm in the winter and from 10.30 am to 4.30 pm in the summer. The new building contains many beautiful carvings in wood and some especially interesting bronze idols. The old building illustrates recent Nepalese history with the uniforms and weapons of Nepalese soldiers and generals from the past two centuries. A sword which Napoleon presented to a Nepalese Prime Minister and leather cannons captured during the war with Tibet in 1856 are particular attractions.

BODHNATH

Bodhnath is one of the biggest stupas in the world and is believed to be at least four or five centuries old. It is located about eight km from the city, quite close to the airport and the Hindu temple of Pashupatinath. The bones of Kashyapa Buddha, one of the Buddhas who preceded Gautama Buddha, are said to be contained in the stupa. It is possible this stupa was constructed after the introduction of Buddhism in Tibet when relations between Nepal and Tibet were amicable.

Bodnath is the centre of Tibetan culture in Nepal and you will see many Tibetan refugees here. Chini Lama, the priest of some of the Tibetan Buddhists, lives here, and close to the stupa there is also a new Tibetan monastery. The stupa is surrounded by small shops selling Tibetan handicrafts and garments. Nepalese call the village where the stupa is located Bodh. Just north-east of the stupa is a big monastery, 'gompa' in Nepali, which is also worth visiting.

Some visitors, deeply interested in Buddhism and meditation, decide to make a prolonged stay at Bodhnath and there are rooms in private homes which can be rented here for as little as Rs 100 per month. About an hour's walk north of Bodhnath is a hill at Kappan with a Buddhist monastery.

Kathmandu Valley

a   A group of Tibetan women at Bodhnath
b   An old gentleman twirls his prayer wheel
c   Shop-houses around the great circle at Bodhnath

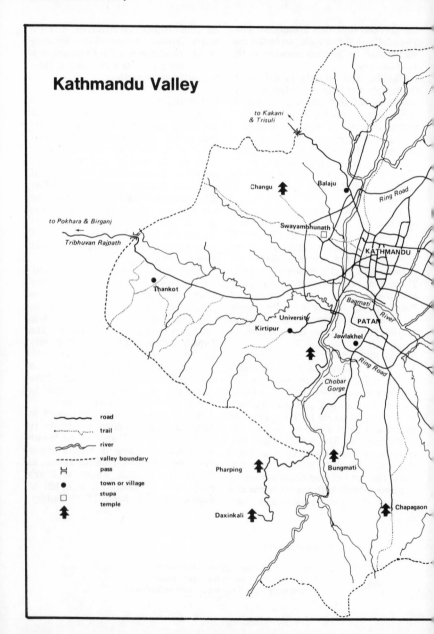

Kathmandu Valley

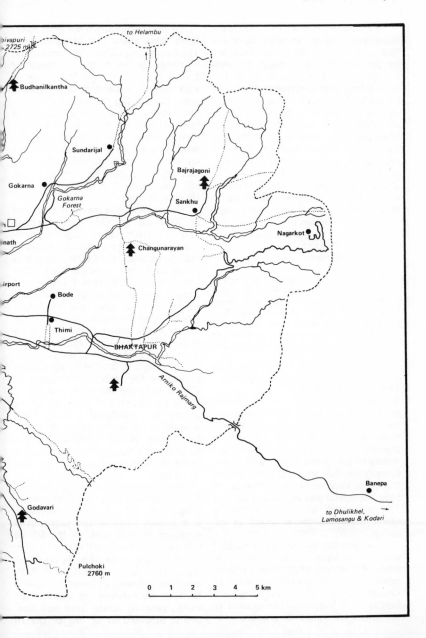

A meditation course on Mahayana Buddhism is given annually from the first week of November to December by the monastery's Tibetan and western monks. In 1981 almost all the 150 participants were westerners. They paid Rs 1800 per month for room and board and were supposed to live a life of strict discipline — no smoking or drinking. They also have courses on painting of Tankas and Tibetan medicine and it is possible to go into retreat. They also have an Institute in Kathmandu at Durbar Marg (near Yak and Yeti Hotel) where they offer free courses on Buddhism on Saturday and Sunday mornings. Write for information to:

Nepal Mahayana Centre
PO Box 817
Kathmandu, Nepal

If you spend even one afternoon talking to the western born Buddhist monks and nuns at Kappan monastery it might change your life. Western students can be found living there year round and rooms are available to those seriously intending to learn.

George Churinoff, USA

CHANGUNARAYAN

The temple of Changunarayan situated on a hilltop north of Bhaktapur and is sufficiently inaccessible that few visitors make the effort to see it. If you are interested in art and architecture and willing to take a few hours' walk in the countryside then you will find a trip to this place very worthwhile. Changunarayan has several masterpieces of 5th and 12th century Nepalese art as well as the oldest stone inscription found in the valley.

It is possible to combine a walking visit to the temple with a trip to the stupa of Bodhnath or the town of Bhaktapur. It is also possible to walk to Changunarayan after watching the sunrise from Nagarkot. The descent to the temple takes about four hours.

To reach Changunarayan from Bhaktapur takes about two hours on foot. The hill, looking rather like Swayambhu, is visible to the north of Bhaktapur from the bus stop but it is best not to walk directly towards it as the trail is poor. For a better trail walk to the Durbar Square then follow any road heading north. Ten minutes walk through narrow alleys will take you to the northern edge of town where you can see the hill clearly. Simply follow the trail until you reach the bottom of the hill from where it is 15 minutes steep climb to the top.

The pagoda style temple is dedicated to Narayana or Vishnu. The temple itself is not very old, perhaps two centuries, but the site is at least 15 centuries old. A Garuda, the mythical man-bird mount of Vishnu, stands in front of the temple with folded hands. It is supposed to have been set up in the fifth century and is one of the most important attractions in the valley. In front of the statue is the oldest stone inscription in the valley made in Gupta script and dating back to the same century.

The temple is flanked by four pillars topped by the traditional weapons of Vishnu including the lotus and conch. There are a number of images of Vishnu around the courtyard holding these weapons in his four hands. In the northeast corner of the courtyard there is an image of Vishnu riding a Garuda, this image is reproduced on the Nepalese Rs 10 note.

The site also contains an image of Vishnu superimposed on top of another image, one of the most picturesque and famous idols in the valley. It is supposed to date back to the 5th or 6th century although half of it is broken. There are a number of other outstanding statues from the 12th and 13th centuries including an image of Narsimha near the entrance. In Sanskrit the word Narsimha means 'man and lion' and is supposed to be one of the 10 incarnations of Vishnu, in this case half-human and half-lion. The statue shows Narsimha killing a demon.

There is an interesting legend of how this incarnation took place — a demon pleased Brahma and in return received a promise that he could not be killed by a man or an animal, day or night, nor by any weapon. Unfortunately the demon then started terrorising the inhabitants of earth and Vishnu himself had to take this man-lion (neither man nor beast) incarnation and use his nails (which were not a weapon) to defeat the demon in the evening (which was neither day or night).

After leaving Changunarayan it is a short, steep descent to the river which can be crossed easily by a temporary bridge during the dry season. Two hours walk — passing the Royal Game Reserve at Gokarna — will take you to the stupa at Bodhnath. If your time is limited you can take a taxi from Kathmandu via Bodhnath along this same road and return the same way.

BUDHANILKANTHA

The image of 'sleeping Vishnu' at Budhanilkantha is probably the largest reclining image of Vishnu in the world. To get there you can take a bus in the morning from near the National Theatre or alternatively you can travel by bus or tempo to Bansbari, the site of a shoe and leather factory set up with Chinese assistance. From there it is about an hour's walk. The energetic could walk all the way from downtown Kathmandu in a couple of hours or, best of all, ride by bicycle.

Vishnu, sleeping on a bed of snakes, is supposed to have been carved from stone in the 11th century. According to legend Vishnu sleeps continuously for four months of each year, falling asleep with the beginning of the monsoon and awakening when it is over. Each November thousands of pilgrims come here for a big fair on the day he

is supposed to wake up. The name Budhanilkantha has nothing to do with Buddha.

Another legend tells of the discovery of the image. A farmer was tilling his field one day and was terrified to find blood coming from the ground at the spot where his plough struck something. An excavation revealed the beautiful image of sleeping Vishnu.

Prayers take place here every morning around 9 am but the kings of Nepal are never allowed to go near the image. Should the king, who is himself supposed to be an incarnation of Vishnu, gaze upon his own image, it is said that he would be cursed. A smaller replica of the image has, therefore, been constructed near the swimming pool at Balaju for the king to visit if he desires. There is also a school, built with British assistance near Budhanilkantha — it is expected to become the best school in Nepal.

Take a trip to Sheopuri — highest mountain peak of the Valley. It is situated in the northern part and you should first go to Budhanilkantha from where it is a three to four hour climb — a full day's trip. The scenery is best because of the over 3000 metre height.

Wolfgang Korn, West Germany

GOKARNA & SUNDARIJAL

A pleasant couple of hours' walk in the vicinity of the Bodhnath stupa will take you to the old Newar village of Gokarna, north of the Royal Game Reserve. From Bodhnath take the road towards the reserve and turn left on to a dirt road after 20 minutes. Another 20 minutes' walk will bring you to the beautiful three-storeyed temple of Shiva called Gokarneswar, Lord of Gokarna. The courtyard has an incredible collection of stone statues of deities from Hindu mythology such as Narad, Surya the Sun God, Chandra the Moon God, Kamadeva the God of Love besides the more conventional images of Shiva and Vishnu. Although they are probably only about a century old I have never seen such a collection in one place in Nepal.

After visiting the temple you can walk up to the village which is inhabited entirely by Newars and is surrounded by the game reserve on three sides. Although the village is so close to Kathmandu the villagers are very poor and many do not even speak Nepali.

Further down the road are the waterfalls of Sundarijal at the edge of the valley; a pleasant bicycle ride down quiet roads.

The Royal Game Reserve at Gokarna is a nice place to relax and get away from the hassles of Kathmandu.
Heidi Bauer, USA

A new company, Safari Park, has recently begun organising tours to the Royal Game Reserve. Its office is located in Durbar Marg and a round trip to the park costs Rs 25. Another way of visiting the park is to buy an excursion ticket for Rs 99. This includes round trip transportation from your hotel, entrance to the park and a one hour elephant ride. Inside the park, it is interesting to watch birds, monkeys and deer. Above all, you can get a glimpse of what the natural landscape and wildlife in the valley must have looked like before human settlement. It is also a popular picnic spot for Kathmanduites.

DAXINKALI

The best known temple to the Goddess Kali, the terrifying, is located on the southern edge of the valley. To get there takes about 45 minutes by car passing the narrow Chobar gorge on the way, through which flows the Bagmati River. A travel agency tour (Everest Travels and Kathmandu Travels) costs Rs 50 or you can travel by bus for Rs 5

round trip. The best day to visit Daxinkali is Saturday when crowds of Nepalese journey there to sacrifice chickens and goats to the blood-thirsty goddess. Tuesday is another, quieter, sacrificial day.

The temple is at the bottom of a steep hill with a small stream flowing close by. After their rapid despatch the animals are butchered in the stream and their carcasses will later be brought home for a feast. It is interesting that sacrifices are always made to goddesses and must always be made with young male animals.

The scene around the altar is one of great chaos, gore and festivity, a visit to Daxinkali recalls the ritual sacrifice of animals which I had only read about in books.

Jack Peters, USA

CHOBAR GORGE

According to legend, when the valley was a lake and Swayambhu an island, Manjushree, the God of Wisdom, struck the rock at Chobar with his sword and released the valley's water. With the water thousands of snakes are supposed to have been swept out of the valley — leaving behind the snake king Karkotak who still lives close to the gorge in a pond called Taudaha. The Chobar Gorge is conveniently visited en route to Daxinkali and the beautiful temple of Pharping can also be included on the trip.

Close to the spectacular gorge is the first cement factory in the valley; unfortunately the Kathmandu Valley has a distressing physical similarity to the Los Angeles basin and major industrialisation or a large growth in the number of motor vehicles could lead to a similar affliction — smog.

The best view both of the mountains and Kathmandu Valley within easy reach (by car) of Kathmandu is obtained by driving out to Nagarjun forest about 3 km north of Balaju in Kathmandu. On payment of Rs 7 you will be allowed to drive through the forest, eventually after 17 km reaching the mountain top, which is surmounted by a Buddhist stupa. An excellent view to the north of all the snow peaks from Annapurna through Langtang is obtained while the entire Kathmandu Valley is laid at your feet to the south.

Steve and Chris Hogan, England

Excursions from the Valley

MOUNTAIN FLIGHT

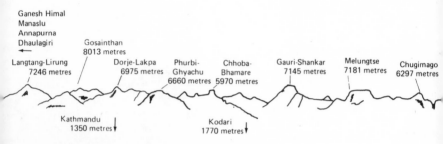

Ganesh Himal
Manaslu
Annapurna
Dhaulagiri

Gosainthan
8013 metres

Langtang-Lirung
7246 metres

Dorje-Lakpa
6975 metres

Phurbi-
Ghyachu
6660 metres

Chhoba-
Bhamare
5970 metres

Gauri-Shankar
7145 metres

Melungtse
7181 metres

Chugimago
6297 metres

Kathmandu
1350 metres

Kodari
1770 metres

If you are in Kathmandu between September and June the mountain flight, with its breathtaking views of the Himalayas, is an experience definitely not to be missed — even at a cost of Rs 655. The flight, made in the early morning lasts about one hour, and the aircraft, a 44-seat pressurised Avro HS 748, flies at an altitude of over 6000 metres. During the flight you can view eight of the 10 highest mountain peaks in the world from a distance of less than 20 km. The aircraft flies along the length of the mountain range in both directions giving passengers on both sides an equal opportunity to view the peaks. In addition you are allowed to admire the view, individually, from the flight deck. A 'mountain profile', to help you identify the peaks is handed out before departure and afterwards the flight passengers are given a certificate to show that they have been 'greeted' by Mount Everest. The flight is especially exciting during the excellent weather and extremely good visibility of late October and November. Royal Nepal Airlines organise the mountain flights.

NAGARKOT

From the vicinity of Kathmandu the best view of the Himalayas, including Everest, can be obtained from the village of Nagarkot. Situated on a ridge to the north-east of the valley Nagarkot offers a view stretching from Dhaulagiri in the west to Kanchenjunga in the east.

Several travel agencies offer tours to Nagarkot from Rs 60 but the impecunious can take a bus to Bhaktapur, walk the several km to the ridge in a few hours, overnight in Nagarkot, and return to Kathmandu for less than Rs 25. During the monsoon period from June to September it is usually cloudy and you will only rarely be rewarded with a glimpse of the mountains. On the other hand the trek to the top will almost always result in a clear view during the months of October to April.

To get to Nagarkot leave the bus stop in Bhaktapur and walk to the centre of town where the Durbar Square is located. Head east from here and ask for the route to Nagarkot. As soon as you leave the city follow the road which passes a Nepalese Army barracks. An

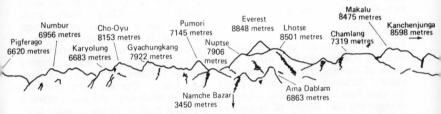

Pigferago 6620 metres — Numbur 6956 metres — Karyolung 6683 metres — Cho-Oyu 8153 metres — Gyachungkang 7922 metres — Pumori 7145 metres — Nuptse 7906 metres — Namche Bazar 3450 metres — Everest 8848 metres — Lhotse 8501 metres — Ama Dablam 6863 metres — Makalu 8475 metres — Chamlang 7319 metres — Kanchenjunga 8598 metres

hour out from Bhaktapur you reach the city water tank by a cluster of bamboo trees and you can take a shortcut which saves two hours walk. Leave the main motorable road and take the trail to the right. Forty minutes walk brings you to a stream, then a steep climb through beautiful pine forests takes you back to the main road.

> *The road to Nagarkot wanders to the left of the river. A trekker would save time if, after one hour's walk from Bhaktapur, he would follow a pipe that is Bhaktapur's water supply straight to the dam then climb the hill and keep the power line in sight all the way.*
>
> Gary Ott, USA

Recently a bus service — it's slow and very crowded, so try to sit up front — has started from Bhaktapur to Nagarkot and buses are available every three hours between 8 am and 4 pm for Rs 3. The buses start from the city bus stations and not from the trolley bus station. It is still pleasant to take the four-hour walk all the way from Bhaktapur except

in the summer and the monsoon.

There are several lodges at Nagarkot. *Everest Cottage* is about 50 metres below the ridge and is situated along the road from Bhaktapur. A double room with attached bathroom costs Rs 33 for a single bed, Rs 44 for two. The dining room has a fireplace where you can enjoy the warmth and get western food. Near the top of the ridge is the *Nagarkot Lodge* where dormitory beds cost Rs 10. *Nagarkot Guest House* is run by a Nepalese woman called Didi; it has an inn-like atmosphere and charges Rs 10 for a bed in the dormitory and Rs 25 for a single room. A good view of the Himalayan Range can be seen from the lodge as it faces the mountains. The relatively expensive *Taragaon-Nagarkot* is expected to open in 1983 which will cost about Rs 200 for a single with bath. *Mount Everest Lodge*, situated slightly downhill from the ridge where Nagarkot is, is the least expensive lodge in town. A single costs Rs 20 and a bed in the dormitory Rs 5.

On a clear day, it is worthwhile walking to the Tower on the ridge north of Nagarkot to get a better view of the peaks. It takes less than an hour and is an easy walk.

If you are overnighting in Nagarkot be certain to bring enough warm clothing as it can get very cold in winter or autumn. There is also camping space available. This trip, with its fine views of eight of the 10 highest mountain peaks in the world, is one the visitor to Kathmandu should not miss.

KAKANI

This village is situated on a ridge northwest of Kathmandu and offers good views of the western and central Himalayas. Although I personally prefer the view from Nagarkot those interested in enjoying the variety of Himalayan scenery, especially magnificent views of Ganesh Himal, should go there. It is quieter than Nagarkot but the food available has less variety and caters less to western tastes. There is a lodge run by the Department of Tourism which charges Rs 10 for a bed or Rs 20 for a single room per night. To get there take a bus or minibus at Sorakhutte (five minutes walk from Thamel) leaving for Trisuli (at 7 am and 1 pm). From there it is about one hour's walk along a dirt road to the top of the ridge.

DHULIKHEL & NAMOBUDDHA

Dhulikhel, a beautiful village just outside the Kathmandu Valley, gives a better view of the Himalayas than anywhere in the valley. In the late sixties the hippies, who had just started coming to Nepal in large numbers, liked this quiet and sleepy Newar village so much that they decided to construct a temple right on the parade ground where you go to view the mountains. Although they were not permitted to do so you may think that their choice would not have been a bad one.

When you are in Dhulikhel, do not miss a visit to Panauti, you reach there after a pleasant two hour walk across ricefields along the course of a small stream. The beauty of this small *town is due to its numerous temples and magnificent wood carvings.*
Michel Thierry, France

Buses leave Kathmandu for Dhulikhel every hour and travel on the excellent road towards the Chinese border. While still in the valley you pass through Thimi, a typical Newar town which produces much of the vegetables for Kathmandu and also has a thriving cottage industry in pottery and mask manufacture. The road then skirts the edge of Bhaktapur and passes through a typical rural landscape of paddy fields at the eastern end of the valley. It winds over the Sanga Pass as it leaves the valley then descends to Banepa, a Newar town with a population of 10,000 and the biggest bazaar in the area.

A steep climb from Banepa brings you to Dhulikhel at 1500 metres. Dhulikhel is the district headquarters and boasts a large number of government offices besides a jail and high school. Its population consists of Newars, although there are people of many other castes in surrounding villages. Many tourists make early morning trips to Dhulikhel to see the awesome sunrise over the mountains. Travel agencies organise these trips from Rs 80. The budget conscious can travel there by bus and stay overnight for less than Rs 20. The best Himalayan view is obtained by climbing — it takes about 30 minutes — the small temple-topped hill to the east.

To see the sun coming up from behind the mighty Himalayas from the little temple up the hill from Dhulikhel is a thrilling sight, even worth getting up at 4 am.
Chris Whinett, England

The *Dhulikhel Lodge* has electricity and hot water and is one of the best cheap places to stay in Nepal. The manager, known as BP to his guests, has visited the US for a few months and is very receptive to western visitors and helpful with trekking information. The spartan rooms at the lodge costs Rs 10 per person or Rs 15 in the rooms with the best view. There are also dormitory beds and should the lodge be crowded you may have to be content with these — the lodge is particularly popular with voluntary workers. It is also a good place to meet other travellers. Nepali food, available at the lodge for Rs 20, also is popular.

If possible while in Dhulikhel you should try to make the trek to Namobuddha, also known as Namura. The walk only takes three hours in each direction and is a good practice run for longer treks. This can even be an enjoyable trek during the monsoon season. BP will supply you with a diagram showing the trail to Namobuddha, it is not difficult and there are not many steep ascents or descents. From the town you pass to the south of the hill with the temple. Although there is a shorter route when returning it is not advisable in the wet season as it may get very slippery.

The trek passes through interesting country and a number of small villages where you can ask for directions. The stupa at Namobuddha is relatively unknown and although it is probably not more than a few centuries old I have not been able to discover its exact age. There is an interesting legend behind the stupa at Namobuddha. One of the earlier Buddhas is said to have come across a tiger at the point of death and unable to find food for its cubs. The Buddha was so moved with compassion that he offered his own flesh to the hungry tiger. If you climb to the top of the hill from the stupa you reach the site where this event is supposed to

have taken place. A carved stone tablet shows the Buddha offering his hands to the tiger. There is an interesting festival at this site in the month of November. You can trek back to Dhulikhel by an alternative route to avoid backtracking.

You can have some very good chang near the stupa of Namobuddha at a very cheap price.
Hans Wagner, West Germany

CHINESE BORDER

Only in Hong Kong is it as easy to get so close to China as you can by Nepal's 'road to the Chinese border'. There is not much to see there but it is nice to boast of having been to the border.

Most of Kathmandu's travel agencies operate tours to the border once or twice a week although it is wise to enquire if the road is blocked by landslides during the monsoon. Kathmandu Travel and Tours (tel 14446) conduct guided tours on Wednesday and Sunday. Everest Travel (tel 12217) has a bus to the border on Sunday, Wednesday and Friday. Both agencies charge Rs 145 for the trip which departs at 8 in the morning and returns at 6 in the evening.

Four times daily a bus service runs between Kathmandu and Barabise via Lamosangu — the starting point for the Everest trek. The first bus leaves at 6 am and the fare is Rs 12. On the way to the border you pass through the beautiful Panchkhal valley between Dhulikhel and Dolalaghat, a well known area for the production of mangoes, guavas, sugarcane and rice. There are no buses beyond Barabise but you can get a ride on one of the many trucks going to the border for about Rs 5 or you can walk there in about five hours. There is a small lodge at Barabise where a single room costs Rs 6. Other ways of getting to the border include a ride on the early morning Post Office bus from Kathmandu to Dhulikhel (which costs Rs 24 round trip) or getting a group together to go on an overland bus or truck.

You can take the mail car to the border or trek, the scenery as you walk is very nice. It is possible to buy tea in villages on the way and sleep on the floor. The road follows the river and there are many waterfalls. It is reasonably easy to hitch-hike along the road (alternatively bargain with lorry drivers) as it is a popular picnic spot.

Jay McLeary, Australia

The last stretch to the border is a dirt road running through a spectacular gorge. Shortly after the tarmac road ends there is a site where rice paper is produced. You can see the rice being ground down in a water-driven stone mill and the sheets of paper stretched out to dry in the sun. A few km south of the border at Tatopani, which means hot water in Nepali, there are hot springs if you fancy having a hot bath and watching China at the same time.

At Kodari, a bridge over the river separates Nepal from China. Sentries stand on both ends of the bridge and on the Chinese side there is a small barracks for soldiers. In the late 1960s a large portrait of Chairman Mao used to stand near the bridge on the Chinese side but it has since been removed. Nepalese traders and porters are permitted to cross the bridge and go into Tibet as far as the town of Khasa but it is not an open border as is the case with India.

No aspect of Nepalese foreign policy has been watched by the outside world with as much interest, concern and sometimes even alarm, as the decisions leading to the construction of this road. Nepal's viewpoint in this respect has not always been understood.

The highway has recently been renamed the Arniko Highway in memory of the renowned Nepalese architect who went to China during the 13th century. The highway starts at Bhaktapur in the Kathmandu Valley; apart from the recently completed trolley bus system between Kathmandu and Bhaktapur the Chinese are also aiding the construction of another road between these two cities. The road leaves the valley through the Sanga Pass and continues through Banepa, Dhulikhel, Panchkhal, Barabise and Tatopani, before reaching the Miteri Sanu or 'Friendship Bridge' at the Bhote Kosi River. A casual glance at the map will show that at this point a chunk of Chinese territory is almost surrounded by Nepal and this is one of the narrowest points in the whole length of Nepal.

The highway generally follows the

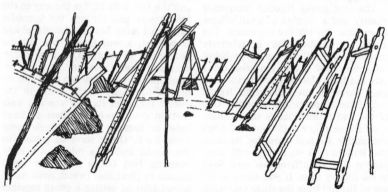

Rice Paper Production

alignment of two rivers, an important characteristic of the Chinese constructed highways in Nepal as the Kathmandu to Pokhara road also follows the course of rivers. The length of the highway is 104 km and it includes one major bridge at Dolalghat. By car it takes about four hours to reach the border from Kathmandu. Kodari, the termination point of the highway, is at 1500 metres while the Tibetan town of Khasa, across the border, is somewhat higher at an elevation of 2200 metres. With the exception of Dhulikhel, few points along the road are noted for their views of the Himalayan range.

The lodge at Tatopani is peaceful and has a lovely setting. The proprietor and his family are hospitable and charming and serve good inexpensive food, dinner is just Rs 2. Upstairs where one sleeps there are mats on the floor for Rs 1 or beds for Rs 2. All clean and attractive.
Sandre Lelaid, Ken Przywaro, USA

The Chinese road has often been called the best highway in Nepal as there are few hairpin bends or steep sections. There are also comparatively few landslides during the monsoons. The bazaar towns along the route, such as Banepa, Dhulikhel and Barabise, are largely Newar but the hinterland is mainly inhabited by Brahmins and Chetris at lower altitudes and by Tamangs and Sherpas at the higher altitudes, particularly in the north.

The agreement for the construction of the road was signed in 1961 and the completed road opened by King Mahendra in 1966. Much of the criticism the road has engendered has been about the threat it could pose to the security of Nepal and India. Nepal has maintained that the road is simply an expansion of a long established trade route and this opening up of a hitherto backward area was essential for its economic development.

Districts connected by the road have become much closer to Kathmandu and the first third of the road as far as Dhulikhel is heavily trafficked. Even as far as Dolalghat, the half-way point, the volume of traffic makes the road economically feasible. My own conclusions after visiting villages along the road four years after its construction were:

'It could definitely be said that most of the villages in the area are better off today than they were four years ago. It is difficult to reach any conclusion regarding an increase in per capita income or agricultural production but there are now schools in almost every village and villagers now have the opportunity to be at least literate. The opportunity of getting education is not solely restricted to people belonging to higher castes; although caste rules continue to be followed there is a new flexibility in their observance. The number of early marriages has declined greatly but the practice of bigamy is still widespread despite preventive legislation. There is an increased tendency for the educated few of the villages to migrate to Kathmandu and settle there. Almost every village has a transistor radio and the villagers now have a chance to know what is happening in Nepal as well as in foreign countries.'

One of the largest magnesite deposits in Asia has been discovered a few km east of the road. If it were not for the road this deposit would never have been economically feasible. A road from Lamosangu to Jiri, built with a Swiss loan, passes through this deposit. The road has also made substantial indirect contributions to Nepal's economic development. Half the materials and machinery used in the construction of other Chinese-aided projects in Nepal — such as the Sun Kosi hydroelectric project producing 10,000 kw near Lamosangu or the Kathmandu-Pokhara highway — are estimated to have been brought along the road. Nevertheless the bordering region in Tibet is sparsely populated and economic activity is still low. It is also a long way from the pop-ulated and industrial areas of China. It is often cheaper to import materials from China by the sea route via Calcutta than directly along the road, but this will change as soon as there is more economic activity in the area.

Where to Stay

ORIENTATION

New Road is the most important road in Kathmandu and its main shopping centre. It starts from the large gate near the airline office and ends at a statue several blocks west. If you continue further west you enter the big Basantapur Square and a littue further on Durbar Square where the old Royal Palace is located. *Durbar* is Nepali for palace and there are also Durbar Squares in Patan and Bhaktapur in front of the old palaces. The Tourist Information Office is situated close to the New Road statue just before you get to Basantapur Square. It can supply a large map of Kathmandu and other material about places to visit. There is also a dairy here where milk products including butter and cheese can be bought.

The road running off Basantapur Square to the south has, since 1973, rejoiced in the unofficial name of 'Freak Street'. It's a wild jumble of cheap hotels, restaurants, hippies, money changers, hash smokers and all the freaky travellers on the road east. Like what used to be the equally well-known 'Chicken Street', in Kabul the capital of Afghanistan, Freak St is known to the travelling fraternity throughout the world, although most of the Nepalese living there are probably unaware that it has been renamed. Many budget travellers do not like the atmosphere there but whether or not you're staying, it makes a fascinating place to visit, and has a large number of shops selling clothes, used trekking equipment, Tibetan handicrafts and wood block prints. However, this area seems to have become less popular recently. The Thamel area has overtaken it as the centre for budget travellers in Kathmandu. Perhaps it is because there are now a few dope dealers, and black marketeers in currency in the area.

A number of streets run out from Durbar Square; the unpaved road running down towards the river from the temple of Ganesh has also been unofficially renamed, this time as 'Pig Alley'. It's not terribly clean, as the name may suggest, but does contain several inexpensive hotels and restaurants and some of Kathmandu's well known pie shops. The narrow street running northeast from Durbar Square through a veritable forest of temples leads to the shopping centres of old Kathmandu called Indrachowk and Asan. In these tiny shops, tightly packed beside the narrow streets, you can find almost anything.

Starting again at the airline terminal end of New Road by the city gate a short walk to the right will bring you to the main post office close to the foot of the high Bhimsen Tower. Walking in the opposite direction will take you by the Government Hospital, past a fenced-in lake, the National Theatre, the American Consul Office, the German Embassy and the Yellow Pagoda Hotel before arriving at the new Royal Palace where the King of Nepal lives. The road continues into the embassy sector where the majority of the foreign embassies can be found. Turning to the left at the Royal Palace a couple of blocks walk will bring you into the Thamel area which has recently emerged as a second centre for low cost, not quite so low as Freak Street, accommodation and restaurants. Thamel is about 10 to 15 minutes walk from the centre of Kathmandu. The street running from the New Royal Palace to the Clock Tower is called 'Durbar Marg', and is a broad street containing most of the airline offices, travel agencies, and entrance to two of the five star hotels in Kathmandu.

WHERE TO STAY

A great number and variety of hotels have opened in Kathmandu in the past five years. There remains a shortage of rooms in four and five star class hotels, particularly during the October-November and March-April high seasons, but current building plans will soon erase this shortage. At the other end of the scale the impecunious traveller can easily find clean, comfortable and decent places to stay for under US$2 a night including hot showers! Few cities in west or south Asia can offer such bargains.

Naturally the list of hotels that follows is by no means exhaustive, but it does include most of the hotels in each category which I assume would be found enjoyable by readers of this book. Some hotels may add a 10% service charge to the prices quoted and all of them will charge the 12% government tax. Don't be surprised if inflation has forced these prices up, although the categorisation will remain the same. Breakfast may be included in the price at some hotels. Many of Nepal's hotels and lodges take their names from high mountain peaks such as Annapurna, Makalu, Manaslu or Lhotse.

Top End Hotels

Soaltee Oberoi — 5* — tel 11211 — cable Obhotel — telex NP203 — 290 rooms, 18 suites, all with bath — fully air conditioned — shuttle bus to the city — 4 restaurants — 2 bars — shopping arcade — swimming pool — casino — out of town location.

Hotel Yak and Yeti — 5* — tel 13580 — cable Yakn Yeti — 130 rooms — restaurant — bar — swimming pool — fully air conditioned — coffee shop — close to city centre.

Hotel de L'Annapurna — 5* — tel 11711 — cable Annapurna — telex NP205 — 155 rooms, 8 suites, all with bath — fully air conditioned — restaurant — bar — coffee shop — shopping arcade — conference hall — close to city centre — swimming pool.

Hotel Malla — 4* — tel 15320 — cable Mallotel — 75 rooms, 8 suites, all with bath — fully air conditioned — restaurant — bar — tennis court — conference hall — outskirts of town.

Hotel Crystal — 3* — tel 12630 — cable Crystal — 53 rooms, all with bath — air conditioned — roof garden — restaurant — very central.

Hotel Yellow Pagoda — 3* — tel 15492 — cable Yelopagoda — 51 rooms all with bath — snack bar — restaurant — roof garden — restaurant — very central.

Hotel Shankar — 4* — tel 12973 — cable Shankar — telex NP230 — 135 rooms — some air conditioned — restaurant — shopping arcade — lawn and gardens — outskirts of town.

Hotel Shangrila — tel 16011 — cable SHANGRILA — telex 276 Sangril NP — restaurant — bar — shopping arcade — garden — outskirts of town.

Hotel Blue Star — 3* — tel 13996 — cable Bluestar — 80 rooms — restaurant — outskirts of town.

Hotel Narayani — 3* — tel 21711 — cable HoNarayani — 75 rooms — restaurant — coffee shop — outskirts of town.

Hotel Mt Makalu — 2* — tel 13955 — cable Montmakalu — 30 rooms — restaurant — bar — centre of town.

Hotel Leo — tel 11252 — 20 rooms — bar — restaurant — central.

Hotel Lhotse — tel 15474 — 15 rooms — outskirts of town.

Hotel Siddhartha — tel 16630 — 16 rooms — restaurant — roof garden — close to town centre.

Hotel Sheraton — tel 16388 — telex-260-HOTEVEST-NP — Cable — MALARI NEPAL — 166 rooms — air conditioned — outskirts of town — coach to city centre — swimming pool — restaurant — bar.

Kathmandu Village Hotel — tel 13770 — 15 rooms — outskirts of town — restaurant.

Hotel Woodlands — tel 12683 — 51 rooms — bar — restaurant — close to town centre.

Kathmandu's oldest luxury hotel is the *Soaltee Oberoi* where a single room costs US$73 to US$78 with all meals and a double costs US$117. Situated a 10-minute taxi ride from downtown Kathmandu, the Oberoi boasts an outdoor swimming pool and Nepal's only casino. The *Hotel Yak and Yeti* is the newest hotel in Kathmandu although the restaurant of the same name has been open for over a decade. A single costs US$40 and a double US$67 a night. The five star *Hotel de L'Annapurna* is a block away from the new Royal Palace in the modern street where most of the airline offices are located. A single room, including breakfast, costs US$45 and the hotel is only a 10-minute walk away from the heart of 'old' Kathmandu. *Hotel Sheraton* charges US$52 for bed & breakfast.

The *Hotel Malla* is one of Kathmandu's newest hotels. Situated in relatively quiet surroundings to the west of the new Royal Palace, the Malla charges US$37 for a single and US$52 for a double with breakfast. The architecture is a mixture of Nepalese and western styles, the gate pillars are topped with lions, fish and peacocks similar to many Nepalese temples. There is a free cultural show for hotel residents every evening except Tuesday.

Somewhat away from the centre of town in pleasant surroundings the *Hotel Shankar* charges US$28 for its three star rooms and does not add any service charges. The building used to be an old Rana palace and still shows the old Rana flair in its big garden and massive building. The only high class hotel in the heart of downtown, old Kathmandu is the three star *Hotel Crystal*. Only a

block from Durbar Square, the Crystal charges US$25 for a single or US$30 for a double including breakfast. If you want a comfortable hotel within walking distance of numerous temples, the old Royal Palace and the temple of the living goddess, I would advise you to stay there. Clean and air conditioned, the Crystal also offers an excellent restaurant and fine views over the city from its upper terraces. *Hotel Narayani* situated across the River Bagmati in Patan charges US$24 for a single.

The *Hotel Yellow Pagoda* is another new hotel; situated near the German Embassy it charges US$21 for a single. *Hotel Siddhartha*, located in the same area, charges US$16 for a single and has an excellent restaurant. A little distance from the town centre the *Hotel Blue Star* can be found near the bridge on the road to Patan. A single room costs US$14 including breakfast and there are no service charges. Several of the more luxurious overland trips, including Penn Overland, use the Blue Star as a starting or finishing point.

Hotel Mt Makalu is just a block away from New Road and Freak Street in downtown Kathmandu. Including breakfast a single room here costs US$17.75. They charge less for rooms above the third floor. *Hotel Leo* charges US$8 for a single with breakfast. Near the immigration office and the Yak and Yeti is the *Hotel Lhotse* where a single room with breakfast costs just US$6. There's music in the rooms, and it has an air conditioned bar. *Hotel Woodlands*, which has recently opened near the Annapurna Hotel, has singles at US$12. Also recently opened the *Kathmandu Village Hotel*, near the temple of Pashupatinath, has a collection of beautiful wood carvings on the windows and is more like a quiet house in the countryside than a hotel. A single costs US$25 with breakfast. *Hotel Shangrila* in Lazimpat is one of the nicest new hotels to be opened in an area of Kath-

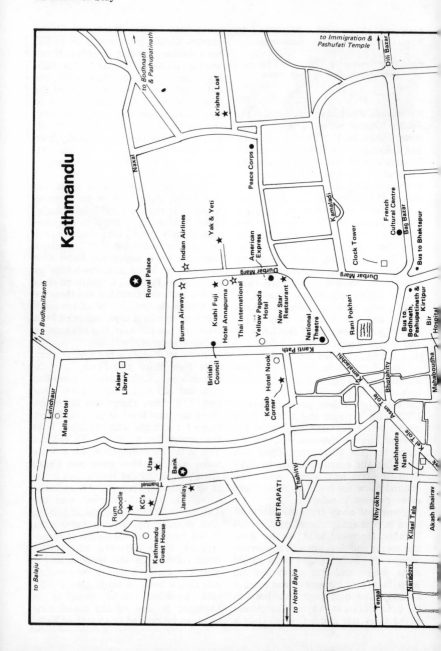

Kathmandu

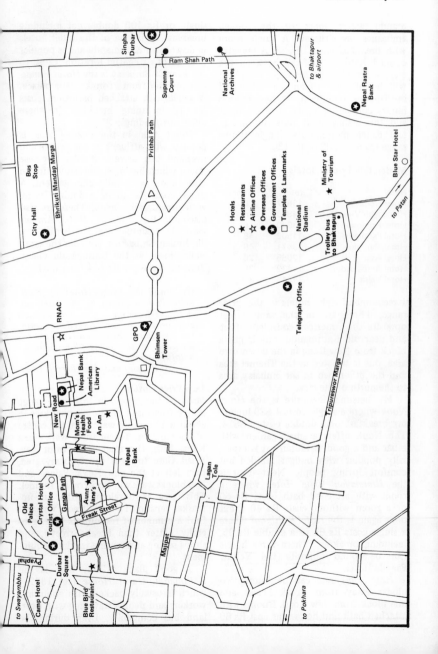

mandu where most of the foreign embassies are situated. A single room with breakfast costs US$28. A recently opened hotel — halfway between the city centre and the Monkey Temple — will be of note to anyone interested in Tibetan Buddhism. It has a good library containing books on this subject and the management puts on theatre and dance programmes. Single rooms range from Rs 100 to Rs 130.

Moderately Priced Hotels

Hotel	tel	Rooms
Hotel Nook	13627	20
Himalayan View Hotel	14890·	14
Hotel Kohinoor	13930	6
Hotel Panorama	11502	48
Hotel Manaslu	13471	45
Hotel Asia	12055	25
Hotel Ambassador	14432	35
Hotel Vajra	14545	38

I recommend eight hotels in this price range. Three are in the same street opposite the American consulate office and near old Kathmandu, one is just a block from New Road in the downtown area, one is situated in the Thamel area and the other two in the embassy area to the north of the city.

My personal favourite is the *Hotel Nook* where a single costs US$9 including breakfast or a double costs US$14. The Nook offers a small garden with a bar and a good restaurant; it is especially popular with budget minded but comfort loving people. Next door is the *Himalayan View Hotel* where a room with attached bath costs Rs 60 or a room without costs Rs 40. Next door again is the *Hotel Kohinoor* where a single costs Rs 65 or a double Rs 95, including breakfast. These three hotels can be found opposite the Yellow Pagoda Hotel.

Hotel Panorama can be found two blocks away from Freak Street and one block from New Road. Rooms with attached bath and hot water cost Rs 60

single or Rs 100 double not including breakfast. It is one of the older hotels in downtown Kathmandu and is popular because of its central location. Close to the French Embassy is the *Hotel Manaslu*, converted from a former Rana palace. A single with attached bathroom costs Rs 72 including breakfast in these quiet surroundings.

Hotel Asia, in the Thamel area, is popular with affluent young people and overland bus drivers. It is a Nepalese house which has been converted into an hotel and has friendly management. A single costs Rs 45 or a double Rs 60 with breakfast included. There are also discounts for students. *Hotel Ambassador*, in Lazimpat near the British and the Indian Embassies, is under the same management as the Kathmandu Guest House and charges Rs 144 for a single.

We found the Savoy Hotel, on Ram Shah Path adjacent to the National Archives Building, to be quiet, clean and very well run. Excellent room service, hot water and breakfast included in the tariff plus friendly, helpful management.
D P Delly and Alan Perrel, USA

Low Price Hotels

Most of the hotels in this price range are concentrated in the Thamel area — about a 15-minute walk from the centre of Kathmandu. To get there walk along Kanti Path, the road north from New Road Gate towards the embassy area, turn left at the new Royal Palace and two blocks walk will find you in Thamel. This area is developing like an up-market version of Freak Street. You will find a number of restaurants here, generally better than Freak Street's, and shops selling and renting trekking equipment.

A good place to stay here is the *Kathmandu Guest House* (tel 13628) which is usually packed with voluntary workers and people travelling with overland bus companies. Even during the slack monsoon season it can be difficult to get a room in this popular hotel without an advance reservation. There is a pleasant small garden and parking space for cars and buses. A double room with attached bathroom costs Rs 100, other rooms cost as little as Rs 25. Reductions are offered to students, peace corps volunteers and long-term visitors. Recently, a travel magazine published in London called it one of the best cheap places in the world outside Europe and North America.

One of the nicest new hotels in the Thamel area, *Hotel Shakti* (tel 16121), has been built in a quiet, garden setting. Singles cost Rs 30 and doubles Rs 36. Highly recommended. *Mahalaxmi Guest House* (tel 16001) in Chetrapati, five minutes' walk from Thamel on the way to the Monkey Temple, is also situated in a quiet area and charges Rs 25 to 30 for a single. Recommended. *Star Hotel* (tel 12803) next door to Kathmandu Guest House has single rooms ranging from Rs 30 to 40. *Tukchey Peak Lodge* has also been popular in the past.

If you want to stay within walking distance of Kathmandu city centre, and be in the middle of fields, the newly opened *Hotel Catnap* is situated in Chhauni across the river Bishnumati in Kathmandu. Rooms are nice and clean and the view of the city of Kathmandu is great. Singles cost Rs 35 and doubles Rs 70.

Rock Bottom Hotels

The wide range of new hotels and lodges in this category offer excellent opportunities for good but inexpensive accommodation for the low budget traveller. So many have opened recently that it is becoming increasingly difficult for their clientele of students, young travellers and freaks to make a choice. The intense competition has led to the provision of some minimum facilities like hot showers.

Most of the lodges in this category can be found in the Freak Street or Pie Alley area but some have also recently opened in the Thamel area. However, the lodges in the latter district are generally more expensive than in Freak Street.

Freak Street In the heart of Freak Street is *Century Lodge*, which is the best place in this price range, and is in a quiet location as it is in the interior away from the main street. A single costs Rs 10 and hot showers cost Rs 2. Luggage can also be stored when you go trekking. There is a library with many books in English available to residents. Suman Shrestha, the amiable manager, is a good source of information on interesting places to see in the valley. Across the street is the *Monumental Lodge* (tel 13065) where a single costs Rs 8 and hot showers are thrown in for free. The *Annapurna Lodge* is in the same street and is slightly more expensive. *Sayami Lodge* is a good, cheap Freak St place where singles cost Rs 20.

Kathmandu's Freak Street with its many tourists, handicrafts and embroidery shops and its many Tibetan and Chinese restaurants reminds me of another street in the St Michel area in the Latin Quarter of Paris. But happily the similarity ends there. In Freak Street, you can still see roaming cows, barking dogs, rickshaws and many smiling Nepalese and Tibetan faces.

Claudine Brette, France

Pig Alley Pig Alley, as Maru Tole has been nicknamed by westerners, is the street containing all the pie shops. It may not look very clean but it does have two good lodges which are popular with many budget travellers. The *Delight Lodge* (tel 15267) charges Rs 10 to 12 for a single or Rs 5 for a bed in the dormitory. *Mount Lodge* located in the same area has also been popular with budget travellers for a long time.

Thamel Area Although most of the lodges in Thamel are more expensive than those in Freak Street or elsewhere in Kathmandu, two lodges recently opened are quite cheap and were liked by those budget travellers preferring to stay in Thamel. They are *Earth House Lodge* and *Pheasant Lodge*. Earth House Lodge (tel 16050) is an old Nepali house converted into a lodge which charges Rs 15 for a single and Rs 25 for a double. Pheasant Lodge situated in a new building off a small side street near Star Lodge charges only Rs 20 for a double.

Elsewhere One of the nicest cheap places to stay in Kathmandu, away from either Freak Street or Thamel, near the Durbar Square, is *Kathmandu Lodge* (tel 13868). Singles here cost Rs 20 and doubles Rs 30. Most of those who have stayed at this lodge, including the more affluent budget travellers, return here whenever they visit Kathmandu.

If you've come to Kathmandu by car and want cheap accommodation plus car parking space, the *Tahachal Lodge* is situated in quiet surroundings across the river in Tahachal — on the road to Swayambhu.

Some of the lodges at the bottom of the rock bottom range are situated in localities which could hardly be called 'clean' as it is understood in the west. On the other hand if you want to live in more indigenous, even mediaeval, surroundings you may well like them. As far as I know, the lodges are quite clean and well cared for and, of course,

very inexpensive. A single room can cost as little as Rs 4 although living there is certain to brand you a hippy! Near the River Bishnumati, three blocks from Durbar Square, is *Bishnumati Lodge* (formerly the Hotch Potch Lodge) in the Pig Alley area.

At Jawlakhel, near the zoo and about 15 minutes walk from the Patan bus stop, is the *Youth Hostel* (tel 21003). If you want to live inexpensively, and don't mind being some distance from Kathmandu, a dormitory bed costs just Rs 6 or a double room Rs 15 to 20.

If you are planning a longer stay it is possible to rent a private home for as little as Rs 100 a month. Main areas are Swayambhu, Bodhnath or in Freak Street, although you can also find long term accommodation in other areas. If you wish to rent a room or apartment contact Major Rana (tel 11542) or find him at his home in Lagen, one block from Freak Street between 7 and 8 am. He does not charge any commission to the lessee. A casual wander around Swayambhunath will usually turn some place up — kids will soon find you. There are various noticeboards which may have information on places to rent — Aunt Jane's, Kathmandu Guest House, Peace Corps Office are just a few. It's often better to take over a place from a departing traveller as finding second-hand furniture may be difficult. Since fridges are virtually unavailable and incredibly expensive, as is electricty, it is wise to ensure that a market is reasonably close to hand for fresh food.

Where to Eat

Kathmandu's restaurants offer an amazing variety of foods. Most overland travellers find the food in Kathmandu to be better and more delicious than anywhere east of Istanbul. Where else in the middle of nowhere could you get sheesh kebab (Afghanistan), wiener schnitzel (German or Austrian), bortsch (Russian), tandoori chicken (northern Indian), masala dosa (southern Indian), kothe (Tibetan), chow mien (Chinese), hamburgers, hot dogs, brownies and banana splits (American), spaghetti (Italian), chicken a la provencal and chateaubriand (French), enchiladas (Mexican), sukiyaki (Japanese) and dal bhat tarkari (Nepali)? Where else but Kathmandu?

Not only that, but Kathmandu's unique pie shops specialise in making pies and cakes, the quality of which approaches those available in the west. This is very surprising to a Kathmanduite who can remember when, in 1955, there was only one restaurant in all of Kathmandu! All this is indicative of the great changes that have taken place in Nepal since it ended its long isolation and flung its doors open to the world. The Tibetan refugees who entered Nepal during this period have been a strong factor in the development of Nepal as the mini-gastronomic paradise of south Asia; many of the Chinese and Tibetan restaurants are run by Tibetans. There are few places in the east where so many different dishes, from so many countries, can be found in so small a city.

Quality Restaurants

Expensive but excellent describes the *Yak and Yeti Chimney Room* which was originally started by Boris. Born in Russia, Boris formerly ran the Royal Hotel, the only high class hotel for westerners in Nepal during the 1950s. Un-doubtedly one of the best restaurants in Nepal it is in an old Rana palace. The elaborately decorated hall has been converted into a dining room, and around the large open fire on a cold night the *Yak and Yeti* has plenty of atmosphere.

Situated in Lal Durbar, about three minutes walk from the Hotel de L'Annapurna, it is often very crowded. Most of the *Yak and Yeti's* clientele consists of well-off tourists, diplomats and a few affluent Nepalese, but some budget-minded tourists do venture in to sample the delights of Nepal's unique restaurant. If you wish to eat here without too much expense then try the Ukrainian bortsch, which is always delicious and only costs Rs 20. Other popular dishes include stroganoff at Rs 60, and a fish dish called bekti.

Perhaps the best Indian food to be found in Kathmandu is from *Kabab-e-ghar*, a restaurant situated in Durbar Marg, just outside the Hotel de L' Annapurna. The decor is very pleasant, it includes Indian miniatures of the Pahari style. Classical Indian music is played in the evenings and 'ghazals' are chanted in Urdu. Its speciality is chicken tandoori dishes, including *chicken peshwari* for Rs 35 which is eaten with the bread called *nan*.

The *Himachuli Room* of the Soaltee Oberoi Hotel serves some of the best food in Kathmandu. Among the more popular dishes are a typically Nepalese soup *alu tama*, for Rs 11, sliced chicken with bamboo shoots for Rs 36 and a tandoori-chicken-type Nepal dish called *Sekuwa* for Rs 34. A variety of Indian, Chinese, continental and Nepalese dishes are featured in the *Soaltee Oberoi's* excellent Rs 131 buffet lunch. Soup and dessert are included with the main dishes and there is no extra charge if you come back for seconds. *Fresco*

Italian Restaurant, alongside the swimming pool at Hotel Soaltee, is also well known for its Italian dishes. Pizzas cost only Rs 22 which is exceptionally good value for a restaurant in a five star hotel.

The Japanese restaurant *Kushi Fuji* is above the offices of Tiger Tops, in the same street as the Hotel de l'Annapurna. You can either take your shoes off and sit in traditional Japanese style or sit up at a table. Lunch here is excellent value, tempura or pork cutlet, soup, a bowl of rice and coffee only costs Rs 20. Dinner is rather more expensive, sukiyaki chicken costs Rs 30, although the food will be cooked right in front of you. One of the best places to try typical Nepali food is *Sunkosi Restaurant*. Prices are somewhat expensive according to Nepalese standards but the food is excellent.

Every evening at seven the *Everest Cultural Society* at Lal Durbar arranges Nepalese folk dances. A typical Nepalese dinner, as eaten by a well-to-do Nepali at home, is served after the show for Rs 75. The meal includes rice, dal and not too spicy curry, vegetables, chutney, dessert (a pudding or a Nepalese dessert called sikarni), washed down with *raksi*. This is one of the best places to try authentic Nepalese food, particularly if you must be careful about your eating. The famous Boris, having left the *Hotel Yak and Yeti* has now started his own restaurant, called simply *Boris*, situated just outside of Kathmandu in Baneshwar on the way to Pashupatinath. A visitor described it as 'Russian in flavour and personality'. It is popular with Kathmandu's diplomatic circles and is rather expensive. Excellent service and the bortsch is still good.

All the restaurants in this category serve well-prepared food and always boil their water — it is unlikely that you will become ill from a visit to one of these restaurants. In winter these places are heated, a luxury many of Kathmandu's hotels and restaurants do not offer.

Moderately Priced Restaurants

Situated on the ground floor of the Crystal Hotel, the *Other Room* offers good western and Indian food and a pleasantly genteel atmosphere in the heart of Kathmandu. Favourite dishes include the chateaubriand (Rs 30 for two people), tandoori chicken (Rs 14), kabuli nan, keema and pillao. Some of the best Indian food in town is available at *Kebab Corner* just around the corner from Hotel Nook. Its speciality is chicken tandoori dishes.

The *Indira Restaurant*, on the first floor on New Road, is one of the older restaurants in Kathmandu and serves good Indian food. The elite of Nepalese society comes here for a cup of tea and a snack while relaxing and talking. It is often quite crowded. This is one of the few places in Kathmandu visited by a large number of westerners in addition to many Nepalese.

The *Annapurna Coffee Shop* is located in the same compound as the Hotel de l'Annapurna and serves excellent coffee, and pastries. The coffee shop's walls are decorated with scenes showing Nepalese dancers and it is kept pleasantly warm in winter. Around noon it is often crowded with westerners and affluent Nepalese. In the Thamel area, *Rum Doodle Restaurant* is a cosy, get together place for trekkers and 'affluent' budget travellers. Its specialties are steak and spaghetti.

Paras is well known for its good Indian food, particularly the chicken curry, biriyani and keema. Although it is not frequented by many westerners, those who do venture in usually praise the quality of food. This restaurant has been open for more than 10 years.

The Taoist symbol hanging outside identifies the *Yin Yang* at Basantapur Square on the fringes of Freak Street. You take off your shoes and sit on the floor in this atmospheric restaurant. Tankas on the wall and photos of Hindu and Buddhist deities add to the mood, as does the excellent selection of music. The chop suey and vegetable rolls are particular favourites here.

The *Blue Bird Restaurant*, under Austrian management (formerly the Swiss Restaurant), is located a block south-west of Durbar Square. Although it can be crowded and the service variable, the french fries are generally thought to be the best in Kathmandu. The goulash, wiener schnitzel and coffee are also very popular. *Kantipur Restaurant* in Thamel is a popular, new place to eat. It specialises in steak and fried chicken.

KC's Restaurant in Thamel was started by a long-haired, bearded Nepalese named Kaysee and has become very popular recently. It serves good steak (for about Rs 20) and is crowded by budget travellers and tourists alike. I meet many people working in embassies in Kathmandu who enjoy eating at this place. I have asked travellers why they like the place so much. Some say it is very clean and reminds them of home, others are impressed by the owner who seems to know exactly what the westerners want; and some think the food has become rather expensive lately. There's also the *Nanglo-China Room*, which has good noodles and stuffed dumplings.

Low Priced Restaurants

Some of the best gastronomic experiences in Kathmandu can be sampled very cheaply in this category. In particular several of the restaurants in the low price range serve excellent Tibetan food which you'd have difficulty finding anywhere else in the world.

Thamel Area

The *Utse Restaurant* in the Thamel area is, for the price, one of the best restaurants for Chinese and Tibetan food. During peak hours, it can get very crowded. Overland bus travellers and voluntary workers are particularly fond of this restaurant. It is one of the few

places in Kathmandu which has remained consistently good for a decade. Its specalities are sweet and sour dishes and Tibetan kothe or momo. Recommended.

In the *Astha Mangalam Restaurant* you can dine on Tibetan or Chinese food surrounded by some of the best decor in Kathmandu. The walls are painted with Tibetan murals, hung with Tankas and you sit on Tibetan rug-covered cushions at elaborately painted tables. *Nankha Dhing Restaurant* serves good momo and also a Tibetan beer called *chang*. *Cimbali Restaurant* at Thamel (on the way to the city centre) has good Italian dishes. Pizzas here cost only Rs 10 to 15 and are excellent. *Tea for Two* is a cosy place and a good spot to meet other travellers.

Freak Street Area

Recently opened in Freak Street, the *Paradise Restaurant*, has become very popular and serves hygienic food including salad. Its specialty is brown rice and 'spinach cake'. Another Freak Street place well known to travellers is the *Mandarin Restaurant* which does Chinese food. *Kumari* is a popular and low priced place situated beside the Century Lodge.

Around the City Centre & New Rd

The present owner of *Aunt Jane's Place* used to work for the USAID office in Nepal. The original Aunt Jane was the wife of a former director of the Peace Corps in Nepal. Situated one block from Freak Street you have to climb stairs to the first floor to find typically American food. Often packed with young travellers this restaurant serves renowned chocolate cake, brownies, pies and ice cream. At breakfast time pancakes top the bill. *An An*, near the Post Office provides good Chinese food. Try the chop suey. It is one of the few places in Kathmandu patronised by well off Nepalese and tourists alike. *Om*

Restaurant, on the way to Freak Street from New Road, serves good Tibetan and Chinese food.

Mom's Health Food is on the street with the tree off New Road. It serves health food similar to that in western vegetarian restaurants. Soyaburgers at Rs 4, enchiladas, soups, vegetables or fruit juices and excellent bread are all popular attractions. Nothing spicy here and you get honey instead of sugar in your tea. *Tripti Restaurant* is a good place for inexpensive Indian food. Apart from the typical dishes of north India you can also try south Indian thalis for Rs 10. It's on a side street off New Rd, opposite to the Bo tree where they sell newspapers.

> *For health food fanatics . . . Mom's is the only place in Nepal which has real whole wheat bread. The food is just as wholesome and tasty as the health food restaurants in California.*
> Carol Pietsch, USA

Elsewhere

A recently opened restaurant, *Mei Hua* in Kanti Path, serves good Chinese food and the specialty is spring rolls. In the same area, down the street and around the corner, next to the Annapurna Hotel, is *Tso Nogono* run by Tibetans. It serves good chow mein and kothe. Back in downtown Kathmandu, the *Moti Mahal* with its good Indian tandoori dishes and the *Lost Horizon* are both popular.

In the late 1960s the *Peace Restaurant* was the only restaurant in Kathmandu serving good Chinese food. If Mr Wong, the Chinese owner, is around you can be sure that the food will be excellent. It has been renamed *Canton Restaurant — Wong's Kitchen* and is situated in Lazimpat near the French Embassy. A little off the beaten track, it's less likely to be crowded. Right across the street is the *Ringmo Restaurant* where the Chinese and Tibetan food is relatively inexpensive.

Rock Bottom Restaurants

It is wise to be careful in restaurants in this category although the ones listed here are adequately clean. There are also many good tea stalls and shops in this same price range that may not even have a name. The most popular meal in this group is probably dal bhat tarkari, the rice, dal and vegetable everyday meal of the vast majority of Nepalese. Most of the westerners you find in these places are overland travellers who have been exposed to this kind of food for months and are quite used to it.

The *Bangalore Coffee House* is adjacent to the American Library and serves good quality south Indian food. You can try masala dosa here for just Rs 2 or for Rs 5 have a full dinner including rice, chapati, curd and four different kinds of dal and vegetables. This place is also frequented by many budget-conscious Nepali intellectuals.

The *Lunch Box Restaurant*, a new place in Freak Street, is clean and serves inexpensive food, so it is often packed with budget travellers. *Dragon Restaurant* still in Freak Street also serves inexpensive food.

The street running down to the river where you find most of the pie shops is also the location for the *Tea Room*. Good music is played throughout the evening and the food is so inexpensive that it has been attracting the low money crowd for nearly a decade.

Pie Shops & Snackbars

Kathmandu's amazing pie shops are not only one of the most memorable aspects of the city they also have very good pies. Three of the best ones can be found within a few minutes walk from Durbar Square in the street which has been named 'Pie Alley' (or less kindly 'Pig Alley') by many westerners. The area may not look particularly clean externally but the pie shops themselves are quite clean and their owners usually learnt their pie-making skills while working as domestic helps to Americans in US AID. *New Style Pie Shop* has excellent apple pie, cakes, brownies and cinnamon rolls — more than 10 different kinds of pie in all. *Pancha's Pastries* in Pie Alley is a new addition to the area. Started by Pancha, who has worked in several of the well-known pie shops in Kathmandu, the pies here are excellent. *Jamaly Restaurant* in Thamel also serves excellent cakes and pies. The pie shops are especially crowded in the evenings and a popular meeting place for overlanders whose paths last crossed in Istanbul or Delhi.

One of the most pleasant and surprising aspects of Kathmandu is the interesting people one meets in the small restaurants and pie shops. This easy-going exchange of information seems more prevalent here than in most other cities on the way to the east.
Jim Wanless, USA

If you want the surroundings to look a little clean then head for the *Krishna Loaf Store* at Kamal Pokhari or *Nanglo* at Durbar Marg. You can get excellent cakes, bread and rolls here. Milk, butter and yak cheese can be bought at the dairy branch on New Road or at the main dairy in Lainchaur near the British Embassy. If you are going trekking make sure to take a few kilograms of cheese along. Cheese costs Rs 52 per kilo and milk Rs 1.75 per bottle.

Western-style *Fresh House* near Freak Street is rather like a grocery store, and is popular with western residents in Kathmandu.

Eating & Drinking Do's and Don'ts
The season you are in Nepal determines whether you need to be very careful about the water you drink and the food you eat. During the dry tourist season from November to April you could drink tap water in Kathmandu, although

it is definitely not advisable. During the wet monsoon season from May through September you should always insist on drinking boiled and filtered water. Lack' of care can result in diarrhoea, dysentery or even hepatitis but most restaurants boil and filter the water as a matter of course. However, the point to remember is that just boiling the water is not enough. It has to be boiled continuously for at least 10 minutes to kill all the bacteria. Most restaurants in Nepal do not do that. Remember that tea is always boiled and, therefore, always safe.

When trekking the quality of the water is the single most important cause of stomach disorders. The golden rule is to only drink water from springs when you are positive that there is no human habitation upstream and to avoid drinking flowing water from rivers or streams. It is still better to boil and filter the water if possible. Above 1500 metres you need to be less careful than in the hotter climate at low altitudes.

As altitude increases, water's boiling point drops — so there is more chance of hardier bacteria (especially typhoid) surviving brief periods of boiling. I'd use sterilising tablets, most of which are chlorine based. I'd regard Nepal as a risky place for the health of the unwary.
Bob Day, England

It is generally quite safe to drink the Tibetan beer known as *chang* which is available very cheaply at places along many of the trekking routes or at Bodhnath and other locations in the valley. It is wise to avoid eating ice cream or any foodstuff which is exposed in the open, particularly from street vendors, but in respectable restaurants ice cream is OK.

If you have any doubts about the quality of meat available in an unfamiliar restaurant then try to order egg dishes instead. Avoid eating meat while trekking unless you are carrying your own canned food or if you are certain that the chicken or goat has been freshly slaughtered.

Stomach Upsets If you are unfortunate enough to develop stomach problems in Nepal the best cure is to avoid solid food, drink only hot tea and let your body fight it naturally. If you decide to give it some help Lomotil and Mexaform tablets are both available in pharmacies in Kathmandu.

Popular Nepalese Food

chang — a mild alcoholic beverage made from barley, similar to western style beer.

thupka — Tibetan soup containing different kinds of meat.

momo or kothe — the Tibetan equivalent of ravioli or dim sums, consists of meat enclosed in dough then steamed or fried.

dal bhat tarkari — the typical Nepali meal consisting of lentil soup, rice and curried vegetables.

sikarni — a sweet dessert made from curd.

gundruk — a typical Nepalese soup made from dried vegetables.

tama — a dried bamboo shoot soup popular in Nepal.

buff — since Hindus can't eat beef, buff (water buffalo) is the normal substitute on many menus — buff steaks, buff noddle soup, even buffburgers.

If you develop a taste for chang and would like to brew some up at home here's the recipe. Get a five or 10 gallon fermenting vessel from a brewery supply shop. For the smaller vessel boil about two kg of millet for several hours. Millet swells considerably so make sure it has plenty of water and doesn't stick. When it cools add water to liquify it, you can also pass it through a blender to smooth it out. Then add burgundy yeast and the juice of a lemon and leave to ferment. This can take several weeks or a couple of months depending on taste. If you like a little extra kick to your chang add sugar, several kg, to the fermenting brew — this is really cheating since in Nepal sugar would be too expensive to be used in this way. The final product will have to be strained through a cloth and racked to remove the yeasty taste. This should not be taken as the only way to produce chang — experiment with it; in Bhutan for example they drink a chang made from half millet and half rice.

recipe from Karel Tiller, Australia

Shopping

Many different souvenirs and handicrafts can be purchased in Nepal but it is important to shop around. Many items, such as the Tibetan and Chinese wood block prints, were not available at all in the late sixties but now are found in all the new shopping areas. Only government emporiums and a very few shops have fixed prices so the golden rule to remember when shopping is bargain! Usually the price first quoted will have a built-in bargaining margin.

Popular buys include:

Masks *Papier mache* masks of many different sizes are used for mask dancing which takes place in Kathmandu in September. Mask images include elephant-headed Ganesh, the terrifying Bhairab and the living Goddess Kumari. Almost all the souvenir shops in Kathmandu sell masks but the best place to buy them inexpensively is the small town of Thimi where they are actually made. Thimi is midway between Kathmandu and Bhaktapur; you can visit the mask painter Kansa Chitrakar on the old Kathmandu to Bhaktapur road about 15 minutes' walk from the bus stop. Prices range from Rs 5 to 30 depending on size. They make good wall decorations. Another good buy in Bhaktapur are the locally manufactured puppets.

Nepali Caps All Nepalese officials are required to wear Nepali caps — topi — when formally dressed. They're black in colour and made in Bhaktapur. Caps are a popular purchase because they look so typically Nepali. There is a cluster of shops selling nothing but caps in an area of old Kathmandu between Asan and Indrachowk; prices run from Rs 15 to 20.

Tibetan Handicrafts Tibetan prayer wheels are possibly the best known Tibetan handicraft: they make good presents to take home. Also popular are musical instruments, charm boxes, dorjes (thunderbolts) and other religious items. Bodhnath used to be a good place for Tibetan items but the large number of short-stay tourists who now rush out there on guided tours and indiscriminately buy anything at the first price asked have pushed prices up to absurd levels.

prayer wheel

Tankas Colour paintings of the deities, called tankas, are painted by Tibetans or by Newars and Tamangs. Many are kept in monasteries but many of the *antique* tankas for sale in Kathmandu are artificially aged over a smoky fire. Tankas can be found for as little as Rs 50 while a good old one could easily cost over Rs 1000. There is no particular place to look for tankas although you will find many in shops at Bodhnath, around Freak Street and in Bhaktapur. There is a new shop in

Bhaktapur, next to the recently renovated Pujahari Math monastery, where you can see the tankas being painted. I also found the prices of tankas to be more reasonable here compared to other places.

Nepalese Handicrafts Patan, where many traditional handicrafts and bronzeworks are manufactured, is the best place to go. Nepal is one of the few places in Asia where they make bronze by the 'lost wax process'. This is perhaps, the most unique feature of artwork in Nepal at present. A bronze statue may cost as little as Rs 150. There are now many small shops around Durbar Square in Patan. You can see handicrafts being made at the Patan Industrial Estate at Lagankhel, the prices here are quite low. The Government Emporium on New Road Kathmandu, also charges fair, fixed prices but the choice is somewhat limited.

> *For good bargains in Nepalese or Tibetan curios go to the vendors who spread their wares on blankets in Basantapur or Durbar Square — but be prepared to bargain.*
> *Stephen Frantz, USA*

Tibetan Carpets, Jackets, Bags It is a good idea to visit the Tibetan refugee camp in Jawlakhel near Patan to see Tibetan carpets being woven. They are also available in the complex of narrow streets between Asan and the National Theatre. The carpets usually cost from US$100 to US$120 each. Their quality is better if wool from the highlands (Tibetan wool) is used. The carpets can be vacuumed, although you should ensure that the dyes are colourfast before buying. Tibetan carpets are vibrantly coloured and have striking designs, but were originally meant as wall hangings rather than floor coverings. The small square carpets are often made into seat cushions. The wool jackets, popularly known as *yakets*

seem to be worn by every visitor to Kathmandu.

Block Prints Block prints of Tibetan, Chinese and Nepalese deities are available in large numbers printed on local rice paper. Many shops around Freak Street sell prints at prices from Rs 5 to Rs 20, but one of the best places to go is the *Print Shop*, next to the Mona Lisa restaurant in Basantapur Square.

> *I would recommend a visit to the bead bazaar, within the main bazaar, north-east of Durbar Square. Here you can buy strings of many coloured beads very cheaply and also several thicknesses of materials to make rings and bracelets.*
> *Annette Mahoney, England*

Khukris The Nepalese knife, traditional weapon of Gurkha soldiers, can be bought for Rs 20 to Rs 500 depending on size and quality.

Khukri

Nepalese Tea Tea is grown in Nepal in the far east of the country in the area bordering Darjeeling. It is claimed to be equal to the famous Darjeeling tea in quality. The best known teas are *Ilam* and *Mountain Gold*, packets of which can be bought for about Rs 15.

Clothes Western women often like Tibetan and Nepalese garments. You'll find all sorts of clothes on sale around the Thamel and Freak Street areas. The traditional Nepalese coats, overlapping at the front and closed with four ties, are another popular purchase — especially in the maroon velvet material from Pokhara.

Jewellery Jewellery of high and low quality is cheap to buy in Kathmandu and designs and carvings can be created to order. One popular buy is a red bead necklace containing a gold ornament known as 'Tilhari'. Worn by almost all married women in Nepal, it serves the same purpose as a ring in the west. The best place to look for a *Tilhari* is in the Indrachowk area near Durbar Square.

> *It will cost you very little to have a Nepalese jeweller working on the street make some article in silver or stone.*
>
> *BB, France*

Terra Cotta A wide variety of attractive terra cotta pots, bowls and flowerpots are made — those shaped like an elephant are favourites. Several shops near Indrachowk sell them. They are made in Thimi.

Other The latest buys include lamp shades of different forms and batik paintings available in Freak Street which were not common before.

Nepal is having, in common with many other Asian countries, a major problem of theft of works of art from temples and monasteries. Many of these masterpieces end up in museums of private collections in America or Europe. If you visit Dhulikhel you can walk down to the temple at the foot of the hill and see the three small pairs of feet that are all that remain of the statues which used to stand in the temple.

Should you buy a work of art which could be more than one hundred years old it is necessary to get permission from the Department of Archaeology before you take it out of the country. If in doubt check — the office is in the National Archives Building (tel 12778), just two blocks from Immigration. Hours are 10 am to 5 pm, but if you go by 1 pm you can expect approval by the same evening. To be on the safe side go there a few days before you depart, customs checks are much more severe on exit than entry to the country.

Every time I visit Kathmandu I take a new pair of jeans with me and get a dragon embroidered on the cuffs. There are a host of little embroidery shops around Kathmandu and they'll produce a brilliant design remarkably quickly and cheaply. Make sure you remember which little shop it was, though. I really thought I'd lost my jeans once!

Tony Wheeler, Australia

Getting it all back Home Unless you are sure about their reliability it is best not to leave articles to be mailed by the shop where you purchased them. There have been instances when articles have never arrived, unfortunately this is also true of some packing companies — I recommend *Sharma and Sons Packers and Movers* in Kantipath (tel 12709). You could also mail your stuff from the Foreign Post Office. For a small fee there are people who will help you pack.

Kathmandu Valley

a Wheels from a temple chariot in Bhaktapur
b Temple struts on the Jagnath Temple in the Durbar Square, Kathmandu
c Children in Kirtipur

Living in Kathmandu

Cultural Programmes

Even if your visit to Nepal is not during the festival season you can still enjoy Nepalese dance and music in Kathmandu. At the National Theatre there are Nepalese operas and musicals almost every day. In addition programmes of folk dancing are put on by:

Everest Cultural Society (tel 15429) shows Nepalese folk dances every evening at 7 pm, the one-hour show costs Rs 45. The dances take place in the extravagantly Victorian 'hall of mirrors' in the same old Rana palace as the Yak and Yeti Restaurant. Dances from the Sherpa highlands, from the Newars of the valley and from other ethnic groups are shown, including the Yak dance, Peacock dance, Mask dance and Witch Doctor dance.

Lalupate (tel 11211) presents Nepalese folk dances from a variety of ethnic groups at 6.30 pm in the Soaltee Oberoi Hotel, admission is Rs 25. At the same time — 6.30 pm — every night *Lali Guras Cultural Group* (tel 13471) puts on a show at the Manaslu Hotel near the French Embassy for Rs 35.

> *On Monday nights you can hear the traditional Nepalese music in a temple a few blocks off New Road in Asantol. Wait for the religious ceremony to end at about 9.30 and just sit in the arcade entrance to the temple and watch the warming up of the musicians. It is done with a large chillum and the music begins when the coughing stops.*
> *Peter Thompson, USA*

Libraries

Kathmandu has an interesting choice of libraries set up by the Americans, British, French, Germans, Russians, Chinese and Indians. Not only can you read recent journals, newspapers and books but there are also film nights.

The *French Cultural Centre* (tel 14326) has a good selection of French publications and is open from 3 to 7 pm on weekdays. There are also film nights from Monday to Thursday each week. Membership costs Rs 10 annually or Rs 3 for admission to one film. More than 100 French films are shown during the course of the year. The centre is located near the Leo Hotel in Bagh Bazaar.

Located near the post office and the tower, the *Goethe Institute* (tel 15528) has a reading room open from 4 to 7 pm daily. Films are shown fairly frequently and there is also an active Nepal-Deutsch club.

The *US Library and Information Service* is on New Road and is open from 11 am to 7 pm Monday to Friday if you want to keep up with *Time* and *Newsweek*. Recent changes in the regulations allow only Nepalese and foreign residents in Nepal to use the library. The *British Council* (tel 11305) is on Kantipath and is open from 11 am to 6 pm Sunday to Friday.

'Rastriya Pustakalaya' or 'Nepal National Library' at Pulchok in Patan has books in English, Sanskrit and Indian languages. A large number of the

Out of the Valley

A	a Bridge at Kodari on the Chinese border
B	b Buddha carving at Namobuddha

books in the library were collected by the Royal Preceptor in Nepal who had been awarded the title of 'jewel of head of scholars' by the King of Nepal. The Tribhuvan University Library of Kirtipur has a nice collection of books and resembles a library in an American university. It is open Sunday to Friday from 9 am to 6 pm.

The Kaiser Library (worth visiting for the building), near the new Royal Palace, has an incredible collection of books, many on Buddhism, Tibet and Nepal that I have never seen before.

Hester Ross, USA

Research Work

If you are undertaking research on economic, social or anthropological aspects of Nepal, the best place to contact is the International Research and Consulting Centre, PO Box 1577, Kathmandu. You can also phone Mr Sharad Sharma on 13438.

Legal Work

Nepal Law Firm (tel 11710) in Ram Shah Path has English speaking lawyers who could assist you if you have any legal problem in Nepal.

Finding Employment in Nepal

Western visitors often wonder if it is possible to find work in Nepal. The answer is, it is very difficult but not impossible. It is easier for those having English as their mother tongue. There are many privately-owned schools in Nepal and they often require trained teachers or just English-speaking adults to teach. Last year, I met a Dutch teacher who wanted to work in Nepal. He visited 15 schools and five of them were willing to hire him. But don't get the impression that it is too easy. The pay is minimal — between US$50 to US$100 a month, however it is cheap to live in Nepal. Finding work in a school might help solve the visa problem,

but it takes a very long time to get things done. Technically, no work permit is required by foreigners and the main problem is getting an extension. Apart from schools, there are many aid missions, travel agencies, consulting firms and airline offices which could be worth approaching. But the number of such openings is small so your chances of getting them would be very remote. This does not mean that it is impossible or not worth trying.

Learning Nepali

If you want to learn Nepali from the same instructors who teach Peace Corps Volunteers who work in Nepal, contact Mr Cheej Shrestha at Naxal (near the Lhotse Hotel) or telephone him at 12551. The charges are Rs 25 to 30 per hour. Another good place is *Training Service Centre* (tel 15926) in Thamel which has similar prices. Nepali is a relatively easy language to learn and a working knowledge could be obtained in three to eight weeks.

Astrologer

If you would like to consult a Nepalese astrologer, there is one person who has a good reputation, whom many westerners have visited. He is Mangal Raj Joshi (tel 21159) who lives in Patan near Kathmandu.

Yoga

If you want to learn Yoga while in Kathmandu, there is a place called Arogya Ashram (tel 16632) at Battisputali near the temple of Pashupati. They teach different postures (including standing on the head) and 'Pranayama'.

Cinemas

Indian films, usually not subtitled, are the usual cinematic fare in the valley although there are occasional English language films. Kathmandu has three cinemas and there are also cinemas in Patan and Bhaktapur. Admission charges range from Rs 3 to Rs 10.

If you do not catch one in India, I suggest a Hindi movie. Even if you do not understand Hindi it will be an interesting, artistic experience. The nicest theatre is near the Palace and Chinese Embassy, price is less than Rs 4.

Bill Cook, USA

Media

The *Rising Nepal* is the main English daily and covers most news from abroad but can be difficult to find if you don't get hold of a copy early in the morning. *Radio Nepal* has English news bulletins at 8 am and 8.30 pm daily. *Time* and *Newsweek* are readily available in Nepal. You can buy the latest issues at the store opposite the big tree in New Road, where Indian dailies, such as *The Statesman* or *The Times of India* are also available. The daily *International Herald Tribune* is also available in many shops.

Bookshops

Kathmandu has a surprising variety of quite good bookshops with particularly interesting selections of books on Nepal — many of which are not available outside the country. There are bookstalls in the main hotels in old Kathmandu and around Freak Street. Probably the best selection of books in Kathmandu is at *Educational Enterprises* near New Road Gate or *Ratna Book Distributors* at Bagh Bazaar. Both have showrooms. Recently several new bookstores have opened in the street around the Clock Tower and National Theatre. *Himalayan Booksellers* near the Clock Tower has a good collection of books on Nepal. In the same area, *Everest Book Store* is also good.

Visit the Chinese book store located in the bazaar area off Indrachowk. They have beautifully illustrated story books and water colour prints, some in English. They also have interesting sets of postcards, reprints of water colour paintings, glimpses of cities, at an extraordinarily cheap price. Ask to see all the different photos of Mao.

Kathleen Bannon, USA

Swimming

The Swimming Pool in the five star Yak and Yeti Hotel is open to outsiders and costs Rs 26 per day. It also has a cheaper rate if you become a member and are staying longer.

During summer, it is possible to swim at the pool at the National Stadium (opposite Telegram Office) for Rs 5 a day. It is open from 10 am to 5 pm. Monday is especially reserved for women. The swimming pool at Balaju Water Gardens is likely to be quite crowded in the summertime. *Narayani Hotel* also has a swimming pool which is open to non-residents for Rs 30 per day. The pools at Soaltee and Annapurna Hotels are only open to residents and their guests.

Nightlife in Kathmandu

Many restaurants and snack bars in Kathmandu are so crowded that they make good places to meet Nepalese and other westerners, but there are few discos or night clubs as they are known in the west. In Kathmandu, people go to bed quite early and in winter you hardly see anyone on the streets after 10 pm. Besides, many visitors are not particularly worried by the lack of night life, it's not what they have come this far for — so the many places that have opened in the past few years have not all had a long or successful life.

For most people a German visitor's comments sum it up: 'If you want night life in Kathmandu, you have to make your own.'

Nevertheless there are some places:

The Soaltee Oberoi Casino — for something to do at night. Black Jack, pontoon and a roulette wheel — you might even come away a few rupees richer. Even if you do not like gambling the music is good and it is fun to watch.

Susan Culkina, USA

There are free buses to the casino from all the leading hotels of Kathmandu from 8 to 11 pm. If you gamble, free drinks are also served. Some hotels also distribute US$5 coupons free which can be exchanged to play at the casino. The Soaltee is one of the very few casinos in this part of the world. You can play in Indian Rs or US$ and take the money out of the country if you win.

There is band music and ballroom dancing at the *Rose Room* of the *Soaltee Oberoi Hotel* almost every evening. The *Up and Down Bar* is perhaps the only disco in Kathmandu. Situated in the Thamel area, it is open every evening except on Fridays. There is no cover charge except on Saturdays when it is really crowded. It is a good place to meet western travellers in Nepal as the Nepalese are required to be members.

The Terai

All travellers who enter Nepal overland from the south pass through the Terai on their way to Kathmandu or Pokhara. Few spend much time in the region however. Such towns as Birganj, Bhairawa, Janakpur are all located in the Terai.

THE TERAI

Besides being the 'granary' of Nepal, the Terai also contains Lumbini, Buddha's birthplace, and the Chitwan National Park where wildlife of the area including the one-horned rhinos can be seen. After the recent opening of the road connecting the Terai with the Kathmandu-Pokhara Highway, both of the above attractions are now so near Sunauli or Narayanghat that they are only a couple of hours away from the main travel route of overland travellers.

The Terai consists of the 'Outer Terai' which is flat and is an extension of the Gangetic Plains; and the 'Inner Terai' which is surrounded by hills in the south and is actually a valley. The Terai extends the length of Nepal, except in two regions where it only contains the Inner Terai. Much of the Terai was heavily forested till the 1960s when the eradication of malaria resulted in mass migration from the hills causing large scale deforestation. A substantial portion of the Terai, especially along the northern foothills still contains large *Sal* forests. The Terai also contains most of the industries of Nepal, and produces more than half of the country's GDP and government revenue.

Most of the people in eastern and central Terai have close ethnic and linguistic ties with the Indians across the border in the states of UP and Bihar. The recent migration of the people from the hills has changed the ethnic character of the Terai. It is also a region of Nepal which has developed more than the hilly region in general. Almost two-

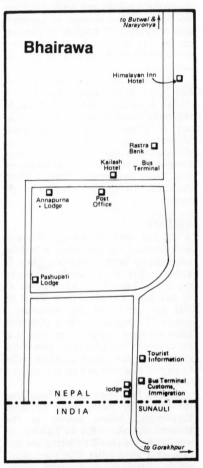

thirds of the Terai contains good, motorable roads connecting Kathmandu and the Indian border and almost all of its towns have electricity laid on.

BHAIRAWA

The city of Bhairawa is a convenient point for an overnight stay if you are planning to visit Lumbini, Buddha's birthplace. It is the headquarters of a

101

small Terai district and contains banks, government offices and hotels. As there are frequent bus services to Lumbini, and everything of interest in Lumbini can be seen in a few hours, it is better to overnight in Bhairawa than in Lumbini.

The best hotel in Bhairawa is *Lumbini Hotel* which charges Rs 75 for a single. *Himalayan Inn* is moderately expensive charging Rs 45 for a single and is popular with slightly more affluent budget travellers. There are cheaper hotels near the city centre which charge Rs 25 to 30. These include *Shambala Guest House* and *Hotel Kailash*. *Pashupati Lodge* has cheaper single rooms.

LUMBINI

A 22 km road connecting Bhairawa with Lumbini, the birthplace of Buddha has recently been completed. There is a bus service every two hours during the day to Lumbini which costs Rs 4. A taxi from Bhairawa costs about Rs 300 for the round trip, including a couple of hours at Lumbini. Although there are some hotels in Lumbini, it is better to stay in Bhairawa as there is not much to see there. Most travellers prefer to stay in Bhairawa and make a day trip to Lumbini.

In 249 BC, when he had been king for about 20 years, King Devanam Pryadarshin, better known as the Emperor Ashoka, came to Lumbini to worship at the Buddha's birthplace and to erect a giant pillar. The main sightseeing attractions at Lumbini, all of which can be seen in a few hours, include this ancient Ashoka pillar. Others are the temple of the Buddha's mother, Maya Devi, and the Tibetan monastery which was established in 1975. It has interesting paintings on the walls and a huge bronze image of the Buddha which was set up by a Raja from Mustang (a region in northern Nepal). There is also a Buddhist monastery with a white Buddha donated by the Burmese, a huge tanka painting and wood carvings on the gate. The entire Lumbini region is expected to be developed, with UN assistance, over the next few years.

The *Lumbini Guest House* is about the only place to stay here. You can probably knock their price of Rs 100 for a double down to about Rs 70, which is still expensive. Food here is also rather pricey and there's not much available. The rooms, however, are clean and very comfortable and there are pleasant gardens and lawns.

CHITWAN NATIONAL PARK

A visit to the park should not be missed as it is one of the finest wildlife experiences in Asia (including the chance to see the one-horned rhinos), and because the park is so easily accessible.

There are several ways of visiting Chitwan National Park. For those with a lot of money to spend, *Tiger Tops Hotel Complex* is connected by air from Kathmandu. It is luxurious and expensive, and can cost more than US$150 a day. The more moderate hotels are within an hour's drive from the city of Narayanghat, which is on the overland route from the Indian border to Kathmandu. These are less than half as expensive as Tiger Tops. It is also possible to visit the park on the cheap for as little as US$15 a day.

Tiger Tops

The Tiger Tops jungle camp is located in the Chitwan Valley 130 km southwest of Kathmandu. The office of Tiger Tops (tel 12706) is located on Durbar Marg close to the Hotel de l'Annapurna. Tiger Tops operates a tent camp on the banks of the Narayani River on the National Park, and also a more comfortable and expensive *Jungle Lodge*. A return flight to Meghauli close to the camp and lodge costs US$70. Accommodation per night in the tent camp

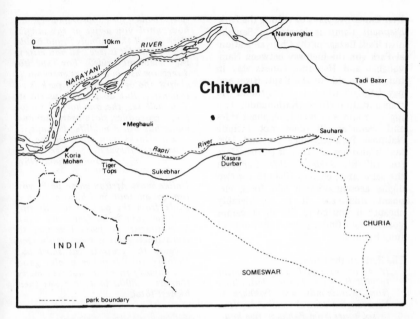

costs US$150 including meals and tours. In addition, there is a Rs 60 entry fee to the park. In the *Jungle Lodge* the fee for the first night is US$170 for a single room, or US$120 for a double room. Accommodation costs include transportation in both cases — you travel by elephant if going to the *Jungle Lodge*. Dr Charles McDougal, who holds a doctorate in anthropology and is an authority on the people and wildlife of Nepal, gives lectures on the area and the animals in the park. A new addition to the activities at Tiger Tops is the village, which shows how indigenous people of the area, known as Tharus, live.

Tiger Tops Lodge — Tiger Tops, PO Box 242 Kathmandu — Telex NP 216 TIGTOP — Kathmandu office tel 12706 — 20 rooms all with bath — bar — restaurant.

In the park there is opportunity for boating and canoeing, visits to native villages, fishing for mahseer in season, nature walks and treks, elephant treks, swimming and, of course, wildlife observation. Unlike African animals which tend to move in large herds, Asian wildlife is more solitary and shy. Observing wildlife involves patience and searching, but animals you may see include various deer, the sloth bear, wild boar, fresh water dolphins, crocodiles (careful where you swim), the rare Great Indian one-horned rhinos, leopards and, with a good deal of luck, the very rare and elusive Royal Bengal tiger. Best season for visiting the park is from October to March when the weather is not too hot. Hunting is strictly prohibited. It is estimated that there are 300 rhinos and 30 tigers in the park, which is only a third of the number 25 years ago. Tiger Tops can also be reached after a two day raft trip on the Trisuli and Narayani Rivers. The trip starts at Mugling on the Kathmandu-Pokhara Highway and reaches Tiger Tops the following day after camping along the river bank.

Less Expensive ways of visiting the Park
Elephant Camp is located in Sauraha near Tadi Bazaar in the Chitwan National Park (on the highway between Narayanghat and Hetaura). Guests stay in huts by the side of the Rapti River and pay US$165 which includes round trip transportation from Kathmandu, two nights' room and board, elephant rides and canoeing. It does not include National Park entrance fee and 10% tax. It also has an office at Durbar Marg (tel 13976). *Gaida Wildlife Camp*, in the same area, charges US$145 for two nights accommodation and food, elephant rides etc. It is considerably cheaper if you go to the above camps yourself and find a place if they are not fully booked.

The Park on the Cheap
It is now extremely easy and cheap to visit the park. Express buses leave from Kathmandu and Pokhara to Narayanghat several times a day (five to six hours from Pokhara; five hours from Kathmandu) where it is a short Rs 3 bus ride to Tadi Bazaar. From Tadi down to Sauraha it is a two hour walk or if you are lucky you can hitch a ride on a jeep. Sauraha has several cheap places to stay and eat. Probably the best place is the Babu Ram Huts where you get your own hut for Rs 10 a single, Rs 20 a double. The owner used to work as a park warden and is very willing to tell you everything about the park. Admission to the park is expensive, (Rs 65 per day), with a canoe trip (Rs 25), and an elephant ride into the jungle (Rs 100 for two). There are ways around this, though. You can spend two or more days in the park for the single admission price by sleeping inside the park in the towers for Rs 10 a night. This allows you to hear and see the animals in the mornings, evenings and all night. The other alternative, and by far the cheapest, is not to go into the park at all, but to stay in Sauraha and then walk along the

river bank for approximately an hour until you arrive at the jungle. Here are all the animals found inside the park and it is free. All you miss is the elephant ride. For specific directions ask in town, as everyone is almost apologetic that the park is so expensive. But do go, it is worth it. You will see the one-horned rhinoceros, crocodiles, sloth bear, deer and numerous other wildlife. Perhaps, if you are lucky you will even see the endangered Royal Bengal Tiger.
Don Graham, USA

Unlike most African game parks you can go on foot in Chitwan, with a guide from the park (a few Rs tip) or from your hotel (generally free). Most tourists go from February to April when game is more easily seen because the grass is cut short but October to December is also good and anyway there are not very many tourists — 8000 in a year was their highest total.

TOWNS OF THE TERAI
Most travellers from the West are not specifically interested in the towns of the Terai (or Inner Terai), although they may pass through on their way from Darjeeling or the Indian border to Kathmandu. Many of the towns seem similar to the towns in the Gangetic Plains in northern India.

Narayanghat is located on the banks of River Narayani which is one of the three biggest in Nepal and drains the central part of Nepal. A large bridge has just been constructed over the river creating a vital link with the East-West Highway of Nepal. Narayanghat, along with its sister city of Bharatpur, is the administrative and commercial centre of the rich agricultural area of Chitwan, which was largely settled by people from the hills in the 1960s. Some of its original inhabitants, the *Tharus* still live here. It is also the gateway to the Chitwan National Park. A large fair takes place every year in mid-January in a town called Deoghat a few km north of Narayanghat. Tens of thousands of pilgrims gather to bathe in the holy waters where the rivers merge to become Narayani. Because of the opening of the new road connecting the Indian border with Kathmandu and Pokhara this town is growing very fast. If you want to stay overnight, *Hotel Bisauni* charges Rs 35 for a double.

Birganj This border town was, a few years ago, the main entry point to Nepal from India. It has lost its importance as more routes into the country have opened up. If you enter Nepal from Raxaul in India you will almost certainly have to spend a night in Birganj.

Almost all of the cheap lodges are found around the bus station. The *Amrapali, Tourist* and *Delicious* are among the better ones — they are quite similar and charge around Rs 12 for a single without bath. *Hotel Diyalo* is somewhat better and single room cost from Rs 36. The *Samjhana Hotel* is situated away from the centre of town and is patronised mainly by overland buses and motorists who require parking space. A single room here costs Rs 30 or you can camp for Rs 5.

Janakpur This town, located in eastern Terai, is famous historically as the birthplace of Sita of the epic Ramayana. There is a temple of Rama and Sita in the town which attracts many pilgrims. It also has a cigarette factory built in the 1960s with aid from the USSR. The local language is known as Maithili, which is also spoken in North Bihar in India.

Biratnagar is the second largest city in Nepal and the largest in the Terai. Being the centre of the jute industry, it is also the major industrial city in Nepal.

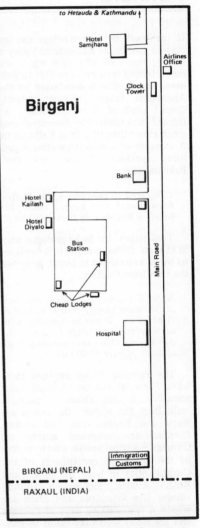

Dharan is situated on the foothills in the eastern Terai and is inhabited by people who migrated from the hills. It also has a camp for Gurkha soldiers in the British Army.

Pokhara

If the work of human-beings has impressed you in the Kathmandu Valley it will be the work of nature which will cast a lasting spell on your visit to Pokhara. The skyline is dominated by the Annapurna range and the perfectly shaped peak of Macchapuchhare, the fish-tail mountain. The Himalaya seem much closer than they do in Kathmandu. A member of a mountaineering expedition, speaking of the view from Pokhara, said:

Compared to that vision, the Matterhorn would have looked crude, the peerless Weisshorn a flattened hump.

Toni Hagen, the Swiss geologist who, in the late fifties, was the first foreigner to travel extensively in Nepal, described the view from Pokhara:

Nepal is a land of contrast. Nowhere is this more clearly seen than here in Pokhara . . . in the background, with no intermediate range between, the Annapurna chain rises abruptly to an altitude of over 8000 metres.

The Pokhara Valley contains three lakes, Phewatal, the most beautiful and accessible, is only about 15 minutes' walk from the airport; the others are Rupa and Begnas. The hills around Pokhara are inhabited largely by Gurungs — a tribal people who form one of the important constituents of the Gurkha rifles in both the Indian and British armies. Picturesque Gurung villages like Ghandruk and Siklis are within a few walking days of Pokhara and are really worth the effort to visit. The population of the valley itself consists largely of Brahmins and Chetris. The tradition of providing Gurkha soldiers from this area means that Pokhara has long been open to outside influence but there is still much population pressure from the surrounding hills. The salaries and pensions received from employment outside — through the army or Indian households — helps to improve conditions in this food deficient area.

The area around Pokhara is currently changing very rapidly. The construction of the road linking Pokhara to the Indian border and to Kathmandu — previously it was accessible only by flying or walking — has a major impact on the area. Pokhara is also the growth centre for mid-western Nepal in the country's four region development programme.

Pokhara is about 700 metres lower than Kathmandu and as a result rather warmer and more pleasant in late autumn and winter. On the other hand it is not a good place to visit in the monsoon as Pokhara gets twice the rainfall of Kathmandu.

GETTING TO POKHARA

There are bus and minibus services between Kathmandu and Pokhara and from there to the Indian border. Public buses from Kathmandu can be found at the foot of the Bhimsen Tower near the Post Office or at the bus stand near the City Hall. The buses leave in the early morning and it is advisable to reserve tickets at least a day in advance, cost is only Rs 33. These are the same kind of public buses that make the trip up from the Indian border. They are not very comfortable and you may have difficulty in stretching your legs.

More comfortable, although slightly more expensive, are the minibuses which are usually ex-overland vehicles. On these buses the cost is Rs 38 and tickets are sold from offices around Freak Street or in hotels. An advantage of travelling by minibus is that they will take you to the lake area of Pokhara. The public buses only go as far as the airport/bus stand from where it is expensive to get a taxi to the lake or entails a half hour walk. The buses will also pick you up from the lake area for the return trip. It takes five or six hours to travel between the two towns.

There are frequent flights between Kathmandu and Pokhara; the short flight offers good Himalayan views and costs Rs 460. If you decide to travel by road, there are few dangerous curves, steep ascents or descents along the excellent Kathmandu-Pokhara highway.

Kathmandu-Pokhara Highway

The Kathmandu-Pokhara highway is 202 km long and for the most part follows the courses of three major rivers — the Trisuli, Marsyangdi and the Seti and crosses over two rivers — the Madi and Marsyangdi. The portion from Naubise, where the road to the Indian border splits off, is 176 km long and was constructed with Chinese assistance. When completed in the early seventies it had cost approximately $14 million.

From the fertile valley of Naubise, the road follows the small stream of Mahesh Khola for 22-km to its junction with the Trisuli River at Galchi Bazaar. The road then follows the Trisuli river through Gajuritar and Benighat, where the big Bidhi Gandaki River joins the Trisuli from the north to the confluence of the Marsyangdi and Trisuli at Mugling. This is the halfway point and a popular lunch stop; at an altitude of only 280 metres it is also the lowest point along the highway. The Chinese have also built a road leading south from Mugling to the Chitwan Valley where Tiger Tops is located. The sacred Hindu temple of Mankamana is only a few km away on the top of a steep hill.

Go to Bandipur, a beautiful Newar town, just off the Kathmandu-Pokhara Road. Before the road was built, it was a major trade centre of western Nepal. Its bazaars still show the prosperity of those times — multi-storeyed houses, a stone paved road and temples. The view of Annapurna and Machhapuchhare from the town is excellent. Get off the bus at Dumre and climb two hours.

David Jarmail, USA

One of the longest suspension bridges in Nepal crosses the Trisuli from Mugling and follows the course of the Marsyangdi. The combination of these two rivers is known as the Gandak, one of the major tributaries of the Ganges. About an hour from Mugling the road passes Dumre, a new town settled after the construction of the highway. Just above it on a hilltop is the beautiful town of Bandipur. The capital of the principality of Gorkha, where the unification of Nepal began, is northeast of this area in the hills. The road then continues through Damauli — the district headquarters which has a good sized bazaar — across the Madi River by a big bridge and on to Khaireni, headquarters of an agricultural extension project being implemented with assistance from West Germany. Improved seed and fertilisers are being provided to many villages in the area from this project: the project buildings are visible from the bus. From there the road follows the River Seti through Sisuwa only 12 km from Pokhara and near the two smaller lakes of the valley. The road enters the town about halfway between the airport and the bazaar. At some points along the route, especially between Mugling and Pokhara, you can glimpse Himalchuli, Manaslu, the Annapurnas and other peaks during the autumn and winter.

Damauli, a small town on the road between Kathmandu and Pokhara, is worth a stopover. The town's main road leads to the Panchayat building. Taking the path to the left of it will take you down to the Madi and Seti

Rivers for bathing, go upstream a hundred or so yards on the right to reach a beach.

Mike Baldwin, USA

The land one sees along the route from Kathmandu to Pokhara is like a patchwork quilt — a composite of swathes of beauty from round the world. I saw rock gorge river scenes from Japanese brush paintings, hills akin to the south-west of the US as well as those from the highlands of Scotland, and the gracefully sculptured terraces, cousins to Java and Bali — consecutive changes in a day's drive.

Judy Benewitz, USA

ORIENTATION IN POKHARA

The main market or bazaar is located to the north of the bus stand while the lake area, where most visitors stay, is south. It is a long walk from the bus stop and taxis are reluctant to drive to the lake for less than Rs 10. On the other hand small taxis and minibuses shuttle between the bazaar and airport. The standard rate is Rs 1 by taxi, only 50 paisa by bus, from the airport to Mahendra Pool, located at the newer part at the beginning of the bazaar. The fare from the airport to Bagar at the far end of the bazaar is Rs 2. There are usually no buses after 5 pm. Recently the buses have started going as far as the lakeside (near the temple) and run almost every 15 minutes, so they are the most practical way of getting around in Pokhara.

Bazaar area Pokhara Bazaar consists of a two km long street, poorly planned and poorly laid out, entailing long walks to get from place to place. Most of the modern shops and the Post Office are located around Mahendra Pool. There are very few shops in the lake area. If you continue along the bazaar from Mahendra Pool and then turn left you reach Pokhara's only cinema. A further 20 minutes walk will take you to the quite modern Shining Mission Hospital which is run by western missionaries and open from 4 to 5 pm on Mondays to Fridays. The campus of Pokhara's only college is also in the vicinity, while in the bazaar itself is an art gallery with paintings by Nepalese artist Durga Baral.

Airport Two of the biggest hotels in Pokhara and the tourist information are all located in this area.

Lake area Perhaps the most touristy part of Nepal, the lake area only had one or two hotels and restaurants just a decade ago. There are now more than 15 hotels with charges ranging from Rs 5 a day to over Rs 250. During the October to April season you will see hundreds of visitors camping, swimming or just sunbathing around the lake.

If you walk from the airport to the lake you come across a cluster of government buildings including the offices of the Zonal Commissioner, highest authority in the region, and the Chief of Police and Immigration. Further on you pass several trees with platforms built around them. The trees are either Banyan or Peepal and were originally planted to provide rest and shade for walkers. It was believed that such deeds resulted in a good life after death. Sometimes two trees are planted together and there is supposed to be a marriage between them.

The dam at the lake was constructed with Indian assistance in the late sixties to provide electricity for Pokhara. Part of the dam collapsed in 1974 and for several months the town was without power, it was rebuilt in 1978. A cluster of budget hotels can be found near the dam. Further around the lake is the Royal Palace and more budget hotels.

The village here is known as Baidam and its inhabitants are mainly of the Chetri caste. Due to the heavy influence of tourism here even children speak

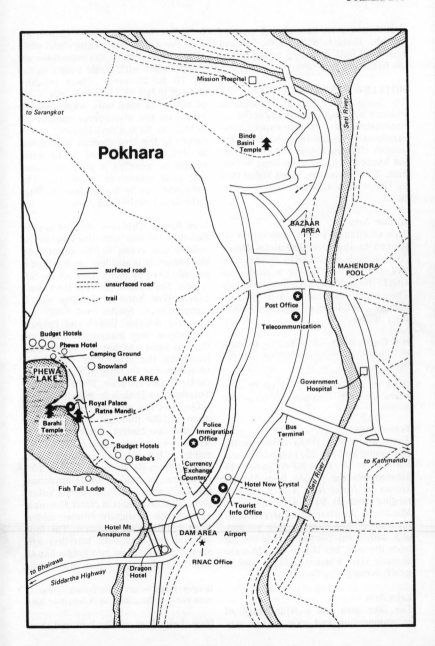

English and some have started smoking hashish. There is a new affluence and even mud huts are being rented out to the freak type travellers.

HOTELS & RESTAURANTS

The hotel and restaurant situation in Pokhara is changing much faster than in Kathmandu so you can expect some variations from the time this book was written. Hotels, lodges and restaurants are located in three main areas in Pokhara. Food prices are rather higher than in Kathmandu and the food is not as good.

Airport Area

Two of Pokhara's three large hotels are located in this area. The Hotel *Mount Annapurna* is decorated in Tibetan style and charges US$12 for a single and US$17 for a double including breakfast. The more expensive *Hotel Crystal* charges US$23 for a single and US$33 for a double.

New Crystal Hotel — 3* — tel 36 — 46 rooms all with bath — full air conditioned — restaurant — bar

Hotel Mt Annapurna — 2* — tel 37 — 32 rooms with bath — restaurant — bar — roof garden

Bazaar Area

There are several cheap hotels (in the price range Rs 15 to 25) in the Mahendra Pool area. A new hotel started by Tibetan-speaking people from Menang known as *Hotel New Asia* has rooms ranging from Rs 30 to 45 a day. *Hotel Mandar* in the same area charges Rs 25 for a single. The bazaar area is not popular with most people as it is too far from the lake, but if you want to make an early start when trekking it may be worth overnighting there.

Lake Area

The lake area has a wide range of accommodation and most visitors stay here. For the more affluent there is the *Fish Tail Lodge* and *Dragon Hotel* while at the other end of the scale there are many lodges with single rooms in the Rs 10 to 25 range. There are also cheaper lodges and private homes, some of them just mud huts, where the impecunious and adventurous can stay for as little as Rs 5 a day. However, many people in the area recently have taken to drugs and you need to be extra careful in selecting a place to ensure that your belongings remain safe. The Lake Area can be divided into the Main Lake Area and the Dam Area.

Dam Area — This area, situated next to the dam, is also near the lake but is quieter and closer to the airport and the bazaar. It is also less touristy and is actually liked by many travellers for this reason. *The Dragon Hotel* is the newest tourist class hotel in Pokhara and is recommended. Singles cost US$9 per day and doubles US$15. As Pokhara abounds in very inexpensive hotels on the one hand and has few tourist class hotels on the other, this hotel helps to reduce the shortage of rooms in the medium class category. The owner, Hari Tulachan, is a Thakali from Kali Gandaki Valley and can give interesting information on the Buddhist religion. There are also two budget hotels in the area which are recommended. *Hotel Garden* run by a Thakali family has single rooms ranging from Rs 20 to 40. It gives 10% reduction to holders of International Student Cards and Peace Corps Volunteers. Just next door is *Hotel Mountain View* which is slightly cheaper and is liked by those on a budget. The food is good here and most travellers who have stayed in these two lodges like to stay there when they return to Pokhara.

Dragon Hotel — air conditioned — bar — restaurant — 20 rooms with attached bath

Main Lake Area — The best and most

pleasant hotel in this area is *Fishtail Lodge* named after Machhapuchhare — the peak which dominates the skyline of Pokhara. To get to the lodge you have to cross the lake by raft. It costs US$19 for a single room and US$26 for a double.

Fishtail Lodge — thatched bungalows — restaurant — bar — 23 rooms with bath

From where the road branches down to the lakeside across from Fishtail Lodge, a cluster of low price hotels and restaurants starts and continues beyond the lake. Pokhara is way above Kathmandu when it comes to finding good places to eat on a small budget. Most travellers head for *Baba's Restaurant* which is run by Babar Singh, a Thakali, who worked for the British army for 18 years. His steak is supposed to be good. This restaurant is a family enterprise and is usually packed with budget tourists, who flock to try the tasty Tibetan and Chinese dishes. *Kantipur Restaurant* along the lake is also good.

There is another group of budget hotels between Baba's and the Snowland (near the temple on the lake), which includes *Hotel Lakeside, Phewa Lodge* and *New Traveller's Lodge*. The price for singles in these lodges ranges from Rs 15 to 30 depending on whether they contain attached bath or not. Doubles are slightly more expensive. *Hotel Snowland* has long been a popular place for budget travellers, and its owner, Kali, has just renovated and rebuilt the entire hotel. He is a good source of information on sightseeing in Pokhara. Just across the street is *Hotel Fewa* where single rooms without baths cost Rs 20, and with Rs 40. For those interested in camping there is an area reserved near the lake temple, often crowded with Kombis and Land Rovers belonging to overlanders.

In the past couple of years several new lodges have opened in the area beyond the Snowland, and some of them are good. Among them are *Fewa Beach Hotel* where singles cost Rs 20, and *Hotel Cosmos* which is slightly more expensive.

SEEING POKHARA

Although the Pokhara Valley does not have the many temples and man-made attractions of the Kathmandu Valley there is still much to see and do. Sightseeing here can be very inexpensive; some popular attractions include:

Phewa Lake The beautiful lake near Pokhara offers pleasant walking and even more pleasant boating. Small dug out canoes can be hired near the temple in the lake. These can be rented for about Rs 5 to 8 per hour.

Rupa and Begnas Lakes The two smaller and less visited lakes in the valley are about 15 km away to the east. They're pretty, unspoilt and wild. If you enjoy trekking the walk to these lakes makes a pleasant day's outing — take a bus to Danda Ko Nak about 12 km from Pokhara on the Kathmandu road. From here a two hour walk on the trail heading north will bring you to the village of Pachabhaiyya. A ridge separates the two lakes here and gives a good view of both.

Sarangkot Another pleasant day's walk will take you to the top of the hill overlooking Phewa Lake. From here you have an incredible view of the whole sweep of the Annapurna range to say nothing of the lake and Pokhara itself. It is possible to climb to Sarangkot in two hours from the lake, but the trail is not well defined. An easier route is to go to the temple of Bindebasani in the bazaar and take the trail from there to Sarangkot. The path back down to the lake is easy to find and the round trip should take four or five hours.

Kahun Danda Another good view of the mountains can be had from the ridge to the east of Pokhara Bazaar known as Kahun Danda. There is a view tower there and the walk from the bazaar takes about three hours.

River Seti The river which flows through Pokhara is interesting in that it often disappears underground. At some places the milky coloured water, due to the limestone in the soil, flows as much as 50 metres below the surface. Pokhara's often heavy rainfall does not lie on the ground but tends to be soaked up immediately. The bridge near the Mission Hospital at the end of the bazaar offers the best view of the Seti River.

Mahendra Gufa These limestone caves have been ransacked by souvenir hunters leaving little to see, but the walk there is very pleasant. The trail to the caves crosses the bridge at Bagar at the end of the bazaar and heads toward the village of Batulechaur. The walk to the caves takes about two hours. Batulechaur used to be well known for its oranges, but a virus epidemic destroyed all the trees in the valley and Pokhara, once renowned for excellent oranges and tangerines must now import them.

Tibetan Refugee Camp The refugee camp at the village of Hengja is about four hours' walk from the airport, a couple of hours shorter if you start out from Bagar at the end of the town. There are many handicrafts for sale and you can see how this colony of displaced persons has now become self-sufficient with the aid of Swiss training. There are smaller workshops near the lake. You can reach one by following the river downstream.

Buddhist Monastery To get to the monastery of the Tibetan speaking Manangis, cross the bridge from Mahendra Pool at the bazaar and walk for 30 minutes along the paved road before you reach a dirt road and see a monastery on the top of a small hill. The monastery is only a few decades old and contains a huge bronze image of Buddha and some colourful paintings on the walls. A visit to this monastery is recommended only if your stay in Pokhara is a long one and you would like to do something new.

Other If you are interested in butterflies, there is a good collection at PN College at the end of town.

Cultural Programme Every evening at *Hotel Dragon*, there is a cultural programme featuring Nepali dances, and costing Rs 20. It is cheaper here than in Kathmandu for a similar one-hour programme. The dancing takes place between 7 and 8.

GORKHA

Gorkha — the ancient capital of the principality of Gorkha that gave the feared Gurkha soldiers their name and from which King Prithvi Narayan Shah set out to unify all of Nepal — is approximately half-way between Pokhara and Kathmandu. Trekkers walking between the two towns on the more southerly route can pass through Gorkha or it can be reached on foot from the Pokhara-Kathmandu highway. The airstrip called Gorkha is actually a considerable walking distance from the town.

Direct buses from Kathmandu to Gorkha leave every day at 7 am and 9 am, take six hours, and cost Rs 23. It is also possible to travel to Gorkha from Pokhara, but it is necessary to take the Pokhara-Kathmandu bus up to Khaireni and change to another bus to Gorkha. *Hotel Gorkha Bisauni* costs Rs 40 for a double and Rs 8 for a bed in the dormitory.

There is not much to see in the historic town itself. To visit the old palace of King Prithvi Narayan Shah, the unifier of Nepal, you have to climb for about 40 minutes to the top of the ridge where his palace was situated. The temple of Gorkhanath with its legendary cave and that of Kali are also there and you will have a fine view of the surroundings including the Annapurna and Himalchuli ranges.

Two centuries ago, when Nepal consisted of many small kingdoms in the hills, the palaces were always constructed on hill tops. After your visit here you will realise the difficulties the ruler of such a small kingdom faced when setting out to defeat the Malla kings of the fertile Kathmandu Valley, and in starting the unification of a country more than a hundred times its size.

The Himalayas

THE MOUNTAINS

The main peaks in the Nepal Himalaya, from east to west, are:

Peak	Height	First Ascent
Kanchenjunga	8598 metres	1955 British
Makalu	8475 metres	1955 French
Lhotse	8501 metres	1955 Swiss
Everest	8848 metres	1953 British
Nuptse	7906 metres	1961 British
Cho Oyu	8153 metres	1954 Austrian
visible from Kathmandu		
Gauri Shankar	7145 metres	—
Phurbi Ghyachu	5722 metres	—
Dorje Lakpa	6975 metres	—
Langtang	7246 metres	1959 Japanese
Ganesh Himal	7406 metres	1955 Franco-Swiss
Himalchuli	7892 metres	1960 Japanese
Manaslu	7850 metres	1956 Japanese
visible from Pokhara		
Annapurna	8090 metres	1950 French
Annapurna 2	7937 metres	1960 British, Indo-Nepal
Annapurna 3	7502 metres	1961 Indian
Annapurna 4	7525 metres	1955 German
Machhapuchhare	7059 metres	—
Dhaulagiri	8137 metres	1960 Swiss

Nepal has the highest peak in the world — Mt Everest — and six others over 8000 metres, and it was mountain climbers attempting to conquer the 'top of the world' who were amongst the first 'tourists' to enter Nepal. Most of the major peaks were climbed in the fifties and sixties but Himalayan mountaineering has lost none of its appeal.

While trekking you are unlikely to go above 3500 metres unless you are walking to the Everest base camp, but breathtaking views are easily found. Mt Everest is not visible from the Kathmandu Valley, but from Nagarkot on top of the ridge to the eastern end of the valley you can pick it out in the distance. The view here extends from the extreme east of Nepal to Dhaulagiri in the west. Dhulikhel also provides a fine Himalayan panorama although Everest is not so clearly visible. Kakani, to the north-west of Kathmandu, provides a good view of the western Himalayas, particularly Ganesh Himal. A very fine view can be had from Daman on the road to the Indian border — a mountain profile to help you identify the peaks from Nagarkot or Daman can be obtained from the tourist information offices. If your stay in Kathmandu permits, visits to Sheopuri to the north and Phulchoki to the south are also worthwhile.

A number of peaks are clearly visible from Kathmandu particularly Ganesh Himal, its three peaks are seen slightly to the north-west. The lesser peaks of

Dorje Lakpa (6975 metres) and Chobha Bhamare (5970 metres) almost dominate the Kathmandu skyline. East of Ganesh Himal the snow-covered peak of Langtang can be seen partially hidden by closer mountains. East of Dorje Lakpa the massive block descending slowly to the east is Phurbi Ghyachu. Further to the east no major peaks are visible until the massive bulk of Gauri Shankar, which can only be seen from the north-east of the valley.

The view from Pokhara is much better than from Kathmandu, and a walk up to Sarangkot is worthwhile for the startling span of the Annapurnas with the perfectly symmetrical shape of Machhapuchhare standing before them. If you are trekking northwest, a trip to Pun Hill, just above Ghodepani, will provide an incredible sight. Machhapuchhare gets its unusual name, the 'fish tail' mountain, from its split apperance when viewed from the east — it is still a 'virgin', unclimbed, peak. In Nepali, Annapurna means 'full of grain' and this long series of ridges does indeed look like the result of a recent harvest.

On the Jomosom trek the view from Pun Hill (near Ghodepani) on a clear morning is the most beautiful sight I have seen anywhere in the world. If it is cloudy at Ghodepani it is worth waiting for as long as it takes to clear.

R McArthur, England

MOUNTAINEERING

The sport of mountaineering came into vogue in Europe during the Victorian era and once the major Alpine peaks had been conquered European mountaineers naturally turned their eyes to the greater challenge of the Himalayas. The natural difficulties in climbing these far higher mountains were compounded, during the 1920s and 1930s, by the continued seclusion of Nepal. Expeditions were chiefly launched from the Tibetan side of the range and, attempting the major prize first, were mainly on Everest.

In 1921, 1922 and 1924 a series of British attempts on the world's high-peak resulted in a maximum height attained at 8572 metres, just 300 metres short of the summit. This height was actually reached, in 1924, without the use of oxygen although the earlier 1922 expedition had used it to reach 8326 metres. Already the pattern for future expeditions with their large contingent of porters had been set — the 1924 expedition used 350.

In 1925 the British climbers Mallory, who coined the famous mountaineer's explanation 'because it's there', and Irvine disappeared in an attempt that may have actually reached the summit — their bodies were never found. A series of less successful attempts followed through the 1930s although several did succeed in climbing to beyond 8000 metres. A strange solo attempt in 1934 by Maurice Wilson added another name to those climbers who lost their lives on Everest.

After the war the greater affluence in the west, improved equipment, skills and oxygen apparatus together with the reopening of Nepal, led to a series of new assaults both on Everest and other peaks. In 1951 a reconnaissance expedition included amongst its numbers the New Zealand climber Edmund Hillary and a Swiss expedition in 1952 sent Sherpa climber Norgay Tensing to 7500 metres. Finally in 1953 John Hunt's British team succeeded in getting Tensing and Hillary to the highest spot on earth.

Once conquered, success on Everest followed repeatedly. A Swiss expedition reached the top in 1956 and in 1960 it was the turn of a party from the Peoples' Republic of China. Members of the massive American expedition in 1963, nearly a thousand climbers and porters, found the Chinese flag on top. An

Indian expedition reached the summit in 1965 and in 1970 a Japanese team not only reached the top but sent one fearless climber back down on skis! Several more attempts included a successful Italian team in 1973 and the International Women's Year victory of the Japanese women's party.

Other Himalayan peaks had also been comprehensively attacked in the fifties and sixties. The successful French expedition under Maurice Herzog on Annapurna in 1950 was probably the best known, for not only was this the first peak over 8000 metres to 'fall', but the mountain fought back, forcing the climbers to descend from the summit in appalling weather. Badly frostbitten, Herzog and his partner paid dearly for their challenge in fingers and toes. While the large expeditions successfully reached the top of one major peak after another, a new breed of up and coming climbers were cutting their teeth on Alpine and North American peaks. Eschewing the 'easy' ridge routes they went for the most difficult faces, attacking them with carefully developed skills and high technology, space age equipment. Chris Bonnington exemplified this trend with his 1970 climb on the south face of Annapurna and following this up with a skilfully orchestrated rush to the top of Everest by the 'impossible' south-west face in 1975.

Mountain climbing is now looked upon by the government of Nepal as a useful source of income as well as a generator of publicity. A royalty has to be paid for each attempt — the higher the peak the greater the fee. Detailed applications have to be made and at present Everest is fully 'booked' for years to come. Until recently only one expedition was allowed on any given peak in each season — the post-monsoon and pre-monsoon parts of the dry season. This rule has now been relaxed and more than one party can climb at once. The Chinese are also allowing attempts on Everest from their side of the border. The Nepalese Government has also started approving winter expeditions to Everest recently. Teams booked on Everest during the late 1980s include French, Japanese, British, French, Italian, Korean, Spanish, Yugoslavian, West German, American, Indian, Polish, New Zealand and French teams.

There are still many major peaks which have not been successfully climbed, some not even attempted. But some observers hope the next wave of activity may be a retreat from the massive, costly, high technology expeditions to a smaller, more manageable scale. Kathmandu's trekking shops have so much high quality equipment gleaned from the left-overs of major expeditions that a small party could be equipped right there. The 1978 Austrian expedition to Everest that put Reinhold Messner and Peter Habler on top without the use of oxygen may be a pointer in that direction.

Trekking

Trekking — hiking along the trails that form the main links between Nepal's isolated villages and settlements — is one of the country's main attractions. The word 'trekking' was almost unheard of in Nepal until the last decade, but many of today's visitors come to Nepal solely to trek.

WHY TREK?

A trek in Nepal is a unique and unforgettable experience for a whole range of reasons, but four in particular stand out:

Scenery Eight of the 10 highest mountains in the world are in Nepal and if you want to see them from close up you must walk. While trekking you'll see far more than mountains — you can walk from tropical lowlands to alpine meadows and glacial moraines, while in the spring Nepal's brilliant rhododendrons will be in bloom and you may see rare species of birds.

Safety Not only is the scenery interesting and ever changing but it can be seen in relative safety. Theft, robbery, assault — all the problems of western civilisation and many Asian countries — are relatively unknown in Nepal. There was a time a few years ago when even women could trek alone in Nepal. Unfortunately, things seem to be changing and trekkers need to be more careful than they used to be. It is advisable to trek in groups of at least two persons and if possible with a porter or guide. But this does not necessarily mean that you need to trek with an organised trekking agency in an expensive way.

Diversity Nepal is a country of contrasts and this extends to the people as well as the landscape. Trekkers pass through picturesque villages inhabited by Sherpas, Gurungs, Magars, Newars, Brahmins, Tamangs and the many other ethnic groups who co-exist in Nepal.

People Trekkers are always impressed by the friendliness of the people they meet along the local trails, which are in constant use and humming with activity. This is a totally different experience from hiking along the often uninhabited trails in the US Rockies, European Alps or Australian bushland. Above all, no household in a village would turn away a weary traveller arriving late in the evening — there are frequent possibilities of staying in Nepali homes.

ON THE TRAIL

A trek can last half a day or for over a month. A short walk up to Nagarkot to see the sunrise only takes about three hours while the walk to the Everest Base Camp will take at least three weeks. Make sure you enjoy walking before setting out on a long trek!

Height Trekking is not mountaineering but it is as well to remember that the Himalayas begin where other mountains finish. An average trek oscillates between 1000 metres and 3000 metres but the trek to the Everest Base Camp will reach 5545 metres. Most of the time you will remain within the altitude range 1500 metres to 2000 metres. It is important to remember that 4000 metres in Nepal is not the same as in Europe or North America as the country is much closer to the equator.

A Day on the Trail Trekking usually consists of a series of ascents or descents, walking five or six hours in the day. To ensure good acclimatisation at high altitudes it is wise to halt for the night at a lower level than the high point reached during the day. A long mid-

POPULAR TREKS

Trek	Location	Time	From — To
Everest	to Solu Khumbu region of east Nepal	1 to 5 weeks	Bus to Lamosangu or fly to Lukla then walk to the base camp
Langtang	North of Kathmandu	12 days	Bus to Trisuli then walk to the Langtang Valley
Helambu	North of Kathmandu	7 days	Bus to Panchka or go via Sundarijal
Kathmandu-Sheopuri	Highest point on the hill north of Kathmandu	8 hours	Walk from Budhanilkantha and return via Sundarijal
Kathmandu-Nagarkot	Hilltop north-east of Kathmandu	3 hours up	Bus to Bhaktapur then walk
Dhulikhel-Namobuddha	East of Kathmandu Valley	One day	Bus to Dhulikhel then walk
Annapurna Sanctuary	North of Pokhara	12 days	Walk from Pokhara via Naudanda, Birethanti and Ghandruk
Ghandruk-Ghodepani	North of Pokhara	7 days	Walk from Pokhara to Ghandruk
Pokhara-Jomosom-Muktinah	North-west of Pokhara	12 days	Routes via Birethanti or via Kusma and Beni
Manang	North-east of Pokhara	2 weeks	Dumre to Manang
Pokhara-Sarangkot	North of Pokhara	One day	Walk from Bindebasini temple in Pokhara bazar

Maximum Height	Interesting Sights	Comments
Tyangboche — 3875 metres, Kala Patar — 5545 metres	Walk through interesting Sherpa villages to stunning views of Everest, Ama Dablam, Nuptse, Lhotse	very touristy from Lukla on
4200 metres	Pass through ethnically Tibetan villages like Tamang, en route to the glacier at the foot of Langtang peak	stay in lodges along trail
Tarkeghyang — 2800 metres	Friendly people and chances to stay in Sherpa homes but poor views of the peaks	—
2700 metres	Walk through forests with excellent mountain views, can overnight in a tent	—
2000 metres	Good scenery including Everest, can overnight in a lodge	—
1700 metres	Pleasant one-day walk along a typical trail to an old stupa marking a legendary spot	—
3725 metres	Pass through Gurung villages en route to the foot of Annapurna, excellent views	2 days through uninhabited areas
2700 metres	Excellent views of Annapurna and Machhapuchhare en route to village of Ghandruk	Need guide from Ghandruk to Ghodepani
2700 metres	Most interesting trek in Nepal, cross the Himalayan range between Annapurna and Dhaulagiri	—
3600 metres	Valley north of Annapurna Range inhabited by Tibetan speaking people known as Manangis	Only open since 1976, can reach Muktinah by 5600 m pass
1700 metres	Excellent views of Annapurna and the Pokhara Valley, see ruins of a 17th century fort	—

day meal stop is usually made and the night can be spent in a village tea shop or in camp — depending on whether you are on your own or with an organised trekking company.

When to Trek The best trekking season is in October and November just after the monsoon — visibility will be clear and the weather mild. March is the next best season and has the added bonus of the rhododendrons and other flowers. Trekking can be done and enjoyed in December, January and February but it can get very cold — particularly at night. April and May are good months for doing high altitude treks, but trekking is not possible between June and September when the monsoon rains make the trails extremely slippery and the leeches come out to make walking miserable. Some people do trek in early June and late September.

Where to Stay If you are trekking independently you stay either in tea houses or in private homes in villages. If you are with an organised trekking group everything is taken care of and you will sleep mainly in tents set up by the porters. Some tea stalls and homes have started making a small charge, Rs 1 to 5, for an overnight stay but usually accommodation is free, providing you take the evening meal there. If you go by yourself to an uninhabited area you may have to sleep in a cave or an abandoned building.

PRELIMINARIES

Trekking Permits Every trekker must carry a trekking permit when away from the areas permitted in the visa. No trekking permits are, however, needed for walking in the Kathmandu or Pokhara Valley or along short treks such as Dhulikhel and Namobuddha. Trekking permits are issued for one destination at a time along proscribed routes. They cost Rs 60 per week initially and Rs 75 per week for the second month. The permits can be obtained in Kathmandu and in Pokhara.

Equipment If you do not already have good equipment it can be bought or rented from one of the trekking shops. The equipment is often top quality but although daily rental charges are reasonable a large deposit may be required — a good down-filled sleeping bag, a rucksack, down pants and down jacket can each be rented for around Rs 5 per day, but the total deposit can easily come to over US$100. It is advisable to have your own strong, comfortable boots — they can be rented but people with large feet may have trouble finding suitable footwear. If a rented sleeping bag does not look perfectly clean have it dry cleaned. *Himal Hiking Home* in Yetkha, one block from Durbar Square and *Annapurna Mountaineering & Trekking* in Thamel have a wide range of gear. You can also find items in Freak Street and equipment can be rented in Pokhara too.

Incidentals The food available along the trail is normally limited in its variety so bring along some cheese, dried fruit and canned food. It will be almost impossible to change money along the way so carry adequate Nepali currency in small denominations. Take cigarettes and matches, they're widely appreciated small gifts. Please don't spoil the children who in some regions come up asking for 'one rupee'. A torch (flashlight) is indispensable for late night trips to the outhouse and matches or salt for getting rid of leeches if you trek in the wet.

Health Medical care along the trail is almost non-existent except for the Edmund Hillary hospital at Khumjung in the Solu Khumbu, so make sure that you are fit and healthy before departing. A rescue helicopter is extremely expensive! Take care of yourself along the trail by ensuring that water is boiled — remember that fresh tea is always safe. Diarrhoea can be the curse of trekkers so bring appropriate medication. At high altitudes almost everyone suffers from headaches so aspirin is advisable as are sleeping tablets to ensure a good sleep. Sunburn can also be a problem at altitude, a barrier cream will protect your skin and good sunglasses are necessary for your eyes. Blisters are another problem for the trekker and adequate supplies of band aids and moleskin are advisable.

The most serious health problem the unwary trekker can fall prey to is the dreaded mountain sickness — this is a major, even deadly, danger for the careless or foolhardy trekker. Mountain sickness is a form of pulmonary oedema and usually hits young and healthy people who do not heed the warnings and go 'too high, too fast'. Prevention is simple — take things easy and ensure plenty of acclimatisation. The first signs often show themselves at night and this is why it is best to sleep at a lower altitude than the maximum reached during the day. The mild symptoms are low urine output, bad headaches, sleeplessness and loss of appetite, followed in extreme cases by nausea, vomiting, severe fatigue, mental confusion, breathlessness and apathy. If 'you get mountain sickness there's just one answer — get down to a lower altitude as quickly and with as little effort as possible.

Maps The series of *Mandala* trekking maps are readily available in shops in Kathmandu. They include Kathmandu to Pokhara, Pokhara to Jomosom, Jomosom to Jumla and Surkhet, Lamosangu to Mt Everest and Helambu-Langtang. All have a useful glossary of Nepali words and walking times along the trails.

ARRANGEMENTS
Independent Trekking   Most of the

young people visiting Nepal trek independently. While the organised treks have all arrangements made by the trekking agency, including porters and food, independent travellers carry their own lugguage (or just hire a porter), spend overnight at tea stalls, lodges and sometimes private homes along the way and eat local food. Although not much English is spoken in the villages along most of the trekking routes, it is becoming more easily understood. There are more than 30 trekking agencies in Nepal. The larger and better established of them are more interested in bigger groups. Smaller agencies are more interested in independent trekkers. There are actually two trekking agencies that specialise in low cost trekking. *Sherpa Trekking Services*, Kamaladi (tel 12489) will help you organise your trek at a minimum cost. It can also arrange the services of an English-speaking guide or rent trekking equipment. If you are interested in joining an organised group with this agency it will cost you less than US$20 a day. If you just want to hire guides, it can provide them at about Rs 60 a day.

Himalayan Nature Treks (tel 21185), also specialises in arranging treks for students and academics. Its office is in Durbar Marg. It also offers special discounts to students. During the off-season, it can organise guides (for about Rs 50 per day plus food) or porters (Rs 50 per day). In 1983, Himalayan Nature Treks plans to organise treks for as little as US$14 a day.

Independent trekking is much easier with the services of a porter who can be hired for Rs 18 to Rs 30 per day. This aid to easy trekking is particularly invaluable at high altitudes where just getting up the ascents will be quite sufficient for most people. When agreeing a price with a porter make sure whether or not you are paying for the porter's meals. In the hills, porters can easily be found at most villages or at the airfields where there will usually be a few who have just despatched a group back to Kathmandu. Porters do not often speak English but will help you find overnight accommodation as well as carry the load and act as a guide. The most popular area for independent trekkers is around Pokhara, possibly because it is comparatively easy to find food and lodging there.

hill country ambulance service

Organised Trekking Several trekking companies in Nepal will arrange sleeping bags, porters, tents, food and also experienced English speaking Sherpa guides. All you need to carry is your own clothes and camera. Trek charges vary from US$17 to US$80 per day depending on the number of people in the group and the duration of the trek. Probably the best known trekking organisation in Nepal is *Mountain Travel* (PO Box 170, tel 12808) whose well-known manager, Col J O M Roberts, has organised many mountaineering expeditions. Its American office is Mountain Travel, 1398 Folano Ave, Albany, California 94706. In England Mountain Travel treks can be booked through Thomas Cook, 45 Berkeley St, London. Treks cost between US$30 and US$40 per day.

Annapurna Mountaineering & Trekking on Durbar Marg (PO Box 795, tel 12736) is also well known and charges

between US$20 and US$24 per day. *Himalayan Journeys* on Kanti Path (PO Box 989, tel 15855) is also popular and its American manager is the author of *Trekking in the Himalayas. Sherpa Co-operatives* (tel 15887) likes to call itself a 'quality oriented organisation' and charges US$24 to US$30 per day in groups which normally number 12 to 15. It also gives a 10% off-season discount. *Himalayan Trekking* on Ramshah Path (PO Box 391, tel 11808) charges US$18 to US$25 per day and has a Sherpa who has conquered Everest.

Ausventure is a very well known and respected name for organising treks from Australia. Its address is PO Box 54, Mosman, NSW 2088. *Australian Himalayan Expeditions*, 28-34 O'Connel St, Sydney, NSW 2000 also brings a large number of Australians to Nepal. Many British trekkers organise their treks through *Sherpa Expeditions*, 3 Bedford Rd, London W4.

All the organised trekking companies require plenty of notice to fix up a trek. Try to allow at least two months.

The Yeti

No description of Nepal can be complete without a mention of the famous yeti — the abominable snowman. This mysterious, ape-like creature lives high in the remotest regions of the Himalayas and has been talked and written about; feared by hill people; searched for by westerners; 'seen' by countless people — but never photographed. Footprints in the snow are the only trace the shy yeti likes to leave, but these are often thought to be normal size human prints that have grown as the sun melted the snow around them. Similarly the yeti scalps in the Solu Khumbu region, in particularly the one at the Pangboche monastery, have all turned out to be fakes. Despite the scientific reluctance to accept the yeti's existence everyone would like to believe in it — so keep your camera handy when trekking!

ROYAL NEPAL AIRLINES

yeti SERVICE

TREKS

There are countless different routes and treks around Nepal. The following are just a few of the most popular 'standard' routes.

EVEREST TREK

The trek to the base camp at the foot of Mt Everest takes three weeks at a minimum. This is not as easy as trekking in the Pokhara area as the trail traverses regions which have remained relatively backward and closed to outside influences. The Sherpa country in the vicinity of Everest is an exception, of course, since there have been so many mountaineering expeditions in this area in the past 25 years.

The usual starting point for the trek is Lamosangu on the road to the Chinese border but if time is limited the trek can be shortened by flying between Kathmandu and Lukla, only a few days walk from the base camp. If you only intend to fly one way it is best to go back from Lukla as this gives greater acclimatisation to the altitude. If you fly directly from Kathmandu at 1300 metres to Lukla at 2800 metres, and then start climbing to the base camp at 5340 metres, great care must be taken to acclimatise yourself sufficiently. Flights to Lukla are now on a regular basis, but at the height of the trekking season, although departures are frequent, cloudy weather can easily shut the hill country STOL fields for several days at a time. Per person cost is about US$55.

The Everest trek is relatively rough as you have many ascents and descents to make. Between Lamosangu and Surkya near Lukla the trail repeatedly climbs over mountain passes as high as 3500 metres and then descends to valleys, as low as 1000 metres, while crossing the rivers that run from the north. There are occasional bazaars and market places along the way. From Surkya at 2343 metres to Namche Bazaar, 3440 metres, and then to the base camp it is an almost continuous ascent. It has been estimated that the trek from Lamosangu to the base camp — taking into account the total number of ascents and descents — approaches twice the height of Everest!

On the way you pass through villages inhabited by Tamangs, Sunuwars, Rais and, finally, Sherpas plus some Brahmin-Chetri villages and occasional Newari ones, mainly the bazaars. In other words you walk from the Nepali speaking, Hindu lowlands to the mongoloid, Tibetan-Buddhist highlands with many opportunities to observe Nepal's rich ethnic mixture. The most interesting area to visit in the Everest trek is the Sherpa country after you reach Changma or Junibesi walking from Lamosangu, or Lukla if you fly in from Kathmandu. According to the findings of a well-known British anthropologist, no other Tibetan speaking people in Nepal can be compared to the Sherpas 'in the high standard of living, spirit of enterprise, sense of civic responsibility, social polish and general devotion to the practice of Buddhism'. Actually, the 'Sherpa Country' is also the safest area in Nepal to trek. Unlike other trails where thefts are beginning to appear, this does not seem to have become a problem here. A portion of the road from Lamosangu to Jiri has now been completed and it is possible to start the trek in Jiri.

The main crop of the Khumbu region is potato. Although the economy of Sherpa villages used to depend solely on potato cultivation — itself a recent introduction — tourism is becoming increasingly important. New Zealand is helping Nepal in setting up the Everest National Park. The park will be located in the catchment area of the Dudh Kosi and Imja Rivers. Under the project, attempts will be made to conserve forest, landscape and wildlife in the area, provide facilities for visitors and raise the standard of living of the local people.

Day 1: Kathmandu-Lamosangu-Pakhar (four hour walking)

Buses leave Kathmandu at 6 am, 10 am and 2 pm on the three to four hour trip to Lamosangu. In Nepali Lamosangu means 'long bridge'. The town is situated on the banks of the Sun Kosi river and is the site for a Chinese-aided 10,000 Kw hydroelectric power plant.

The first part of the trek involves a steep eight-hour ascent from Lamosangu at 770 metres to Muldi at 2345 metres but you can stop at Pakhar, four hours from Lamosangu.

Day 2: Pakhar-Busti (eight hours walking)

From Pakhar you continue to ascend for five hours to Muldi, then commence to descend to Surkhe (1750 metres) and finally Shera at 1448 metres. For a short distance from Shera you walk through pine forests before reaching Kiratichap (1320 metres) then descend to the Bhote Kosi River.

Day 3: Busti-Jiri (eight hours walking)

A steep climb brings you to the village of Kavre and Namdu and to the Chisapani Pass from where you have a good view of the eastern Himalayas and, in particular, Gauri Shankar which lies immediately to the north. An overnight stay in the beautiful 1860 metre high valley of Jiri is worthwhile; the valley was developed with Swiss assistance in the 1960s and has a STOL field and hospital. It costs Rs 270 if you were to fly from Kathmandu directly to Jiri and start your trek from there. The guest house here costs only Rs 2 per night and has private rooms and running water, very pleasant after three days walking. The weekly market, or 'hat', is held on Saturdays and is well worth seeing.

On the Everest trek it is a good idea to rest for a day or two at the Government Agricultural Centre at Jiri, which is about three days trek from Lamosangu. Tourists can stay in modern stone bungalows (two beds to each room for Rs 2 per bed per night) and eat at the staff canteen where the food is superb. You can also buy fresh milk, bread and cake — the only place between Kathmandu and Everest. This is a comparative oasis in the wilderness.

John Anderson, England

Day 4

It is worthwhile taking a day's rest in either Jiri or Thodung.

Day 5: Jiri-Thodung (eight hours walking)

The fair-sized Newar town of Those is only a few hours walk from Jiri. It used to be famous for the extraction of iron ore and the manufacture of khukris. This is a good place to buy supplies and in spring, summer or autumn a trip to the Thodung cheese factory is a must. Thodung at 3091 metres is only two hours from the main trail and you can buy yak cheese and other luxuries. On the way you pass through Changma (2040 metres), the first of many Sherpa villages with typical mani walls.

Do not miss stopping at the Thodung Cheese Factory for great cheese omelettes, fine hospitality and a cup of coffee that is out of this world. It is only an hour away from the main trail.

Robert Hanchett, USA

Day 6: Thodung-Sete (six hours walking)

A 500 metre descent brings you to the Likhu Khola River followed by a 2000 metre ascent to the Lamjura Pass at 3530 metres. That would be too much for one day so it is best to stop at the village of Sete (3575 metres), still a thousand metre climb from the river.

Day 7: Sete-Junibesi (six hours walking)

The Lamjura Pass will reward you with rhododendron flowers in spring and snow in the winter. From the top it is a thousand metre descent to the village of Junibesi at 2675 metres. It is very popular with most visitors and there is a beautiful monastery, supposed to be the oldest in the Solu Khumbu area, just an hour away from the main trail. A good view of Numbur peak can be seen from the village.

Day 8: Junibesi-Manidingma (six hours walking)

A 700-metre ascent takes you to the Salung Ridge, then a 500-metre descent follows to the Solu Khola River. The beautiful village of Ringmo, with apple orchards, is just three hours from Junibesi and is followed by another climb to the Taksindu Pass at 3200 metres. There is a monastery with a guest house and cheese factory nearby and the view from the pass includes the mountains and the Dudh Kosi River. A descent follows to the village of Manidingma at 2316 metres.

Day 9 & 10: Manidingma-Kharekhola-Kharte

The Dudh Kosi River is an 800 metre descent from Manidingma. The river carries water melted from Everest itself. It is a climb once more up to the village of Kharekhola (2073 metres) and then the village of Puiyan (2835 metres). Lukla, with its STOL field, is slightly off the main trail and higher up. It is situated on a 'terrace' at an altitude of 3000 metres. It also contains a modern Sherpa hotel where singles cost US$10 and up, while a more reasonably priced STS charges Rs 5 in the dormitory.

Day 11: Lukla-Ghat-Namche Bazaar (eight hours walking)

From this point it is almost all up into the Sherpa country. You descend to the Dudh Kosi River and follow it, crossing it twice up to Jorsale. Before Jorsale there is a pleasant hotel at Manjo, site of a vegetable farm for the Everest View Hotel. You can get a good quality green salad at this place! Namche, at 3440 metres, is the 'Sherpa capital', and the best known of the Sherpa villages because of the many Sherpas from around here who go on mountaineering expeditions. It is also the centre of the handicrafts industry and the place where trekking permits may be checked. Saturday is the market day in Namche. The village of Kunde near Namche has a hospital built with New Zealand aid. A mica plant is being set up in Namche with Austrian assistance. A good place to stay here is the

International Footrest. The expensive Everest View Hotel is higher up the hill.

Hotel Everest View — Kathmandu office tel 13854 — 12 rooms, all with bath & view of Mt Everest — restaurant — bar — electricity — oxygen if needed — yak hire — solar heating — singles US$86, doubles US$156 — STOL flight from Kathmandu US$120 — open from October to May

Day 12. Namche-Tyangboche (five hours walking)

The Syangboche STOL field is a short climb above Namche. Slightly higher than this is the Everest View Hotel which may be expensive but then not only does every room have a view of Everest, but you can also see it from your bathtub! From here the trail descends to meet the main Namche-Tyangboche trail and continues down to the Dudh Kosi where there is a small tea shop and a series of picturesque water-driven prayer wheels. A steep ascent brings you to the famous monastery of Tyangboche (3875 metres). The monastery is totally surrounded by mountain peaks and offers a fine view of Everest and Ama Dablam. In the full moon night of the month of November the colourful Mani Rimdu festival is held here with much singing and dancing.

The most scenic part of the Everest trek is between Tyangboche and Pangboche and it is at this altitude where the good points of trekking can really be appreciated.

Phil Martin, England

Day 13 & 14: Tyangboche-Pheriche-Lobuche

Beyond Tyangboche it is important to ensure that you are in good physical shape. A descent and ascent takes you to Pangboche where the monastery has a 'yeti scalp'. Pheriche is the last Sherpa village and has a first aid post, where there is usually a doctor. It also offers an excellent view of Everest. There are tea shops at Lobuche (4930 metres) but little shelter is available beyond this point and unless you are on an organised trek with tents it is best to use Lobuche as a base and make day treks from here. Kala Pathar (5545 metres) offers the best view of Everest obtainable anywhere. The mountain is not actually visible from the base camp (5340 metres) but it's still worth visiting, as is the lake at Gorak Shep (5160 metres).

Important Note The number of days given here are the minimum number of walking days. It is important to be adequately rested and acclimatised, and a day's rest at Namche and Tyangboche is particularly advisable. Remember that the victims of altitude sickness are often the fittest and healthiest people who foolishly over-extend themselves.

If you have walked all the way from Lamosangu you may like to consider extending the trek by walking south to Katari in the Terai, via Salleri, a four-day walk. It is especially pleasant in the winter and is still not frequented by many western trekkers. From Katari you can take a bus to Kathmandu or to Darjeeling via the East-West Highway.

Sherpa

HELAMBU TREK
If your time is limited and you cannot go far from the Kathmandu Valley the Helambu trek takes you to a Sherpa area where you can see how these fine Buddhist people differ from their lowland neighbours. The trek lasts a week or 10 days and does not go above 3000 metres.

The two main villages of Helambu, Tarkeghyang and Sermathan, are situated at 2800 metres and 2600 metres respectively so you are not in really high country. It is possible to climb higher to the Gosainkund lake (4290 metres) or go to the Langtang Valley through the Ganja La Pass (5106 metres), but this high altitude pass is only feasible between May and September. Spectacular views of the Himalayan peaks are only to be found if you go higher on this trek. But as compensation the people are friendly and hospitable and almost every Sherpa house in the region will be quickly converted to a 'hotel' to welcome tourists as 'paying guests'.

During the Rana period the Helambu region was well known for its beautiful Sherpa girls many of whom worked for aristocratic Rana families in Kathmandu. The area has, therefore, been open to outside influence for a long time and almost everybody understands Nepali. Recently many people have gone to work on road construction in north-east India but almost all of them come back during February-March. In the summer most of the people left in the villages are either very young or very old.

In the Tibetan language the word for Helambu means both radish and potato, and the area is heavily dependent economically on both these products. Rice and wheat cannot be grown at this altitude. Large quantities of radishes and potatoes are exported to the lowlands in exchange for rice and other commodities. Apples are also grown in the Helambu area.

Helambu is a region, not a specific village. There are two ways to get to Helambu from Kathmandu and it is probably best to go one way and return the other. From Panchkal on the road to the Chinese border you can follow the Melemchi River to Tarkeghyang, the most important village in the region. This route also involves only two days of uphill walking whereas the alternate route from Sundarijal requires an ascent followed by two days of descent, before more uphill work. The Sundarijal route offers a good view of the mountains from Patibhanjyang, and both routes meet in the village of Taran Maran before the steepest ascent. Sundarijal,

at the northern end of the Kathmandu Valley, can be reached by taxi or you can bus to Bodhnath and walk there in three hours.

Trek to Helambu to see Sherpa houses, wood carved cabinets and fantastic brass and copper pots. The people will serve you rice, dal and Sherpa tea consisting of tea, ghee and salt.

Ludi Grothelaw, Australia

Day 1: Panchkal-Bahunpati (seven hours walking)

An early start from Kathmandu is essential to reach Bahunpati on the first day. The 6 am bus will get you to Panchkal by 9 am. The trail follows the Indrawati River and involves no steep ascents or descents. Bahunpati is a small bazaar and has some government offices and a recently constructed tourist bungalow.

Day 2: Bahunpati-Taran Maran (four hours walking)

You continue to follow the Indrawati River to the village of Melemchi (820 metres) from where the trail follows the Melemchi River to Taran Maran at 1204 metres. The Sundarijal Trail joins this one here. There are also a number of places to stay here, and the short walk allows plenty of rest before the steep climb the next day.

Day 3: Taran Maran-Tarkeghyang

If you are a good walker you may be able to reach Tarkeghyang the same evening you start from Taran Maran. As

Pokhara

A | a Rural home near Pokhara
B | b Machhapuchhare from the Bindebasini Temple in Pokhara

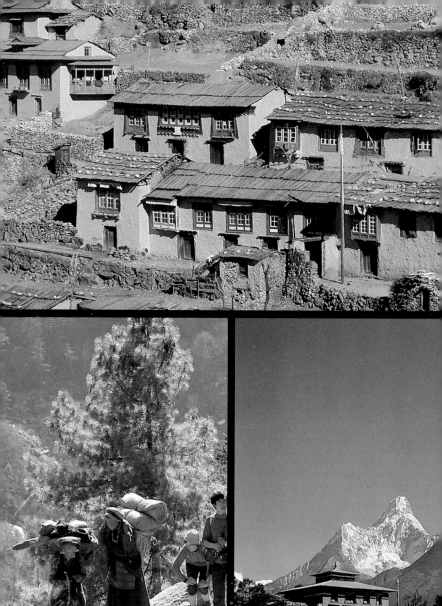

it is a climb of almost 1800 metres to the village you may not make it and may have to stop in Kiul at 1500 metres, Thimpu at 1680 metres, or Kakani at 1850 metres.

The trek to Helambu offers altern-ative routes of three to four days and friendly homes for overnight stays along most of the way. Individual farms and homes are preferable especially in Tarkeghyang which has a landing pad for helicopter tourists and a noticeably higher standard of living.

Ron Bitzer, USA

Day 4: Tarkeghyang-Sermathan (four hours walking)

A French student once told me that Tarkeghyang resembled a village in the alps. You'll reach it on the fourth day if not before. There is a festival in the village on the full moon in March with a feast in the evening and a masked dance, which goes on till midnight. The ceremony takes place in a new monas-tery. The houses are clustered together in Tarkeghyang in contrast to the next village of Sermathan, only three to four hours' walk away with no steep ascents or descents. Sermathan is at an altitude of 2600 metres and the trail runs through a beautiful forest. Less commercialised than Tarkeghyang, Ser-mathan is also an important apple growing area and has a government horticulture farm. Although the mount-ains visible are not particularly notable the view is scenic and the beautiful natural setting also gives a good view of the valley of the Melemchi River to the south.

Day 5: Sermathan-Taran Maran

On your way back you can reach Taran Maran in one day or if you are in a hurry go back via Bahunpati on the road to the Chinese border. Alternatively you can enjoy good scenery by return-ing via the picturesque village of Pati-bhanjyang (2200 metres). Follow the Taran Maran Khola which flows from the west, then make a steep thousand metre climb to the village. The trail then descends through the village of Mulkharka and passes through beautiful forests with good views of the mountain range before reaching Sundarijal.

LANGTANG TREK

The peak of Langtang can be seen to the north of Kathmandu on a clear day. In the course of the trek, which takes two weeks, you go to a pleasant valley at the foot of the peak where the glacier ends and the base camp is located. On the way to Langtang you get a good view of Ganesh Himal between Betrawati and Dhunche.

The trek starts from Trisuli Bazaar, a short bus ride from Kathmandu, and for

The Himalayas

a   Namche Bazar in the Solu Kumbhu
b   On the trail from Namche to Tyangboche
c   Tyangeboche Monastery and Ama Dablam

the most part follows the Trisuli River and the Langtang Khola. It passes through Tamang and Tibetan villages like Ramche, Dhunche and Langtang, and finally reaches the cheese factory at 3871 metres set up with Swiss and New Zealand aid.

In comparison to other treks this one passes through relatively undeveloped areas despite the proximity to Kathmandu. This is a more backward region than Pokhara where employment abroad has made some difference. Many Tamangs from this area still serve as porters around the Kathmandu Valley.

An interesting addition to the Langtang trek — if you are physically fit and the weather is warm enough — is a visit to the high altitude lake of Gosainkund at 4313 metres. A different route must be taken from Dhunche and on the way back you can visit Helambu and enter the valley at Sundarijal. The big annual pilgrimage to Gosainkund at the August full moon is unfortunately a bad time for trekking — the middle of the monsoon when the leeches will be out in force.

Most of the Trisuli River's water comes from the Bhote Kosi River across the main Himalayan range in Tibet. It may be advisable to bring some food along on this trek as the Nepalese food obtainable can get very monotonous.

Day 1: Trisuli-Betrawati-Manegaon (six hours walking)

Buses run to Trisuli Bazaar (541 metres) which is 72 km from Kathmandu. Trisuli is the administrative headquarters of a small district and has a 21,000 kw hydroelectric power plant which was built with Indian aid and supplies a large part of Kathmandu's power supply. The climb from Trisuli is quite gradual until you reach Betrawati (641 metres) where a steep climb starts to Manegaon (1196 metres).

Day 2: Manegaon-Ramche-Bokejhundra (five hours walking)

The steep climb continues to Ramche at 1791 metres after which there are no steep ascents or descents as you pass through Grang (1890 metres) and Thade (1989 metres) before reaching Bokejhundra at 1890 metres.

Day 3: Bokejhundra-Dhunche-Syabrubensi (six hours walking)

The trail goes through dense jungle from Bokejhundra before reaching Dhunche (1966 metres) which is the headquarters of the district. The route then descends to Syabrubensi at 1463 metres.

Day 4: Syabrubensi-Sharpu (six hours walking)

The six-hour walk from Syabrubensi brings you to the village of Sharpu (2590 metres) which is the first village in the Langtang valley.

Day 5: Sharpu-Ghoratabla (Langtang) (five hours walking)

Many people prefer not to stay in the village of Langtang but continue to Ghoratabla where there is a lodge and you might even find steak and french fries! The climb from Sharpu to Ghoratabla is very steep and difficult.

The Langtang trek offers the greatest diversity with the least effort of any trek in Nepal. From 700 metres at Trisuli Bazaar to 3000 metres at Kanchen Gompa, the trail climbs steadily through everchanging climates and cultural areas. For those who wish to see as much variety of Nepalese countryside and people as possible in a short time, this trek is a must.

Ted Lowe, USA

POKHARA TREKS

The area around Pokhara offers the best opportunities for independent trekking in Nepal, primarily because finding food and a place for an overnight stay is comparatively easy. The Thakali people from the Thak Khola area of the Mustang District have set up many bhattis along the trails. Provided you take your meals there you can usually stay in them for free. These places are quite clean and the food is well prepared although slightly expensive by Nepali standards. In some villages along the trail you can even get pies and bottled beer — due to the influx of tourists in the area. Thakali women are quite liberated and you will find inns run by women whose brothers or husbands have gone to different towns in the course of business.

There are treks lasting from three to 15 days from Pokhara. Some of the most popular include:

Pokhara-Ghandruk This eight-day trek takes you to the beautiful Gurung village of Ghandruk and affords spectacular views of the Annapurnas and Machhapuchhare. A guide is required if you continue on through the forest to Ghodepani; the view from the top of Pun Hill is one of the most fantastic in Nepal. It is possible to reach Ghandruk via Chandrakot on the Jomosom trek and return via Landruk, Dhampus and Hengja. Ghandruk is at an altitude of 2000 metres and is spread out over the whole ridge. It is one of the most famous Gurung villages in Nepal. Many Gurkha soldiers are employed in the British and Indian armies from this village.

Himalayan Lodge, in the upper part of the village, is run by an ex-British Army Gurkha soldier and it's a good place to stay.

Pokhara-Annapurna Sanctuary This 12-day trek continues from Ghandruk to the Annapurna base camp. You must carry some food as it is not available beyond Chomrung and you may even have to overnight in a cave.

Pokhara-Ghachok Lasting only three days this trek reaches 2800 metres and offers beautiful scenery and interesting Gurung villages to those with limited time.

Pokhara-Jomosom-Muktinath This 15-day trek is the best known in the area and some other shorter treks form part of it. It's the 'best' trek in Nepal for many reasons. The trekker passes from the paddy fields and forests of the southern hill region right through to the arid desert-like landscape of the Tibetan plateau. The trek crosses right over the Himalayas, although it remains well within Nepalese territory. Between Dhaulagiri at 8137 metres and Annapurna at 8090 metres the Kali Gandaki River carves the deepest gorge in the world; it's crossed at an altitude of 2800 metres. You will see a wide variety of ethnic groups in the many villages you pass through. The trail is surprisingly good, despite the rugged terrain, as it was once a main trade artery linking central Nepal with Tibet.

The first four days of the trek, which goes from 819 metres to 2713 metres, is the same for some of the other Pokhara area treks. From Pokhara you head directly north, crossing a pass at 2835 metres then descend to the hot springs at Tatopani (1190 metres). You then follow the course of the Kali Gandaki River, gradually ascending to Jomosom at 2713 metres. Alternatively you can travel south to Naudanda on the road to the Indian border and follow the course of the Andhi River, cross the minor pass at Karkineta (1600 metres) and pass through Kusma and Baglung before following the Kali Gandaki. Although most trekkers take the first route up and back it is better to go via Karkineta and Kusma and return on the other route as the climb is more gradual. The fare for flying from Kathmandu to Jomosom is Rs 580. It costs slightly more to fly on a charter.

Day 1: Pokhara-Naudanda (four hours walking)

To make an early start either spend the night in Pokhara Bazaar or take a taxi from the lake area. There are two routes out of Pokhara as far as Naudanda (not the same Naudanda as the one on the road to India). The first route goes up the ridge from the temple of Binde-basini and follows the ridge, known as Kaski, to Naudanda at 1458 metres. This route offers beautiful views of the mountains, Pokhara and the lake. Just before reaching Naudanda you can see the ruins of the palace of the king of the small principality of Kaski. Nepal was once divided into many such small principalities. The alternative route is to walk to the Tibetan refugee centre at Hengja in the north-western part of the Pokhara Valley and then make the stiff climb to Naudanda.

Day 2: Naudanda-Birethanti (six hours walking)

The trail on to Lumle passes through Brahmin and Chetri villages. Lumle has a British-aided agricultural extension project for retired Gurkha service-men from the British army. Three hours walk from Lumle takes you down to Birethanti (1037 metres) on the banks of the Modi River. There are some nice lodges here which make it a good place for an overnight stop and the river has beautiful waterfalls and good swimming in the summer. The route to the Gurung village of Ghandruk starts at Chandrakot.

If you go to Pokhara take the time to visit Birethanti which is only about two days' walk from Pokhara. It is the most beautiful village I saw while in Nepal. The people are very friendly and a series of four waterfalls provides excellent swimming.
Leslie Gill, USA

Birethanti is the closest approxim-ation of heaven on earth — at least for the tourist who can eat bananas while relaxing by the waterfalls!
Steven Smith, USA

Day 3: Birethanti-Ghodepani (nine hours walking)

A straight walk to Tirkhe (1440 metres) takes four hours, followed by a steep climb of 1500 metres to Ghodepani (2835 metres) passing the Magar village of Ulieri and a dense forest on the way. This is one of the highest points on the trail to Jomosom. If you diverge to Ghandruk be sure to take a guide though the forest. This area is very bad for leeches during the monsoon. In the spring there are many rhododendrons and in winter there will be snow. An hour away from Ghodepani, which means 'horse and water' in Nepali, is Pun Hill.

On the Pokhara-Jomosom trek, stop at Ghodepani and the next day climb the hill nearby and you will see about 30 peaks of the Himalayan range.
M Bonnemaison, France

Day 4: Ghodepani-Tatopani (six hours walking)

A long descent through the pretty Magar village of Sikha (2012 metres) leads to Tatopani at 1190 metres. There is hardly a household in the village which does not have someone who has done military service in the British or Indian armies. The village gives a partic-ularly good view of the Dhaulagiri range and has a ropeway project set up with Japanese assistance. Tatopani has good food and, of course, the hot springs after which the village is named. From here you follow the Kali Gandaki River, one of Nepal's major rivers.

Day 5: Tatopani-Lete (eight hours walking)

Almost all the villages from here on are Thakali and you can expect to be welcomed in all of their homes and offered excellent food. The gradual climb from Tatopani passes through Dana (1448 metres) and Ghasa (2012 metres) to the beautiful village of Lete (2438 metres). Except for a small stretch between Dana and Ghasa the trail is surprisingly good. Lete is in the middle of a deep gorge and offers an incredibly impressive sight of the whole of the western flank of Dhaulagiri.

On the Jomosom trek stay in Lete for one night. If it is cloudy have patience, you will see an incredible sunset on Annapurna and the silver Dhaulagiri melting under sunshine.
Gerhard Blias, West Germany

Day 6: Lete-Jomosom (seven hours walking)

The trail continues to follow the Kali Gandaki through many picturesque Thakali villages to Tukuche (2600 metres) the unofficial centre of the whole region of Thak Khola. The relatively affluent Thakalis have migrated to Pokhara, Bhairawa and Kathmandu since the decline in trade with Tibet. Marfa, further along, has narrow streets and a mediaeval look as well as a government-established horticulture farm which supplies fruit and vegetables to the whole region. Jomosom village, the headquarters of the Mustang district, is only two hours further walk. There is a STOL field, police check point and hospital here. This is the last Thakali village as all the villages further north are inhabited by people ethnically Tibetan. The famous temple of Muk-

tinath is only a day's walk from Jomosom.

Jomosom is in an area geographically part of the Tibetan plateau although politically it is still deep inside Nepalese territory. The monsoon never reaches this side of the Himalayas and you will rarely see trees or grass. Just north of Jomosom you may find the black fossil remains of marine animals known as 'saligram' in Nepali. They are from the Jurassic period millions of years ago and are worshipped in many Nepalese homes.

Walk up to the yak pastures from Marfa — best done in the warm season when the yak herds are taken up to the high grassy slopes. The walk up and down takes a full day and the path is very dry with little or no water available, so it is best to carry a little. The first part is very steep and rocky but the path gets easier higher up, although the altitude (more than 4000 metres) may make it difficult. The last part involves a walk round a wide grassy bowl on a slope that carries on up to the snow. From this vantage, the Nilgiri Range is clearly visible directly opposite and one can see a long way north towards Mustang and Tibet; Jomosom and the Muktinath Valley can also be seen.

P H England

Day 7: Jomosom-Muktinath (six hours walking)

The famous Hindu temple of Muktinath is situated at an altitude of 4000 metres and is the final destination of the Pokhara-Jomosom trek. The temple, also revered by Buddhists, is situated at the foot of a snow covered ridge near a cluster of four villages inhabited entirely by Tibetan speaking people. There are also eternal flames which are revered by the pilgrims. Trekkers on their way to Manang climb a 5000 metre pass after Muktinath and descend to the pleasant valley north of the

Annapurna Ranges. But it is much easier to do it from the Manang side. The village of Kagbeni situated on the banks of the Kali has also been enjoyed by almost all visitors.

Rafting

Rafting along Nepal's mountain rivers has become increasingly popular and Nepal has become almost as well known for its whitewater rafting as for its trekking. In fact many of the adventure trips to Nepal now combine a trek with a rafting expedition. The rafting trips mainly take place on the Sun Kosi, the Trisuli and the Kali Gandaki Rivers. *Adventure Travel Magazine* rated the Sun Kosi as one of the world's 10 best rivers for rafting.

RAFTING

No special experience is required for a rafting trip although kayaking, which also takes place in Nepal but to a much lesser extent, is a sport for the experts only. As long as you don't mind doing some paddling and have no objections to wet clothes you're a suitable candidate for a whitewater trip. There are more than a dozen rafting operators in Nepal now but they all follow a generally similar pattern. Costs range from around US$20 to US$75 a day. The tours generally last from about three to nine days and there are usually between seven and 17 people on each trip. Each raft will have an experienced helmsman, to ensure you stay upright through the tricky bits. More expensive

trips may include Nepali cooks and paddlers; on the lower priced trips you take turns at fixing the food and do the paddling.

WHEN TO RAFT

The rafting 'season' follows the trekking season very closely. As with trekking the monsoon season is unsuitable. It's cloudy, damp and miserable and the rivers are often too high. In October, with the close of the monsoon, conditions are at their best. The weather is clear, the harvests are on and the rivers are running well with the run-off from the monsoon. Winter can, as for trekking, be a bit chilly but that doesn't stop the rafting enthusiasts. With spring it's warmer once again and melting snow from the high peaks again provides good river conditions.

WHERE TO RAFT

There are three main rafting rivers in Nepal, all quite easily reached from Kathmandu. They provide a variety of rafting experiences to suit every taste and level of expertise. The Sun Kosi, Trisuli and Kali Gandaki are the three main rivers used for rafting trips. The first two are the most popular.

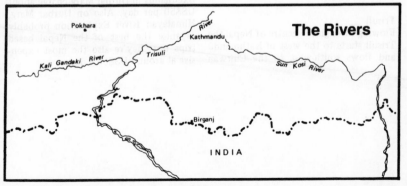

Sun Kosi River

The Sun Kosi is to the east of Kathmandu and is the river for those who want a longer, wilder and more remote adventure. This is the river rated in the world's top 10 for rafting enthusiasts. The starting point for Sun Kosi trips is Dolaghat, about 2½ hours out of Kathmandu on the road to the Chinese border. From there you're out of touch with 'civilisation' for eight to 10 days for the Sun Kosi runs through a region devoid of roads or towns. All you'll find along the way are small villages and settlements in the occasional open valleys which the river runs through.

The first couple of days are an easy paddle but then you have five to seven days of real whitewater with more smaller rivers adding their flow to the mighty Sun Kosi. The final two days are on the Terai as the river leaves the mountains and you drift gently down to Chatra where the Sun Kosi trip finishes. From put-in to put-out is about 210 km.

The Sun Kosi drains from some of the highest mountains in the eastern Himalayas including Everest. You raft through narrow gorges and quiet open areas where dug out canoes ferry villagers across the river. Upriver there are forests of pine while downriver you find lush vegetation, ferns, groves of bamboo and groups of monkeys and colourful birds.

Trisuli

Flowing through the centre of Nepal the Trisuli starts to the west of Kathmandu and flows south-west to the Chitwan National Park in the Terai. If the Sun Kosi is Nepal's river for the more experienced rafter then this is the river for beginners or at least those with less experience. A road follows the river for much of its length. Trisuli trips generally last from three to seven days. The most popular trips are a short 2½ day introduction to rafting — first an easy day's paddling, then a day of whitewater and then an easy morning's drift down into the Terai. Longer trips will usually include more whitewater rafting in the narrow gorges further upriver.

Trisuli trips start from the Kathmandu-Pokhara road. The river flows through Magyar and Gurung areas and in places you'll see high footbridges crossing the river. As you reach the Terai the Trisuli merges with the Kali Gandaki and becomes the Narayani, a wider, easier river. Trisuli trips end at Narayanghat from where many visitors continue to the Chitwan National Park.

OPERATORS

There are many US or European based rafting operators with trips costing from US$30 to $75 per day. You can also organise rafting trips right in Kathmandu. Encounter Overland, who have an office in the Kathmandu Guest House, organise the cheapest rafting trips with costs from just US$20 per day. Lama Excursions in Durbar Marg charge about US$50 per day. Also on Durbar Marg, Himalayan River Exploration probably organise the best of the Nepal based trips but they're also the most expensive at around US$65 a day.

Booklist

An amazing number of books have been written about exploring Nepal, mountaineering in Nepal and on its culture, art, religions and architecture. The list that follows is simply a selection of some of the more interesting books. Some of them may only be readily available in Nepal, others are long out of print and may only be found in libraries.

GENERAL

The Wildest Dreams of Kew Jeremy Bernstein, Simon and Schuster, New York, 1970 — a very readable account of Nepal's history and an evocative description of the trek to the Everest base camp.

Nepal — the Kingdom in the Himalayas Toni Hagen, Kummerley and Frey, Berne, 1980 — the definitive record of the geology and people of Nepal by the same man who, until the early sixties, had probably seen more of the country than anyone else — Westerner or Nepali. Numerous personal insights make it particularly interesting and it has the added bonus of excellent colour photography.

Mustang — a Lost Tibetan Kingdom Michel Peissel, Collins and Harvill Press, 1968 — a somewhat over excited description of a visit to the isolated region of Mustang north of the Annapurnas and close to the Tibetan border.

Nepal Namaste Robert Rieffel, Sahayogi Prakashan, Kathmandu, 1978 — a good general guidebook to Nepal.

Katmandu Colin Simpson, Angus and Robertson, Sydney, 1967 — an attractive book about a visit to Kathmandu and Pokhara, with some fine photographs.

The Mountain is Young Han Suyin, Jonathan Cape, London, 1971 — a flowery women's magazine-style, fictional romance set in Nepal in the mid-fifties.

CULTURE, PEOPLES, FESTIVALS

Festivals of Nepal Mary Anderson, George Allen and Unwin, London, 1971 — covers the many festivals celebrated in Nepal.

People of Nepal Dor Bahadur Bista, Ratna Pustak Bhandar, Kathmandu — deals in detail with the different ethnic groups of Nepal.

Sherpas of Nepal C Von Furer-Haimendorf, John Murray, London 1964 — a rather dry study of the Sherpas of the Everest region.

Tigers for Breakfast Michel Peissel, Hodder and Stoughton, London, 1966 — a biography of the well known Boris Lissanevith of the Royal Hotel and Yak and Yeti Restaurant.

The Gods of Nepal Mary Rubel, Shivaratna Harsharatna, Kathmandu, 1968 — a detailed description of the Hindu and Buddhist deities.

A Nepalese Discovers his Country Prakash A Raj, Sajha Prakashan Kathmandu, describes the social, economic, and political transformation of Nepal since 1951 when it ended its isolation.

Nepal in Crisis Blaikie, Cameron and Seddon, Oxford University Press, 1978, London — describes the reason for lack of development in Nepal in the decades of the sixties and seventies in the context of the construction of roads.

ART AND ARCHITECTURE

Kathmandu Valley Towns Fran Hosken, Weatherhill, New York, 1974 — more than 500 colour and black and white photographs of the towns, temples and people of the valley and an introduction to its history and festivals.

Nepal — Art Treasues from the Himalayas Waldschmidt, Oxford & IBH, London, 1969 — good description of many works of art in Nepal including photographs of objects.

Himalayan Art Madanjeet Sing, Macmillan, London, 1968 — an introduction to the art of the whole Himalayan region with beautiful pictures.

An Introduction to the Hanuman Dhoka stitute of Nepal and Asian Studies, Kir 1975 — an excellent description of

Royal Palace and the many buildings clustered in Kathmandu's Durbar Square.

TREKKING

Trekking in the Himalayas Stan Armington, Lonely Planet, Melbourne, 1982 — everything you need to know before setting out for a trek in Nepal, plus day by day coverage of all the main trekking routes and very good maps.

Trekking in the Himalayas T Iozawa, Yama Kei, Tokyo, 1980 — translated from Japanese, the book contains good maps and descriptions of trekking trails.

A Guide to Trekking in Nepal Stephen Bezruchka, Sahayogi Press, Kathmandu & The Mountaineers, Seattle, 1981 — a detailed description of the main trekking routes for the independent trekker.

Sherpa, Himalaya, Nepal Mario Fantin — good photographs and a detailed description of the Everest trek and the Sherpas of that region.

Trekking in Mt Everest and Solu Khumbu, Trekking North of Pokhara and Helambu, Langtang Valley and Ganja la John L Hayes, Peter Purna Books, Kathmandu, 1976 — This series of trekking guides gives a detailed description of each of the above treks and even an altitude profile.

A Winter in Nepal John Morris, Rupert Hart-Davis, London, 1964 — a very readable account of a Kathmandu to Pokhara trek by a retired British army Gurkha officer whose fluent Nepali allowed him to make some interesting observations of Nepalese life.

Nepal Himalaya H W Tillman, Cambridge University Press, London, 1952 — if you can find this book in libraries, it gives a fascinating account of some easy going rambles around Nepal by an Everest pioneer of the thirties together with some astonishingly unplanned (by today's standards) mountain assaults.

MOUNTAINS & MOUNTAINEERING

Annapurna South Face Chris Bonnington, Cassell, London, 1971 — an interesting account of the new highly technical assaults on difficult mountain faces plus the problems of expedition organisation and the sheer logistics of carrying out the climb.

Everest the Hard Way Chris Bonnington, Hodder and Stoughton, London, 1976 (also available in paperback) — the exciting story of the perfectly timed and executed rush to the summit in 1975, the first successful ascent by the south-west face. Backed up by some of the most amazing mountaineering photographs ever taken.

Everest South-West Face Chris Bonnington, Hodder and Stoughton, London, 1973 — an account of the author's earlier, and unsuccessful, attempt on the most difficult Everest face.

Many People Come, Looking, Looking Galen Rowell, George, Allen & Unwin, London, 1981 — an interesting study on the impact of mountaineering and trekking on the Himalayan region. Many excellent photographs but a rather steep price.

To the Third Pole G O Dhyrenfurth, Munich, 1960 — the post war attacks on the world's highest peaks, the third pole of the world according to the expedition leader.

Annapurna Maurice Herzog, Jonathan Cape, London, 1952 — a classic description of the first successful conquest of an 8000 metre peak and the harrowing, frostbitten aftermath.

The Conquest of Everest Sir John Hunt, Hodder and Stoughton, London, 1953 — the first successful climb of the world's highest mountain.

Annapurna to Dhaulagiri Dr Harka Gurung, Department of Information, HMG, Kathmandu — describes the mountaineering activity in Nepal between 1950 and 1960 when almost all the major peaks were conquered.

The Himalayas — a Journey to Nepal Takehide Kazami, Kodanshi International, 1968 — one of the Japanese 'This Beautiful World' series with stunningly beautiful colour photographs of many of Nepal's peaks.

Himalaya Herbert Tichy, Robert Hale, London, 1970 — a chatty series of incidents and anecdotes from the author's Himalayan wanderings since the thirties, including the ascent of Cho Oyu, at the time the third highet peak climbed.

Faces of Everest — Major Ahluwalliah, Vikas Publications, Delhi 1977, describes mountaineering activity on Everest in detail.

Hashish

One of the reasons for the increasing popularity of Kathmandu in the late sixties and early seventies, particularly amongst the *freak* community, was the unlimited availability of hashish and even stronger drugs. Although the smoking of hashish had been free in Nepal until 1973 few local people smoked it apart from the *sadhus* or holy men. Some young Nepalese were starting to smoke as a result of association with freaks however. Hash smoking is now supposed to be banned but people say it still goes on. Taking hash out of the country is strictly prohibited and several people have been arrested at the airport trying to smuggle it out. A recent study conducted by the government showed that many areas in the hills of western Nepal where people were financially dependent on the cultivation of marijuana had been adversely effected by the ban.

CENTRAL HASHISH STORE

Glossary

Apron — colourful aprons are worn by all married Tibetan women.

Ashoka — Indian emperor who did much to spread Buddhism 2500 years ago, including to Nepal.

Asla — river trout.

Avalokitesvara — Hindu/Buddhist god whose incarnation is Machhendranath.

Bakba — Tibetan clay mask.

Bajra — see Dorje.

Bazar — market area, a market town is called a bazar.

Bel Tree — young Newari girls are symbolically 'wed' to a bel tree to ensure that the death of any future husband does not leave them a widow.

Bhairab — the fearful manifestation of Shiva.

Bhati — tea shop/rest house in western Nepal.

Bon Po — the animist pre-Buddhist religion of Tibet.

Brahmins — the priestly caste of Hindus who also form one of Nepal's major ethnic groups.

Chakra — disc-like weapon of Vishnu.

Chang — Tibetan rice beer.

Chappati — unleavened Indian bread.

Chautara — stone platforms built around trees along walking trails as resting places for walkers.

Chetris — prince and warrior caste of Hindus, the present king and all the Ranas were chetris.

China Lama — the chief lama at Bodhnath.

Chomolongma — Tibetan name for Mt Everest, 'Mother Goddess of the World'.

Chortens — Tibetan Buddhist stupas. .

Chowk — courtyard or market place, as Kumari Chowk (house of the living goddess) or Indrachowk (market area of Kathmandu).

Chuba — long woolen coats worn by Sherpas.

Crow — the messenger of Yama.

Curd — yoghurt, a speciality of Bhaktapur.

Dal — lentil soup that forms part of the Nepali diet.

Deval — Nepali word for temple.

Devanagari — Nepali script, identical to Hindi nd Sanskrit.

Dhwaja — metal plate ribbon leading up to the roof of a temple as the pathway for the gods.

Dorje — 'thunderbolt' symbol of Buddhist power.

Durbar — palace, the main valley towns each have a Durbar Square, the square in front of the palace.

Durga — terrible manifestation of Parvati, can often be seen killing a demon in the form of a buffalo.

Earthquakes — are rare in Nepal but major ones shook the valley in 1833 and 1934.

Everest — the highest mountain in the world, named after George Everest, the British Surveyor General of India at the time the British discovered it.

Flag — Nepal is the only country in the world which does not have a rectangular flag.

Freaks — the young westerners who wander the east and can be found congregating in Bali, Kabul, Goa and Kathmandu.

Gaines — beggar minstrels.

Ganesh — elephant-headed son of Shiva and Parvati.

Ganja — hashish.

Garuda — man-bird vehicle of Vishnu, often found kneeling before shrines to Vishnu — human-like except for wings.

Ghee — clarified butter.

Ghat — steps down to a river, bodies are cremated on a 'burning ghat'.

Gompa — Tibetan Buddhist monastery.

Gopis — cow herd girls, Shiva is said to have dallied with them on the river banks at Pashupatinath.

Gurkha — originally derived from the name of the region of Gorkha, it came to be used for all soldiers recruited from Nepal for the British army.

Gurkhali — another name for the Nepali language.

140

Gurr — a baked, grated potato dish prepared by the Sherpas.

Gurungs — people from the western hill regions, particularly around Gorkha and Annapurna.

Hanuman — Monkey God.

Hashish — dried resin from the marijuana plant.

Indra — King of the Vedic Gods.

Kali Gandaki — between Annapurna and Dhaulagiri this river cuts the deepest gorge in the world.

Kali — terrifying manifestation of Goddess.

Kartikiya — God of War and son of Shiva.

Kata — Tibetan prayer shawl, traditionally given to a lama when one is brought to his presence.

Khukri — curved, traditional knife of the Nepalese, used with devasting ability by the Gurkhas.

Kinkinimali — temple wind bells.

Krishna — the eighth incarnation of Vishnu, often coloured blue.

Kumari — more peaceful incarnation of Kali. The Nepali name of the living goddess in Kathmandu is also Kumari.

Lama — Tibetan Buddhist priest or holy man, also respectful name.

Laxmi — Goddess of Wealth, consort of Vishnu.

Leeches — unpleasant blood-sucking creatures that appear in great numbers along the trekking trails during the monsoon — to get rid of them use a lighted cigarette, salt or insect spray, but do not try to pull them off.

Lingam — phallically shaped symbol of Shiva's creative powers.

Machendranath — patron God of the Kathmandu Valley.

Mahabharata — ancient Hindu epic.

Mahseer — giant game fish caught in the rivers of the Terai.

Malla — dynasty which ruled the valley from the 13th to the 18th century and created some of the finest art and architecture in the valley.

Mandala — geometrical and astrological representation of the world.

Mandir — Nepalese word for temple.

Manjushree — God who cut the Chobar Gorge and drained the dammed-up waters from the valley.

Mani Stone — stone carved with the Buddhist chant 'Om mani padme hum' — oh you jewel in the lotus.

Mani Wall — wall built of these stones in the hill country, always walk by one with the wall on your right.

Mantra — prayer formula or chant.

Mara — Buddhist God of Death, has three eyes and holds the wheel of life.

Mirror — usually found on temples to help devotees place their tikas.

Monsoon — rainy period from mid-June to late-September when there is rainfall virtually every day; there is also a very short winter monsoon, lasting a day or two usually in late January.

Mutinath — holy place north of Pokhara where a natural gas flame and water issue from the same rock.

Naga —serpent deity.

Namaste — Nepalese greeting.

Names — male Sherpas are named after the day of the week they were born; Monday — Dawa, Tuesday — Mingma, Wednesday — Lakpa, Thursday — Phurbu, Friday — Pasang, Saturday — Pemba, Sunday — Nyima.

Nandi — the bull, animal of Shiva.

Narayan — incarnation of Vishnu.

Narsimha (Narsingha) — man-lion incarnation of Vishnu.

Newars — original people of the Kathmandu Valley who were responsible for the architectural style of the valley.

Nilakantha — form of Shiva with blue throat caused by swallowing poison that would have ruined the world.

Oriflammes — prayer flags, prayers written on them are carried off by the breeze.

Pagoda — multi-storied Nepalese temple, this style originated in Nepal and was later taken up in China and Japan.

Panchayat — village democracy, the party-less government of Nepal.

Pashupati — incarnation of Shiva.

Patakas — see dhwajas.

Porters — hill people who carry goods the trails of roadless Nepal.

Prashad — consecrated food.

Prayer Wheels — cylindrical wheel inscribed with a Buddhist prayer which devotees spin round; in the hill country there are water-driven prayer wheels.

Puja — religious ritual or observance.

Raksi — rice spirit.

Ramayana — Hindu epic telling of the adventures of Prince Rama and his beautiful wife Sita and the demon King Ravana.

Rana — the series of hereditary Prime Ministers who ruled Nepal from 1841 to 1951.

Refugees — thousands of refugees fled to Nepal from Tibet after the Chinese invasion.

Reincarnate Lama — lama who has been selected for his position due to indications that he is the reincarnated form of a previous lama.

Rhododendrons — in Nepal rhododendrons are not a small decorative bush but a huge, brilliant tree which blooms in March and April above 2000 metres.

Ropeway — built from Thankot in the valley to Dharsing in 1929, to bring goods up from India, still in use today.

Sagarmatha — Nepalese name for Mt Everest.

Sankha — conch shell symbol of Vishnu.

Sarangi — violins played by the gaines.

Sherpas — hill people of eastern Nepal who became famous for their exploits with mountaineering expeditions, literally means 'people from the east'.

Sherpanis — female Sherpas.

Shivaratri — birthday of Shiva.

Sirdar — leader/organiser of a group of porters.

Solu Khumbu — Everest region of eastern Nepal where the majority of the Sherpas live.

Sonam — kharma built up during successive incarnations.

STOL — short take-off and landing aircraft.

Stupa — Buddhist religious structure like a circular mound surmounted by a spire, always walk around stupas clockwise.

Shikara — Indian-style temple like Krishna Mandir or Mahabouddha temple in Patan.

Tanka — rectangular Tibetan paintings on cotton, framed with brocade strips.

Tantra — symbolic and metaphysical religious philosophy evolved in the 10th to 15th century that binds Hindu and Buddhist people in Nepal.

Tempos — small three-wheeled transports commonly used in Kathmandu — similar to Thai samlors or Balinese bemos.

Terai — flat land of southern Nepal.

Thakalis — people of western Nepal around Jomosom who specialise in running hotels and bhatis.

Tika — red sandalwood paste spot marked on the forehead as a religious mark and on women as an indication of marriage.

Tribhuvan — grandfather of the present king who ended the period of Rana rule in 1951, the road to the Indian border from Kathmandu and the Kathmandu airport are named after him.

Trisul — trident weapon of Shiva.

Topi — traditional Nepalese cap.

Torana — ornament above temple doors which indicate to which God the temple is dedicated.

Tsampa — barley-flour porridge of the Sherpas.

Valley — until fairly recently the Kathmandu Valley was almost synonymous with Nepal, the country is still a conglomeration of many different peoples and ethnic groups.

Vihar — religious buildings comprising sanctuaries and lodgings for pilgrims.

Vishnu — the preserver, has many incarnations in Nepal.

Yak — main beast of burden and form of cattle in the high country above 3000 metres.

Yama — God of Death.

Yeti — the abonimable snowman.

Yoni — female sexual symbol usually found with lingams.

Zhum — female offspring of a yak and a cow.

To watch a sunset, preferably alone near the temple on the river, and see a Nepalese day end is an experience both interesting and educational. You see the water buffaloes washed, the goats being driven home and the sun fade away behind the mountains with Swayambhu in the distance.

Suzi Albright, USA

Index

LONELY PLANET NEWSLETTER

OTHER LONELY PLANET PRODUCTS